STEAMPUNK BANDITOS

Sex Slaves of Shark Island

MARIO ACEVEDO

WFP
WORDFIRE PRESS

ISBN: 978-1-61475-660-6

Cover art and design by Eric Matelski

Kevin J. Anderson, Art Director

Published by
WordFire Press, an imprint of
WordFire, LLC
PO Box 1840
Monument CO 80132

Kevin J. Anderson & Rebecca Moesta, Publishers

WordFire Press Trade Paperback Edition 2018
Printed in the USA
Join our WordFire Press Readers Group and get free books,
sneak previews, updates on new projects, and other giveaways.
Sign up for free at wordfirepress.com

❀ Created with Vellum

CHAPTER ONE

Y ou'll never know what to expect, so be ready," the bartender said to me. I puzzled over what she meant, and I hoped it was an inviting tease. She handed over my check.

I was in a brewpub on Walnut Street in my hometown of Denver, Colorado. A hundred years ago the building had started life as a boiler factory, then it became a warehouse, then sat idle for decades, was converted into an artist colony, which was then swallowed by the gentrification spreading northward from LoDo like herpes. In this latest reincarnation the place was a noisy faux-dive offering local craft beers, single-malt scotches, and fancified bar food. The bartender—a Chicana *prieta* who did a nice job filling out her Los Mocosos t-shirt—had attracted my eye even before she took my order. I couldn't help but crank up the charm and flirt. Sure, I could've gotten into her pants using vampire-hypnosis, but that would've been the equivalent of a supernatural roofie. If I couldn't get laid using my natural charisma, then it was time to improve my social skills.

She turned to serve another customer. I read the check and felt like I'd been given a wedgie. Besides my two beers, I'd been charged with four more beers, two shots of Lagavulin, and a cheesesteak sandwich.

I beckoned her and shouted to be heard over the din of conversation. "What's this?"

"That guy said to put it on your tab." She pointed down the bar.

I scanned the line of tattooed hipsters, and they parted just enough for me to make out a familiar face. Imagine a brown, wizened mutt grinning a mouthful of yellowed teeth like he'd scored a bucket of fried chicken from the dumpster. Who else could it be but the sketchiest vampire ever? Coyote.

He raised his glass to salute me. My kundalini noir, the supernatural force that animates my undead bloodsucking form, coiled in suspicion. I hadn't seen him since our last adventure together over a year ago. We had rescued our vampire friend Carmen Arellano from her alien captors, then quelled a vampire rebellion, and frankly I was still recuperating. It's never a coincidence when Coyote shows up, so I knew he was after more than a free lunch.

"I was going to throw the bum out," the bartender said, "until he told me you were good for the tab."

I slapped my Visa card on the bar and scowled at Coyote. He kept grinning.

With the tab settled, I put my sunglasses on, made my exit, and started for my car. The bright August sun baked through my layers of Dermablend and makeup.

Just when I thought I might make it to the car, he popped from behind the corner and waited on the dirt shoulder of the street, a diminutive scarecrow in frayed denim. Strands of oily hair jutted from under a grease-stained ball cap. A wispy mustache colored his upper lip. Cheap wraparound sunglasses with a paperclip inserted into one of the temples made him look more *rasquache* than usual. "Hey *vato*, you slipped out of the bar without saying hello."

"Hello."

"*Chale* man, don't be this way."

"Coyote, every time I run into you, I get a dent in my wallet." I kept walking toward my car. He fell in step beside me. This close, he brought the tangy and sweet smell of over-ripe onions and melons.

"Life is more than money, *ese*," he replied.

"Says the man with no money."

"Sorry, I had to do this."

I raised an eyebrow. "You're apologizing to me for mooching?"

"No, not that *ese*. I meant using that *ruca*."

"What girl?"

"Angelica. The bartender." He nodded back toward the brew-pub. "Took some doing, también. Is costing me a big favor."

And what favor could he possibly offer in return? The guy owed me enough money to pay off the mortgage of a small condo. "You want something. What?"

"A ride, *ese*."

"Where to?"

"My *chante*."

"No way am I driving you back to New Mexico."

"I've moved."

"Oh? What happened to Rainella?" She was his most recent girlfriend. Together they shared a doublewide in the high desert south of Farmington, and their home had been the base for our last supernatural odyssey.

"Things happen, *ese*," he quipped and didn't elaborate. He pointed to the left. "I live a few blocks from here."

"How many is a few?"

He squinted and counted on his fingers. "Twenty-one and a half."

"Okay. I can do that." We reached my car.

He gave my silver Lexus sedan the once-over. "What happened to your Cadillac?"

"I needed a change." I palmed the remote.

But before I could press the button to unlock the car, he waved a hand and the doors clicked open. He slipped into the front passenger's seat. "This will do."

I worried that the leather seats would absorb his funk. He directed me to Downing Street, then Brighton Boulevard, and we made our way to Globeville, a tiny enclave zoned for cheap rents and light industry, bounded by Interstates 25 and 70, the railroad tracks, and the Platte River. Along the way he fished peanuts from a pocket in his denim jacket, cracked them open, munched, and tossed the shells out his window. The breeze carried at least half of the shells back into my car.

When I asked again about Rainella, Coyote turned on the stereo and increased the volume of KUVO until it was just shy of being uncomfortably loud. Obviously he didn't want to talk about New Mexico or her. Not now anyway. Maybe never.

We drove past a trailer park and down a block of ramshackle adobe shacks, which looked as forlorn as a collection of rain-warped cardboard boxes.

He turned the radio off. "Stop here."

Not surprisingly, we parked outside the most rundown of the little houses. Ribbons of discolored paint curled from the wooden door, the adjacent window frames, and the eaves. Rusted nails secured the door. Scabs of stucco had fallen loose, exposing mud bricks underneath.

Coyote cracked his car door open. "Well *vato*, don't you want the grand tour?"

"Not especially."

"I got something to show you."

I kept my hands on the steering wheel.

"You'll be out of here in *diez minutos*. Tops."

"And that's it?"

"In, out, like you're delivering pizza."

There was a catch to his offer, but if I didn't humor him, he'd be under my feet for days.

We got out of my car. Denver's skyline peeked above the

mountains of wrecks in the auto salvage yard next door. I followed Coyote along a weedy path beside the house. We ducked through a gap in the sagging chain-link fence that enclosed a barren dirt lot, littered with old tires and rusted, discarded water heaters, washing machines, and stoves.

Coyote approached the back door and grasped a steel lock the size of a coffee cup. Quite the lock to protect this dump. He blinked, the lock popped open, and he slipped it off the hasp. He pushed the door and it wobbled open, creaking and releasing a heavy musty odor.

We took off our sunglasses. I removed my contacts to take the measure of Coyote's aura. It shimmered around his skinny frame like he was wrapped in burning yellow fluff.

We entered a kitchen that was in no better condition than the exterior. Stained and warped counter tops. Cabinet doors hanging crooked or missing altogether. A set of vice-grips served as a handle for the faucet. The spigot dripped into stagnant dish-water. The linoleum floor felt spongy beneath my feet. A spray can of Febreze rested on an empty shelf, lying on its side like it had surrendered.

Coyote continued to the darkened front room and further into his dilapidated labyrinth. Sunlight filtered through gaps around the plywood in the windows. The ceiling drooped in places where the roof had leaked. Mushrooms grew in random patches on the carpet. The edges of their caps shined purple in the gloom.

A coffee table rested in the middle of the room, between a threadbare sofa and a vinyl recliner patched with duct tape. Candles, tin cans, bottles, a small tattered book, and a chipped, ceramic bowl decorated in a Southwestern motif sat on the table. A clutter of more items rested beneath. The book looked like a vintage-style diary, a hardback with the covers torn off.

I said, "You might want to clean this place up before the homeowners' association files a complaint."

"*Vato*, laugh all you want. But if I told you what I pay in rent, you wouldn't believe me."

"You're right. I don't believe that you pay rent at all."

"Speaking of rent." He tapped his trouser pockets. "I'm a little light this month."

"Seriously, you pay to live here?"

He stared at me, his aura sizzling in a low burn.

"You really don't need rent money, do you?" I asked. "You're squatting here, right?"

"If I was squatting, don't you think I'd choose a classier place than this?"

"No."

He pruned his lips. "Okay, you got me. I need *feria*."

"You could work."

"Would you hire me, *ese?*"

"Good point," I replied. "Before I hand over any cash, tell me why we're here."

Coyote sat cross-legged on one side of the table. He motioned that I sit opposite him.

"I have a job for you," he said.

"What kind of a job?"

"*Algo bien diferente. Y muy importante.*" He flipped through the book, showing me dog-eared pages filled with scribbles and sketches. "This has everything you need to know."

I reached for the book, but he pulled it away. "It's not for reading."

My brow furrowed. "Then what good—"

"*Vato*," he interrupted, "you're thinking too linearly." A glowing spot lifted from his aura and hovered inches above his head. The spot spread into a horizontal line that resembled a length of sputtering neon. The line wiggled and shook, made loopy curves, then shrank back into the dot, which plopped into his aura. His demo did little to enlighten me.

"Explain," I said.

"*El dinero, por favor*," he replied.

I counted two Jacksons from my wallet and dropped them on

the table.

He looked the money. "Kinda light, *vato*."

"That's all you're going—"

He palmed the bills into a shirt pocket. "So-kay. You can owe me." Without elaborating about the book he centered the bowl between us. He sprinkled crushed leaves and powder from the tin cans into the bowl. Next he plucked mushrooms from the carpet and gathered them on the table to mince with a pocketknife. As he sliced and diced, the pieces crackled and emitted purple sparks. After whisking the mushroom pieces into his other hand, he dumped them in the bowl. He dug a chrome cigar lighter from his pocket and used its blue flame to set a corner of the book on fire. Its pages darkened and crinkled. He dropped the book into the bowl and jabbed at the burning pages with a long wooden spoon.

I traced the flight of embers lifting from the bowl, watched them float about the room, expecting the carpet and sofa to start smoldering. "Other than setting this place on fire, what are you trying to do?"

"Patience, *vato*, patience." He spooned the pages until they crumbled into ash. He doused the fire with liquid he poured from two of the bottles. I smelled mescal and goat's blood. He stirred the soupy mix until it stiffened into a fist of black, smelly dough. Reaching into the bowl, he scooped a handful of the mixture and mashed it with both palms like he was making a mud pie. Then he rolled it between his hands. Pieces fell back into the bowl. He held one hand open and showed that he had fashioned something the size and shape of an almond. The thing began to squirm like a maggot.

I didn't know if he had conjured the disgusting thing or it had been buried in the mix. "The hell is that?"

He rose to his knees and leaned toward me. "Remember *Star Trek II: The Wrath of Khan?*"

"Yeah. And?"

"Remember that part when Khan planted a mind worm in

Chekov's ear?"

My kundalini noir zinging in panic, I flinched from Coyote.

But too late. He reached across the table and snagged my hair with his free hand. For a five-hundred-year-old vampire who was as scrawny as his namesake, he was surprisingly quick and strong. He slapped his other hand against my left ear and jammed the maggot into my ear canal. Once he let go I jumped to my feet and bolted backwards.

Extending a talon from my fingertip, I tried in vain to dig the wiggling, disgusting creature free. But it had burrowed too far and kept worming deeper and deeper. I spun in circles, stomping my feet, yelling, "What did you do, Coyote, you crazy bastard!"

The maggot reached my eardrum, and as it pushed through, the pain was like getting my head skewered by a red-hot poker. I fell and thrashed on the carpet, screaming and rubbing my ear.

The pain ebbed and I lay on my back, gasping, and followed the path of the maggot as it crawled through my brain. It inched behind my eyeballs, pushing them against the front of their sockets. I pressed my hands over my eyes, horrified that this thing might eat its way through them.

"Coyote," I hollered, "I am going to skin you alive!"

"Don't panic, *ese*. Everything in that book is now in your memory."

"What the hell are you talking about?" The image of the maggot crawling through the folds of my gray matter had me cringing in terror.

"Hold on." He lifted me by the hair into a sitting position and smacked the back of my head. The worst sinus pain of all time flooded my cranium. He cupped my nose and again smacked the back of my skull.

"Blow your nose," he ordered. "Blow!"

I closed my mouth and blasted air through my nose. A gooey ball descended from my nostrils. Coyote pinched my nose and withdrew his hand, slimy with snot. I saw him brush his fingers over the bowl, and the maggot tumbled in.

I wiped my nose with the tail of my shirt, relieved that the pain had eased and the maggot was out. But I still shivered with disgust from the phantom sensation of the squirming horror crawling through my brain. Coyote uncapped a small red fuel can, splashed kerosene into the bowl, and lit it. A flame whooshed to the ceiling.

I watched, blinking. "You're going to torch this place for sure, *cabron loco*."

Coyote crouched beside the table and slapped his hands over the bowl. "Come here quick."

"Now what?" I kept my distance.

Smoke seeped between his fingers. "Hurry, get over here, *pendejo*. Before I lose it."

"Lose what?"

He glowered. "Just move your hairy *nalgas*. *Ya!*"

I crawled to the table. He lifted his hands and released a puff of smoke. He grabbed the back of my neck and pulled my face into the malodorous vapor.

"Breathe it," he demanded. "Breathe it."

I sucked in a deep breath. The acrid smoke burned my throat, and I curled into a ball, choking and coughing.

"We did it, *vato*," Coyote said, relaxing. Fire darted about his fingers and he rubbed them on his jeans to put out the flames.

"Did what?" Too woozy to sit upright, I collapsed against the floor.

His face loomed over mine. "Sent you on your way."

"My way? Where?" I mouthed the words but they faded from my hearing.

Coyote's face dissolved into a Cheshire's Cat grin floating in the gray haze. "Someplace close and faraway."

"To do what?" My body felt untethered, weightless.

He mumbled an answer, but all I caught was a whisper at the end. "You'll never know what to expect, so be ready."

"What does that mean ..."

CHAPTER TWO

I blinked myself awake. My eyes focused on a wooden chest of drawers, then closer to me, a blanket and sheets bundled around my body. Seconds ago I had been in Globeville, on the floor of Coyote's hovel.

Now where am I?

Startled, I jerked and knocked my skull against a headboard. My gaze roved across a bedroom, lit by a smoking flame inside the glass chimney of an antique oil lamp. I sat up and took in the rest of my surroundings.

A ceramic pitcher and a large bowl sat on a washstand. Also antique. A rug stretched between the bed and a door. Bustiers, garter belts, and stockings dangled inside an open armoire. Framed pictures hung from walls papered in an Art Nouveau pattern. Heavy drapes covered a set of windows. Clothes —*somehow I knew these were my clothes*—lay on the seat of a plush armchair in the far corner. A pair of tall shiny boots stood alongside the chair. *My boots.* A wide-brimmed black hat was perched on a gun belt coiled on the back of the chair. *My hat. My gun.*

Everything looked like props from a western. Piano music, laughter, and the murmur of lively conversation from downstairs completed the perception. Where was I? A saloon? The air smelled of lilac perfume and spunk. I contemplated the armoire and its display of women's undergarments. Not a saloon. A bordello.

I tucked my arm under the pillow, and my fingers touched the cold metal form of a pistol. I slipped out a bird's head pocket revolver, what was known in the Wild West as a hideout gun. The markings on the barrel read Johnson & Bye .32 caliber. It was nickel plated with mother-of-pearl grips—a pimp's heater. I also knew it was mine, which begged the question: Was I a pimp? Why the need for a loaded gun under my pillow? Was I here for business or pleasure?

Or was this a dream?

I weighed the little pistol in my hand and looked about the room. Sniffed. No dream—the details were too real. Then what was going on?

As I slid the revolver back under the pillow, a hazy memory floated through my mind. That of Coyote and the smoke and the maggot and his last words before I had fallen unconscious.

You'll never know what to expect, so be ready.

Be ready for what? Had Coyote transported me through a psychic portal like he'd done last year, when he sent Jolie and me to a different planet to rescue Carmen? No, this felt different. This was more than a new place; this was a new time, a new reality.

I was naked beneath the covers, and I extended my hairy leg from under the blanket. Why couldn't I see my aura? I blinked and realized I wasn't wearing my contacts. *I should see my aura!*

I caught my reflection in a floor mirror that faced the bed. *My reflection?* How was this possible? I locked in on my image, the panic settling into wonder. A very macho shoe brush of a mustache obscured my upper lip. When the hell had I grown that womb-broom? And when was the last time I had seen my reflection? Not since before I was turned. Studying my eyes, I realized they didn't shine with a vampire's red glow as they should. They looked ... normal. *Human.*

I held my arm over the bedcover and noticed a shadow. I waved my arm and the shadow followed. I waved both of my arms, and they both cast a shadow. My shadow. The first time I'd seen mine in years.

My mood sagged. Was I no longer an immortal bloodsucker?

Then deep inside, my kundalini noir stirred, as if it too had been knocked out for the journey, stretching and squirming like a serpent crawling out of its den. That was good news. A kundalini noir confirmed that I was still a vampire.

I willed my fangs to extend. They snapped out, and I ran my tongue across their sharp points. Fangs, check. I opened my hands and spread my fingers. Talons, check.

Examining my hands and arms, I noticed they were a nice shade of Mexican brown. I scrubbed my skin to see if any makeup rubbed off. None did. This complexion was all Felix Gomez. A similar phenomenon had happened years before, the result of a rare spider's bite, and it hadn't ended well. I hoped this was different.

Scars blemished my arms, both legs, my torso. Welted flesh with stitch marks, wrinkled burned skin, puckered bullet wounds. Some old, some fresh, and more than I had earlier. I must have pissed off a lot of people in this place, just like home. And more disturbingly, the welter of scars across my belly looked like I had sustained a fatal wound. Yet here I was.

A hundred questions piled inside my mind. Were there other vampires? Did I have to hide my supernatural persona? How about the *Araneum*—the underground network of vampires—did they exist? Why did Coyote send me here? What did he expect me to do? How was I supposed to get back?

Disconnected thoughts tumbled through my head. Fragmented images. Passages from Coyote's book, scribbled on pages that had shriveled into black ash. Large chunks of awareness failed to congeal like I was suffering from amnesia.

Footfalls approached outside the door. Footfalls that echoed in a hallway. The quick steps of a woman wearing heels.

My kundalini noir remained calm, alert, cautious. Not certain if supernaturals had to hide in this world, I retracted my fangs and talons, just in case. I fixed my eyes on the door, to a crystal doorknob with an old-fashioned keyhole underneath. The knob turned.

A woman entered. Cherubic face with rouged cheeks. Curls of brunette hair were pinned to the top of her head, exposing the nape of a graceful neck. A short robe in a floral print was cinched around her curvy frame. Dark stockings covered her legs and she wore heeled sandals fastened with silk ribbons.

She hung a fresh towel on a rack of the washstand. I was staring at her back when a name popped into my head. I said, "Eunice." That was her name, I was certain. But how did I know?

She turned and swiveled large blue eyes toward me. One eyebrow lifted. "What's that look? Ready for another throw?"

"Depends." A roll in the sack with her sounded like a great welcome to wherever I was, but somehow I felt like I had to be somewhere soon. I was not a pimp; I made my living solving other people's problems, and a big problem needed my attention. "What time is it?"

She grasped a gold pocket watch—*my watch*—from the washstand and flicked it open. "Nine twenty-two."

I looked to the curtains and didn't see any light spill past them. It should be dark outside but just to make sure, I asked, "AM or PM?"

Her brow knit. "What?"

"Morning or night?"

She gave her pretty head a slow shake, and a smile curved her painted lips. "Did I rattle your brain that much, Felix? If so, I should charge you extra."

She got my name right, and that reassured me. "Then which is it? Night or day?"

"Night," she answered, puzzled. "Just an hour since I left you."

I considered Eunice and my vintage surroundings. "What year is this?"

Her expression wilted. "Now you're being worrisome."

"Humor me. What year?"

"Eighteen eighty-seven. June 3rd. *Friday*."

I let the date sink in. "Where are we?"

"Quit acting loopy. You haven't turned into a hop-head, have you?"

"A what?" Then I remembered that vintage slang, hop-head—opium fiend. I sat up and swung my legs off the bed. "No, I haven't been hitting the pipe. Please, Eunice, where are we?"

She sauntered dramatically to the window and threw the drapes back. Windows panes divided a night sky into dark rectangles. The reflection of streetlamps smeared the glass. She extended one hand, palm upward, and announced, "Behold, St. Charles on the Platte River of the West Kansas Territories."

Her statement hammered me square. I was still in Denver, but if this was 1887, the name she offered was wrong by about thirty years. St. Charles was the original moniker for the town before William Larimer and a bunch of other cronies—make that founding fathers—jumped an earlier claim on the settlement. They greased their subterfuge by offering to name the place after the then-governor of Kansas. Hence, Denver. And by 1887 the West Kansas Territories had become the state of Colorado. But none of that had happened here. How much else had changed from what I knew as history?

A set of men's drawers lay on the rug by the bed. My drawers for sure. I stepped into them and padded barefoot to the window. I looked down from a second story onto a bustling street. A crowd of mostly men, in late nineteenth-century frontier or city clothes, wandered the sidewalks below. The few women wore Victorian dress. Shadows shrank and grew from people as they circulated past gas lanterns perched on tall poles at the street corners. More light spilled from windows and doors facing the sidewalk. Horses with riders trotted over the hard-packed, dirt street. Other horses plodded along, pulling wagons. People milled about, chatting with one another, while others darted across the busy intersection. The ambiance seemed unusually festive.

"Why the crowd?" I asked. "Is it a holiday?"

"Holiday?" she replied. "It's a payday weekend. Folks come into town spending money like lonely sailors on liberty, thank goodness."

A three-story, brick building stood across the road, flanked by similar structures to the left and right. The location seemed vaguely familiar. "We're at the corner of Market and 20th," I said, a memory gathering.

"Yeah," Eunice said. "But given all the nonsense you've been talking, I'm surprised anything came to mind."

A horseless wagon rumbled down Market, smoke and sparks puffing from a tall stack fixed to a barrel-like engine at the front of the vehicle. Levers and pistons jutted from the engine, steering the front wheels. A circular port on the engine, with an orange light shining through, made the machine resemble a mechanical Cyclops. A man sitting at the rear of the bed guarded the load of crates. I studied the vehicle to find the driver and didn't see one. The wagon stuttered and lurched along a crooked path as if it were blind. People scrambled out of its way.

"What is that?" I asked.

Eunice peeked out the window. "An automatic buckboard."

That did not sound familiar. "Who is driving it?"

"It's *automatic*. It steers itself. More or less, anyway." She squinted at my face. "You seemed sane and sober when you came in. Did you fall off a horse and the concussion is just catching up? Maybe another woman kicked you in the head?"

I turned back to the mirror and focused on my face. Besides the mustache, my hair was longer. Greasy strands curled past the tops of my ears and down my neck. I'd always kept it short and neat. My eyes gleamed from inside chiseled sockets, accented by thick eyebrows.

I was looking at myself, of that I was certain. But I was new here. What happened to the Felix I'd replaced? Had he taken my place back in Coyote's shack in Globeville? Was he as confused as I was? Or was there only one Felix—me—and I had been dropped mid-stream into another existence? I thought hard about what Coyote had told me, hoping for clues to help me understand my predicament, but none came.

"You're not *that* easy on one's constitution, Felix," Eunice said, breaking me out of my fugue. "So quit staring at yourself. You'll wear out the mirror."

"Sorry, I'm a little distracted."

"A little? A man looks at his reflection in this place, he should be expecting to see a girl bent over in front of him, her titties slapping together, the two of them making a show."

Glancing to Eunice, I grinned. *Maybe next time.*

I stepped to the washstand. My pocket watch lay beside the bowl, and I examined the fob at the end of the gold chain. A bronze medallion. Make that a medal; a military award. It featured a trident and a musket forming a cross, a silver star shined where they intersected. Two sharks flanked the trident. The words along the top of the medal read: *Por Valor*—For Valor. And along the bottom: *Batalla por Isla Tiburón, Golfo de California* —Battle for Shark Island, Gulf of California. *Shark Island? Was there such a place? And when did this happen?* I turned the medal over. The reverse featured a stylized eagle, spread wings with squared tips, and beneath the bird's claws: *Ejercito de Aztlan*— Army of Aztlan.

Aztlan, the mythical birthplace of the Aztecs. *Aztlan exists? And it had an army? And they gave me a medal?*

I clasped the medal in my hand and closed my eyes. I saw Asian men, Chinese infantry fighting with and against Mexican soldiers. Water surged around my ankles, water that ran red and warm from bodies strewn along a beach, mowed down by steam-powered Gatling guns. Artillery blasts and screams jolted me, and my eyes sprang open, ending the vision.

I set the medal beside a bunch of coins I assumed were mine. Choosing a silver half-dollar (Seated Liberty, United States of America), I read its date: 1872. To see if I retained my supernatural strength, I levered the coin over the knuckle of my index finger and used my thumb and middle finger to crease it. The coin bent, though not as easily as I remembered it should.

Eunice watched, astonished.

Apparently, she didn't know I had preternatural powers. I pressed the coin between my hands until it was flat again. "It's a parlor trick, that's all." I flipped the coin to her. "Keep it."

She snatched the coin midair and then tried to bend it. "How did you—"

"It's a trick, I just told you."

I approached the armchair and gave my clothing the once-over. Nice duds. I did dress well. Curious about my choice of primary shooting iron, I slipped the revolver from its holster on the cartridge belt, waxed brown leather with polished brass fittings. The pistol was a Richards-Mason cartridge conversion of a Colt Navy, the octagonal barrel shortened for a quick draw. Its bluing was worn, the metal nicked and scratched like a well-used tool. A saloon girl had been carved into both ivory grips, yellowed with hairline cracks.

I flipped open the loading gate to see a nice fat cartridge waiting to do its duty. The markings stamped on the rim read .45 Colt. You hit a man with a slug from this, he goes down and he stays down. Hmmm, an original Navy was .36 caliber so mine had been bored out and modified to accept a bigger round. I levered the hammer to half-cock and rotated the cylinder, the mechanism indexing with precise and satisfying clicks. Odd that I carried this antiquated, custom-made piece given the more modern choices that should be available. So even in this alternative setting I marched out of step. I lowered the hammer onto an empty chamber and returned the revolver to its holster. Brass cartridges filled the loops stitched to the gun belt and brought a menacing heft to my rig. People fucked with me, I was going to fuck back.

Eunice chuckled.

"What's so funny?" I asked.

"You're such a typical *pistolero*. You come to a whorehouse and spend more time playing with your gun than with pussy."

"Guns keep me alive, darling." I set my gaze on her crotch. "The day that little clam kills someone, let me know and I'll put it in my holster."

"It's broken plenty of hearts, does that count?"

"Unfortunately, no." I scooped my clothes and laid them on one of the arms of the chair. I pulled on a white undershirt and sat on the seat cushion.

"Are you leaving?" she asked.

"I've got to be someplace at ten." How did I know this?

"Will you be back?"

I also knew that I wouldn't. "Don't hesitate to take another customer." I plucked socks from inside my boots. My right boot had a sheath, with dagger, sewn inside the calf. My left boot, a small leather holster, most certainly for the Johnson & Bye. Only a rough man would be so well armed.

"You paid for the night," Eunice noted, sadly. I must've been a favorite client.

I slipped my socks on, then my trousers.

"No refunds," she added, "or credit for the next time."

I shrugged.

"Where are you going?" she asked, still petulant.

The answer came to me without thinking, yet the thought of my destination was ice-cold with foreboding.

"To see the Dragon."

CHAPTER THREE

Memories trickled through my brain, guiding me. I walked as if by remote control from the bordello, across 20th Avenue, to a warren of ramshackle shops arranged along the mouth of a narrow street, the entrance to Denver's—make that St. Charles's—Chinatown, aka Hop Alley. Dim lights flickered behind curtained windows. Chinese men watched from gloomy doorways. The younger ones were dressed like American big-city toughs, while the older ones wore baggy smocks over pajama-like trousers. Braided pigtails dangled from the back of their shaved heads.

Two women in voluminous Victorian clothing—faces hidden beneath veiled hats—climbed the steps to a loading dock. A Chinese woman opened a door for them and out wafted the flowery, musky fragrance of opium smoke. All three women disappeared inside and the door shut behind them.

As I continued down the alley, I noted the differences between my abilities in this world and my abilities at home. For one, my night vision wasn't as sharp. Previously, my eyes were as keen as a wolf's. Now, the details weren't as clear, the images not as distinct. But still better than a mortal's.

Speaking of which, could I still transmutate into a wolf? Did shape-shifters exist in this new reality?

I halted suddenly, then turned to face a wooden door recessed into the brick wall of a three-story building. My destination. I noticed nothing remarkable about the door besides the absence of a doorknob or handle. The paint was mostly gone, exposing weathered and marred wood. Rusted hinges held it in place.

I pulled at the chain of my pocket watch and snapped it open. Ten on the dot. I dropped the watch back into my vest pocket and knocked. Seconds later the door swung toward me, and a feeble yellow light spilled out. A wizened Chinese woman emerged to hold the door open. She held a mop and wore a soiled apron over a loose blouse, its sleeves rolled past her elbows. She beckoned with a fussy manner and motioned that I step carefully across the wet entrance and into a hall. I didn't remove my hat. Frontier protocol allowed a man carrying a gun and on business to keep his lid on, and this was not a social call.

A heavy, dank smell hit my nose. Cool. Ripe with decayed flesh. Grimacing, I glanced to my left and right. I didn't see a dead body but the odor reminded me of a morgue.

At the end of the hall, a Chinese man grinned as if amused by my sensitive nose. He added a dismissive smirk: *the Dragon sent for you, prissy fuck?*

The man—a guard—wore no shirt, only striped military trousers tucked into suede leggings, fitted over laced boots. He was dark, unusually tall, and the tattoo at the center of his muscular chest—a Chinese dragon inside a ring of flames—was framed by leather suspenders clipped to a wide leather belt. A white sash under the belt further accentuated his lean waist and sculpted, V-shaped torso.

I expected him to carry a sword, something exotic and curved like a scimitar, instead, a massive Walker revolver hung in a cross-draw holster attached to his belt.

The old woman nudged me forward and closed the door.

When its latch clicked, the walls seemed to shrink in and gave the impression I was no longer on the western plains but deep in an Asian mountain fortress. I continued down the hall toward the guard. Splashes of weak light fanned from the amber wall sconces, providing more shadow than illumination. Burning gas hissed within the sconces.

Three steps from the guard I halted for him to search and disarm me. But the guard only grunted and nodded to the stairs rising behind him.

I was allowed to proceed without surrendering my weapons? Maybe that corpse smell came from a failed assassin, as a warning.

The staircase banister and railings were one long sinuous carving of Chinese imagery: maidens in repose, rabbits, fish, tigers, dragons. As we climbed the steps, the guard trailing, I noticed the air lost its rotted meat odor and became cooler, more pleasant. Something mechanical rumbled above the ceiling.

At the landing, a second guard opened another door. A wave of refreshing air burst out and the rumbling became louder.

I paused at the threshold.

A gas lamp chandelier lit the room. A slender man in a simple olive-green suit sat behind an enormous, black-lacquered desk. A young, red-haired woman was seated close beside him.

Wispy hair crowned his bald, bony head. Beady eyes swam within the lenses of wire-rimmed spectacles. His features crowded the bottom of his small face, which in turn made his forehead seem too big—almost grotesque.

His face I recognized from an etching that I'd never seen, yet the image was crisp in my mind. His identity came to me in one gush of memory, the details so fresh it was as if I'd just finished reading a California broadsheet warning about the Yellow Peril incarnate, the most feared of the Chinese crime bosses outside of the Orient.

Wu Fei. The Dragon.

My kundalini noir coiled like a serpent, wary, defensive.

Anywhere else, this skinny old man would be wearing an

accountant's eyeshade and fussing with an abacus. Yet here, one snap of his thin fingers and the gutters would run with blood.

A tall bell jar sat in the middle of his desk. A white opaque mist fogged the inside of the jar. A brass trivet sat beside the jar, next to a brass lever with a large emerald knob that protruded from a slot in the desk.

Behind the gangster hung a crimson silk tapestry bearing a golden image of a Chinese dragon identical to the guard's tattoo. Cool, moist air and plumes of white vapor blasted from metal vents in the ceiling, above which was the source of the rumbling.

Wu Fei raised one arm and motioned benevolently. "Come in, Mister Gomez." His voice came out in a strained raspy tenor, spoken loud enough to be heard over the noise. "Enjoy refreshment of my newly acquired swamp cooler. Steam makes cold. Truly amazing."

All right, he knew my name. What else did he know? That I was a vampire?

I touched the brim of my hat in salutation. Coming closer, I saw the reason for his gravelly voice. A necklace of scar tissue circled Wu Fei's throat: the mark of a man who had been hanged —and lived.

The woman at his right looked Irish. Freckles. Fair complexion. The breeze from the vents tugged at coppery strands spilling from under her black skullcap, which was decorated with elaborate golden filigree. Her fingers were splayed on the desk, showing off manicured and lacquered nails and jeweled gold rings. She wore an azure silk tunic with a Mandarin collar. Chinese characters and symbols of the western zodiac embroidered in gold bullion decorated the collar and the black trim of the tunic. These clothes and the tattoos around her wrists confirmed her presence here. She was a psychic messenger—a telepath.

Her piercing gaze gave the disconcerting impression that she could read my mind. That double-downed on the odds stacking against me.

More of Coyote's planted memories bubbled into my consciousness. Apparently in this world, clairvoyants existed and they were used to transmit and receive messages. In other words, human psychic radios.

And another thought. This gangster must be growing money if he could afford to keep one of her kind on his payroll.

She spoke to Wu Fei. In Chinese.

He tipped his head and considered her words. He looked back up—eyes widening as if privy to a new secret—and gave me a crocodile's smile. What had she told him? My kundalini noir twisted and bared its fangs.

Wu Fei pointed to a wooden chair in front of his desk.

Droplets from the vents sprayed across my face. I sat and pondered how to survive intact should this appointment unravel into a double-cross.

Armed guards watched. The gangster and his Irish witch might have pistols. The chair might have a grenade under the seat cushion. Poisoned darts might be aimed at me.

This is crazy. Do I really have to do this? Why was I here?

I reflected on the medal on my watch chain. *The Battle for Shark Island.* A line of scars on my belly began to ache, reminding me of where I'd been hit with rifle bullets.

I was a veteran of a war that I'd never been in, carried wounds that I'd never received, and earned a living settling scores for strangers. I was a gunslinger with a past that was phantom even to me. Now I sat in front of the most dangerous man between the Mississippi and Yangtze Rivers. Why had Coyote sent me? What did the Dragon want?

Was this about a job? Wu Fei had the wealth to buy politicians and cops by the ward. By a simple command, he could send a band of cutthroats to slaughter an orphanage.

Perhaps Wu Fei owed a favor to an enemy of mine, and the debt would be settled by the delivery of my carcass. Fear prickled my skin and despite the chilled air, sweat formed inside my hatband. My eyes flicked to the bell jar.

Wu Fei read my curiosity. He grasped the knob on top of the bell jar and lifted.

He revealed the head of a man inside the jar. The man was still alive and pumping choppy breaths through the nostrils of his long, tapered nose. A wooden dowel secured with a leather strap was cinched tight across his mouth, drawing his lips back, exposing teeth glistening with saliva and blood. Sweat poured down his Slavic features. His dark eyes stared through me to a place far from his misery.

His neck was corded with strain and I could see his naked shoulders through the hole in the desk. He must be trussed within and subjected to some fiendish, quiet torture. Razors? An acid bath? Scorpions? Leeches with barbed mouths crawling up his ass?

Whatever tormented him, I was sure the telepath knew because her face blanched with disgust and terror.

Wu Fei set the bell jar on the trivet. The vapor inside of the bell jar condensed into clear trails that dribbled to the rim of the glass.

I didn't know what the wretch had done to deserve this attention but I couldn't help but feel sorry for him. "Is this necessary?"

"Of course it is necessary," Wu Fei answered. He spoke in the stilted cadence of a coolie railroad worker. The dangerous bastard could be pretending he wasn't far from his roots as a simple peasant. But there was no pretense in the sadistic cunning of those bespectacled eyes. "This is a lesson for all concerned. To him. To his associates. To my constituents. And most importantly, to you, Mister Gomez."

I rubbed an elbow across the waistline of my coat and felt the comforting swell of my Colt Navy. I pulled my legs close until my boots bumped against the chair so my hideout revolver and boot dagger would be within quick reach.

Wu Fei replaced the bell jar over the man's head. When it

sealed against the desk, the fog returned and within a few of the man's breaths, the inside of the glass was again white.

Wu Fei pointed to the brass lever jutting from a slot beside the bell jar. The telepath gulped. With trembling fingers, she reached for the lever. Grasping it, she gave a firm pull. Gears meshed inside the desk. She pushed the lever, leaning into it, and a metallic snap shot from the desk. Instantly, blood sprayed the inside of the jar, coating it red. She sat back against her chair, looking green and nauseated.

He nodded to the guards. One of them barked a command.

Two barefoot Chinese girls—slender as reeds—and hopefully too young to be prostitutes, but this was St. Charles, appeared from behind a silken screen at the far right. Abbreviated robes barely covered their thighs. One draped a silk cozy over the bell jar, as if by disguising it we would overlook the macabre contents. The other brought a tray with a porcelain teapot and three matching cups. She set the tray on the desk and filled the cups. A leaf of steam lifted from each serving of tea. Then both girls bowed and shuffled backwards to disappear behind the screen.

Wu Fei took a cup from the tray and with avuncular deference, handed it to his telepath. He picked up a second cup for himself and I raised mine. We gave each other a silent toast, but as we brought the cups to our lips, I paused and fixed a suspicious gaze at my tea. If I had a tail, it would've been twitching like a cat's.

"Drink, Mister Gomez," the telepath said. "Please enjoy our hospitality." I could hear the milk and cream of the upper Midwest in her voice.

Wu Fei studied me, and it was apparent that he took pleasure in my discomfort. I made a slurping sound but didn't drink. With my sleeve, I wiped my lips. I smiled at him, then at her. My hand edged to the Colt Navy. The instant I felt woozy, both would die.

Setting his cup aside, Wu Fei asked, "You have much experience with Chinese?"

I replied, "I served on a Cantonese gun boat during the fight for Baja." I paused, surprised by what I'd just said.

"Ba-Ha?"

"California," I answered, again without thinking. "The flotilla was from San Diego. They were good sailors at sea and damn fine infantry on land."

Wu Fei nodded, pleased by the accolades I had given his countrymen.

I put my cup on the edge of his desk and slowly reached into an inside coat pocket. I could feel the gaze of the guards. I fished out a small memo pad and withdrew an onionskin telegram—my invitation here—that was folded between the pages. Another surprise for me since how did I know about the telegram? "Wu Fei, with all due respect, you're a man with a considerable reputation."

He nodded again, even more pleased.

I showed him the telegram.

Wu Fei only glanced at it. He tapped the woman's arm. She opened a drawer on her side of the desk, pulled out a manila envelope, and handed it to her boss. He undid the string closure. Shaking the envelope over his other hand, he caught the tintype that slipped out. The metallic rectangle was the size of a playing card. He offered it to me. I tucked the telegram back into the memo pad and accepted the tintype.

On closer inspection, it was a tintype of another tintype, the era's way to make photocopies. The subject was an attractive young woman with high cheekbones, almond eyes, and shiny dark hair gathered into long braids. Chinese but she could've been an Apache or Navajo.

I moved to return the tintype.

Wu Fei said, "Keep. You need to find girl."

I turned my attention back to her face. "Who is she?"

"My daughter. Ling Zhu Han."

This admission took me aback ... quite a bit, actually. I never figured the Dragon to be a family man.

"How do you know she is missing?"

Wu Fei explained in his tortured English that she was en route to St. Charles when she disappeared in Tucson six weeks ago, and he hadn't heard from her since.

Tucson? "Any ideas? Suspects?" Someone must have a death wish if they had kidnapped Wu Fei's kin.

"That why I hire you, Mister Gomez."

I withdrew a pencil in a silver extender from inside my coat. As I asked for more details I jotted notes in the memo pad. Age? Eighteen. Married? No. Home? La Jolla, a village north of San Diego.

"Occupation?"

"I believe scholar. She is bright girl."

"Scholar of what?"

"When you find, ask her."

Since Ling was living in California and Wu Fei was here, I guessed they were estranged. My questions and Wu Fei's answers volleyed back and forth. Mother? Dead. Sisters, brothers? Perhaps.

Friends? You find. Traveling companions? Again, you find. No reason to ask about enemies since Wu Fei had more than a stray mongrel had fleas. Motives? Ransom?

"That your job to learn, Mister Gomez."

The gangster offered more information, enough for me to make plans for Tucson. Wu Fei's voice never faltered when he talked about the disappearance of his daughter.

She could've run away or her body could be rotting in a hole. Either way, for a grieving father, he acted too composed, too self-assured, too aware.

"Another thing, Mister Gomez." He reached into a desk drawer and handed me a silver ring banded with turquoise. "She wore an identical ring on a right finger. It will help in identifying her."

He said that as in, *identifying her corpse*. I examined the ring and gave it back.

I pulled at the fabric of Wu Fei's story and picked at the weave of its tattered truth. I read the telepath's face for clues but her expression remained an opaque, placid mask. Wu Fei whispered into her ear. She said, "You have doubts, Mister Gomez?"

Plenty. But what brought me here was my reputation as a *pistolero*. If I walked away, I might as well shave off my mustache, pawn my guns, and pay the rent cleaning spittoons.

Closing the memo pad, I said, "I appreciate that you've asked me for help but understand that looking for your daughter would be more than a favor. Before I accept, we have to come to terms on compensation."

Wu Fei snapped his fingers. One of the guards brought a strongbox and rested it on the floor beside the desk. He opened the lid and lifted a heavy canvas satchel. The frayed and weather-beaten bag looked like it had been dragged behind an overland steam-ferry. The guard placed the satchel on the desk, careful not to disturb the bell jar.

Wu Fei draped one gnarled hand on the satchel. "Five thousand dollar in gold American eagle and Aztlan sol." He pointed a mangled finger at the tintype. "Bring her to me and I deliver another ten. That fifteen thousand dollars, Mister Gomez. Much money. Very good compensation."

A total of fifteen thousand dollars? A governor's salary. More than much money, a fortune.

I took the satchel and opened the flap. Thick coins in fifty-dollar denominations lay in neat glittering rolls. I had never held this much gold in my life, here or back in the other world. It weighed like ... trouble and danger.

The red-headed psychic stared at me. Her eyes were as green and sharp as the edges of chiseled emeralds. She whispered to Wu Fei.

Smiling, he turned to me. "Miss O'Laughlin wishes you luck

and success. I not paying for luck. I only pay for success." Wu Fei patted the silk cloth over the bell jar. "You pay for failure."

The gangster blurted something in Chinese and I caught *gou za zhong*, their equivalent of *gringo*.

A guard tapped my arm. I became aware that I was no longer welcome and felt like a trespassing foreigner. The rumbling behind the vents made the silence among us stifling. I fastened the satchel flap and lifted the bag to sling it over one shoulder. Its heft surprised me. The two guards opened the doors and without further ceremony, I gave a parting glance to the bell jar, left the room, and continued to the bottom of the stairs.

The old Chinese woman and the tattooed guard crouched beside a wooden crate that blocked my path. She wrapped a severed arm—lacerated and mottled with rot—in waxed paper and fit the bundle into excelsior, filling the crate.

No mystery about the morgue smell now.

The guard fit a lid over the crate and secured it with nails. The dragon in the flaming ring design had been branded on the lid. A line of Chinese characters, also scorched into the wood, followed one edge. *Return to Sender, perhaps?*

The old woman made an angry chattering sound, and the guard dragged the crate out of my way. I proceeded down the hall to the exterior door. It opened eerily as I approached and shut after I had passed. I walked into the hot, sticky night and through the alley back to Market Street. My kundalini noir relaxed and I breathed deep, appreciating that I wasn't dead. But the serenity didn't last. The reek of horseshit, garbage, burning coal and tobacco, and the sidewalks teeming with crowds looking for cheap thrills reminded me that I was back on the gritty streets of the city.

At the corner of 20th, four drunken cowboys argued with a prostitute, who was dressed in an open robe thrown over lingerie. They wanted a group rate, ten bits; she wanted to charge them individually. "It's the same amount of work, one at a time or all at once, you cheap bastards. You wanna sport, it'll cost you each a buck."

Anxiety over this assignment upset my guts like a bad meal. I read my watch. 11:10. Had I spent an hour with the gangster?

Who was stupid enough to kidnap a child of Wu Fei? What was to gain? And the gangster? He didn't act like a father desperate to find his daughter. The Dragon was a powerful man, why wouldn't he use his army of thugs instead of hiring me? So many vexing questions and when I groped my memory for answers, all I gathered were cobwebs.

And worse, I was walking onto the lawless boulevards of St. Charles with a bag of gold coins hanging on my shoulder.

My kundalini trilled an alarm.

Someone watched. Someone waited.

CHAPTER FOUR

Paranoia tugged at my nerves. I scoped the faces in the busy intersection, probing to see if anyone showed more than a passing interest. But everyone seemed too busy getting drunk and whoring, or fleecing the drunks and johns. But that paranoia kept tugging, cinching anxiety like a noose around my kundalini noir.

I searched the streets and raked my gaze across the tops of the surrounding buildings. A lone figure stood stock still on the roof of the Marcus Hotel. Dread wrapped icy fingers around my undead heart. The hood of a cloak obscured the figure's face, yet I could have sworn its shadowed eyes were focused right on me.

Horses pulled a coach in front of me, blocking my view. When the coach passed the stranger had disappeared. I blinked, wondering if I had been hallucinating.

My kundalini noir writhed—unsettled, apprehensive— confirming that my eyes hadn't deceived me.

One of the Dragon's spies? Or a spy from a rival gang? Or someone who kept lookout on the comings and goings through Wu Fei's door for a target of opportunity like me with this weighty bag of gold on my shoulder?

My fangs extended and I kept my mouth closed tight to keep them from showing. Hooking my right thumb over the front of my coat, I got ready to flip it back so I could make an easy reach for my Colt Navy.

Retreating from the curb, I put my back against the wall. My nerves were raw, tingling with dread and foreboding. What spooked me most was that I felt marooned, cast off in this strange world. I grew to hate Coyote. Why had he sent me here? When and how could I get back?

I felt vulnerable, like it was only a matter of time before crosshairs found me. I wished I wasn't alone. I needed vampires I could trust. My friends Jolie and Carmen. We'd been through horrific scrapes together, and I was sure they could've helped me find my way home. But they were unreachable on the far side of whatever supernatural wall Coyote had flung me over. Were they even looking for me? Did they even know I was missing?

Then I perceived a new feeling, one that caused my fears to loosen.

I had a friend here.

A face coalesced in my memory, like a photo coming into focus. A lean, drawn face. Caucasian skin weathered and bronzed by hard life under the open Western sky. Gray eyes the color of storm clouds, as ready to smile as they were to squint down the barrel of a Sharps rifle. Lanky, powerful limbs that moved quick as a panther's. A man as good on a horse as I was. A mustache that rivaled mine.

Then another thought made me wince. Since when could I ride a horse?

His name hovered on the edge of my awareness.

I couldn't let myself get distracted. I put my mind back on locating who had been watching from the roof. I let my gaze range across the street, from face to window, from window to door, from door to rooftop. No one that I could see hunted me.

Hunted. Of course. Hunted. Hunter.

My friend's name was Malachi Hunter. He was my longtime

friend and business associate. Together we had administered plenty of justice. And on occasion, he was my partner in crime. Together we were expert in exploiting the slack between right and wrong.

Malachi was where? My thoughts lagged as I groped through the sparse memories Coyote had drizzled into my mind. I looked south, down Market Street, then realized I should be one street over on Larimer. At the Dizzy Ute Saloon. I tapped my shirt pocket where I kept the telegram. I had shown Malachi the message earlier today. He and I were to rendezvous at the saloon after my meeting with Wu Fei.

New worries added to my angst. Did Malachi know I was a vampire? Was he? Or was he my chalice? Did that mean we were more than business partners? Maybe it was Coyote's idea of a joke to send me here to snuggle with a gay lover. In which case I'd be sucking more than Malachi's blood.

Tamping down a tide of dismay, I resigned myself to roll with whatever life and relationships I had here. Still, Malachi didn't seem my type, and hopefully, he wasn't.

I clamped an arm against the bag and navigated through a gaggle of revelers to 19th and east to Larimer. In the streets, horses, buggies, and buckboards jostled for right of way.

An automatic tractor chugged down Larimer, belching smoke and sparks from its engine stack. Its small, forward-feeler wheels clattered on long whip-like struts like an insect's forelegs. Steam vented from pistons rotating the drive wheels. A yellow glow pulsed erratically from the port at the front of the boiler. Behind the tractor, an enclosed trailer rumbled over the hard-packed road. A slogan painted on the side of the trailer read: Sure-Safe Delivery. Our Drivers Never Get Drunk.

The tractor hooted a blast of steam for the other traffic to stay clear. Horses whinnied and strained at their traces. Pedestrians scurried to safety before they were trampled by beast or machine. I darted behind the wagon to cross the street. Steam plumed over me. Halting beside the wooden Indian outside a tobacco shop, I surveyed the way I had come. Nothing suspicious.

But paranoia still tweaked my nerves. My vampire sixth sense whispered danger.

Continuing toward Larimer, I turned south at the first alley. The illumination from kitchen windows threw pools of dirty light into the murk. A couple of drunks teetered against a lamppost. Above them, a gas jet's meager flame hissed inside the broken glass lantern. Moths fluttered dangerously close, and one burst into flames. Down the alley, a back door opened and someone emptied a bucket, its contents sloshing across the ground. I studied the alley with vampire night vision. Rats and raccoons picked through garbage.

Grimacing at the smell, I stepped around the drunks, pools of vomit, and scattered trash. I passed the kitchen windows and service doors of the public halls and saloons. With my hand firm on the grip of my .45, I halted occasionally and checked behind me and along the roofs to make sure no one followed. Still that prickle of paranoia wouldn't go away.

I reached the kitchen behind the Dizzy Ute Saloon, lifted my feet over piles of garbage, and climbed the back stoop to the open door. I entered a steamy cloud of smells: hot stew and fried meat mixed with the alley's rank odors.

Three cooks—a large black man and a couple of Mexican *paisanos*—worked at the stove and a cutting table. They paused to regard me. The black man's gaze cut to a coach gun hanging with the pots and pans above the table. The *paisanos* menacingly adjusted their grips on the cleavers. I showed my open hands and shook my head, indicating I wasn't here for trouble. The black man nodded curtly to the other door and let me pass.

Once at the far side of the kitchen, I stopped at the end of the short hall. Straight ahead, beneath layers of tobacco smoke, businessmen, saddle tramps, and saloon girls leaned against the bar and crowded around tables. A piano and mandolin accompanied peals of crude laughter. No one acted like they cared two road apples about me.

To my left, stairs to the second floor. To my right, a row of three snugs.

The snugs were enclosed booths with room barely enough for four. The perfect setting to make secret deals, deliver bribes, and act as favored hideaways for respectable gentlemen and ladies seeking to indulge in unrespectable recreation. You had to be careful to make sure the tables had been wiped clean. You never knew what happened on top of them.

The doors to the snugs were closed except for the one nearest me. It was ajar. A broken lucifer protruded from a crack in the adjacent paneling. Door barely open, matchstick in the wall. Malachi's signal that the rendezvous was on.

Still, my paranoia did not relax. I looked back to the kitchen. To the bar. To stairs and the landing above. I halted by the snug's entrance and listened. Aside from the merriment in the saloon and the rattle of kitchen implements, nothing.

I sniffed. Tobacco. Spilled beer. Faint perfume. All normal for a place like this.

Yet the alarm kept plucking my nerves. I was missing something.

I drew the Colt Navy and slowly levered the hammer back. The pistol cocked and ready, I pushed the door, cracking it open just enough to see a man with a rangy physique occupying one of the benches. Flickering light from a ceiling oil lamp etched shadows on his craggy face. Hard eyes stared at me.

Malachi Hunter. Looking stoic as always. He could have a scorpion in his union suit and wouldn't act bothered. His derby was tipped back and the shaggy, blond hair draped over his ears shimmered in the shifting light. His open hands rested on the table.

A man in a rumpled black duster sat on the bench opposite Malachi. Elbow propped on the table, he pointed a gleaming snub-nose revolver at Malachi's face. One twitch on the trigger, and a slug would've blasted my friend's nose right through the back of his skull.

The identity of the man aiming the revolver bloomed in my memory, like a bloodstain spreading through cloth. The gruesome scar that started at his jaw and tore its way up his left cheek to bisect his eyebrow, gave him away. *El Cicatriz*—"the Scar"—Saul Sanchez. Bag man and thumb breaker.

"Felix, put your gun on the table," Cicatriz ordered with a twitch of his pistol. "Get in and sit down. Tell me what news you bring from our good pal, Mr. Wu Fei."

CHAPTER FIVE

I placed my revolver on the table and slid next to Malachi.
Cicatriz scowled. His hair was a greasy mop of black
and silver. The nubby whiskers of his unshaven face glistened like the points of a barbed-wire fence. "Hands on the table. Now."

I obeyed.

"Close the door."

With the toe of my boot, I nudged it shut. I glanced at Malachi.

He looked at me and grumbled, "Nice move, jackass."

Cicatriz's black hat rested on the table. Beneath the brim peeked the ivory grips of two Schofields—Malachi's revolvers. I replied, "I'm the dumbass? He got the drop on you first, goober."

"Both of you," Cicatriz barked, "shut up."

When I turned back to him, I noticed a fleeting red iridescence in his irises, and then realized what my sixth sense was warning me about.

A werewolf had been waiting nearby. Cicatriz.

Back in the other world, the musky smell of a lycanthrope

would've been as obvious to me as the odor of a kennel that needed a good scrubbing. Did werewolves not stink here?

As for Malachi, my memory confirmed he was human. Did he know Cicatriz was a werewolf? I wasn't sure. But my gunslinger friend was so hard-boiled that even a lycanthrope wouldn't faze him.

And did Cicatriz know I was a vampire? I was betting that he did. Was he going to reveal my undead identity or was there an *omerta* between us supernaturals?

A small leather pouch dangled just below Cicatriz's open collar. Beads decorating the pouch glittered in the light of the oil lamp hanging over the table. The decorative fringe and the pattern of the beads—a red and yellow circle inside a ring of black and white—identified it as a Sioux medicine bag. The magical concoction of herbs and powders inside masked werewolf stench like supernatural deodorant.

Cicatriz noticed my interest in the bag. In a self-conscious move, his free hand tucked it back inside his shirt.

He swung his revolver in my direction. The gun was a nickel-plated Merwin Hulbert, probably a .44. The hammer wasn't cocked back, but no matter. The pistol was a double-action so a quick squeeze of the trigger would be enough to write the first lines of my obituary.

As a vampire I could take one, two lead slugs, provided they didn't drill my skull or break a major bone. But if the Merwin Hulbert was loaded with silver bullets, then all bets were off. Malachi was human. He had taken his share of gunshot wounds and kept fighting, but his body was a lot more vulnerable to bullets than mine. If we attacked simultaneously, one of us could take Cicatriz. The other would die. Not odds I'd gamble on.

Cicatriz studied me with quick stabs of his eyes. "What was your business with Wu Fei?"

"I was in the neighborhood and he wanted to chat. We had tea."

His gaze fixed on the satchel slung over my shoulder. "Let's see what's in your bag."

I didn't move.

"You deaf?" Cicatriz asked. "The bag. What's in your goddamn bag?"

I reached to slip its sling off my shoulder.

"Easy," cautioned Cicatriz.

Slowly, carefully, I dragged the heavy satchel from my arm and let it go *thunk* on the wooden surface. Cicatriz and Malachi shifted in their seats, curious about the hefty, metallic sound.

"Open it," Cicatriz commanded. His beady, wolfish eyes kept darting from me to Malachi and back.

I unfastened the brass buckles and lifted the canvas flap. Turning the satchel onto its side, I let its gold coins roll onto the table. Their reeded edges rattled hypnotically on the wood. I was hoping to distract Cicatriz, but he didn't take the bait.

His left hand slapped over the coins. He scooped one and slid back on the bench until he wedged himself in the far corner of the snug. Lifting the coin, he brought it to eye level beside the Merwin Hulbert. His gaze flicked from me to the glittering coin, but only briefly. One furry eyebrow lifted.

"A fifty-dollar Sol." He glanced at the other coins and grinned. "It seems you and Wu Fei had an interesting conversation." As Cicatriz placed the coin back on the table, he asked Malachi, "What made the Dragon so generous? What does he want from you two?"

My buddy shrugged. "Wu Fei doesn't want buffalo scat from me. If there's a deal, it's strictly between him and Felix."

Keeping the revolver trained on us, Cicatriz scratched the whiskers on his jaw. Were we close to a full moon?

He said, "You present me with an interesting and advantageous conundrum."

"How so?" I asked. My kundalini noir coiled against the floor of my belly, waiting for the moment to strike.

"The biggest problem is getting both of you out of here and

to a safe place," Cicatriz said. "Safe, I mean, for me." He groped at his waist, unsheathed a Bowie knife and stabbed the table. "Once there, Felix, you will have the pleasure of watching me skin your friend until you tell me everything I want to know about your meeting with Wu Fei."

Malachi sucked his teeth, unimpressed.

"Save yourself the trouble." I chuckled and began to raise my hands. Cicatriz's snarl made me lay them flat again. "Just head on over to the Dragon's door and ask him. I found he can be a very reasonable man."

Cicatriz glowered and touched his scar. "That reasonableness is up to interpretation."

Malachi balled his fists and pushed up from the table. "Enough jawing. Let's get this show going."

"Sit back down," Cicatriz ordered. "We're not leaving yet."

"What are you going to do?" Malachi replied, sitting. "Stare at us all night with that ugly puss of yours. Now that's torture."

"Quit running your mouth, gringo. How about I ask Felix one more time, right here, right now? If he bullshits me, I shoot you in the shoulder. I ask him again and if I get more bullshit, I put a bullet in your gut. And you should be plenty worried because Felix is always full of bullshit."

"How many times do you intend to shoot him?" I asked. "Not that I care. I'm simply curious."

"Four times ought to do it. I'll keep the last two bullets for you."

"Kill me and you won't know about my business with Wu Fei."

"Now that I have this gold, that's a mystery that can wait until another day."

"People will hear the gunshots."

Cicatriz laughed, a coarse rattle from deep in his throat. "This is St. Charles. Gunshots from a snug can be forgotten with a simple exchange of money." He patted the pile of gold coins.

A knock on the door. We all sat up, surprised.

The doorknob turned and the door swung open to bang into the table. A woman bumbled in, her form swaddled in a dark-blue, slim-waisted jacket. Her pleated skirt draped past the tops of tall boots. A brimmed hat with a gauzy veil masked her face. She sidestepped noisily—boots scuffing the floor, clothes rustling—as she squeezed against the table to close the door.

Cicatriz braced himself against the wall opposite the door. His confused gaze darted from the woman to me. I shrugged to let him know I had no idea what this intrusion was about. He looked at Malachi, who also shrugged, then looked back at the woman. His grip tightened on the Merwin Hulbert.

If the stranger had been a man, I'm sure Cicatriz would've plugged him twice by now. But the appearance of a woman had left all equally bewildered.

He growled, "Who the hell are you?"

She planted herself on the bench next to him. I smelled her perfume and perspiration. Definitely human. She gushed, "Okay, I'm here." Her tone confident, assertive, almost too big for the snug. "But I was told to expect only one of you. I see, *un, deux, trois*. That'll bump up my gratuity."

I recognized her voice and her brusque, impatient manner. A choker with an ivory cameo grazed the collar of her white blouse. She had stolen that cameo from me. Slowly, the memory of her congealed, and it brought a bitter taste.

She examined the confines of the snug. "Not much room for the four of us, but we can make it work provided you fellows don't mind bumping swords." She faced Cicatriz and tapped a lacy finger against the muzzle of his revolver, acting unconcerned that it was aimed at her chest. "You, my roughneck friend with such a lovely shiny gun, get to go first."

She withdrew her hand and deftly unbuttoned her jacket. All the tension in the snug spiraled around her. The front of the jacket parted and it swelled open to reveal the full bosom of her blouse. The air was electrified with the anticipation of seeing more of her feminine charms. And as dangerous as those charms were, even I wanted to see them again.

Bringing her gloved hands to the table, she drummed her fingers, then stopped, abruptly, dramatically. My kundalini noir hitched. Her head jerked and tilted to regard the gold coins as if she had just noticed them. She raised her veil and folded the hat brim to better examine the coins in the dim light. "Oh my. Such a treasure. We are going to have a *very* good time."

She lifted her head and the overhead lamp caught her face, though her eyes remained in shadow. Her face: oval-shaped, high cheekbones. A sharply sculpted proud nose, almost too big. A wide, too-big mouth with mismatched lips. The upper was a thin line while the lower drooped like a plump slice of ripe fruit. A lot of her parts were too big, yet amalgamated as they were on her, they were perfect for the kind of woman that she was. Seductive. Scheming. Treacherous.

Hermosa Singer.

We were all in trouble.

CHAPTER SIX

S o it was the four of us in the snug, bathed in the
uncertain piss-yellow glow of the overhead lamp. Malachi
and me on this side of the table, Hermosa directly opposite me, Cicatriz next to her. His menacing glare cut from face to
face, and the muzzle of his revolver tracked wherever he looked.

That pistol didn't concern me as much as Hermosa's unex-
pected arrival. Staring at her, memories exploded in a glittering,
brilliant shower. But it wasn't all confetti, some of those memories pelted me like shards from a broken mirror.

One random sliver of memory: contentment, she and I riding
together, laughing in the aftermath of a naughty escapade, our
horses splashing across a sun-dappled creek. Another sliver: the
sadness of awakening alone on a cool morning, her side of the
bed empty, unkempt, and still warm. Another: the raw heat of
her naked body pressing down on mine during a moist humid
night, her hair cascading over my face, my skin electric from the
caress of her hands and lips. Yet another: the burn of treachery
when I realized my saddlebags had been pilfered and once again,
she had run off with my cash and my self-respect.

Hermosa Singer, she could wreak more havoc than a dozen

tornadoes. Named She-Who-Sings-With-The-Owl by her adoptive Caddo parents, her blood was as mixed up as a stray mongrel's. Pick a tribe, a nation, a people. Shawnee. Huron. Manso. German. Creole. Irish. If there was a possible coupling between two random strangers, then it was in her bloodline.

At fourteen, she had escaped the reservation and with the ease of a chameleon blending into the brush she changed her surname to Singer and submerged herself into the white man's world. Knowing that men did stupid things for beautiful women, she decided to grease that inclination by naming herself Hermosa.

I wondered how many of these recollections came from Coyote's book and how many already resided in the brain of this alternate Felix.

Slowly, Hermosa removed her hat and laid it beside her on the bench. The lantern shined on her face. In its yellow light, her complexion took on an amber cast, lighter than mine. Even though her eyes remained in shadow, they glistened as bright as her jeweled earrings. Her hair was pinned up in layers of voluptuous curls. Loose strands teased over her ears. My undead heart waited for her to unpin her locks and shake them free, an invitation for me to reach across the table and cup the back of her slender, graceful neck.

My kundalini noir buzzed, conflicted between the desire to jump her bones or to sit tight and hope that she went away. Soon.

Her eyes were not on me but on the gold coins. When she went for one, Cicatriz growled, "Those are mine."

She withdrew her hand.

He aimed his revolver at Malachi and me. "You know these two clowns?"

She smirked. "Maybe I've seen them before. In a circus."

That made him chuckle.

I kept my expression tight, resentful that my insides were twisted over her while she could be so flippant. Then I saw a gleam in her eyes; she had a plan for Cicatriz. The poor bastard was doomed.

"Who sent you here?" he asked.

"Dale Prichard, the concierge of this fine establishment. Normally I do my business upstairs." She leaned close to Cicatriz. "Listen, the meter is running. I get paid whether we sport or we sit here and look at each other."

"You'll get paid once I bed you," Cicatriz replied. "If there was another deal involving these bums, then too bad."

"Mr. Prichard won't like that."

"Mr. Prichard can go fuck himself."

"Let her go," I said. "There's no reason for the *little* lady—" at this, Hermosa glowered spitefully, "—to attend to the business between us."

"There's a reason," he answered. "She can watch me shoot you two shit heels and then tell the world that I'm somebody you don't fuck with."

"You might want to buy a dictionary," Malachi said. "Expand your vocabulary."

"Whaddaya mean?"

"That way you can use another word besides 'fuck.'"

Cicatriz furrowed his scarred brow. "*Fuck* you." He jabbed the Merwin Hulbert at my friend.

As fast as a scorpion flicking its tail, Hermosa thrust both arms at Cicatriz. Her left index finger threaded into the revolver's trigger guard, binding the trigger and keeping him from squeezing off a round. The knife edge of her right hand cracked across his Adam's apple, *hard*. Even though he was a werewolf, the blow stunned him.

Seeing my chance, I got ready to spring over the table and jam my thumbs into his eye sockets. I would twist his neck until his skull snapped from the spinal cord.

Hermosa stayed me with a wave of her right hand. *I got this.*

Eyes bugged out, his jaw clenched and unclenched as he tried to suck air down his smashed windpipe. His left hand clutched at his collar.

Her left hand remained knotted around his revolver. With her other hand, she reached under the lapel of her jacket and slipped forth a slender glass syringe. With a flick of her finger, she knocked free the tiny cork on the needle. Aiming the syringe at Cicatriz's neck, she jabbed the needle into his jugular and depressed the plunger.

His neck corded, and he trembled. His eyes glowed with pain. She withdrew the syringe and a dot of blood beaded on the wound. Both of his arms fell against the table and he slumped backwards, his body twitching to the cadence of his dwindling pulse.

Hermosa wrestled the revolver from his limp hand. She examined the nickel-plated gun and then placed it on the table. "Should bring me some nice pin money from a pawn broker."

He wheezed a final death rattle. Hermosa grabbed his hat from the table and covered his face. "Now hush. Die quietly, you smelly son of a bitch."

Back in my former world, a freshly dead lycanthrope would've cycled to his wolf shape by now. What to expect here I couldn't guess.

Hermosa reached into the pleats of her skirt and produced a long jewelry case. She popped it open, slid the syringe through loops in its velvet lining, snapped the case shut and tucked it back into her skirt. As the final gesture in her act of murder—cold-blooded though well-deserved—she wiped her gloved hands.

"Felix, Malachi," she hooked strands of hair behind her ears, "a gentleman would've thanked me by now." She pushed the Schofields across the table toward Malachi. "I think these belong to you." She wagged a finger. "And I caught that look you gave me earlier. Shame, shame. You're a married man."

My friend pruned his lips and retrieved his revolvers.

I palmed my Colt Navy and dropped it back in its holster. I

tipped my head at Cicatriz's corpse. It still remained in human form. "What about him?"

"He's not going anywhere," Hermosa answered. "Not soon, anyway. Let's discuss business."

A hunch prompted me to ask, "It was you on the roof of the Marcus, wasn't it? Watching me."

She touched her chin and looked to the ceiling. "Felix Gomez dipping his wick in Mattie's House of Mirrors, that's not news." She dropped her hand and beamed excitedly. "But Felix visiting the Dragon, that's news."

"Who told you I'd be there? A little bird?"

"I have a flock of little birds telling me all kinds of things. But before we continue." She tallied the gold coins using her fingers. "Knowing that Wu Fei likes to work in round numbers, this looks like it should be five thousand dollars. Split three ways, that would be ..."

"What the hell you talking about?" Malachi asked, crossly.

"We're partners," she replied, feigning surprise.

"I don't remember asking," I said.

She laughed. "You and your formalities. If it hadn't been for my serendipitous arrival, this ugly rascal would've added two more notches to his gun."

"You only saved me the trouble of killing him myself," I replied. "In another minute, I would've sent his twisted soul to Hell."

"How so?" Malachi asked. "Seemed to me like he had us both by the nether parts."

"I had something cooking, don't you worry," I said. "Besides, other than sitting on your lazy ass waiting for me, you didn't seem keen on a—"

"Boys, boys," Hermosa thumped the table. She pointed at the coins. "What's this money for?"

I couldn't risk telling her. "How about I give you a third and you go about your merry way?"

"Oh no," she replied. "I smell a bigger payoff. That third is only my retainer."

Malachi shook his head. He knew as well as I did that if we brought Hermosa into our fold, there was a good chance she would hogtie us with her self-serving schemes. I knew Wu Fei was playing with a marked deck, and we didn't need another cheater in this poker game.

I stared at her. Malachi stared at her. She busied herself dividing the gold coins into three piles.

Malachi asked, "What would it take for you to leave us be?"

She sat upright and crossed her arms. "All right. I can tell I'm not exactly welcome. So let's make a bet."

Betting against Hermosa was like getting into a kicking contest with a mule. You would always lose. But accepting her challenge seemed like our only recourse other than shooting her, and we hadn't yet crossed that bridge.

She plucked one Eagle off the table and held it between us. "You tell me why Wu Fei hired you. If I can't be of any use, then I'll keep this one coin and call it a night. On the other hand, if I can provide worthwhile utility, other than my charming company, then I'm in for a third of everything."

"Hell," Malachi relented with a heavy sigh, "Felix hasn't yet told *me* what's going on with Wu Fei."

"In that case," Hermosa said, "fill *us* in."

My kundalini noir curled in my belly, waiting, hoping that I wouldn't do something stupid because of her. Again.

"Here's the story." I reached into my coat pocket and withdrew the envelope Wu Fei had given me. I opened it and fished out the tintype. "The Dragon wants me to find this girl."

Malachi took the photograph and held it to the light. "Who is she?"

"Her name is Ling Zhu Han. She's Wu Fei's daughter."

Malachi mumbled under his breath. "I was hoping he wasn't allowed to breed," His eyebrows arched in curiosity. "What happened to her?"

"She's gone missing."

"Was she kidnapped? Did she run away?"

I shrugged.

Hermosa beckoned with her fingers. Malachi passed the tintype to her. She studied the image, her eyes shrinking to a squint. "I know her."

"You do?"

"If that's Ling, sure." Hermosa handed the tintype back to me.

"Do you know where she is?"

"I do."

My nerves strummed with excitement. This might be the easiest bounty I'd yet collected. "Where?"

"Oh no. First, do I get a third of the payoff?"

Malachi and I looked at each other. We both nodded.

"All right," I said, "you're in."

She looped an arm around a third of the coins and raked them to her side of the table.

"Hold on," I slapped my hand on hers. "Tell us where we can find the girl."

Hermosa pulled free. "She's in a grave. Dead."

CHAPTER SEVEN

Malachi and I sat stunned by the news. Ling Zhu Han was dead? I rested the tintype on the table. I studied her visage. Her youthful, serious face framed by braids. The moody, judgmental eyes. She was an attractive young woman, and I wondered how pretty she would look with a smile. What a shame she was dead.

"Are you sure it's the same woman?" I asked.

Hermosa nodded.

"Did you know Ling was Wu Fei's daughter?"

"At the time, no."

"Time?" Malachi pressed. "What time? When was this?"

I didn't let her answer, "And you're sure she's dead?"

Another nod. Her eyes dimmed with an emotion I'd never before read in them: guilt. "I blame myself for what happened to her."

"How so?"

"Last month I met Ling in San Diego. She and several other Chinese women had organized a venture with the Continental Sisters of Benevolent Light. It's a charity to help girls and young women in unfortunate circumstances." Hermosa mimed having a large belly.

"Ling was pregnant?" I returned the tintype to my coat pocket.

"You mean *with child?*" Hermosa raised an eyebrow. "No."

Even though a murdered werewolf lay slumped beside Hermosa, I realized that in this world and time, certain words crossed the line of propriety. Apparently, "pregnant" was one of them.

Hermosa continued, "Ling was helping prostitutes from the Orient. The charity provided room and board, education, medical attention, correspondence with adoption agencies. The Sisters had approached me to provide protection services."

"Protection services?" Malachi asked. "Against diseases? Or other unfortunate circumstances?" He patted his belly. "Like a little bastard."

"Of course not," she replied, tersely. "This kind of protection." She reached into the pleats of her skirt, pulled out the butt end of a revolver, and slid the weapon back into its pocket. "The group was heading to El Paso del Norte to visit the border brothels. They would be traveling by train through rough territory in southern Aztlan. I was hired as a guard with the understanding I'd get three dollars a day plus expenses. Once on the way, the head patroness, Mrs. Abigail Widmark, reneged on the deal, saying that in the true spirit of benevolent assistance, I should've offered to serve for free. Meanwhile, Mrs. Widmark was riding first class with a personal maid and a hairdresser, all paid by the charity, I must add. I jumped the train at Yuma and returned to California ... Monterey. Two weeks ago I read in a broadsheet that Ling had been murdered." Hermosa fell silent, brooding.

I let her have a minute of introspection before asking, "Murdered? How? When?"

"By the time I got the news she'd already been dead for four weeks. She died in Tucson after their train had been attacked and robbed. Ling was one of two women killed. The other was Chen Li."

"Anything special about her?"

"Chen Li? Not that I could find. She was just at the wrong place at the wrong time."

"What happened to the rest of the party?" I asked. "Mrs. Wid—?"

"Hold on," Malachi interrupted. He rubbed his chin and stared blankly in the direction of Cicatriz as if his corpse was a party in our conversation. "Wu Fei's daughter is murdered and weeks later he hires us to find her killers? This puzzle is not fitting together."

"Actually," I amended, "Wu Fei never said that we had to find her killers. When he told me about Ling, he gave no indication that she was dead. If fact, he acted like he had no idea what happened to her."

"How could the Dragon not know that his daughter had been murdered?" Hermosa asked. "Seems as soon as he heard the news, he would've sent an army of thugs south to rip out tongues until someone ratted on the killers."

"Or," Malachi's mustache twitched as he sneered, "Wu Fei is after something else, and Ling's death is only an excuse to secure our services."

To do what? And why? Now it was my turn to keep silent and brood.

Malachi's arm sallied across the table and returned with a gold coin. He examined the fifty-dollar Eagle and muttered, "The shit we do for some shiny metal."

"What you don't want," Hermosa said, "you can give to me."

"First try taking it from my wife," Malachi replied. "You'll find more mercy stealing from Wu Fei."

"Where is Ling buried?" I asked.

"I'm guessing Tucson," Hermosa answered.

"Wu Fei only hired me to find her and bring her back," I noted. "He mentioned nothing about her being alive or dead. We find her body, dig it up, and bring it to him. She's wearing a silver and turquoise ring that should help identify her. With that, it's case closed, and we get the rest of our money."

Malachi dropped the coin back on the pile where it landed with a heavy *ping*. "That easy?"

My jaw clenched. A sarcastic reply died in my throat, strangled by an abrupt hunger that climbed from my belly and clawed up my neck. My vision turned opaque and crimson, as if blood had flooded into my eyes.

Blood.

Blinded behind this curtain of red, my kundalini noir writhed, torn between panic and the call to feed. What was happening? My fangs yearned to extend and puncture a neck. I closed my fists to hide my talons. My head swam, dizzy with the lust for warm human nectar. I fought to keep control, something that wasn't a problem in the other world. But here, my nerves jittered and ached for blood like a junkie starving for a fix.

My brow burned feverishly hot. The inside of my nose tingled with the smell of the rich, delicious blood of my companions. The ravenous hunger spread through me, swelling into my flesh, like a rabid Felix was fitting himself into my skin. This could be doom for Malachi and Hermosa.

Horrified, I wrestled against this sensation. My mind squared off against my kundalini noir, like a tamer whipping a lion, forcing it to yield, to back away. The hunger retreated down my throat, down my chest until it lay simmering in my belly. The red film ebbed from my eyes, and the details within the snug emerged back in focus.

Still confused yet relieved, and thirsty, I let my gaze rove across the table in a vain search for a bottle. A belt of whiskey would help soothe my nerves.

Paranoid that my companions had witnessed the beginning of my metamorphosis into a bloodsucking monster, I gave them both a sheepish look while I sought words for an explanation.

Then it was as if the moment had snapped closed.

A metallic pinging faded in my ears. Malachi was just drawing his hand back from the pile of coins. Hermosa was appraising me, and her expression betrayed no surprise or terror.

The rush of hunger and my reaction to contain it had passed faster than the blink of an eye. But my thoughts remained off-kilter and a lingering panic still plucked at my nerves.

What had caused this onset of vampiric blood lust? A need for sustenance? When had I last fed? In the old world, yesterday. No telling when in this world. And where would I feed? From who? As far as I could tell, Eunice at the bordello was not a chalice. Neither were Malachi nor Hermosa. Did chalices exist here? Or did I have to slip away and hunt for necks?

Malachi reached inside his coat and fished out a leather cigar case. He opened it and offered one to me. Did I smoke? If my friend so casually offered a stogie, then I guess I did. I accepted one. He proffered another to Hermosa, which she took.

Malachi put his case away and struck a lucifer. Its flare brightened the room and the odor of burning sulfur stung my eyes. I stuck the cigar into my mouth and leaned toward the lit match cupped in his hand.

"You might want to bite off the end first," he suggested.

Of course. I chomped the end of the stogie and followed Malachi's example by spitting my nub on the floor. Hermosa used a small penknife with a mother-of-pearl handle to trim her cigar.

Seconds later, we were puffing like chimneys. Ironically, the aromatic tobacco smoke cleared my head and chased away the vestiges of my vampiric doppelganger. For now, I felt safe. My thoughts swung back to Ling.

"What next?" Hermosa tapped ash on the floor.

"Tucson," Malachi replied.

I motioned to the gold coins. "We shouldn't travel with all this money. It's better that we convert these Eagles and Sols into smaller change and put the rest in a safe."

"What safe?" Hermosa asked, the gears and cams in her head already working the angles.

"Banks don't open until ten tomorrow morning." Malachi plumed smoke at Cicatriz. "In the meantime, we need to get rid of him."

"I'll handle it." Hermosa withdrew her cigar and flicked her fingers against its ember. The cigar extinguished, she slipped it into a pocket of her jacket.

"You going somewhere?" Malachi asked.

"I am." She reached into Cicatriz's shirt and jerked free his Sioux medicine bag.

"What do you need that for?" I asked.

She held it to the light, and its beaded surface glittered like the scales of a snake. "It's pretty. And now it's mine." She stood and reached for the doorknob. "Give me a half hour. When you hear my signal, drag his carcass out the front door."

"What signal?" I asked. "What are you planning?"

She collected the Merwin Hulbert she'd taken from Cicatriz and two of the gold coins. "Use your imagination. Just be ready." She palmed the revolver and edged between the table and the door to let herself out. For the brief moment the door was open, laughter and piano music wafted from the bar into the snug.

As I gathered the remaining coins in the satchel, Malachi watched Cicatriz. He asked, "We're supposed to drag him out? Like no one would notice?"

"Why not leave him here?"

"Can't do that," Malachi replied. "St. Charles isn't so wide open that we can leave a dead body behind and not expect to arouse suspicions."

I didn't relish touching this deceased man cur. "How about we walk him out, carried between us like a drunk?"

"That might work, depending on how inebriated the rest of the clientele is. Let's get him ready." Malachi climbed on the table, stooping to avoid banging his head against the overhead lamp. I scooted around the table and grabbed the dead were-wolf's arm.

He was as limp as a dressed turkey. I could've easily handled him but for the sake of concealing my supernatural powers, I helped Malachi lift and slide the corpse until we had it sitting on the edge of the table, propped between us. I adjusted his hat.

Our tobacco smoke thickened into a dense fog. Malachi coughed. He ground out his cigar on the table. "Getting hard to breathe."

Since I didn't have to breathe, I hadn't noticed. But to share my friend's concern, I knocked the ember off my stogie and pinched the end to make sure it was out. I tucked the cigar butt into a vest pocket.

"I gotta ask you something," he said.

"Something personal?"

"Damn right, it's personal. Otherwise I would've come right out with it."

I couldn't imagine what Malachi intended to ask and considered this an opportunity to learn more about myself in this world. "I guess if I say no, you're going to ask anyway."

"Pretty much."

We sat perched on the table and stared at the door, waiting for Hermosa to return.

"Then ask, already."

More waiting.

"You gonna ask, or are we going to drop dead from old age?"

"Okay." Malachi leaned forward to peer around Cicatriz's slumped form. "What the hell is wrong with you?"

Plenty, but nothing I wanted to share.

"You're acting like you fell out of the sky and landed on your head."

What had he picked up on? I looked at my hands as if I was giving off clues that were invisible to me.

"See what I mean," he explained. "Normally, you're sharp as a barber's razor. Now you're kinda dull. You turning into a hophead? A *grifo?*"

"Nothing like that."

"Then what?"

I had to give him something. "I dunno. When I woke up earlier in Mattie's I was feeling somewhat off."

"You pick up the clap?"

"God, no."

"What girl did you see?" Malachi was still leaning forward and he was squinting out one eye.

"Eunice. Why?"

His face relaxed and he sat up straight. He coughed and I thought he was choking. The coughs erupted into laughter. "Every time she milks a pecker it rings a man's brain like a bell."

"You speaking from experience? Does Lupe know?"

"Me cheat? Lupe would castrate me like a shoat," Malachi replied with mock horror. "It's only what I heard."

If Eunice rang my bell, it was nothing compared to the reverberations Hermosa sent through me. She and I had a history that was more mixed up than her bloodline. She knew I had been at Mattie's cathouse, and yet I hadn't detected a whiff of jealousy. Were the tables turned, would I be as cool?

Minutes passed. Malachi checked his watch. More minutes passed. I checked mine.

"You notice this guy is starting to smell like a dead dog," Malachi commented.

Without his pouch of protective magic, Cicatriz's lycanthrope nature was seeping out his pores. Would his corpse shape shift? I said nothing. I waited and worried about myself. What had awakened my frightening wild and unrecognizable vampiric persona? Were my friends in danger? Could I keep the evil Felix dormant?

"I figured you would've picked up on that," Malachi said.

"On what?"

"What else?" He gestured toward Cicatriz. "His stink."

I regarded the corpse. All I sniffed was the lingering cigar smoke.

"Figured you of all people would've picked up his scent and wouldn't have let him get the drop on you."

"What are you getting at?" I asked, wary about Malachi's interrogation. As in Cicatriz was a werewolf and I was a vampire?

Malachi let my question sit, and I was left stewing over whether or not he knew anything about the supernatural world. The quiet in the room amplified the muffled chatter and music sifting through the walls.

He asked, "You think Hermosa double-crossed us?"

I was glad he'd changed subjects. "Too early in the game for that," I said. "Besides, she's rattled by Ling's death. I think she's taking it personally. Whatever snipe hunt Wu Fei has planned for us, Hermosa's going to see it through to the end."

"Did she skip out on us?"

I patted the satchel. "Not without her share of the gold."

"Then where the hell is she?"

"Cooking up a scheme."

"Like what?"

A string of rapid-fire gunshots tore from outside. Men and women shouted in panic. More gunshots. These were closer, as if returning fire. Boots stomped the floor. Tables crashed. Glass shattered.

"Goddamn," Malachi exclaimed. "It's pandemonium out there."

"No," I corrected. "It's Hermosa. Let's go."

CHAPTER EIGHT

Malachi and I hoisted Cicatriz's corpse upright and propped him between us. I made sure the bag of gold coins was tight against my side.

Gunfire and commotion shook the walls. I pulled the door open, and we shuffled sideways out of the snug and into the hall, dragging Cicatriz. Gun smoke fouled the air. Fleeing men and women barreled into us. Others lay flat on the saloon floor, hands clasped over their heads. Still others crouched behind tables or the bar and unloaded their smoke wagons toward the entrance. Glass sprayed from shattered windows. A soiled dove pushed a fat well-dressed businessman—her john no doubt—behind an over-turned table as she emptied a derringer. A ragged-looking cowpoke crawled like a lizard through puddles of spilled booze and pocketed the loose change scattered across the floor.

Malachi jerked his head toward the kitchen, then to the saloon. "Which way?"

Another string of rapid-fire gunshots crackled from the street. These shots smeared into one another and I knew of no gun that could fire that fast. Those weren't gunshots, but firecrackers—Hermosa's handiwork. I pulled us toward the front door. "This way."

Malachi and I tromped to the entrance, right through the riot of panic and gunfire. We hauled Cicatriz along, like the whole bunch of us were invisible, slugs zipping past, plaster falling from the ceiling, splinters flinging from the floor and the furniture. A bullet ricocheted against a spittoon and sent the brass vessel spinning and spraying its vile brown liquid.

A bullet broke the last remaining windowpane and whined past my head. Apparently Hermosa was using real ammo as well as firecrackers for her ruse.

We barged through the front doors and emerged into the cool night air. Bullets swarmed around us. Buckshot ripped clapboard siding to our left and right. We were taking fire from all sides. Gunshots from the Dizzy Ute must have zinged through the saloons across the street, because their patrons had also opened up with their guns, which only added to the confusion as to who was shooting at who. People ran pell-mell through the street, hollering and waving pistols, rifles, and shotguns, shooting at whatever spooked them. Cowboys on horses galloped in circles, shouting drunkenly and blasting away.

A buckboard sat against the sidewalk. Steam and smoke plumed from the head of an imposing horse-like contraption—a mechanical-Clydesdale made of brass and iron—strapped to its harness. Hermosa sat in the driver's seat of the wagon, and she twisted around to face us, her identity masked by a bandanna tied bandito-style and the brim of her hat pulled low. She held a smoldering fusee and used it to light a string of firecrackers, which she tossed on the sidewalk where they detonated in a rip of sharp reports. Dropping the fusee, she reached into her lap to brandish the Merwin Hulbert. She squeezed shots back into the saloon, aiming high so she wouldn't hit anyone but still stoking the ruckus. She shoved the pistol into the pleats of her skirt, planted her boots against the front of the wagon, and hollered, "Jump in."

Grabbing a set of levers connected to the mechanical-Clydesdale, she worked them back-and-forth. The machine's enormous iron hoofs churned against the dirt street, and the buckboard lurched forward.

Malachi and I pitched Cicatriz into the wagon. We leapt from the sidewalk and landed on the bed just as it pulled away. The bag of gold coins slammed against my ribs.

The mechanical-Clydesdale stutter-trotted toward the cowboys riding amok in front of us. Hermosa tugged on a lanyard and jets of steam shrieked from the machine's nostrils, making the horses scream and rear up. The cowboys unloaded on us with curses and revolvers. Bullets clanged against the metal hide of the mechanical-Clydesdale but otherwise, we chugged away unscathed.

I climbed onto the front seat beside Hermosa. Malachi crouched behind us and kept a concerned eye trained back on the chaos.

We turned the first corner and headed east on 19th Street, the wagon bouncing and rumbling beneath us. The mechanical-Clydesdale pistoned its legs and pulled us along at an accelerating clip. Its abrupt, vibrating movements rattled us like beads in a maraca.

"Int-t-t-teresting m-m-machine," I managed to say. I coughed and waved away the smoke streaming from its head. "B-b-but why not st-st-steal a real horse?"

Hermosa yanked the bandanna past her chin and let it settle around her neck. "St-st-steal a real horse and you sw-sw-swing," she answered, a cautious gaze fixed on a circular gauge on the mechanical-Clydesdale's butt. "T-t-technically, this is not a h-h-horse."

I could've argued the legal distinctions but the wagon's jittering motion about shook my teeth out every time I opened my mouth.

Arriving at Welton Street, we steered north to Five Points and continued past shuttered shops and noisy saloons, those patrons oblivious to the carnival of fireworks we had left behind. We kept going, on past the last trolley stop, until the graded road ran out and we bounced along a rutted trail. Countless stars glittered above us. A crescent moon washed the landscape with its dim, silvery light. We proceeded past small, darkened farmhouses and halted near a line of dense brush. Gears gnashed inside the mechanical-Clydesdale's belly. Steam feathered from its nose. Its ears and the rivets on its neck glowed a faint red.

Water gurgled and splashed from the gloom in front of us, and when I stood to get my bearings, I spied the Platte River glinting through gaps in the brush. "Why did we stop? To dump Cicatriz into the river?"

Hermosa tapped the toe of her boot against the machine's butt gauge. The needle hovered near the red zone. "Gotta let this thing cool down. And I've got other plans for Cicatriz."

"Like what?"

She pulled the Merwin Hulbert from her skirt and twisted it open, scattering the spent shells. She fished a handful of loose cartridges from a pocket and after reloading the revolver, snapped it closed.

"You expecting trouble?" I asked.

"Tell me, what's the point of carrying an empty gun?" She turned to Malachi. "Anyone following us?"

"No one I can see. How about you, Felix?"

The question implied I could see through this murk. Did that mean Malachi knew I was a vampire?

"Well?"

I scanned the trail behind us with my night vision and confirmed that no one followed. "We're good." My suspicions made my kundalini noir twitch, and my stomach grumbled. I hoped I didn't get another bout of blood lust. No telling what or who I'd eat before I got the answers I needed.

Hermosa tucked the Merwin Hulbert into a skirt pocket. She tweaked the levers and the mechanical-Clydesdale squirted steam out its nose. I glanced at the gauge. The needle was back in the green. Smoke and embers puffed out the machine's ears, and those big legs started to articulate. She steered the wagon to the right. We rumbled back to the trail and climbed a slight incline. The brush on either side of the path grew higher, blending with willows and oaks crowding against us. The cover became especially thick, and even with my vampire eyes, I might not be able to see someone waiting in ambush, especially considering the way we shook because of this mechanical beast. I rested a hand on my Colt Navy, thumb on the hammer, and glanced back at Malachi. He must've been equally concerned, having drawn one of his Schofields.

Sniffing smoke, I looked around for a campfire. Aching for a meal, I took another sniff and wished for a steaming bowl of blood.

We'd gone about two hundred yards when the trees gave way to a meadow. On the rise before us, lazy moonlit clouds outlined the silhouette of a broad house with a turret. Slivers of light peeked through curtained windows. A banner of smoke twisted from a stack behind the house.

Feet scrambled across the ground, heralding a pack of large dogs racing at us from the shadows. Seven big mongrels with necks thick as railroad ties, eyes menacing and teeth glistening. Hermosa slapped a hand across my arm, cautioning me not to shoot.

Looking back at Malachi, I noticed he had put his revolver away. Evidently, there was something about our destination I should know but didn't.

I looked at the dogs the way one might scrutinize a lobster in a tank. If I didn't eat soon, one of these curs might be on my menu.

The dogs escorted us to the house. Hermosa guided the wagon toward the entrance and braked. The mechanical-Clydesdale stood trembling, its engine puttering, steam seeping from its nostrils. The dogs sat on their haunches, panting, ears quirking at muted, random sounds.

Curtains parted in a window and light spilled out. A moment later, the front door opened. A tall, slender man in a high-crowned, flat-brimmed hat lumbered into the doorway, his body outlined in the warm tones of oil lamplight, his face shrouded in darkness.

"Who's there?" he shouted. He carried no firearm, which I thought naive considering he opened his door to strangers. Then again, this pack of killer dogs was a pretty intimidating guard force.

"It's me," Hermosa shouted back.

"I know a lot of 'me's,'" he replied. "You'll have to be more specific."

"Hermosa Singer."

"Felix and Malachi with you?"

He knew us?

"Chief Flaco Talaco," Malachi called out. "How are you?"

"Busy, as if that mattered to you. Give me a minute." The chief disappeared into the house. I didn't know if he was a chief, but he did have the guttural accent of an Indian. Sounded Sioux. Cheyenne?

"Does he know what you want?" I asked Hermosa.

"You visit Flaco Talaco this time of night, there is only one thing you want." She reached over the seat and rapped Cicatriz's skull with her knuckles. "To get rid of one of these."

The chief emerged again, this time with a metal bucket. He rested it on the threshold, reached in and began tossing hunks of raw meat at the dogs. "Good *chunkas*." The dogs lunged and snatched the meat in midair, their jaws snapping like bear traps. The aroma of the bloody flesh made my fangs itch, and I fought the urge to dive among the dogs and fight for my share. The bucket empty, the chief set it by his feet. One of the dogs rushed over to stick its big head in the bucket and eagerly lapped the insides, making it clatter against the ground. The chief said, "Meet me at the barn." He went back inside and closed the door.

Hermosa drove us around the house to a long wooden barn

detached from the house. The dogs remained behind, tearing at the meat, gnawing on bone, and fighting over the bucket. As we approached the barn I heard the growl of a furnace and the smell of smoke became stronger. Light shined through cracks in the barn.

When we reached the other side of the barn, wide double doors creaked open. Lamplight bathed the threshold, illuminating Chief Flaco. I wondered how he got here from the house. Through a tunnel? He was very thin, as his name implied. A red-and-white checkered shirt hung on his lanky form like a sack. Small eyes peered from wrinkled sockets on either side of a large, hatchet-like nose. Two long plaits of braided hair hung over his ears, and silver conches glittered around the crown of his hat.

Behind him, inside the barn, bizarre bronze statues cluttered the stone floor. The sculptures—bent tubes, curvy petals, sieve-like cups—ranged in size from squat pieces a foot tall to spindly shapes that towered above the chief. Broken clay molds, sprue, and lumps of red wax littered the floor. I didn't take the chief as a sculptor.

Chains hung from the ceiling. Stacks of crucibles stood beside the mouth of a furnace sunk into the floor. Its chimney pipe led to the ceiling. The fire inside the furnace growled like a hungry beast.

Hungry beast. That was me. I closed my eyes so I wouldn't look at my companions the same way I had at the dogs. As chow.

"Before we proceed," Chief Flaco said. I opened my eyes and saw him displaying an open hand.

Hermosa flipped him one of the gold coins. The chief pushed the barn doors fully open. She ordered, "Drop the tailgate," and Malachi and I climbed off the buckboard.

Popping loose the pins holding the gate, we let it fall open. She manipulated the levers of the mechanical-Clydesdale to steer the wagon backwards into the barn. The chief grasped a loop of chain hanging from the ceiling and put his weight on it. A mechanism in the rafters rattled, pivoting rods connected to the floor. A long hatch of false stones pivoted open, then a metal chute angled up toward the back of the wagon. A door at the far end of the chute slid open, and intense heat from burning coals surged out, making me wince. Hermosa drove the wagon until it bumped against the chute.

"Okay," she said, "in he goes."

Malachi and I yanked Cicatriz by the legs and fed him into the chute. At the instant gravity took hold, we let go and he slid into the furnace where he disappeared in the flames with a belch of sparks. Cicatriz the werewolf would soon be roasted to ash. Goodbye. Good riddance.

The chief let go of the chain and the mechanism in the rafters rattled again. The chute retracted flat and the hatch folded shut.

"Is that all?" he asked.

"We need a place to spend the night," Hermosa said. "Let things settle."

"What about the horse?" He pointed. "And the wagon?"

"Uh," she hesitated, "You want them? They're yours."

"Park them over there." He walked from the door a few feet and waved toward a collection of steam machines and wagons along a corral behind the barn. "I could use the spare parts."

Hermosa drove the wagon from the barn and parked among the other machines. The mechanical-Clydesdale clattered to a stop and a final breath of steam leaked from its mouth and nostrils. The fire in its eyes dimmed. Hermosa returned to the barn and she and Malachi headed for the house like they were familiar with the place. I started after them when the chief asked me to wait.

"What do you need?" I asked, famished and irritable.

"It's not what I need, but what you need." He tipped his head, motioning that I proceed inside the barn.

Perplexed by his comment, I waited among the bronze sculptures. Some looked like thick nets. Others were like barren trees or long spirals. All resembled pieces of jerky cast in bronze. "What are these?"

"Signal collectors." He closed and latched the barn doors.

I shook my head, perplexed by the use of a term that didn't seem to belong in this place or time. Maybe Flaco Talaco was more than an Indian chief. Maybe he was some kind of mad scientist.

"Collect what kind of signals?" I asked.

"Psychic energy. The telepaths use them."

Again with the psychic energy. My last run-in with psychic energy had taken me to another planet and almost killed me. My thoughts turned to Wu Fei's red-headed clairvoyant. I didn't know how psychic messaging worked but hadn't thought it needed mechanical help.

As he made his way to the far end of the barn, he avoided heaps of coal, stacks of bronze ingots, and wire armatures of those weird shapes. I had no trouble following him, though I was surprised how well he navigated the clutter without tripping or hitting his head.

The bag of gold coins sagged from my shoulder and that caused bothersome thoughts to wiggle down my spine. Why was the chief so interested in me? But Hermosa and Malachi trusted him, and I decided that I had to as well.

The chief and I stepped behind a wall and toward a stairwell that sank into the floor. So this was how the chief got here from his house.

At the bottom of the stairwell, the walls and ceiling glowed bright green, as if they'd been painted with the luminescent juice of lighting bugs. We turned a corner, walked down a short hall, and entered a small room, stifling hot.

But it wasn't the temperature that made my kundalini noir scream *Danger! Danger!* The floor, the walls, the ceiling of the room were covered with diagrams and sketches etched in thick black lines against the radiant green paint, and they were drawings I recognized from the book Coyote had burned and then implanted in my memory. I froze in place, dizzy with confusion. And when I'm in a strange place and confused, my instincts take over. My claws and fangs extended and I reached for my revolver, just in case.

If the chief saw that I was contemplating massaging his guts with .45 caliber lead, he made no notice. Rather, he turned his back to me and leaned over a metal locker to open it and reach inside. I backed up a step, nerves tingling, my revolver drawn, the hammer cocked, finger on the trigger. I resisted the urge to gape at the drawings and instead kept my gaze focused on the chief and the spot where I'd pop him.

"Easy now, Felix," he said in a soothing tone. He stood and turned around to show that he cradled a gallon-sized glass jar in one arm. He uncorked the jar and the mouth-watering scent of human blood wafted to me.

The chief's eyes burned vampire red and his broad mouth parted in a smile that revealed a pair of fangs. "Here you go, brother bloodsucker. *Bon appétit.*"

CHAPTER NINE

A poke in the side jolted me awake. I opened my eyes. An Indian woman with a mop of cropped hair was staring at me. After that initial impression of her, an intense light flooded my eyes and her image dissolved in the dazzle.

"You want coffee?" she asked.

Startled, confused, I sat up and bumped my head. Squinting at the blur around me I realized I was on a roof high above ground. Then I realized the source of the blinding light was the sun. I cringed, terrified. The first rays of the morning sun were deadly to vampires and if I had been exposed like this at daybreak, I should've been cremated. But I wasn't. Another change in the supernatural rules?

I was facing east, directly at the rising sun. Its warmth caressed me, and my fear melted away.

I blinked the haze and sleepiness from my eyes, but the bright sun stung and I raised my hand to shade my face. The details about where I was came into focus. A balcony on the roof. On the ground below me, a corral. In the corral, three horses soaked up the sun. Chickens pecked around their hooves.

Outside the corral stood the mechanical-Clydesdale and the other assorted steam engines. I was on top of Chief Flaco's barn.

The woman poked me again. She was using a stick and wore a checked blouse over a denim skirt. "Coffee?" She gazed at me from the edge of the balcony, so she must've been standing on a ladder.

A metallic, funky taste lingered in my mouth. "Yeah, coffee would be great. Thanks."

"Then come down and serve yourself." She disappeared past the edge of the platform.

Disoriented, I turned to see what I had bumped my head against. It was a large brass telescope mounted on a trunnion like a cannon. Scooting to the edge of the balcony and looking down a drop of about twenty feet, I saw that the Indian woman had stepped away from the ladder and was walking toward Chief Flaco's house.

He was pissing against a fence post. In one hand he held a cup of coffee, in the other, he held his crank. He tipped his head up to glimpse me past the brim of his hat.

"Morning." He hailed with a wave of the cup. He set the cup on top of the fence post, gave himself a shake, and buttoned his fly.

"Yeah, good morning," I drawled.

"Get your ass down," the chief said.

I took that to mean, *no problem, levitate to the ground.* I pushed off the roof and—*oh shit!*—plummeted to the earth, where I landed feet first and collapsed to my side. My revolver bounced out of its holster and clattered against the hard dirt. I picked myself up, shaken, embarrassed—*some gunslinger I am*—but unhurt.

"What the hell did you do that for?" the chief demanded, looking amused. "Are you afraid of ladders?"

A new mental note: *I have no power of levitation.* "I slipped," I explained as I retrieved my pistol, wiped it clean, and jammed it back in the holster. I used my hat to beat dust from my trousers and coat, and I braced myself against the wall of the barn, still confused, still hung over. I squinted to keep the sun from hurting my eyes.

My bag of gold should've slammed into me when I hit the ground. I groped at my sides. The satchel was gone. "Where's my bag?"

The chief sipped again from his cup, then flung the dregs into a patch of weeds.

As I waited for an answer, memories from last night bubbled into my consciousness. Seemed that since my arrival into this alternate place and time, I'd been cursed by bouts of fragmented memory.

What I recalled: The jug of blood, which he and I had decanted like a bottle of fine wine. The heady aroma of type A-negative. Its succulent meaty taste had smothered me like kisses from a big, horny woman.

Laughter. More blood. Then mescal. *Mescal! What was I thinking?* Obviously I hadn't been thinking. Then more blood. Mescal. Blood.

Sometime during that drunken conversation I had asked Chief Flaco about his business with Wu Fei. Whatever the chief answered remained lost in the fog. Same for what he told me about psychic energy and our lives as vampires. In vain I picked at the recess of my brain for his explanations.

I remembered also asking him if he knew Coyote and felt elation when he answered, "Sure," thinking that I'd at last have found a link between here and home.

But the chief elaborated by reciting a string of names such as, "Coyote-Peyote? Hairless-Coyote-Who-Shivers-In-The-Winter? Coyote-Squints-Too-Much? Coyote Five Legs?"

Since none of those names sounded familiar, I then described the Coyote I knew with as much detail as I could. Everything from his height, his scrawny build, his weathered face, his wispy mustache and soul patch. His accent. His manner.

The chief had replied, "You'll have to be more specific. That sounds like half the Coyotes I know."

So besides those scraps of memory, at the moment all I had was this stale taste in my mouth.

"You asked about your bag?" The chief now winged a thumb toward his house. "This way." Shambling at first, I followed him, my legs growing steady, my head clearing. His pack of dogs were scattered about the yard, watching me with the same distrustful stare from last night.

"Your bag is inside the house," the chief reassured me. "I was worried you'd lose it so sometime after we uncorked the second jug—"

A second jug?

"I had one of my wives take it away for safekeeping."

Relieved by that scrap of good news, I asked, "How did I end up on the roof?"

"Actually, we both ended up on the roof. When we began drinking I showed you my astronomy charts, then you wanted to show me something in the heavens so we climbed on the balcony to look through my telescope. Then you babbled about alien creatures on another planet and a couple of women."

"Did I mention Carmen? Jolie?"

The chief gazed down his big nose. "You tell me. You were the one doing the talking. Besides, I was drinking as much as you were."

My thoughts spiraled back to the one crucial detail I was certain he couldn't deny. I said, "You called me 'brother vampire.'"

The chief adjusted his hat so it sat low on his brow, and he flung his braids behind his shoulders. He turned his craggy face in profile to mine. "If you have a question, I'll answer on the condition that this time you won't forget."

"Just 'a' question? I have many."

"Then start asking."

"Who knows we're vampires?"

The chief brought his dark eyes to mine. "That's a rather

simple-minded question. Like asking which way is up."

"Just answer me."

"Only us."

"Us who? Vampires? What about werewolves?"

The chief grimaced like he'd stepped in dog shit. Good, I had the same reaction at the mention of lycanthropes. "We know about them. They know about us."

"What about the humans?"

"My squaws know."

"What about Hermosa? Malachi?"

"They think that on occasion you have one too many holes in your tipi. But as far as being a vampire ..." The chief shrugged. "You'll have to ask them."

We reached the back stoop of his house.

I asked, "What about if—"

Chief Flaco halted and whirled to face me. "Just be careful." His large hand grasped my shoulder and he gave me an avuncular shake. "Keep your secret for as long as you can." With that terse advice, and adding nothing about the consequences if my vampire identity was revealed, he let go and pulled the door open.

We passed through a room filled with the eye-watering stench of lye. Piles of clothes soaked in large tin washbasins. In the next room, Malachi and Hermosa were sitting at a small table against a large window and drinking coffee. I took in the aroma of elk sausage, fried eggs, and fresh bread. Sunlight gleamed across silverware and plates of food on the table. And the satchel. My friends greeted my entrance with identical condescending stares, which I deserved.

Malachi's hair was neatly combed, his face recently shaved. Hermosa's tresses were drawn up and held in place with a silver and tortoise-shell hairclip.

Two young Indian women—or rather, girls—waited barefoot between the table and the kitchen. Calico blouses over simple cotton skirts draped their nubile bodies. Chief Flaco had mentioned his squaws, and I didn't know if these two were wives or daughters.

Cocking an eyebrow, Hermosa appraised me over the rim of her cup, then looked at the bag, then me again. "Here you stagger in as usual. Late, hung over, and with empty pockets."

I raised my hand to forestall any more snide comments. "Before we discuss anything, let me have a cup of coffee."

One of the girls brought a cup and a coffee pot. I took an empty chair at the table.

Malachi pushed the bag of coins toward me. "The last time you were this careless was when the Gonzales brothers grazed you with buckshot."

I didn't know the Gonzales brothers or remember getting hit by a shotgun. That must've been the other Felix. "I'll be more careful."

"That's what you said the previous time." Malachi speared a hunk of sausage with a fork. "The gold's all there," he added as an aside.

I sipped the java, brooding. I was the leader in our quest to find Wu Fei's daughter, and I couldn't make it through the night without bumbling like the fall guy in a comedy.

Malachi wiped dots of grease from his mustache. "Chief, would you have a map of the territories? Something that illustrates the roads from here through Aztlan?"

The chief said that he did. He left and returned a few minutes later. We cleared the table to unroll a map and secured the corners with silverware. I leaned over the map, fascinated to learn more about the differences between this world and the one I had left behind.

The map showed the southwestern corner of the U.S. and northwest Mexico. What used to be New Mexico, Arizona, California south of Monterey, northern Chihuahua and Sonora, plus Baja California were now joined as the nation of Aztlan. New Mexico had been renamed Mogollon after one of its Indian tribes.

Malachi traced his finger from St. Charles south to the border of Mogollon and the West Kansas Territories (what had been Colorado). "We can take the train from here to Tucson. Once there, hopefully we'll find out what happened to Ling Zhu Han."

Still curious, I studied the map to see how in this time continuum (Oh God, I'm now in a cheesy episode of *Star Trek TNG!*), politics had rearranged the borders. I had so many questions about how this had happened. But considering I'd already mishandled the gold and was acting quite a bit "off," I decided to pretend that I hadn't perceived anything unusual.

"We shouldn't travel with all this gold," Hermosa said. "Why tempt the undeserving?"

"What do you suggest?" I asked.

"Decide how much we need. Convert that amount into smaller gold pieces, silver, and paper notes. Stash the rest in a bank."

The plan sounded reasonable but that it came from Hermosa made the back of my neck prickle. Malachi waited for my reply, one of his eyes narrowed.

"All right," I said. "Only we choose the bank." I put my hand on Malachi's shoulder. He nodded in agreement.

Hermosa raised her chin and turned away. "You don't trust me, don't be shy to say so."

Malachi and I replied in unison. "We don't trust you."

An hour later the chief had his older squaw, the one who had poked me with the stick, drive us back into town in a sharp little buggy pulled along by a nice-looking mare. I had cleaned up and reeked of cologne, but I didn't care. As we passed through downtown I kept my eyes peeled in case someone remembered us from last night. Glaziers knocked broken glass from shattered windows. Empty brass cartridges littered the street. Bullet-riddled signs dangled from lampposts. No one gave us a second glance.

Outside the Confluence Territorial Bank on Wazee Street,

the squaw halted the buggy to let us dismount. Inside the bank, three tellers—all men wearing green eyeshades—sat behind a counter, each separated from the lobby by a brass grid. A sunburnt, ruddy-faced guard in a gray uniform tracked our entry, his arms cradling a coach gun. Malachi and I then took off our hats to show we were here on polite business.

We made a beeline toward the desk of a bank officer, a portly man in a neatly pressed business suit. He set his papers down and watched us expectantly. Rising in place, he extended a large soft hand to shake mine. His grip felt like a lump of warm dough. "Chester Dahlgreen, vice president. How may I help you?"

Hermosa stepped back to let me do the talking. "We'd like to change some gold into tender and rent a safe deposit box."

"Which would you like to do first?" Dahlgreen's thin, droopy mustache framed a small mouth with tiny teeth, no doubt an overworked eating apparatus for such a well-fed man.

"The safe deposit box," Malachi answered.

"This way." Dahlgreen led us to an anteroom between the lobby and the vault. He unlocked and slid open a rolltop desk and prepared three sets of forms.

"I'd like a box and two keys," I said. "In case we lose one."

"Of course," Dahlgreen replied.

I added, "And three signatures to get into the vault."

"Not a problem, sir."

He sat in the desk chair and placed a quill pen beside an ink well. "Whose names shall I enter in the vault access authorization?"

I looked at my companions. "Her name, Hermosa Singer. His name, Malachi Hunter. And mine. Felix Gomez."

Dahlgreen swiveled the chair to face us. "Before we proceed, I need some identification."

ID? Here? Puzzled, I turned to my friends for help.

"What kind of identification?" Malachi asked.

"The usual. A birth or marriage certificate. Baptismal papers.

Military discharge. Records from another bank or other such reputable institution."

I blinked at Dahlgreen.

He shrugged. "Or someone who can vouch for your identity."

Hermosa pointed at me. "He is Felix Gomez." She pointed at Malachi. "Malachi Hunter."

I pointed to her and Malachi and recited their names. Just to be sure, Malachi pointed to Hermosa and me and repeated the process.

Dahlgreen dipped his pen in the ink well. "Good enough." He wrote Hermosa's and my names on the forms. We signed. Malachi served as witness. Dahlgreen gave us one copy of the forms. We went through the ritual again for him to issue a set of two safe deposit keys, one for me, one for Malachi. I didn't need to explain my strategy. To retrieve our stash of gold, all three of us needed to sign the access form, only I didn't trust Hermosa enough to let her have a key. As long as she got her third of the final tally—which she would—she'd have to accept my arrangement.

Each of the safe deposit keys was stamped with FORTIS and the box number. I asked Dahlgreen if he had any cords handy. He did and gave Malachi and me two thin leather cinches that we used to tie the keys around our necks.

Dahlgreen approached the vault door and heaved against a lever. The massive circular door glided open. He high-stepped over the threshold and lit oil lamps hanging from the low roof. He stepped out. "Your box is on the left."

The three of us climbed into the vault and clustered around a small table in the middle of the floor. The yellow glow from the lamps cast gray shadows across the rows of boxes. I set the satchel on the table and unfastened its buckles. With the flap pulled back, the coins inside glittered like the talisman from an oracle, an oracle that remained mute about what lay ahead.

Next stop, Tucson.

CHAPTER TEN

W e bought tickets on the Valley Steam-Comet, which left St. Charles at noon. We'd pass through Santa Fe at nine this evening, then on to Deming and end up in Tucson at eight tomorrow morning. Malachi and I bought tickets to a private compartment while Hermosa paid for a berth in the women's Pullman.

I looked out the window, fascinated by the vista as we rolled south, amazed at how the region looked a hundred years before my birth. My mind's eye stuttered as if I was watching scenes unfold from *The Time Machine*. What I knew as Interstate 25 became the Valley Highway, then State Highway 1, then the valley road, then the Ute Trail.

I had bought a couple of gazettes to help fill in the blanks about what had happened to the United States that I knew. The big change was that the Civil War had dragged into a stalemate, which bankrupted both the North and the South, and ended with the Armistice of 1866. The war-weary and impoverished Union fell apart. Texas left the Confederacy to become its own sovereign republic (again). California had split in two, the northern part joining Washington, Oregon, Idaho, Montana,

British Columbia, and Yukon to form Cascadia. The New Mexico territory also divided in two, the northern part naming itself Mogollon, the southern, Arizona. Likewise, Mexico had broken into pieces. Sonora and Baja California joined Mogollon, Arizona, Southern California, and Nevada to create a new nation in the southwest: Aztlan.

Besides reflecting on how much the political landscape had changed, I thought much about my situation as a vampire. Chief Flaco had cautioned about revealing my undead self to others. The problem was that here, unlike in the other world, my companions were human. I had to be more cautious. I couldn't remember if I had asked the chief if the Araneum existed here. Or maybe I had and he answered, but that detail didn't stick in my mescal-addled head.

Malachi sat opposite me in the compartment, munching on a sandwich and drinking coffee he poured from a vacuum flask. He had offered to buy me a meal from the diner car, but I was still full from last night's blood meal so I declined.

I did accept a cup of coffee and it rested in my hand, as warm as the camaraderie I shared with my friend. Hopefully, if the day arrived that I had to reveal my vampiric side to him—and Hermosa—the news wouldn't affect our friendship. When the coffee turned cold, I dumped the brew out the window and returned the cup to Malachi.

He finished his sandwich and tossed its newspaper wrapper into a small trashcan. After whisking crumbs from his mustache, he dug into his coat pocket and flipped a large coin to me. I snatched it from the air.

He said, "I'll bet you this. We'll run into trouble before the night's done."

The coin was a silver dollar. "You know something I don't?"

"If I noted anything worthy of my attention, you think I'd be in here talking to you?" He stretched his long legs across the floor. "Consider it a professional hunch adjusted for the law of averages."

"All right. Why not?" I pocketed the coin. "But if something does happen, it'll be me who gets us out of trouble."

"Deal." Malachi lit himself a stogie.

The door slid open and Hermosa scooted into the compartment. Without asking, she plopped beside me.

"I thought you wanted time alone," Malachi said. "Catch up on some reading."

"That was the idea," she replied. "Until one of the girls in the sleeper car decided to entertain a man in her berth."

"Can't fault a couple for seeking true love," he said.

"Love had nothing to do with it. She was charging him two bucks. Said she'd split an extra three if I joined in. No thanks," she added with a sneer of disgust.

The train paused in Castle Rock, then Colorado City, Pueblo, and Trinidad. At each stop Malachi and I left the compartment to stand in our car's vestibule and survey the people milling outside. A few passengers disembarked, others climbed on. Hermosa mingled her way through the other cars to troll for gossip. In the afternoon our train finally began the climb to Raton Pass, Malachi and I returning to our compartment, Hermosa remaining at large.

A spur curved away from the mainline. Armored cars on the tracks pointed the long, slender barrels of rifle cannon at the sky over the border with Aztlan. A placard on the closest car read: *U.S. Army, 11th Anti-Airship Artillery Brigade. If it flies, it dies.* Apparently, relations between the U.S. and our neighbors to the south weren't always cordial.

As we rolled into the train station at the top of the mesa, we passed a large sign that welcomed us to the nation of Aztlan and the state of Mogollon. In English and Spanish the sign advised us to have visas or passports ready.

A jolt of concern made me sit up straight. I had neither. Malachi reached into his coat and removed his billfold. He plucked a five-dollar note, creased it lengthwise, and held it between his fingers. He raised an eyebrow at me, seeming to ask, *What are you waiting for?*

I followed his example. The train eased to a halt at the station. Soldiers in khaki uniforms climbed aboard. Their red armbands read *Customs—Aduana* in embroidered gold letters. Since Raton Pass was but an entry point, not many passengers left the train. Outside the windows, vendors hustled food and drink.

Heavy steps tramped down the aisle to our door, and it was whisked open. One of the customs soldiers—a sergeant judging by the chevrons on his sleeve—leaned in, a thin mustache decorating his wide, dark face. "Papers, please."

Malachi raised his hand, and the sergeant plucked the bill. I extended my hand, and the soldier helped himself.

"What is your final destination?" He slipped the money into a tunic pocket.

"Tucson," Malachi said.

"And the nature of your trip?"

"Business."

"Ah well," the sergeant said. He fished two business cards from another pocket and gave one to Malachi and one to me. "At one point in every business trip, a man must allow himself a little pleasure." He saluted, said, "Enjoy your stay in Aztlan," and withdrew from the compartment, sliding the door closed.

The card read:

Doña Juanita's Parlor of Refinement
42 Grand Avenue, City of Tucson, State of Arizona
Music. Refreshments. Beautiful girls.
This card good for one intimate handshake
or as credit toward the procurement of other entertainment.

The reverse provided the same message in Spanish. Malachi gave his card to me. "The wife wouldn't be pleased," he said.

We continued to Santa Fe. As I had done in Colorado—

rather, the West Kansas Territories—I compared the landscape to what I remembered from the future. With only the occasional settlement astride meager dirt trails, the high desert looked more desolate than I recalled.

In the late afternoon I headed alone to the vestibule at the end of our railcar. The car behind us bucked and strained at its coupling. The wind slapped my clothing, and I screwed my hat tight on my head. I watched the sunset over the ragged *llano*, awed by the beauty, and the fact that I was alive in such strange circumstances.

The door opened, and Hermosa joined me on the vestibule.

"Don't tell me," I raised my voice to be heard over the clack of wheels, "your amorous friend in the sleeper car has another appointment."

"She's quite the entrepreneur," Hermosa replied. "And noisy. Here I thought by getting a private berth I'd be getting some rest."

I made room for her against the railing. We stood side-by-side and admired the changing view. The sun settled below the horizon and its wake of orange clouds darkened to red, then purple. Sparks from the locomotive stack zipped through the twilight.

Hermosa lifted my arm and wrapped hers around my waist. She pressed her head against my shoulder. "Romantic, isn't it?"

I had to admit that it was. The swaying of the train, the aroma of sage mixed with the smell of burning coal, an adventure calling me forward, a beautiful woman leaning her warm body against mine.

But it was Hermosa, and a small voice beneath the swell of emotion whispered, *Beware. Beware.*

She removed pins from her hat and whisked it off. Strands of hair fluttered in the breeze. "It's been a long time, Felix," she said, in segue to what I knew would be the start of a lot of bad decisions on my part.

"We've done this before," she said. "You. Me. On the train."

"I'm sure we have."

"What do you mean? You say that like you don't remember."

That was true. I didn't remember.

She pivoted and brushed her hips against mine. "We did it like this. Outside, just like now." Her hat gripped tight, she leaned over the railing, her dark tresses swirling like smoke from a fire. "I held onto the railing and you held onto me." She yelled so I could hear her over the clatter of the train. "We were so naughty. So wicked."

"You were complaining about your bunk mate's lack of decorum," I said.

"That is different," Hermosa rubbed her butt against my thigh. "This is about me."

The smart thing would've been to spin her around and interrogate her about her true intensions, but Hermosa's charms smothered that small voice of caution.

She teased that fine rump against my crotch. When I leaned over her to scoop her in my arms, she guided my hands to her breasts, though they were well packaged inside layers of clothing. I nuzzled her neck and inhaled the delirious fragrance of sandalwood, lilac, and vanilla. My hands roamed down her side and gathered her skirt.

"Okay, love birds," a voice menaced. "Freeze."

My hands remained where they had been fumbling with Hermosa's drawers. Slowly, I turned my head.

A man clung to the outside of the railing on the other side of the vestibule. He hadn't arrived through the door or jumped from the car behind us. The only way he could've reached that spot was by inching his way along the outside of the train. The ballsy effort of an acrobat—a sniff confirmed a lupine odor—or a werewolf.

The wind buffeted his coat's lapels and the brim of his hat. Keeping a large Colt revolver trained on us, he climbed over the railing and growled, "Tell me what you did with Cicatriz."

CHAPTER ELEVEN

T he werewolf *pistolero* advanced toward Hermosa and me. "Hands in the air, the both of you."
I raised my hands and pivoted slowly toward the gunman. Had he showed up a minute later, I'd be standing with my pants down and my pecker *in flagrante delicto*. Hermosa fluffed her skirt so that it draped over her legs.

"I said freeze!" he barked.

"Please, allow a lady to retain her dignity." She turned very deliberately to face him.

The train rocked beneath us and the werewolf shifted his weight to hold his revolver steady. Light from the vestibule door's window highlighted a scarred brow and a twisted nose that looked like it had been visited by one fist too many. "Where's Cicatriz?" he shouted.

"Why are you asking us?" I replied.

"Okay, wise ass. How about I shoot this bitch 'til you tell me what I want to hear." He trained the muzzle of that Single Action Army on Hermosa. A sneer took over his scowl, and he pointed the gun at me. "Naw, I bet she knows. So I'll shoot you instead. That way, after she talks, she can show her appreciation that I let her live. Isn't that right, darling?"

Even with my vampire reflexes I couldn't reach my pistol before this werewolf plugged me. My kundalini noir shrank inside me as if to make itself a smaller target.

He raised a bony hand and gave Hermosa a curt wave. "Step aside so I don't get any blood on that pretty dress of yours."

She was still pressed against me and I felt her grow tense. She was getting ready to try something. Pull a knife? Another poisoned needle? A pistol? I didn't know, but whatever she had in mind, it had better be quick before this lupine asshole ventilated my ribcage.

He snarled and said, "Before you try anything stupid, I know why Wu Fei has sent you to find his daughter. And it's not what you think. Too bad you'll never get to Tucson, otherwise Matthew Randolph would tell you everything."

"Who?"

"Matthew knows that Wu Fei has more tricks up his sleeve than the dev—"

The vestibule door burst open and smacked into the werewolf. The window shattered and sprayed glass against his face. Malachi sprang from where he'd been crouching behind the door. He hooked his left arm around the door to jam the barrel of his Schofield into the werewolf's belly. The gunshot boomed through the air, and Malachi's revolver spat a cloud of smoke.

Hermosa whisked a hand underneath her jacket and lunged for the werewolf, a pocket revolver at the ready. By the time I had my Colt Navy in hand, she had unloaded twice into the werewolf's face, the two rounds flaring in the darkness and cracking like bullwhips. Malachi added another thunderclap of fire and smoke when he again stitched the werewolf's guts with the Schofield. The bullet tore through the lycanthrope and pinged against the car behind us. Dense smoke fouled the vestibule before getting sucked away by the wind.

The werewolf toppled over the railing across the back of the vestibule. He tumbled against the coupling and bounced under the car behind us.

Malachi clamped a hand on his derby and leaned over the railing. He leaned back in. "Fell right under the wheels." He shouted to be heard over the clatter of the train. "Whoever polices that mess better bring a rake and a basket."

Though I breathed easier, I wished I'd gotten the chance to ask the werewolf what he meant by *I know why Wu Fei has sent you to find his daughter. And it's not what you think. Too bad you'll never get to Tucson, otherwise Matthew Randolph would tell you everything.* That confirmed my suspicions that Wu Fei had another agenda hidden behind this assignment. And it further bothered me that the werewolf and this Matthew Randolph knew why when I didn't have a clue.

Malachi broke open his Schofield and two empty shells ejected from the cylinder. "Good thing I needed a cigar and saw what was happening. Otherwise, it might have been you getting rolled and sliced beneath the train." He replenished the cylinder with cartridges from his gun belt and snapped the revolver closed. "Was it a stick up? What was he waiting for? Why the hell didn't he just gun you down?"

"He asked about Cicatriz," Hermosa replied. "But more importantly he said he knows why Wu Fei sent us here."

I added, "He said that someone in Tucson by the name of Matthew Randolph also knows."

Malachi's eyes crinkled. "Never heard of him."

I wanted to ask Malachi and Hermosa what they knew about the supernatural. But instead I said, "Apparently our traipsing after Ling Zhu Han is a ruse. Wu Fei is playing us."

"Figures." Malachi holstered his Schofield. "Which does not bode well." In a sudden flurry of interest he studied the layout of the vestibule. "How the hell did that shootist get the drop on you anyway?"

Hermosa cleared her throat.

I answered, "We were a bit distracted."

Malachi worked his mouth and sucked on his teeth. Then he flashed a grin at me. "By the way." He held his hand up and curled his fingers.

I dug into my coat and returned his silver dollar.

"That was the ante," he noted. "Pay what you owe me."

I dug back into my coat and gave him another dollar. He touched the brim of his derby in a sarcastic salute.

"You guys had a bet?" Hermosa asked. "About what?"

Gloating, Malachi explained, "Told Felix we'd have trouble tonight, and I'd have to save his hide."

"Next time," Hermosa said, "I want a piece of that action." She reloaded her little Remington and slid it back under her jacket, tapping the slight bulge to make sure the pistol remained snug.

"Another bet?" I prompted. "Double or nothing?"

Malachi tucked against the wall of the vestibule and pivoted from the wind to relight his cigar. He flung the match over the side. "Let me think about it. Cicatriz and our recently departed guest could've been acting alone. Or with someone else. We'll see. Either way, they might be reconsidering their options on account they're naught for two against us, and we left their last envoy cut into pieces like a salami."

Hermosa screwed her hat back on and tucked stray strands of hair beneath its crown. She removed long pins from under her lapel and used them to secure the hat.

Two men stepped through the vestibule door, the white-whiskered conductor in a blue uniform, and he was followed by a muscular stump of a leathery faced half-breed wearing a buff-colored barn coat. The conductor's jacket was hooked over a revolver tucked in his trousers. The other man's coat was flipped over a pistol in a cross-draw holster on his left hip. In his right hand he carried a coach gun. He wore a badge: a star within a circle. The circle said *Ferrocarril Nationale—Guardia Superior* in embossed letters.

The conductor considered me, then Malachi, then Hermosa. "What was the shooting all about?"

"My apologies," I replied. "We were celebrating some good news and got carried away."

He stepped to the vestibule railing and peered over the tail end of the car. Nodding suspiciously, he swept a questioning gaze over us. His attention dropped to the floor and he bent down to scrape a fingertip across the wooden planking. He stood and held the finger to the light glowing through the vestibule door. His fingertip was stained red with blood. Brow furrowed, he looked back at us.

Malachi shrugged. Hermosa shrugged. I shrugged. The conductor pulled a handkerchief from a trouser pocket and wiped his finger.

The guard was studying the door and raked his boots through the broken glass. He cut us an accusing look, and Malachi pointed at me.

The guard said, "*Cinco sols, por favor.*"

Spearing Malachi with the most pointed glare I could manage, I fished my billfold from my coat. "*Solamente tengo dólares.*" I handed the guard a five-dollar note.

He shook his head. "*Papel, no. Oro.*"

I replaced the bill and dug into another pocket for a five-dollar gold coin. I held it out.

He snatched the coin and rubbed it with his thumb. He held the thumb to the light to see if any finish had rubbed off. Satisfied that the coin was legit, he dropped it into a trouser pocket. "*Portense bien, sinvergüenzas.*" With those words of caution, he returned the car, the conductor trailing after him.

Hermosa and I let Malachi finish his cigar and as a group, we returned to our compartment. Hermosa called it a night and continued to the women's Pullman.

"I could also use some shut eye." Malachi yawned. "Felix, you take first watch. That is, if you don't mind."

I wasn't sleepy so I told him to go ahead and bed down. We

snuffed the oil lamps. I could see well enough but my friend fumbled in the darkness. He stretched himself on one of the benches and covered his face with his derby. Within moments, he began snoring a chorus to the click-clack rhythm of the wheels.

I stared out the window at a star-crowded sky and a landscape black as the depths of an abyss. Distant lights floated in the darkness. Lone homesteads, campfires, I didn't know. Illuminated squares cast by the train's windows raced across dirt and brush. Occasionally, the eyes of animals—deer, coyote, raccoons, rabbits—flashed by, fleeting as specters.

I couldn't help but think of this trip to Arizona as a metaphor for the way I was receding from my other life. Somehow I was certain that I'd return to 21st century Felix. But staring at the infinite gloom like I was now, I resigned myself to being stuck here for long while in the body of this other Felix.

I wondered if he was in my skin back in the Denver? If so, what was his reaction to that world and its different rules? Was he friends with Coyote? Jolie? Carmen? Imagining him with Carmen lashed me with jealousy. Even if he was me, he didn't deserve her.

Would I ever meet my doppelganger? Suppose the supernatural switcheroo got out of sync and we ran into each other? Would we bond as twins? Or would I regard him as my rival and duel him to the death? Or would we acknowledge one another and move along with a shrug and a wave goodbye?

The train reached Santa Fe and rumbled to a halt. That time of night, people shambled across the station platform clumsy as sleepy ghosts. Malachi lifted his hat off his face, raised his head to look around, yawned, and went back to cutting Zs. I didn't mind giving up my turn to sleep because the thoughts cranking in my head wouldn't let me rest.

At a quarter after one in the morning, the train started again and within minutes we chugged south along the Rio Grande valley through Belen, then Socorro, and after a quick stop in

Deming we were at last heading west to Tucson. The collections of adobe and pine-lumber shacks that we passed through seemed barely worthy of a name. I kept track of our progress by marking the time with my pocket watch.

The morning sun began its climb to claim the day, and it brought the blossom of a pink sky over the Black Hills. I stared out the window, fascinated that I could admire so casually the once-feared sunrise. Minute by minute, the landscape lightened from purple to blue to brown to shades of beige. Shrubs and cacti emerged from the retreating shadows. I was watching the world reborn and with it came the optimism and freshness of a new day, a feeling that I hadn't known since I'd become a vampire.

Malachi sat up, blinking, and rubbed his grizzled face. He groped for his watch chain but I saved him the bother of checking the time.

"It's six twenty."

"Where are we?"

"Almost at Lordsburg."

He coughed and with a stamp of his boots, he stood. "Hungry? Let's get to the dining car."

"Go on. I'm enjoying the sunrise."

"Suit yourself. I'm famished, and I gotta see a man about a horse." Malachi stumbled out of the compartment.

Roadrunners and jackrabbits darted alongside the train. Up close, the desert landscape was sand and dirt dotted with random creosote and mesquite. Solitary Joshua trees stood like neglected outcasts. But as the landscape scrolled toward the horizon, the vegetation blended into a sumptuous olive-green carpet.

The door slid open and Hermosa let herself in. She sat opposite me on Malachi's bench, wearing the same outfit from last night and looking a bit haggard.

"Doesn't look like you got much rest," I noted.

"Finally, but only after I put laudanum in that horny tramp's tea. Far be it from me to pass judgment on how another woman earns her keep in this world, but honestly, rutting goats have more discretion."

Hermosa's voice faded into a blur. I stared at her, wondering why her lips moved but she didn't appear to say anything. Then I noticed I couldn't hear the rattle of the wheels over the track.

A faint hum started in my head. My throat constricted. I tensed, acknowledging that the noise sounded too much like the terrifying hum of the deadly morning sun from the other world.

The hum grew louder, then it faded. I relaxed, wondering what was going on.

The hum returned, this time stronger, and it twisted a stab of hunger—blood lust—deep in my belly. My brow heated. I drew my nerves tight, in fear of losing control. The blood fever I felt two days ago was back but even stronger than before.

Again, the hum faded, and while my muscles eased, my kundalini noir remained taut as strung wire.

The hum returned, increasing in volume, stoking my appetite, only to fade again. The hum rose and dimmed in the cadence of measured breaths. Each interval ratcheted the blood lust up from my guts, up my throat, to my mouth until my tongue felt parched without the moist caress of human nectar. The red film from before returned to color my vision.

That hum exploded into the grating shriek of a fire alarm. My brain felt like it was boiling. My vision blurred to a red haze. The scent of human blood flooded my nose. Then my head cooled, the haze evaporated, and I was staring right at Hermosa. At her face. At her throat. At the spot where her carotid artery throbbed, waiting to be tapped.

For her part, Hermosa acted as if she had no clue about the maelstrom of confused and dangerous thoughts swirling inside my head,

My fangs extended and I kept my mouth clamped tight to keep them from showing. I couldn't feed from Hermosa. In the other world, I could pump amnesia-causing enzymes into my victim, which would erase all memory of my feeding on them. But I didn't know if I had that ability here. Plus, somehow I knew that drinking Hermosa's blood would cause complications I didn't want to deal with. So I wrestled against the compulsion to fang her, and the hunger ebbed. Then another scent of blood beckoned and teased me to the door.

I pushed upright to follow the smell. My mind swam, disconnected from my body yet still tethered to that new scent.

Hermosa started to rise. "Where are you going?"

I patted her shoulder to reassure her. "Stay here." I staggered out the door and up the passageway between the compartments toward the front of the train. The awareness of other passengers floated on the edge of my peripheral vision. Step by awkward step I made my way to the front of the car. I exited onto the forward vestibule, only vaguely concerned with the wind batting my hat and clothes. All I heard was that hum keening through my ears.

I hopped to the next car and continued my journey, navigating toward the aroma of human blood, but it was sweet, as though braided with another ingredient. I made my way through a car crowded with third-class passengers packed on wooden benches, their arms and legs splayed protectively over luggage and crates. Mostly down-and-out sodbusters, Mexicans, blacks, American Indians.

At the forward end of the passageway a Chinese man in a silk tunic of an Oriental pattern, worn over canvas trousers tucked into boots, and a fedora on his head, watched as if he was expecting me. By this time I was drowning in that aroma of tainted blood. He stepped back, smiling, like he knew the answer to this riddle of the blood scent but wasn't sharing. He twisted a doorknob and a narrow door on the left opened. The blood smell swirled out and I stumbled past him as if drunk on the fragrance.

Inside the windowless compartment, a woman lounged on silk pillows piled on a bench against the wall. She was a blonde with features so severe and sculpted it was as if her face had been whittled into shape—relaxed in green silk pajamas, her lanky legs crossed, black felt slippers on her feet. A teenage girl in pajamas relaxed on a quilt in front of her. She looked fifteen, maybe sixteen. Colorful pajamas clung to the soft curves of her ripe, young body. Neither acted surprised by my arrival.

A string of paper lanterns swayed above, illuminating the compartment with a warm, muted light. The woman held in her slender fingers a long, elegant wooden pipe. A ribbon of smoke unraveled from the pipe's bowl, and now I recognized one of the fragrances blending with the meaty notes of the blood.

Opium and something else. Something light. Delicate. Floral.

Her icy blue eyes held mine as she brought the pipe to her lacquered, crimson lips. She drew a languid breath. The ember in the bowl flared bright orange and the hum returned to squeeze my brain and feed the blood lust. She exhaled smoke and the hum faded. Faded until I could again hear the steady click-clack of the train wheels.

"Welcome, Felix," the woman purred. "I figured you could use breakfast."

Questions about her and the strange floral aroma cascaded through my brain, but they were smothered by my appetite and the promise of satisfaction.

She sucked leisurely on the opium pipe and as the ember glowed and dimmed in the bowl, the hum returned and then slackened. Smoke drifted from her nostrils and her eyes hooded in euphoric gratification. "Eat," she said. "Only the best for you."

The girl on the quilt sat straight, pulled a ribbon from her hair and with a toss of her pretty head, let her black tresses drape to her shoulders. Her large hazel eyes smoldered with the guarantee of forbidden pleasure. She raised her arms, bent her hands backwards, and presented her wrists. "For you, Mr. Vampire."

CHAPTER TWELVE

F angs sprouting, I sank to my knees and seized the girl's wrists. I held them to my mouth and bit through the skin, greedily going back and forth between each wrist, the hot blood spurting rich and succulent. Rivulets coursed down one arm, and I lapped the blood as if it were melted ice cream dribbling down a cone.

My kundalini noir vibrated with heavenly bliss. The waves of blood coursing down my throat washed away the hunger.

Her body tightened in pain, and I settled on one wrist and sank my fangs deep into the veins. In reflex, I pumped my enzymes into her. She loosened at the torrent of pleasure and moaned. Her head lolled away from me, eyes scrolling upwards, eyelids fluttering.

My blood lust satiated, I burped and gave each wrist a final lick to seal its wounds and then let go. She collapsed against the quilt, spent.

I sat back on my heels and locked bleary eyes with the blonde who regarded me with an amused, judgmental smirk. She took another languid draw on her opium pipe. Her gaze dropped to the girl splayed on the quilt and then back to me.

I wiped my mouth with my sleeve, suddenly disgusted with myself. Somehow I had allowed this woman to manipulate me into this shameful, feral display of vampiric gluttony.

I slapped the pipe out of her hand and jumped to my feet. "Who the hell are you?"

The pipe clattered against the wall. The lit ember flew out of the bowl and landed on the quilt. The blonde jerked upright and stomped her foot on the smoldering knot of opium. "Who the hell am I? The question should be, what the hell is wrong with you? Trying to start a fire?"

She collected her pipe from where it had landed on the bench and examined it. "Good. It's not scratched." Bending forward and reaching with the pipe, she used one of her long manicured nails to nudge the opium back into its bowl.

The girl stirred on the quilt and propped herself on an arm. Her eyes narrowed in feline expectation as she sat up and raked her hair into place. Slipping her hands under her pajama blouse, she raised her butt and slid the bottoms off. Her eyes stayed on me.

"What's going on?" I asked, my thoughts still in a haze.

The woman blinked, incredulous. She stared at the pipe's bowl. "Hmm, I switched blends. Maybe that accounts for your craziness."

I stepped backwards until I thumped against the compartment door. "Blends? What are you talking about? Who are you?"

She shook her head, clearly puzzled. "No, the question is, who are *you*?" She pointed at the girl. "If you were the Felix I know, you'd be riding her caboose by now. Maybe asking me to join in."

I set my hand on the grip of my Colt Navy. Now that my head was clearing, I surveyed the room in darting glances yet kept this woman at the center of my attention. She and the girl wore Chinese clothing. The guard outside was Chinese. Banners with Chinese characters decorated the walls. Chinese lanterns swayed from the ceiling. A leather suitcase engraved with

Chinese symbols sat against the corner. A thought chilled my brain.

Wu Fei.

Last night, before Malachi put the first of four bullets into him, the werewolf was about to reveal a secret regarding Wu Fei and me.

My nerves hardened at the notion that I was being played. Bile soured the back of my throat and I needed to know if this woman and her chums were part of Wu Fei's double-dealing.

The door pushed behind me. I drew my revolver and whirled around. The Chinese guard was leaning in. In one lightning-fast motion, I grabbed him by the collar, hauled him into the compartment, and slammed him to his knees. I shouldered the door closed. The hammer cocked, I screwed the muzzle of my pistol into his temple. I knocked the hat off his head, then yanked the Webley Bulldog from his hip holster and tossed it aside. I did the same for the dagger I found in the shaft of one boot.

Reaching for the suitcase, I opened it with my free hand. I scooped out a small box in black lacquer and mother-of-pearl.

"What are you doing?" the woman shrieked.

"Stay quiet," I replied.

The guard flinched, and I jammed the muzzle deeper against his skin. "Move again," I menaced, "and I'll splatter your brains." I glowered at the woman and the girl to let them know that my threat was meant for them as well.

I dumped the box and its contents—jeweled necklaces and brooches—on the floor. I scooped another box and emptied that, too. More jewelry. Another box. This was filled with small vials that smelled of perfume. Another box. Ribbons and pins. Yet another box. More vials, but these had a medicinal odor.

"Wu Fei," I explained in a whisper. That reptile had to be behind this. "If I find one thing of his, I'm going to tear you all apart."

"Wu Fei," the woman gasped, face draining of color, eyes

widening. "No. What makes you think we're here because of him?"

"No, not Wu Fei," the guard repeated, his eyes clenched tight in case I was to blast a hole through his skull.

Even the girl blanched and recoiled at the sound of the Dragon's name. She drew her legs up and clutched her throat as if to melt into the corner of the bench. Not from me, but from the specter of Wu Fei.

Their terror seemed genuine. So I relaxed, eased the revolver's hammer down and holstered the gun. "Okay, so you're not here on Wu Fei's business."

"Of course not," the woman replied. She gulped.

"Then why are you here?"

The guard looked up at me over his shoulder, his brow furrowed. The woman's forehead also knit.

"You're chalices," I said.

"Chalices?" she asked. "What are you talking about?"

If they didn't know, then no need to explain.

She unfolded her legs and as her forehead smoothed, I noticed small tattoos on the insides of her wrists. I remembered Miss O'Laughlin—Wu Fei's telepath—and her tattoos. Was this woman also a telepath?

She tilted her head as she looked at me. "What's the matter?" She picked up the opium pipe. "Maybe you need a hit."

I waved her off. "Just tell me who you are and what the hell is going on."

She held the flame of the lighter over the bowl and sucked on the pipe. "Gladys," she said as she puffed.

"Gladys, who?"

"Gladys. You asked who I am. My name is Gladys Vesna."

"Gladys?" I chuckled. When I thought of femme fatales holding court with underage prostitutes in a rolling opium den, the name Gladys wasn't the first to come to mind.

"What's so damn funny?" Smoke curled around her face.

"Not much," I answered.

Legs crossed, the girl reached for the pipe. The hem of her pajama top sagged across the gap between her thighs but I still caught a glimpse of her hairy hoo-ha. Sucking expertly on the pipe's mouthpiece, she winked at me as if demonstrating what I was missing.

I had better leave before some vestigial trace of that other Felix made me do something I'd regret. But I still had questions. I snatched the guard's hat from the floor and slapped it on his head. "Get up." I kicked his pistol and knife toward him. The muzzle of my Colt had left a red circle on his temple.

"How did you know I was on this train?" I asked.

"I didn't," Gladys answered, surprised by my question. "I play a tune on the pipe, and guys like you show up."

Evidently, some humans knew about the supernatural. By guys like me, she meant vampires. I wanted to ask her how many of "us" she had as clients but decided that I'd already let on that there was much I didn't know but should. I reached for the doorknob.

"Twelve bucks," Gladys said.

"For what?"

"For your meal." She stroked the girl's head. "And to keep waifs like poor Louisa off the street."

I snagged two five-dollar coins and tossed them to Gladys. She caught them. "This is only ten dollars."

I pointed to the guard. "He's good for the difference."

Leaving the compartment, I headed back to mine, more perplexed than ever about this mysterious world I'd been dunked into. Aside from the time-jump, on the surface, this place seemed similar to my own. But every day, I was learning more and more but understanding less and less. One thing was for sure, this other Felix lived a very loose life, even by my sketchy standards.

I had just jumped onto my rail car and passed through the vestibule door when a hand clasped my arm. I whirled about, my hand ready to strike with talon or gun.

Hermosa released me. "Where have you been?"

"Getting fresh air."

"You always say that when you disappear like this," she replied. "For once, give me a straight answer."

"How come you never give me a straight answer when you disappear?"

"That's different," she said. "I'm a woman." She pulled close and sniffed. "So where did you go? Visiting hop heads?"

"Something like that."

"What for?"

"Lay off," I jerked away and continued down the passageway. "Since when are you my mother?"

Hermosa kicked at me and her boot glanced across the back of my pants. "If I was your mother, I'd beat your ass sideways. Answer me, goddammit."

"I'll answer when I have answers."

"What does that mean?" She followed me to my compartment. Malachi waited, reading a small book and smoking a cigar. He greeted my return with a questioning gaze.

I sat on the bench opposite him. Hermosa dropped herself next to him so that I had two people giving me one big stink-eye.

"What the hell is your problem?" I asked.

"What the hell is yours?" Malachi replied. He tucked the book into a coat pocket. "Ever since I met you at the saloon back in Denver, you've been acting like your rails aren't quite parallel."

"I've got things on my mind." I slumped in the bench, as frustrated with myself as Malachi and Hermosa were with me. This world was a curious place with new rules and strange players who popped in at random moments to stir an already boiling pot.

"Like what?" Hermosa crossed her arms.

I answered, "Like once we get to Tucson, finding Matthew Randolph."

CHAPTER THIRTEEN

Our train rolled past the tiny village of Willcox and continued through the gap in the Galiuro Mountains. Cactus and sage clung to the rocky palisades on either side. Bighorn sheep grazed on wild grasses clumped across the rocky terrain. From the vantage in the aft vestibule of our car, Malachi and I kept a wary eye on the rugged landscape. He braced against the side railing, looking south, Chiricahua Peak looming past his head.

I had to raise my voice to be heard over the clatter of the train. "What do you see?"

Malachi took the cigar out of his mouth and spit a piece of tobacco. He pointed the stogie up the steep incline to what at first appeared to be mule deer in the distance.

On closer study I saw that the deer were actually horses with mounted riders whose clothes blended with the beige and gray behind them. I picked through what I remembered from the area's history. "Apaches?"

"They're not Mohicans," he replied, looking at me, slanting one eyebrow dismissively. He gave another pull on his cigar and tipped his head toward the Indians. "As long as they keep their distance, we'll be safe."

We continued past Benson, where the mountains smoothed into rounded hills dotted with mesquite and chaparral. Our train rolled into a rustic and shabby settlement clustered around the train depot, remarkable only in that it was larger than every other rustic and shabby settlement we had passed through since Santa Fe. Fences made of crude posts and rails lined the dirt streets, where stray dogs trotted about their business. At the outskirts of town, the streets and the buildings seemed to melt into the desert. We chugged under a smoke-stained wooden arch painted

**WELCOME TO TUCSON, POPULATION 8,340
CAPITAL OF THE GREAT STATE OF ARIZONA
REPUBLIC OF AZTLAN**

I contrasted this dusty and hardscrabble little town against my recollection of the other Tucson—which sprawled in a rash of asphalt and strip malls across the flat desert basin to the surrounding hills.

Bell clanging, the train coasted toward the station platform, a wooden expanse with offices and shops along the opposite side. People gaped at the bullet-riddled cars. A man in a gray coat and black derby waited on the platform, his mustached face bunched into a scowl. A marshal's star glittered on his coat's lapel. His hands were hooked on either side of the buckle of his gun belt.

A group of armed men—five, six, seven—flanked him, outfitted with bandoliers heavy with cartridges and bearing Winchesters and the smaller stars of deputies. Revolvers jutted from the yellow sashes cinched around their waists. All shared his grim demeanor.

Just in case they were looking for us, Malachi and I ducked back inside the car and watched from behind a compartment window. Hermosa hustled toward us from the passageway. She dropped her suitcase and joined us at the window.

Two more gunmen on the edge of the platform observed the train's arrival. They were of shorter stature with complexions like rawhide. Their raven-black hair was combed back over their ears to brush against their shoulders. Loose tunics sagged beneath their gun leather, and their baggy trousers were gathered into cloth leggings. The bright red bandannas tied around their heads seemed to blaze against the rest of their faded, dust-colored clothing.

Apaches.

The one with the fiercest glower wore a copper shield on his breast.

I asked, "Who's Prince Charming with the badge, the one who looks like he's shitting a piece of hot coal?"

"That's Snake-Who-Smiles-At-Nothing," Hermosa answered. "He's the commander of the Chiricahua Scouts."

The train was still rolling when the marshal, his deputies, and the Apache scouts rushed onboard.

Malachi and I pulled away from the window. These lawmen were looking for someone and I hoped it better not be us. The train jolted to a stop. Heavy boots tromped down the passageway from both ends of the car. I gripped my Colt Navy when Hermosa pulled my hand away. Her eyes told me *Let's see what's going on.*

The boots shuffled, paused, then resumed shuffling, coming closer. I heard voices, then the boots halted outside our compartment. The door slid open, and the marshal and a deputy glared at us.

The man wearing the derby introduced himself. "Marshal Justin Boudreau. We're looking for Gladys Vesna, and her accomplices, Sun Zhipeng and Louisa Davidson."

His deputy held up a dog-eared handbill, illustrated with crude portraits of Gladys, Sun, and Louisa. In bold print beneath their faces, lettering said, *Wanted for Larceny, Fraud, Counterfeiting,*

Prostitution, Horse Thievery. Below that, smaller print listed a string of lesser crimes.

"Have you seen any them?" the marshal asked.

Another man abruptly joined them. It was the railroad guard. He shouldered his way past the deputy to point at me. *"El se junto con los que buscan. Yo lo vi cuando visito el compartimento del los forajidos."*

I wanted to glower at him, but I kept a poker face.

Malachi and Hermosa shot me identical looks of disapproval. *What have you done now?*

The marshal narrowed his eyes. "Is that true?"

Better that I not deny it. "Gladys owed me money."

The guard said, *"Acompañanos."*

When I stepped forward, Malachi and Hermosa moved to leave with me.

"Just you," the marshal said.

The guard and the marshal gave way and I crowded past them, my hands relaxed and away from my sides. We marched down the narrow passageway. Deputies and Apaches watched over the other passengers. Nervous eyes tracked us.

We reached the car where I had met Gladys. The conductor waited beside her compartment's door, now open. Since the marshal and his men were searching for Gladys and crew, it didn't surprise me when I peered into the compartment and found it deserted. Paper lanterns swayed from the ceiling. The silk pillows remained on the bench and the rug on the floor. What confirmed Gladys's recent presence was the lingering scent of opium smoke.

"I was here," I admitted.

"What was your business?" Marshal Boudreau asked, gruffly.

"Like I told you. She owed me money. Which she didn't have on her. Told me that once we got to Tucson she'd make good." I gestured into the empty compartment. "Which I doubt is going to happen."

"If you see her," the marshal emphasized, "you let me know."

He nodded curtly to one side, indicating that our business was done.

Malachi and Hermosa were waiting for me when I returned to the compartment.

"Who is this Gladys Vesna?" Hermosa asked.

"Someone who's mucked up my life almost as much as you have," I replied.

Hermosa made a face. "Is she the one you so mysteriously disappeared to visit?"

"Yeah. And like I told Marshal Boudreau, it was about money."

"What kind of an answer is that? Most everything in this world is about money."

"And not everything in this world is about you, Hermosa. Sometimes—"

Malachi interrupted. "Why don't you two chattering squirrels continue this conversation off the train? Let's meet at the Presidio. I'll stay behind to poke about for useful information."

Hermosa spun on her heels toward the door.

I called after her. "What about your bag?"

Without breaking stride, she turned her head to give a coquettish smirk. "A true gentleman always looks for the opportunity to help a lady."

What gentleman? What lady? I lifted the suitcase by its handle and was surprised by its heft. What had she packed? Lead bloomers?

She scrambled onto the vestibule, lifted the hem of her skirt, and hopped onto the platform. Her suitcase banging against my knee, I caught up to her. We made our way to Toole Avenue where we mixed with the traffic—pedestrians, buggies, and wagons—and continued to Pennington Street, the main drag of this desert mini-megapolis. She led us to the El Presidio Hotel, a glamorous moniker for what was a simple, two-story building covered in white-washed stucco. A black bellhop beckoned us through the entrance, the double-doors propped open.

The exterior might have been dreary drab but the interior dazzled with color. Shafts of sunlight spilled through the many open windows. Bright green fronds sprouted from planters covered in garish tile. Large, gaily rendered paintings hung from the walls to match the red velvet furniture trimmed with gold tassels. Panels of tinted glass and large slices of geodesic rocks reflected and refracted the light, filling the lobby with sparkles of jeweled hues.

The clerks behind the counter were all Chinese. Hermosa asked for two rooms.

"Baths?" our clerk asked.

Hermosa slapped a fifty-cent piece on the counter. "At once, kind sir. In our separate rooms of course."

An hour later I was finishing a bath in a portable tub between the beds in the hotel room I was to share with Malachi. The FORTIS key remained tied around my neck. I was hoping the bath would've invigorated me, but as I rinsed away the last of the funk, a growing fatigue began smothering my thoughts. I hadn't slept one moment since leaving St. Charles.

After toweling off, I slipped back into my clothes. A pair of shoes shuffled outside my door. Someone knocked. I quietly cocked my Colt Navy and tucked it under a dry towel on the dresser.

"Room service," a man's voice said. "Sir, if you're done with your bath, I'm here to empty the tub and collect the wet towels."

I told him to come in. The door lock was keyed open, and a bellhop entered to go about his chores. He used a bucket to bale the tub out one window, gathered the damp towels, and left.

I sat on the bed, laid the little Johnson & Bye beside me and emptied my Colt to clean it. In my frock coat I carried a brass pocket box that contained sections of a cleaning rod that screwed together, assorted brushes, screwdrivers, and a tiny oiler. I scrubbed the black powder fouling off as best I could with a rag, ran a brush and patches through the bore until it shined bright, then oiled the lock work and tightened the screws.

Finished with this chore, I reloaded the Colt, tucked the hideout gun back in my boot, and put the cleaning supplies back in their box.

I was wiping my gun belt clean when a pair of boots clomped to my door. A key clicked the lock. Holding the Colt, I waited.

"It's me," Malachi announced. He added, "I didn't run into any skunks." Code that all was well. If he had said, *Things are fine*, then that meant things were not fine and we were in danger.

"Come on in." I pushed the revolver into its holster.

Malachi entered and pocketed a key. He appraised the room, which was barely wide enough for our two narrow cots and the tub. "Damn, it's small. One of us would have to leave to make room for the other to fart. Brothel cribs offer more elbow room."

"The hotel only had two rooms left."

"And Hermosa took the larger?"

"A suite actually."

"Figures." He placed a box of .45 cartridges on the dresser. "Bought you these."

"What did you find out?"

"A couple of folks have heard of Matthew Randolph." Malachi's gaze fell on the gun belt in my hands. "You about done? I need to treat myself to a decent meal. Then we'll poke around and see what more we can dig up on Matthew Randolph."

"Give me a few minutes. I'll track you down."

"Suit yourself." He let himself out.

I locked the door and lay on my bed. I promised myself just a short nap. After coiling the gun belt by my pillow, I had barely closed my eyes when a train whistle filled my ears. My eyes jerked open.

The room was pitch dark. With a start I sat up, my nerves brittle with trepidation that while I slumbered something terrible might have unraveled. The moon's glow illuminated the drapes hanging limp in front of the open window. I scanned the room and saw nothing but furniture and the gray metal of the tub. I listened to plodding horse hoofs and the rattle of wagons. From below rose the tinkle of piano keys and the cackle of laughter. I tugged at my watch chain and checked the time. 9:32.

I slipped out of bed and, walking lightly, approached the window and peeked past the drapes. Light spilled from the saloons and cafes down the darkened street. People in the streets appeared to be in good spirits—or stumbled from being full of them. Gazing down the blocks toward the train depot, lamps seemed to illuminate every window in view. Dusty, little Tucson teemed with life, and it was night, the best time to be a vampire.

Now to learn what had happened to Ling Zhu Han.

Besides tracking down Matthew Randolph, where to start? Should I prowl around Tucson, flash her portrait, and expect someone to recognize her? The chances were best that someone in the Chinese community knew her, and if they did, then they probably also knew that she was kin to Wu Fei. In that case, anyone with anything of help would clam up.

Before heading out after Malachi I stopped by Hermosa's room. The door was open and a maid was kneeling beside a tub in the center of the room. She was using a small pail to empty the tub into a bucket. A flowery, soapy fragrance and the smell from oil lamps lingered in the air.

The maid, a diminutive Mexican, pushed up from the rim of the tub. "Are you looking for *la señorita?*" she asked.

"*Sí.* Where did she go?"

"*Quién sabe.* But she was *muy guapa. Bien vestida.*"

Which meant Hermosa was dolled up for her temptress routine. For who? Marshal Boudreau?

I left the hotel, wondering how to find Malachi. In short order I listed his priorities. A meal. A drink ... or two. A shave. A cigar.

I found him outside the closest tobacco shop. He was keeping company with the wooden Indian and lighting a stogie, his presence clouded by bay rum aftershave and whiskey aroma.

"Let's look for Randolph," I said.

Malachi puffed on the cigar. "I'm ahead of you, partner. In these parts, Randolph is known as Colonel Matthew Randolph and is a proud member of the Sons of the Rebellion. Hold out Confederates who won't admit they lost the war. Their meeting hall is here in Tucson. If he's within earshot of town, I predict we'll run into him before midnight."

"You sure about that?"

Malachi reached into a coat pocket. "Last you mentioned a bet, you said double or nothing. Catch." He flipped two coins at me in rapid succession. A pair of silver dollars.

If I lost this wager but found Randolph, it would be worth it.

"This way." Malachi stepped off the sidewalk and started in the direction away from the center of town. We dodged piles of horse crap and horse-piss mud puddles. "The meeting hall is in a watering hole where the scalawags and roughnecks hang out. We kick that hornet's nest, and I'm sure Colonel Matthew Randolph will come out."

"Let's start kicking."

CHAPTER FOURTEEN

Malachi and I walked toward the outskirts of town. We tromped past well-lit saloons and cafés brimming with activity. Music from a variety of instruments carried over peals of laughter. Men and women in working or fancy clothes strolled over the wooden sidewalks and across the street, oblivious to the horses and wagons. A drunk stumbled out of one saloon and like a moth drawn to a flame, collided with a lamppost, and crumpled onto the dirt.

A woman yelled at us from a nearby second-story window. A wooden sign on the building said *Doña Juanita's Parlor of Refinement*. I remembered the card in my pocket.

"Hey, you boys interested in a throw?" she asked. "My bed's empty between ten and ten-thirty."

Malachi didn't bother to look, and I gave her a wave.

As the largest settlement between El Paso del Norte to the east and Yuma to the west, Tucson was certainly a testament to the best of western culture.

"The name is Lily," she said. "Lily of the Lovely Lips. Both sets."

"Can't say that I'm even tempted," I remarked to Malachi.

"Tempted about what?" He puffed absently on his cigar. All business, his eyes remained fixed on our path down the street.

"Are you certain we're going to find Randolph?" I asked.

"Nothing's a given but sitting on our asses won't get us past nowhere."

A loud bell clanged behind us. I turned and the bright lamp of a mechanical beast dazzled me. I pulled Malachi aside. The machine *chugga-chugged* past us, horses and pedestrians darting out of its way. Moving on four tall, spindly legs, it resembled a giraffe, except one that walked backwards. What should have been the neck was a smoke stack jutting from the back end. The front light shined from where the butthole would've normally been. A man and a woman in Victorian finery and goggles sat in the cockpit located in the torso. They trembled in rhythm to the vehicle's stuttering gait. Another clang rang from the bell. The machine ambled precariously for a block, then turned right, sparks floating in its wake of smoke.

Traffic surged back into the street, and Malachi and I continued on our way. As we approached the outskirts of town, the shops and saloons became intermingled with stables and animal pens. The buildings looked more ramshackle, more tumbled down. A sow and her piglets scurried past one house and shimmied through a hole in the neighboring fence.

A small fire burned in a metal barrel where the street emptied into desert. A circle of saddle tramps stood around the flames and shared a bottle. They sang and yodeled a cappella in a tipsy, off-key western version of New Jersey doo-wop. One of them held a note that sounded suspiciously like the howl of a wolf. Or was it a werewolf?

Malachi slowed his step. "You got the ammo I left you?"

"What's not in my pistol and on my gun belt is here." I tapped my pockets. "Why? You worried about these guys?"

"It's not them." He gestured to our destination, a crude adobe structure, the last building before Tucson petered out into the Sonora wilderness. A canvas tarp functioned as the door, and raucous conversation poured forth. Slivers of yellow light escaped from around the tarp and from cracks under the eaves.

The fire from the barrel illuminated a painting on the building's cracked stucco facade, an amateurish rendering of a pair of owls surrounded by glasses of foaming beer and bottles of wine and whiskey. The birds were perched on ragged script that spelled out *Naki Muh*.

"What is this place?" I asked. "Hooters?"

Malachi halted, stared at the painting and considered what I had said. "Yeah, hooters. Why not?" He pointed to the birds. "*Naki Muh* in Apache means Two Owls."

A detail floated from what Coyote had planted in my memory. "To the Apaches isn't the owl a harbinger of death? Doesn't seem like an inviting name for a saloon."

"It does, sorta." Malachi extended one finger. "You go in this place, the first death comes from whatever rotgut you get plastered on." He extended another finger. "The second death comes from the hangover."

Made sense.

We climbed onto the porch, a low simple platform of wooden planks, scuffed with mud and horseshit. We skirted past the tarp draped over the entrance and stepped into an interior bathed with yellow light filtered through layers of tobacco smoke.

Dozens of oil lamps hung from the ceiling, smudged by soot and pockmarked by what I guessed were bullet holes. Roughnecks and lowlifes crowded the wooden floor, clustered around small tables or along the walls and the bar to the left. The tinny notes of a badly tuned piano floated above the din. A large Confederate flag hung across the far wall along with a banner labeled *Sons of the Rebellion, Local 101*. Colonel Matthew Randolph couldn't be too far off. To the right of the flag, a tough-looking *pistolero* in a slouch hat guarded a narrow door.

Few of the patrons lifted eyebrows at our arrival while most remained interested in their card games or drink. Malachi and I made our way to the far end of the bar, and placing our backs to the wall, scouted the room.

The *pistolero* by the flag stepped aside and a man with a smooth, baby face exited from the door. He wandered about the room, pausing at tables, slapping backs and making small talk like a politician currying votes.

Baby Face reached the bar, where a drink waited for him. Malachi stepped behind him and elbowed his way in to take a place on his left. I slid to his right.

"Say friend," Malachi asked. "What's in the back room?"

"You've got no friends here." Baby Face guzzled his booze. "And you've got no business asking."

I sidled closer. "How about we make it our business?"

Smirking, he slammed his glass on the counter and turned towards me, his right hand sliding toward his revolver.

"You touch that and you die," I said. With my hand low and between us, no one could see that I extended a talon and poked him in the lower back. He froze, convinced it had to be a dagger. "Do anything funny," I whispered, "and I'll feed your kidneys to the swine."

"You have no idea the—"

"You have a name?" Malachi interrupted. "I'm less likely to shoot a man I'm acquainted with."

"Lemuel."

"Very well, Lemuel. Why don't you lead us to the back and make introductions?"

"Proceed," I ordered.

Lemuel led us down the sides of the room. Curious faces tracked us. Lemuel nodded to the guard, who was chewing a toothpick. Brow pinched in skepticism, he stepped aside. I retracted my talon and—my kundalini noir snapping like a flag in a storm—placed my hand on the grip of my Colt Navy. Malachi brought up the rear and made sure the door closed behind us.

We entered the proverbial smoke-filled back room, one with a second door along the opposite wall. Two large men—one of them Marshal Boudreau—sat side-by-side in throne-like chairs at the far end of a long table, puffing on cigars. Ten other men were arranged around the table, engrossed with stacks of bills and coins.

Women in saloon-girl attire flitted about the room, replenishing drinks and cigars. They took notice of us as we advanced through the smoke but acted as though we were expected. I nudged Lemuel forward.

"Colonel," Lemuel said.

The man beside the marshal raised his eyes from the table and set them on Lemuel. We had found Matthew Randolph.

"You're back already. I—" Randolph's gaze clicked left and right between Malachi and me. His mouth fell open and the cigar tumbled out, trailing ash down his beard and vest. Though until now we didn't know him, he certainly knew who we were.

The other men caught his surprise and heads rotated towards us. Hands blurred after pistols and chairs scratched across the floor, halting abruptly when Malachi and I brandished our revolvers and clicked the hammers back.

"Before anyone does anything stupid," I offered, "ask yourself. Are you here because of principle or profit? If it's principle, then things might not turn out well because my friend and I will put bullets up your hairy nostrils before you can blink. But if it's about profit, then put your hands on the table and you'll live to appreciate your money."

Hands lifted and fingers splayed across the table.

Boudreau skewered us with a you're-about-to-die glare.

"Marshal, we met previously." Malachi pointed to me. "Felix Gomez."

I pointed back. "Malachi Hunter."

Randolph's mouth closed and his lips compressed. The set of his brow lowered as if it was squeezing blood into his reddening face.

Boudreau reached carefully across his chest and flipped the

edge of his coat to reveal his star. "I trust you know what you're risking."

"Don't worry, Marshal, we're not interested in what you reap from this town." Malachi waved the barrel of his Schofield to the cash in front of Boudreau.

"What is it that you want?" he asked.

"Just Randolph," I answered.

"Why?"

"Let's just say he has friends who might want a seat at your table," Malachi answered.

"What friend?"

"Wu Fei."

An oppressive hush fell across the room. The saloon girls cleared their throats and shuffled uncomfortably. Boudreau squirmed with unease. "And what do I get out of this," he cleared his throat, "keeping in mind that I don't take kindly bargaining with a pair of six guns trained on my aspect."

"For starters, we get out of your hair. Plus you get rid of Matthew Randolph. That's one less snout at your trough."

Boudreau steepled his fingers and looked at Lemuel. "Well?"

Lemuel's gaze tripped across the men as he counted heads. He deadpanned, "Thirteen is an unlucky number."

"Judas!" cried Randolph. He stabbed a finger at Lemuel. "Traitor. Judas."

Lemuel stepped away from Malachi and me. "I was never one much for Bible stories or you, Colonel Randolph. I believe that you're sitting in my chair."

Randolph stood and stumbled backwards. His fingers clawed toward his holster but stopped short. "Justin," he gasped, pleading to the marshal. "You can't do this. You can't give me up. Not after what I've done for you."

Boudreau grinned and took a hearty drag on his cigar. "I hereby annul my debts to you."

Marching to Randolph, I plucked his Colt revolver from its holster. I admired it, a shiny and expensive black Peacemaker decorated with gold scrollwork and Mexican eagles carved into the mother of pearl grips. But I preferred my Navy. So I set his revolver on the table and patted Randolph down. He also carried a matching dagger and hideaway pepperbox. I ordered him to unfasten his gun belt and let it fall to the floor.

"These men are criminals. Killers!" Randolph shouted. "I'll pay a bounty to bring them down."

"Which anyone is free to collect," I emphasized. "Anyone?" I implored to the rest of the men.

All shook their heads.

"One more thing," I said. "Who knows anything about Ling Zhu Han?"

A second chill braced the room. Boudreau pointed a finger at Randolph. "Ask him."

Bingo.

"Then you'll definitely want to get rid of him." I pushed Randolph toward the back door.

"Marshal, you can't let this happen!" he shrieked. "Goddamn you, Justin Boudreau."

"Colonel, taking the Lord's name in vain is not helping your case."

A saloon girl unlatched the door and stood aside, motioning that the way was clear like she was a frontier spokesmodel.

I pushed Randolph over the threshold. He blundered down the fan of light spilling from the door, our shadows stretching before us. I prodded him again to keep moving. Malachi was at my heels, his Schofield trained on the door. It closed and the night swallowed us, the darkness relieved only by the saddle tramps' trembling fire and by the stars above.

I wasn't sure where we were taking Randolph. Someplace secure to interrogate him. But he turned and staggered to the left.

"Hold up," Malachi said. "Where are you going?"

Randolph lifted his arm and pointed a crooked finger. "That way. To the Chinaman's cemetery. I'll show you."

"Show us what?" I asked.

"The answer to your question." Randolph leaned in the direction he had indicated and tottered like he was possessed. "You asked about Ling Zhu Han." We met with a dirt road and Randolph followed it away from town. Malachi and I stayed with him. We remained quiet, alert in case he was leading us into a trap.

Once Randolph told us what we wanted to know, then what? I couldn't kill him in cold blood—neither could Malachi—and we couldn't let him simply walk away and not expect retaliation.

Randolph seemed to have realized the same thing. With every step, his gait weakened like his spirit was dribbling out of him. Maybe he had decided that he was going to die and was in no hurry to meet his maker. I chose not to console him. Better that he imagine the worst and so freely spill his secrets. Then maybe I'd let him live.

"You want to know how we found you?" Malachi asked.

"Not particularly," Randolph muttered, "unless it changes my circumstance."

"It was your shootist friend on the train who gave us your name."

Randolph shook his head. "Diego is as stupid as he is hot-headed."

"You mean was," Malachi corrected.

I wanted to ask Randolph how he came to pal around with two werewolf gunmen, or would that be gun-werewolves?

Randolph mumbled, "Cicatriz got greedy. When he learned Wu Fei hired you, he wanted to get his hands on your loot. Then after you killed him, Diego wanted revenge and saw that as another opportunity to take your money."

"How do you figure into this?" I asked.

"Obviously a bad decision on my part," Randolph replied.

We proceeded past the iron gate of the main cemetery with its collection of tombstones, crypts, and simple crosses. The road curved down a shallow gully and on the next rise bypassed the cemetery marked with a fancy wooden sign that said *Negroes' Burial—Final Resting Place for the Freed-man.*

Randolph continued down the road to the next cemetery, his composure withering as if crushed by a great weight. What was tearing at him? Guilt? Remorse?

With faltering steps, he bumbled under an arch with upturned Oriental corners. I slowed to listen. All I heard were the crunch of our boots and Randolph's labored breathing. I sniffed. Nothing but desert sage, the faint odor of a skunk, and the trace of a distant fire.

Malachi and I followed Randolph into the cemetery. The markers were stone slabs laid flat into the ground. I saw no tombstones for anyone to hide behind. The closest cover was the brush on the adjacent swells of ground, too far and too dark for anyone to pick us off.

Garlands and necklaces draped small statues of Confucius and of the Buddha. Bouquets of dried flowers lay on top of a few markers. Malachi caught his toe and almost tripped. I didn't have a problem picking my way through the darkness. However Randolph wended his way through the cemetery with eerie precision.

He arrived at one marker and sank to his knees.

"Ling Zhu Han?" I asked, hopeful that maybe this quest of ours had come to an abbreviated end.

Randolph clumsily brushed dust from the stone marker. He leaned to one side and thrust a hand into his coat pocket.

"Easy," I warned.

He produced a lighter and flicked the starter. The flame, though tiny, flared bright as a bonfire in the gloom. Malachi and I shielded our eyes. Randolph brought the lighter close to the marker and illuminated Chinese characters and in English, *Chen Li.*

I asked, "This the Chen Li who was with Ling Zhu Han?"

"She is." Randolph extinguished the flame and it left spots dancing in my eyes.

"And Ling?" Malachi asked.

"Not here." Randolph's answer was practically a moan.

"Is she alive?" I asked, my kundalini noir quivering in apprehension.

"That I don't know."

"What do you know?" Malachi demanded.

"I was put up to it." Randolph's voice cracked.

"What do you mean?" I asked, impatient, irritated. "It, what?"

"It was us who robbed the train. But the robbery was a diversion for us to kidnap Ling Zhu Han."

"Kidnap her why? On whose orders?"

"And then we let her escape."

My kundalini noir twisted upon itself in confusion.

"Escape?" Malachi seethed. "To where? Or is she dead? Quit playing games."

"She had to get away," Randolph replied. "That was part of the plan."

"What plan? Then Ling is alive? Where is she?"

"I can't tell you." Randolph curled into a ball, crying. "If I talk he'll kill my family. Skin them alive while I watch."

"Who are you talking about?" I shoved my revolver into its holster, reached down, and hoisted him to his feet. "If you don't give us a straight answer, then we'll drag your miserable hide to Wu Fei and you can try keeping your secrets from him."

"I've said enough," Randolph pleaded, his words dissolving into sobs. "This is my punishment for making a deal with Wu Fei. He's the devil."

"Wu Fei?" I traded an incredulous glance with Malachi. "What deal?"

Randolph's legs buckled and I let him sag against the marker. He writhed onto his belly and then one hand slid to his lips.

"What are you doing?" Malachi kicked Randolph and crouched beside him. "He stuck something into his mouth."

I knelt and drew my knife to pry open Randolph's mouth to

retrieve what he had put in there. Then I caught the almond odor, sickly sweet. Cyanide.

Randolph retched and clutched his throat. Malachi and I stood and backed away, alarmed, disturbed. Randolph thrashed as he struggled for breath. Malachi adjusted his grip on his pistol, contemplating if he should put the wretched colonel out of his misery. But he didn't. I backed away from Randolph, scanning our surroundings.

He wheezed and gagged in the throes of poisonous strangulation. His clothes rustled against the ground. Then he lay still.

"Give him a minute," Malachi suggested. "Make sure he's stone-cold dead."

A coyote skulked close. It raised its muzzle, sniffed, and darted away, no doubt spooked by the cyanide's aroma.

Moments ago, the trail leading to Ling Zhu Han had shined as bright as morning. Now it was as dark as the night around us. Once again, Wu Fei had blurred the trail.

CHAPTER FIFTEEN

Malachi and I stared at Matthew Randolph's corpse, which lay in a macabre, twisted pose with its butt sticking straight at us.

"Well hell," Malachi lamented. "We find ourselves looking at yet another dead end ... if you don't mind the pun."

I tossed a suspicious glance about the cemetery. Though my kundalini noir pulsed with no unusual vibration, I remained worried that someone watched. Having a dead man at your feet will make you think these things. But other than small critters scuttling about their business through the night, we were alone. Even so, we kept our pistols drawn.

"Unless you're planning a séance to talk with the recently departed," I said, "let's go."

We left the cemetery and hiked the dirt road leading to Tucson. My mind spun in frustrated circles. Had Randolph not decided to do himself in, and had he kept talking, Malachi and I would know where Ling Zhu Han was and more about this deal with Wu Fei. As it was, all we knew for sure was that she had been in Tucson and now wasn't. That and Wu Fei was stringing us along.

Malachi pulled a cigar out of his coat and stuck it in his mouth.

"I wouldn't light that," I cautioned. If someone was tracking us through the sights of a rifle, the flare of a match and the glowing ember of the cigar in the darkness would make for a ready aiming point.

"I wasn't going to."

Curious about the time, I pulled at my watch chain; the wrong end because the fob slipped into my hand. When I palmed the bronze medal, I was prompted to ask, "Why did we fight in the war?"

"Which war? Be more specific."

"The one for Aztlan independence." Though my roots were north in St. Charles, I wanted to know why I still carried this memento of my military service.

Malachi kept a steady pace. "What's so damn important that you're asking about that now?"

"We got to talk about something," I replied, "and I got nothing to offer about Ling."

"Me neither."

"So tell me. Why were we fighting for Aztlan?"

"The usual reason."

"Which is?"

"Misguided patriotism, though I surmise there is no such thing as guided patriotism since they both lead you to the same misbegotten place." His footfalls marked a passing beat. "Some goddamn battlefield where you fight and bleed for honor. For virtue. For liberty. The perennial bullshit." Another passing beat. "That and we needed the money."

I tucked the medal back into my pocket. I still had questions about that war and other conflicts that rumbled in my memory like the echo from distant artillery. But Malachi's cynicism didn't illuminate much so I kept quiet and thought about what our next moves should be. Wu Fei was playing us, but we'd already taken his money so we couldn't back out of our contract without owing him.

We followed the road as it dipped and curved. We rounded the blacks' cemetery, then the whites' and Tucson came into view, as illuminated and festive as a carnival. As we entered the edge of town, several streets removed from the *Naki Muh* and a prudent distance away, we holstered our pistols. Malachi lit his cigar.

At the hotel, Malachi made a beeline for the front desk. He asked for paper and a pen. The doughy-faced clerk handed him a single sheet of stationary, a small bottle of ink, and a dip pen, which Malachi carried to a tall writing desk. He tipped his derby back and pushed the paper close to a reading lamp.

"What are you writing?" I asked.

"I'm doing my Christian duty. Someone needs to claim Randolph before he rots."

Malachi dipped the pen into the ink and wrote in neat cursive. Pausing occasionally, brow wrinkled in concentration, he would ink the pen nib and continue. When finished, he set the pen aside and angled the note for me to read.

Marshal Boudreau,

It should not surprise you to learn that Colonel Matthew Randolph has met an untimely end this night, though not by any hand other than his own. I, and my partner Felix Gomez, are innocent in the matter. The late colonel chose to expire voluntarily by ingesting poison, a fatal amount. You may find his corpse where he fell and passed away in the Chinese citizens' cemetery.

Regards,

Malachi Hunter

A bit wordy but accurate. I said, "Looks fine."

"My ass it looks fine." Grinning wryly, Malachi held the note by a corner and waved it to dry the ink. "This is a goddamn masterpiece. Did I ever tell you I'm working on my memoirs?"

"Several times."

He dabbed one finger on his script. Seeing that it didn't

smudge, he folded the note in half. When he returned the pen and ink to the desk, he said, "I need a message delivered."

The clerk reached under the counter and produced a menu of options and prices. "Not a problem, sir. Shall that be via telegraph or telepath?"

"Neither." Malachi presented the note. "It's local."

"Ah then," the clerk replied. He turned and opened a door behind the desk. He leaned in and yelled in Chinese. Holding the door ajar, he faced us and smiled awkwardly.

We waited. The clerk's smile withered into a pained scowl. He raised a finger. *One moment, please.*

He leaned back into the doorway and unleashed a tirade in Chinese. From my days fighting alongside the Cantonese infantry, I caught only the choicest of swear words. *Lazy fucker of chickens. Good-for-nothing fellator of goats.*

The clerk faced us again, smiling obsequiously. He closed the door and stepped to the counter to put the inkbottle in a drawer and wipe the pen with a rag.

The door opened and a mop-haired kid, fifteen maybe, tossed out a pair of slippers and followed them, barefoot. After he stepped into the shoes, he looked from me to Malachi. "Whaddaya need, boss?"

The clerk unleashed another tongue-lashing and swatted him across the back of his head.

The kid deflected a second swat and bowed half-heartedly. "Sir, how may I help you?"

Malachi eyed him. "You old enough to deliver this?"

"I know every cathouse and hooch joint in town. Where I've never been, you don't want to go." The boy held out his hand.

"The *Naki Muh*." Malachi offered the note.

"The where?"

"I thought you knew every joint in town."

The kid mimicked the clerk's smile and cupped his fingers.

"Here's a dime," I offered.

"The *Naki Muh* is on the far edge of town." The kid cupped his fingers again. "A long way to go this time of evening."

I added a coin. "All right, two bits."

"And it's a dangerous place."

I dropped a nickel into his greedy young hand. "And that's all you get. Otherwise you'll deliver the note for free with my boot in your ass."

"No need for threats." With a smug grin, he pocketed the coins and, note in hand, jogged out of the lobby.

"Is there anything else, kind and generous sirs?" the clerk asked.

"Unless William Shakespeare has another opus to write," I replied, "we'll help ourselves to the hotel bar."

We crossed the lobby and took seats at a table with our backs to the wall. Malachi faced the entrance into the bar, and I watched the lobby. We ordered sarsaparilla over ice and whiskey on the side.

A mechanical horse-machine clanged to a halt outside the hotel. Coal smoke slithered into the bar. A moment later, Hermosa stamped into the lobby, lifting the hem of her skirt to reveal pointed, western-style boots. A miniature top hat sat askew on her messy hair. With the back of one hand, she wiped soot from her cheek. Black smudges spotted the short cape attached to her red velvet jacket. Her expression seemed unfocused as if she were exhausted, but when she caught sight of us, she beamed and waddled on crooked legs to our table.

Malachi and I stood to greet her. I pulled a chair for her.

"That's the first gentlemanly act I've been treated to all night." She scoped out our drinks. "Whatever you're having, make mine a double."

I shouted the order to the barkeep and then asked her, "Where have you been?"

She settled into her chair, knees apart, the posture hardly ladylike. "Getting answers. What about you?"

"More like half an answer," Malachi replied. "Hopefully you

did better."

"Of that, I'm sure. Like always." She fluffed her skirt as if to cool her knickers. "What did you learn?"

"Colonel Randolph was the one who attacked Ling's train, along with Cicatriz and Diego, the shootist who attacked us on our train. He took us to Chen Li's grave."

"Which you saw?"

"We did," I replied.

Hermosa fluffed her skirt again. "And Ling?"

"She wasn't buried there. Randolph told us Ling wasn't in Tucson though he wouldn't say where she went or if she was alive or dead."

"Wouldn't say?" Hermosa snapped. "Why didn't you force him?"

"Because Randolph took poison rather than spill all of his secrets."

"Oh dear." Hermosa's expression softened. "Why would he kill himself?"

"Didn't want to get crossways with Wu Fei."

"Who by the way," Malachi said, "apparently engineered the robbery, which was itself a ruse so Randolph and his gang could kidnap Ling. And then let her go."

"So why put out the word that she was dead?" Hermosa asked.

"Maybe she is dead," I replied, "though buried someplace else."

"I hope not," Hermosa said. "Because aside from that, what Randolph told you jibes with what I found out. That when Ling left Tucson, she was quite alive."

"How did you learn that?" I asked.

"In due time." Hermosa answered. The barkeep brought her drinks. She sipped the iced sarsaparilla and then batted her skirt. "Excuse me for being crude, but I'm tempted to fling this cold drink up my dress."

"What the hell did you sit on?" I asked, annoyed.

"I did more than sit."

"On what?"

"Not what, but who."

Malachi and I narrowed our eyes at her.

She answered, "The commander of the Chiricahua Scouts, Snake-Who-Smiles-At-Nothing. In exchange for some information I managed to make him grin a little. Twice." She fluffed her skirt.

I teased, "I thought he would've satisfied your itch rather than give you one."

"It's no itch. My missus down below is worn out. Snake had a big snake."

Malachi cleared his throat. "Let's keep this conversation on a decent topic. What information did Snake provide? And why would he know?"

"Just because white people don't think much of Indians doesn't mean that they aren't paying attention to what's going on," she explained. "But this information didn't come easily. Believe me, to make Snake talk I used every technique that came to mind. Even the French ones." She drank her whiskey and chased it with a gulp of the sarsaparilla. She swallowed delicately, and I got the impression it wasn't just her lady parts that were sore.

"Snake's men told him that Ling survived the train robbery and continued south to Sonora."

Malachi and I perked up.

"Where in Sonora?" Malachi pressed. "The state is nothing but desert and mountains."

"And coastline," she offered.

"What are you getting at?" I asked.

"Guaymas?" I ventured.

"Close," Hermosa replied. Her expression darkened with foreboding. "*Isla Tiburón.*"

With that news my kundalini noir sagged in apprehension. Blood-soaked memories flooded my thoughts. *Shark Island.*

CHAPTER SIXTEEN

Hermosa glanced from me to Malachi. He chewed nervously on his cigar. Her foreboding expression darkened another shade. Seconds ago she had revealed a promising clue that would lead us to Ling Zhu Han, but it was to a place none of us wanted to visit.

Coyote had planted disjointed memories within me, but the mention of Shark Island unlocked a vault of horror. One particularly savage battle in the War for Aztlan Independence came into focus. My ears rang with the sounds of chaos and death. A storm of bullets from the island's defenses clipped the air around me. I heard myself shouting to my soldiers—an infantry unit of mustered-out Union veterans, freed slaves, plus Mexicans, Chinese, Yaqui and Papago Indians—as we scrambled down the sloping deck of our burning paddlewheel gunboat. We tumbled into the water, our desperate circumstances becoming more frantic as we raced against drowning, enemy shot and shell, and the sharks tearing through our ranks. Dying friends called out my name, but all I could do was tread water and keep splashing forward with a wounded comrade hanging onto my neck. My temple pulsed at the murderous recollection and I began to tremble and rock back and forth.

The trance broke with Malachi slapping my back. He knuckled a tear from his eyes for he had been at that battle, too. I blinked myself back to the present. Hermosa was staring at me, her face drawn with compassion. She pushed her shot glass of whiskey toward me and I gulped it down.

Malachi exhaled a thick blast of smoke to rid the air of its bad juju. "So what happens now?"

"We head south," Hermosa replied. She laid a handbill on the table. "I booked us passage on the land yacht from Nogales to Guaymas."

Land yacht? I wanted to ask why, but since I've been in this world I've been asking a lot of stupid questions, and it must've been obvious to everyone else why we couldn't take a train.

I examined the handbill and its illustration of a ship-like vehicle mounted on enormous spoke wheels. Tiny human figures in shadow beneath its hull provided a measure of scale. The land yacht appeared two-hundred feet long. The sales copy promised *deluxe hygienic* accommodations, *nutritious and salubrious* dining, and lastly, *a safe and secure passage.** At the bottom of the page, the asterisk noted, in fine print: *Passengers are advised to bring firearms and ammunition and be proficient in the use of such.*

Malachi took the handbill and perused it as he alternated between smoking his cigar and sipping his whiskey and sarsaparilla. He dropped the handbill back on the table. "I guess we have no choice."

"We're in luck," Hermosa offered with a veneer of optimism. "That land yacht was supposed to have left today but got delayed on account that its steward took suddenly ill. Fortunately another steward signed on. Otherwise we would've had to wait a week for the next voyage."

"When are we leaving?" I asked.

"At eight tomorrow morning we catch the narrow gauge for Nogales. The land yacht leaves at noon sharp."

She summoned the waiter and asked for another whiskey, which she stirred into her glass of iced sarsaparilla. Pointing to us, she told the waiter, "One of these two gentlemen will take care of the bill." She straightened her little hat and adjusted her collar. Glass in hand, she excused herself, "Tomorrow then, bright and early," and walked bowlegged out of the bar and into the hotel lobby.

The waiter remained at our table. Malachi looked at me. "Another sarsaparilla and whiskey?"

"Actually, I'm done." The thought of returning to *Isla Tiburón* brought a new thirst, one I couldn't quench with any drink from the bar. I needed fresh blood to settle my nerves. I rose to my feet. "Go ahead without me. I need some fresh air."

"Be careful getting that fresh air," Malachi said wryly.

With a wave, I tromped outside, away from the hotel's light and into the middle of the street, where the gloom matched my mood. Traffic had thinned to a few solitary pedestrians, either drunks stumbling in search of a place to lie down or others like me, in search of someone to lie with.

My fangs began to itch. My mouth salivated at the prospect of a blood meal. I needed a victim who wouldn't mind if I got close. I remembered Lucy of the Luscious Lips and the offer she yelled from her window when Malachi and I had walked by. Her bed was scheduled to be free from ten to ten-thirty. I yanked the chain of my pocket watch and read its face by the moonlight. 11:52. I hope this wasn't past her bedtime. Then again, in her profession it should never be past her bedtime.

Retracing my steps from earlier this evening, I found the entrance to *Doña Juanita's* bawdy house. The door was unlocked, and I entered a corridor illuminated by candle sconces. At the end of the corridor, a matronly woman sat behind a counter that blocked a stairway. When I asked if Lucy was still available, the woman checked a ledger on the counter and tugged a numbered cord from a dozen that dangled from small holes in the ceiling. A muffled chime answered.

The woman said, "Lucy is now available. Room 311. The house fee is two dollars."

After I handed over the cash, the woman lifted the center of the counter to let me pass to the stairs. I ascended creaking steps to the third floor. Flickering light from a ceiling oil lamp reflected across silver numbers tacked to the doors. The door to 311 was ajar, and a weak amber light seeped around its edge.

I knocked softly and entered. A candle burned inside a small hurricane lamp. Dressed in a filmy nightgown, Lucy sat in front of a vanity and brushed her long dark tresses. She regarded me in the mirror. "Welcome traveler, where's your handsome friend?"

I hung my hat on a wall peg. "It's just me."

She pivoted on her stool to look at me and hooked her ankles together, leaning to one side to show off the curve of her hip. "What's your pleasure this late hour? A three-dollar gallop? A more leisurely five-dollar ride?" She played with the top buttons of her gown. "Ten dollars gets my entire amorous repertoire, my bunk for the night, and some spit polish for any morning wood you might sprout. Plus complimentary coffee. But you'll have to leave by nine."

"It'll be quick, I promise." I crossed the room and counted three silver dollars into her hand.

She clasped the coins and pouted. "I was hoping for more from a stud like you."

Which she was going to get. The blood thirst pulled at the back of my throat, and my fangs threatened to jut out, fully extended. I unbuckled my gun belt and looped it on a bedpost.

Lucy slipped out of her gown and stretched across her mattress, naked, writhing seductively on her belly to draw my attention to her long legs and tempting round ass. But as I undressed, my eyes homed in on her neck. She winked as she rose to her hands and knees, tits dangling. "Saddle up, *vaquero*. This filly is hot and lathered."

When I crouched behind her, she arched her back and raised her head, shaking her hair, tempting me to grab a handful.

Which I did as I eased into her. She responded with a rehearsed and well-timed moan.

The blood lust flared inside of me, demanding that I feed, that I take. With my free arm, I hugged her torso while I pulled her head to one side. Pushing her flat against the mattress, I pressed my mouth to her neck. At the instant my fangs punctured her skin, she struggled and cried out, "Hey, rough stuff is an extra two dollars!"

I savored the initial rush of delicious blood filling my mouth. I worked my fangs and injected her with a good dose of enzymes to jolt her pleasure receptors. She flushed fever-hot and went slack beneath me. Her sultry flesh invited me to put all my weight on her and soak up the heat.

Her human nectar flowed down my throat and its warmth unloosened the kinks and knots in my kundalini noir. I relaxed my hold and slid off her. She turned to face me, and—eyes hooded in euphoric pleasure—she reached for me, one hand for my neck, the other for my erection. Opening her legs, she pulled me on top of her, guiding my mouth to her throat and my hard-on to her pussy.

I lay on top of her and helped myself to seconds. She clasped me with her arms and legs, and finding a rhythm, we pumped my balls dry. I gave her another dose of enzymes and she seemed to melt into the bed sheets.

I took a moment to let the blissful aftermath fade into a pleasing memory. In the other world, this was how I fed, and I appreciated the familiarity. I pushed off the bed, wet a towel in the washbasin on the vanity, and wiped the spunk from my junk. Leaving a three-dollar tip, I got dressed and headed downstairs. I paused at the front door to gather my wits. More than one complacent and satisfied customer had been gunned down as he exited a whorehouse, still distracted by his host's lingering charms. The blood meal had diluted my apprehension, and my nerves gleamed sharp and ready for our adventures in Guaymas.

Returning to El Presidio Hotel, the aroma of Malachi's cigar smoke greeted me in the hall outside our room. I announced myself by whispering our code that all was fine. "I didn't run into any skunks." When I heard the hammer of his Schofield revolver give that distinctive click of moving from cocked to uncocked, I eased the door open.

Malachi was sitting up in his bed, in the dark, stripped to his drawers, his face lit by the ember of his cigar. His FORTIS key hung from a leather cord—similar to the one I wore—from around his neck. The Schofield rested beside his right hip, and his left hand cupped a glass. A bottle of whiskey stood on the floor beside his bed.

I slipped into the room and closed the door. "Thought you'd be asleep by now."

"So did I," he replied.

"What are you doing?"

"Thinking about my wife. Drinking. Was doing some reading." He waved the small book he'd been toting around. "Virgil."

I coiled my gun belt under the pillow on my bed, the grip of my Colt Navy within quick reach. I sat on my bed and yanked off my boots.

Malachi slurped from his glass. "How much did that fresh air set you back?"

"Eight bucks."

"You got everything out of your system?"

His question tugged at my kundalini noir, and I had to know what he meant. "Can I ask you something?"

He released a jet of smoke. "You can ask all you want. Getting answers is a different matter."

"How well do you know me?"

He squinted a moment. "Well enough. What's eating you?"

I'm a vampire, that's what is eating me. My kundalini noir withdrew into a fearful ball, not certain how my closest friend in this world would react.

While I dithered, Malachi read my face.

"You do this once in a while," he said.

"Do wha—"

"I know who you are, and what you are. And that's between you and the Almighty. For the record, I wouldn't trade places."

"So you know what I am?"

"I was there, remember?"

His reply sent my thoughts spinning. *No, I didn't remember.* "Malachi, I need to ask."

"Well, I'm done answering." He said this like we were treading onto forbidden ground. "Now it's my turn to ask a question of my own. You ready for tomorrow?" He stabbed the butt of his cigar into the glass, where the ember drowned with a hiss in the remaining drops of whiskey.

"I am."

"Good." He set the glass on the floor and fluffed the blankets over his body. "Whoever is waiting down south will be deserving our utmost attention."

We were up at six AM. I felt fine though I'd been awake all night wondering about my place in this world as a vampire. Malachi knew my true identity, at least, that's what I gathered. As did Gladys and her crew of thieves. What about Hermosa? Wu Fei? His telepath certainly gave that indication.

By seven Malachi and I walked out of the hotel barbershop, freshly shaved and full of hot coffee and fresh donuts. Hermosa waited for us in a one-horse cab outside the hotel. "Good morning."

I tipped my hat and replied in kind. Right after the three of us climbed into cab, the driver flicked the reins, and the horse pulled us forward.

Along the way, I watched Hermosa and Malachi, studying how they seemed to enjoy the morning ride, lost in tranquil musings while my mind was bursting with questions. Our road skirted the coal yard west of town. As we passed the mountain of coal, she explained that the factory processed the material into bricks of wonder-fuel used to power the land yachts.

Once we arrived at the train stop, I carried Hermosa's valise to our passenger coach hitched behind freight cars loaded with hexagonal bricks of the wonder-fuel. We occupied a cramped bench—Hermosa sandwiched between Malachi and me—and watched a guard force of Apache tribal police board the train.

At eight sharp, with a loud blast from its steam whistle, our train began the two-hour trip to Nogales. As we picked up speed, the wind blended the smell of engine smoke and the fragrance of sage and Hermosa's perfume. The soothing aroma and the gentle rocking motion lulled me into pretending that I wasn't an undead bloodsucker and that we weren't plunging into danger. Occasionally, the chirp of a songbird slipped through the mechanical racket of the train. Eventually the clutter of Nogales crept into view. The train slowed and stopped at the station.

Hermosa flipped her jacket's lapel and read the small watch pinned underneath. "Perfect. I have an hour to shop. A proper woman should have the right attire for any occasion." She adjusted her gloves and regarded Malachi and me. "You two might want to secure equipage necessary for our journey."

"We're about to do that." Malachi slapped my arm. "Let's go."

Hermosa summoned a porter and he tagged her valise for the land yacht.

Malachi and I wandered the main street in search of an adequately stocked mercantile. I bought a shaving kit that we'd share, and he picked up a box of cigars. We each purchased a leather stowaway satchel—our war bags—and stuffed them with extra clothes, engineer boots, hand towels, and two hundred rounds of .45 ammo, plus a box of .32s for our hideaways.

At eleven we caught up with Hermosa who had secured a steamer trunk to tote the additions to her wardrobe. She paraded in her new outfit, a khaki hunting jacket and matching jodhpur pants. Tall riding boots, a new holster for the Merwin

Hulbert revolver, and a safari hat with a white scarf completed her ensemble. She hired a wagon to take us to the land yacht.

I had wondered about this improbable vehicle, our ride through the Sonoran desert. What happened to the train from Nogales to Guaymas? And why not take a stagecoach? When the land yacht came into view, I stared in amazement. A single example was parked—or should I say "berthed"—along an elevated platform teeming with dock hands and passengers. While the illustration on the handbill had given me an idea of the size of a land yacht, up close, the vehicle appeared gargantuan.

It sat on a chassis of eight colossal wheels. Sunlight sparkled along its white superstructure, busy with windows, hatches, and ladders. The upper half of the hull was white with pastel blue-gray and crimson trim, and the lower half painted black.

The yacht's iron wheels were twelve feet tall and a yard wide, and cleats the size of fists studded the rims. Workers in greasy overalls climbed over the gigantic springs and along the huge drive shafts linked to the wheels.

Black smoke curled lazily from the stack behind the wheel-house and a second, smaller compartment. From the roof of this compartment jutted a strange, radar antenna-looking device, which resembled psychic signal collectors. Two cargo cranes swiveled over the yacht, one hoisting pallets of wonder-fuel from the train and the other hauling a net laden with crates.

A porter hefted Hermosa's luggage from the coach toward stairs leading up to the dock. I let Malachi proceed and I followed. We halted at the end of a queue of passengers by a shed near the boarding ramp. We shuffled toward the shed and when Hermosa was close, she offered our boarding passes to the steward in the shed and pointed to Malachi and me.

The steward—a woman with short, inky black hair—took the passes and leaned out the office window to verify the count. Blue eyes gazed from a slender face with angular features, a face that I instantly recognized. Her gaze didn't dwell on mine but I was glued to hers.

Distress bubbled inside of me. We hadn't even left Nogales and already this trip was veering in a very bad direction. The ship's steward was somebody I had hoped to never see again.

That blonde hop head and whore-monger on the train from St. Charles, now sported a new haircut and dye job. She was that duplicitous lizard, Gladys Vesna.

CHAPTER SEVENTEEN

What was Gladys doing? Was she here by design or was it just my bad luck? I fought the urge to grab her by the arms and shake the truth out of her.

She responded to my glare with a look of innocent surprise. As she arched her eyebrows, the brim of her officer's cap tipped up. "Yes sir?" She ran her finger down the yacht's manifest. "Mr. Felix Gomez?" which she mispronounced as "Goams."

Hermosa leaned close. "Is there a problem?"

Gladys kept acting like she didn't know me. "I don't think so." She extended her hand to me. "Vanessa Glades." With her other hand she pointed to her epaulet, royal blue with an embroidered golden key superimposed over a spoked wheel. Signs of the zodiac decorated the rest of the field. "The yacht's steward as if that wasn't obvious."

I recalled what Hermosa had said last night; that the land yacht's departure was delayed because the steward had taken ill. And by pure chance, Gladys happened to arrive to take the now vacant position? I didn't need a kundalini noir to detect the sham.

"A pleasure to meet you, Vanessa." I clasped her hand and squeezed until she winced, then let go. "Rather lucky for the yacht company that you arrived when you did."

"Am I missing something?" Hermosa interjected.

"Not at all," I insisted. "The steward and I were making our acquaintance."

Vanessa, aka Gladys, massaged her hand. She punched my boarding ticket and offered it to me. "Please continue up the ramp. Your berth assignments are on the passes. Welcome to *La Poderosa.*" This name she pronounced correctly.

Hermosa took my wrist and led me up the boarding ramp, our boots clomping on the wooden planks. The passengers behind us stepped to the steward's office. When we were out of earshot from Gladys, Hermosa slid her hand over mine and dug her fingernails into the back of my hand.

"Who is she?" she demanded.

I twisted my hand free. Even so, I had to admit that her nails had stung. "Like she said, the steward."

Hermosa paused at the top of the ramp and faced me. "If there's something I need to know, go ahead and spill it. Once we leave Nogales, our circumstances are bound to become precarious if not downright dangerous. I don't want to be blindsided."

"And neither do I."

"Quit talking in circles, Felix. Who is she? An old lover? I thought you would know better than to take up with a psychic."

"How do you know she's a psychic?"

Hermosa did an eye roll. "The wrist tattoos. Plus, yacht stewards are required to serve as telepaths. The zodiac emblems on her epaulets should've clued you to that."

So Gladys was both the steward and the psychic messenger? Great, now she had two ways to screw with us.

"Well?" Hermosa frowned. "Is she an old lover?"

"Vanessa and I were definitely not lovers. Can we leave it at that?"

A young blonde in a yacht crew uniform hailed Hermosa and me. "Please, clear the ramp. The passenger cabins are to your left."

"We'll discuss this later," Hermosa said. She glanced back at Gladys with claws in her eyes, then continued down the narrow deck to find her room.

The crew woman grinned politely as I walked by. I did a double take. I recognized her face—the thin eyebrows over bright eyes, slender cheeks and pronounced jawline—and realized she was Louisa Davidson, Gladys's ingénue accomplice. Like her boss, Louisa had cut and dyed her hair. If both of them were on the yacht, then the third member of their grifter triumvirate had to be onboard. I halted and asked, "Louisa, where is Sun Zhipeng?"

To her credit, Louisa didn't let her façade slip. "Who sir? Another passenger? And why are you calling me Louisa?"

"And you are?"

She knit her eyebrows. "Dorothy Leahy, the yeoman's assistant."

"How long have you been on this yacht?"

"Sir, if you have a problem with me you're more than welcome to take it up with the captain."

"Hey pal, can you move it?" a passenger complained from the ramp. He struggled with two carpetbags in each hand.

"I'll see you around, Yeoman Leahy."

"Enjoy your trip, *sir*."

I had no doubt that Sun Zhipeng was on the yacht, and I hoped that he, Gladys, and Louisa were trying to put distance between themselves and another set of problems that I had nothing to do with. Even so, the three of them were like smoldering matches set atop a keg of gunpowder.

Malachi was waiting in our quarters. The cabin was less than half the size of our hotel room, which had been cramped enough. Fortunately we had bunk beds. I called top bunk.

"Fine with me," Malachi said. "When you start snoring I can kick you in the ass."

We stowed our bags in the footlockers under the bottom bunk and ventured to get a layout of *La Poderosa*. The passenger cabins were on the main deck, in the superstructure behind the galley. The officer's mess and quarters were on the deck above. And above those sat the wheelhouse and the telepath's booth. Below the main deck were the crew's bunks, the engine room, cargo holds, and under that, more cargo holds and the bunkers of the wonder-fuel.

We wandered toward the bow on the port side of the main deck and examined a circular gun tub that stuck out from the hull. A canvas cover had been folded back from a Gatling gun mounted on a pedestal in the center of the tub. A crewman polished the gun's brass receiver and fittings.

New thoughts flooded my mind, but my body responded like they were familiar memories. I stepped into the tub, and the crewman retreated to make room. As I lowered myself onto the tractor seat behind the pedestal, my right foot automatically found the firing switch on the footrest. I admired the cluster of eleven steel barrels protruding from the receiver. This was a steam-powered Gatling gun, mass murder in .45-70 caliber.

I inspected the gauges, and my hands guided themselves over the levers and cranks as if I had done this a thousand times before. Coyote must've added pages from the gun's operating manual to his magical journal.

"You act like you know what you're doing," a baritone voice remarked, the accent a deep New Orleans Creole. A barrel-chested black man in the yacht captain's uniform watched from the deck, a gold tooth glistening in his smile. "God willing, we won't need your skills."

I rose from the gun and joined Malachi in introducing ourselves.

"André Labatut," the captain said. His dusky-brown eyes

matched the color of his dimpled complexion. Labatut wasn't much taller than Hermosa, but I'd bet he weighed over two hundred pounds. Heavy, jeweled rings shone on his thick fingers. I studied him for a moment, hoping that we hadn't crossed paths before because I didn't need yet another awkward moment.

"Come this way," he directed. We proceeded around the bow to a gun tub on the starboard side. A quick-firing 37mm Hotchkiss sat on the pedestal. No memories came to me, though I recognized the cannon from a military history book in the other world.

Malachi crouched and squeezed himself onto the small seat on the left side of the pedestal. "Felix, let's show Captain Labatut how it's done." Malachi's tone was uncharacteristically nostalgic. "Like that time we were on the ramparts of Durango, and we beat back that charge by the *lanceros*. Canister shot. *Boom!* Explosive shell. *Blam!*" He gestured to the seat on the right side. "Go on. You and me were the number one sharp-shooters on this piece."

I gazed at the gun—its confusion of cranks, levers, and knobs —and had no idea what to do.

"Goddammit," he cursed, "well get to it."

Labatut stared at me. After a moment, he allowed an empathetic grin and said, "It might have been a while, no?"

"It has, yes," I muttered, glad that the captain had given me a way out.

Malachi stamped his boots against the metal deck and stood. He gave me the stink eye and stormed off toward the rear of the ship. I followed him past the open holds. Down below, the crew was busy lashing down large heavy crates.

Malachi stopped to light a cigar and watch them work. Without looking at me, he said, "How come you act like you fell off a horse and whacked your head?"

"You've already asked me that."

"Maybe you fell off another horse."

"I don't know what to tell you."

"Tell me you won't forget what to do at the appropriate time." He gestured with his stogie to the forward gun tub. "Not like what you did in front of the captain." He sounded concerned, like my amnesia was a symptom of a worse ailment.

"Listen," I screwed up the courage to broach my supernatural concerns, "I have things to discuss. I'm not who you think I am."

He planted one boot forward and leaned toward me, his face uncomfortably close. His eyes crinkled, and the crease along his brow deepened until it looked like a slot for a coin. "Let it go, Felix. I was there. In fact it was me who took you. I didn't want to do it, but I couldn't let you die." His eyes glistened with heavy emotion.

What? What? WHAT was Malachi talking about?

Then a broad smile took over his face, and he straightened. "But we're here, on the cusp of yet another adventure. A couple of pirates, you and me." He reached into his coat and withdrew a silver flask. He unscrewed the cap and handed the flask. "*Gan bay*, my good friend."

My crossover memories told me *gan bay* meant cheers in Chinese. The fraternal kinship radiated from Malachi like heat from a stove. I took a pull from the flask and the sharp, honeyed, notes of a good whiskey caressed my palate. "*Gan bay*, brother."

"Brother?" he winced and grasped the flask. "Let's not get carried away with ourselves. Here's mud in your eye." He gulped a hearty swallow and slapped my arm. "Now let's go refresh that creaky memory of yours."

Turns out what he meant were the yacht's guns. We inspected a second set of gun tubs that stuck out from the hull near the stern, another Gatling gun and another Hotchkiss. I was certain we didn't pack this much firepower for show.

Hermosa was mingling with about thirty other passengers in the shade beneath a canvas awning stretched over the fantail.

Our fellow travelers looked like businessmen or wealthy sojourners on holiday. The group suddenly perked up and crowded against the railing. Curious about the commotion, I pressed against Hermosa to see.

A formation of twenty Apaches on ponies trotted from the desert. They halted near the yacht. Feathers dangled from the long barrels of Winchesters carried at the ready. Bandoliers crisscrossed leathery torsos.

"Chiricahua Scouts?" I asked.

"No," Hermosa answered. "See their colors?" These Apaches wore blue-and-white checkered scarves around their necks and blue sashes around their waists. "They're guards contracted by the land yacht company. Our escorts through the outlaw territory between here and Guaymas."

A heavily armed yacht, Apache scouts dressed for the warpath—"outlaw" seemed like a tame description of what might await us.

At eleven-thirty, the yacht's steam whistle let loose a piercing shriek. The smoke rising from the stack thickened and darkened. At a quarter to noon, clouds of steam vented from the stack and mixed with the black smoke.

Passengers puffed on cigars or fanned their faces, watches in hand as they waited for departure. A deep *whompa-whompa* reverberated from below, and the yacht began to shake from the churning of the engine's big pistons. At noon on the dot, the whistle let loose another shriek, and the immense vehicle creaked and rumbled from the dock. *Whompa, whompa.* Pennants flapped from the superstructure. At the dock, people waved goodbye. Our Apaches broke formation to either gallop ahead or lag behind as rear guard.

La Poderosa swayed and trembled as it plodded over a dirt road braided with the wide ruts left by the previous land yachts.

After a few minutes the novelty of the ride wore off and the realization settled that we were in for a long, boring, bone-shaking voyage. Passengers withdrew from the railing. Some disappeared into their cabins, others tried to get comfortable on the cushioned lounge chairs under the awning.

Hermosa and I remained at the railing and clung tight as the deck stuttered and rolled beneath us. She looked over both shoulders to make sure nobody stood close. "So," she began in segue to an interrogation, "tell me about our steward, Vanessa Glades."

"There's not much to say," I replied, though there was. "She's been involved in plenty of scams. Cheats. Frauds. Shady exploits *you* know plenty about."

Hermosa pursed her lips. Score one for me.

"And you know her, how?" she asked. "Is she the Gladys Vesna that Marshal Boudreau was so keen on finding back in Tucson? The one you visited on the train?"

"I'll tell you this much," I said. "You're right to be concerned. And about the yeoman's assistant, Dorothy Leahy."

"That pretty young thing?"

"Yeah, her." Before Hermosa could skewer me with a snide question, I blurted, "I've never touched her." Of that I was certain, but that other Felix might have been all over her nubile cootchie. "And there's a Chinese man with them. I haven't seen him yet but I'll bet he's aboard. His name is Sun Zhipeng, but he might be using an alias."

"I don't know why you're so cagey about Vanessa," she said, "After all, confession is good for—"

A planted memory came to mind. Something juicy. "Don't lecture me about coming clean about my past. Seems you once attended an artists and models party in San Francisco, nude models I have to add."

Hermosa blushed and looked away.

"And during the gala someone spiked the punch with laudanum. The safe in the host's study was cracked open and—"

"I have an alibi."

"Three thousand dollars in gold bullion went missing."

She jerked tight the scarf knotted under her chin. "This conversation is getting boring. You're getting boring. All right then, I'll keep my eyes open for Vanessa, Dorothy, and their suspicious Chinese friend." Hermosa spun away from me and fought to keep her balance as she negotiated the tipping, shaking deck back to her cabin.

I stayed at the railing to study the wide, flat valley for clues about what had happened to the railroad. An hour south of Nogales I found part of my answer when our path ran parallel to what remained of the old tracks. A few railroad ties sat on the elevated bed, but most lay scattered along the way. Iron rails lay twisted and bent. Eroded craters marked long-ago demolitions.

La Poderosa skirted a small canyon. The remnants of bridge abutments clung to the top of the opposing cliffs. At the bottom, smashed rail cars lay in a pile like the carcasses of prehistoric beasts. I tried to imagine the mayhem surrounding that disaster and couldn't see anything that would tell me who that train had belonged to. The remains of the empty and scorched cars and the accompanying death filled the air with a creepy foreboding.

Now I realized what had happened to the railroad that had linked Nogales with Guaymas. As the main thoroughfare through this province, the route had been the object of a bitter campaign by both sides to control it, and if they couldn't, to destroy everything.

Our Apache escorts trotted with us—the vanguard up ahead, outliers to the side, and rear guard—and all were unmoved by the devastation.

A couple of hours later we passed to the west of a sandy plain, the abandoned rail line running down its middle like a scar. What was left of locomotives and railcars cluttered the landscape, half-submerged in the sand dunes like wrecked ships. The sound of our engine echoed across the desolation. *Whompa, whompa.*

Passengers leaned from the railing for a better look. Someone pointed to the ground around our wheels. Human bones and fragments littered the ground. None formed a recognizable skeleton as the corpses had been ravaged years ago by scavengers. Here, there, sun-bleached skulls faced us, and their black sockets seemed to track us, to taunt us.

Scattered among the weeds and in the dirt, tarnished buttons, pieces of faded, tattered uniforms, and rusted broken rifles added to the eerie sense of an enormous tragedy. Tumbled adobe heaps along the vista ahead marked the remnants of abandoned dugouts and battlements.

I saw no evidence of recent civilization. Although this was now part of Aztlan—our side had won the war—destruction and death seemed to have condemned the land to perpetual ruin.

But not everyone shared my somber appraisal. A female passenger chirped, "We should ask the captain to stop. I would love to collect souvenirs. A skull and officer's insignia would look splendid in my library."

We continued through the decay of more forgotten battlefields. As the hours waned, long shadows stretched across our path from the hills to our west.

I scoped the terrain around us and realized I hadn't seen our Apache escorts in some time. I wasn't the only one to have noticed because a worried, anonymous voice cried out, "What happened to our Indians?"

Someone else answered, "They've either deserted or sold us out, the treacherous bastards!"

La Poderosa jerked abruptly to the left, to put distance between us and a line of hills to our right. I looked to the superstructure and a crewman wearing crossed bandoliers and carrying a rifle scrambled toward us along the upper deck. He stopped where a bell hung from a stanchion on the railing. He yanked on the bell's rope and its brassy peal plucked my nerves with alarm.

"Get your weapons," he yelled, "or take cover."

Passengers gasped in fright. A few brandished their pistols. All scurried toward their cabins.

Bringing my attention back to the hills, I spotted flickering lights in the shadowy folds of the rising ground. I didn't need Coyote's memories to tell me what I was seeing.

Gunfire.

CHAPTER EIGHTEEN

Bullets pinged against the iron hull of *La Poderosa*. Another volley chopped splinters from the wooden gunnel. A window shattered. Men and women hugged the deck and screamed.

I dropped behind the gunnel and palmed my Colt Navy but held fire. The shots were coming from at least five hundred yards away, beyond the range of my revolver.

The land yacht careened to the left, skewing so fast she threatened to roll over. Passengers, me included, slid across the deck as more bullets cracked by our ears. For a moment I thought the helmsman might be a traitor attempting to crash the yacht. Then a gigantic explosion slammed the hull and bounced us against the deck.

Passengers let loose cries of terror. Dust and sand pelted us. A curtain of smoke traced over the starboard side, and the stench of burned gunpowder stung my nostrils.

La Poderosa rocked from side-to-side and found its balance. I scrambled to my feet and ran back to the gunnel. Smoke and embers hung in the air above a huge crater just to the right of the yacht. An explosion that big had to have come from a land-mine. Thankfully someone on the crew had spotted the bomb, and the abrupt turn kept us from getting blown to pieces.

As the smoke and dust cleared, I studied the attack. That initial gunfire was meant to keep our heads down so we wouldn't see the bomb. And then what? Someone had to pick over the wreckage.

Who was responsible? Our treacherous Apache escorts? Or were there others?

Gunfire from behind answered that question.

Revolver in hand, I made for the fantail. A score of outlaws leapt from behind the creosote and cactus, and sprinted after us on foot. More sprang up as a fresh volley from the distant rifles tore into the yacht. Two men dashed for the stern. One of them whirled a grappling hook and rope over his head. He let it fly and it sailed upward to catch the fantail railing. He and his partner leapt for the rope and scaled it effortlessly hand-over-hand.

Humans couldn't move like that. These two were definitely werewolves, and werewolves meant bad trouble.

Leaning over the railing, I took aim at the first werewolf ascending the rope. My Colt Navy roared fire and smoke. The werewolf slipped from the rope, his nose cleaved by a bullet. He tumbled over the werewolf behind him and slammed to the ground. His buddy clung to the rope and snarled at me.

I let go another round but the jolting motion of the yacht threw off my aim. Rather than waste another bullet, I extended my talons and sliced the rope. The werewolf fell, his eyes burning with hate. The feeling was mutual. He smashed into the dirt and collapsed to one side. Just as I put my sights on him again, more bullets snapped the air like hornets, and I ducked.

Another six desperadoes raced after us on horses. Eventually we would outrun them, but before that, some would manage to climb on board.

The young crewman who had sounded the alarm bell dropped into the rear starboard gun tub. He tore the canvas cover off the Gatling gun, but his moves were panicked and uncertain.

I pounced into the gun tub and beat him to the gunner's seat. "No hard feelings," I said, "but a little urgency is required."

Reaching to the bottom of the pedestal, I opened the spigot to pressurize the power accumulator with steam. The needle on the gauge swung to READY. After releasing the locks, I traversed the gun at the mounted outlaws shooting at us from the right, a hundred yards away. I yanked on the charging handle. Cartridges clattered down the chute from the ammo box and cycled into the receiver. Aligning the sights, I mashed the foot trigger. Steam whistled through the receiver, and the cluster of barrels spun in a blur. Each of the eleven barrels shot twice a second, allowing me to hose the attackers at a rate of 1,320 bullets per minute.

The Gatling gun spewed a buffalo fart of flame and smoke. Heat from the muzzle blast spanked my face. A wall of lead stitched across the outlaws and their horses, and they disappeared in the storm of dust. Lifting my foot off the trigger switch, I held tight to the aiming cranks. I savored the vapor of hot oil lifting from the barrels, the odor of burned gunpowder, the exhilaration of the Gatling's power.

Then through the staccato gunfire, a piercing shriek tore at my nerves. The dust settled, revealing two horses thrashing on the ground, crippled and screaming in pain.

My kundalini noir clutched in sudden despair. The terrible wail tore at my memory—at my real memory—of the time during the War in Iraq when my soldiers and I ambushed a family of innocent civilians. Our bullets had ripped open a little girl, and her agonized dying cries seared themselves into my psyche.

The horses kicked and screeched in misery. I could kill humans and supernaturals and feel no remorse except that I hadn't knocked them off earlier. But what had these horses done to deserve this gruesome fate other than to serve and trust us?

A desperado untangled himself from the bloody mess and limped to his feet. He didn't move like a wounded werewolf, but like a mortal in a lot of pain. He aimed his revolver at me, hesitated, then turned to the horses. He fired twice and put the tortured creatures out of their misery. He faced me again and lowered his pistol. I didn't know if he was out of bullets or if he was done fighting and wanted me to finish him off. His baleful eyes drilled deep into me. He was a hundred feet away, close enough for his silhouette to fill my gun sight. One quick burst and I'd blast him to pulp.

My kundalini froze. I couldn't shoot, and I watched him recede past the hull of the yacht.

Someone punched my shoulder. It was Hermosa, in her safari clothes, yelling, "Shoot him! Kill him!"

I didn't move.

She snatched the Spencer repeater rifle from the crewman's hands and dashed to the fantail. Propping one thigh against the railing, she held steady, aimed, and fired. Smoke and flame spat from the muzzle. She cranked the rifle's lever. A spent shell twirled over her head. Aimed and fired. More smoke. Sent another shell flying. Aimed. Fired. The smoke veiling her body slipped away. Lips pursed in grim satisfaction, she pushed away from the railing and cranked the lever once more. The last spent cartridge pinged by her boots.

La Poderosa groaned to the right and the horses, their riders, and this one desperado returned into view, all of them dead, all of them outlined by a bloody stain.

A Hotchkiss boomed from a forward gun tub, the horrendous clap smacking my ears. Then another boom. And another. The cannon shells exploded where the long-range gunfire had started. I heard Malachi holler, "You weasels came to dance, then enjoy the music."

The rest of the desperadoes scattered like roaches behind rocks and into dips in the ground. The swarm of bullets thinned and died. Hermosa tossed the rifle to the crewman.

Passengers peeled themselves off the deck and slithered to the gunnel to peek at what was left of the attack. A couple of them fired their pistols halfheartedly.

Another bell clanged, followed by Gladys yelling, "Cease fire." I wondered what she had done during this gunfight. I slid the Gatling's charging handle to SAFE, gears in the gun meshed, and the unfired cartridges clattered back up the chute into the ammo box. *La Poderosa* continued forward. *Whompa, whompa*.

I beckoned the crewman. "Have at it." I rose from the seat to let him attend to the gun.

Hermosa glared at me. "You picked a hell of a time to get soft-hearted. How much you wanna bet that outlaw would've come back another day to slit your throat?"

I said, "Maybe I left him for you."

"Next occurrence," she jabbed my chest, "don't do me any such favors. There is a time for mercy and this wasn't one of them. Someone comes gunning for us, you send him to hell."

She fixed my eyes with a hard gaze of her own. She huffed in frustration and rested one hand on the grip of her holstered revolver.

A lot was going on inside her head, but at the moment I didn't want her to share. So I eased past her to go forward and see Malachi. Along the way I replaced the spent shells in my revolver and pondered the attack. Werewolves and humans working side-by-side? Did the mortals know about their supernatural cohorts? What about our crew and passengers? No one seemed to act as if they did.

Malachi sat perched on the edge of the gun tub, his boots propped on the cannon's barrel, smoke curling from its muzzle and breech. He had just lit a cigar. Two crewmen tossed spent cannon shells overboard.

Captain Labatut stood beside him, feet planted firmly apart on the rolling deck. He puffed on a meerschaum pipe that had mellowed to a rich amber color. Considering he had almost lost his yacht, his life, and ours as well, he seemed to be in a casual mood. But the keening shriek of the mangled horses still rang in my ears.

"Nothing like a little excitement to get the pulse racing," Labatut said between teeth clenched around the pipe's stem.

I appraised the passengers and his crew. Many still looked shaken and none seemed anywhere as relaxed as the captain. "It could have gone badly," I replied.

"True, but it didn't." He drew his lips back to give a big smile, and the sun caught the diamond in his gold tooth. "I've been through worse scrapes, Mr. Gomez."

"The captain and I were just theorizing the reason for the ambush," Malachi offered.

"I figure the outlaws lost about eight, ten men," Labatut said. "They attacked in numbers, so whatever they were after must've been worth the risk."

"What's your cargo?" I asked instead. "Gold? Treasure?"

"A treasure indeed." Labatut guffawed a booming laugh. "Better than gold. I'm transporting heavy industrial equipment. Drill presses. Lathes. Milling machines. With those devices you can make tools to either excavate gold or fashion weapons to take it."

"How likely that's what they were after? Cargo that heavy, how would they get it out of the desert?"

The captain drew deep puffs from his pipe. "An interesting speculation," he said in his Creole lilt. "The logistics would be troublesome but not impossible. I've heard tell of a gang who once dragged a five-ton iron safe through the bayous of Terrebonne parish."

"Heard tell?" I asked.

"A rumor and let us leave it at that."

"What about our passengers?" I pressed.

"A few socialites. Some well-heeled businessmen," Malachi answered. "Might be worth the bother of a ransom."

"Where is ..." I was about to say Gladys and remembered to say instead, "The steward?"

Labatut pointed with his pipe up the ladder to the topmost deck. "She's sending a report of the attack back to Nogales."

I started to climb the ladder when Labatut mentioned that telepaths did not like to be disturbed when transmitting messages.

"It's all right. She won't mind. We're old friends." I clambered up the ladder to the bridge of the wheelhouse and proceeded aft along the tiny deck to the telepath's booth. Up here the sway of the yacht was more pronounced. I clung to a handrail, leaned against the door, and peeked through a gap between a curtain and the edge of the window. Louisa was leaning against the door and I found myself looking over her shoulder. No surprise she was here. She and Gladys were the opposite sides of the same marked card.

Shafts of light from bullet holes in the wall bored through the darkness. Gladys wobbled on a stool behind a small table, circles of light scuttling across her blouse and face. A copper band decorated with sapphires sat like a crown across the front of her head. She clasped a set of brass knobs on either end of a device that resembled a ticker tape machine. Her eyes were shut and she appeared to be in deep concentration.

Since Gladys didn't mind interrupting my work, then she shouldn't mind if I interrupted hers. I tried the doorknob but it was locked. I gave it a vampire twist, broke the lock, and yanked the door open.

Louisa stumbled backwards into my arms. I pushed her back in and squeezed against her to pull the door closed.

If Gladys was in a trance, she needed no time snapping into the present because she pointed a Colt Cloverleaf pocket pistol at me. Louisa scooted to the far corner and turned around. Her fingers inched to the big revolver holstered at her waist. The dust and gunpowder soot on her and Gladys's white uniforms told me they had been in the thick of the fighting.

"Easy, ladies," I cautioned. "I'm only here to ask a question."

"One question," Gladys snapped. "Then get out."

"Did you have anything to do with the attack?"

Gladys winced. "Why are you asking me?"

"Because you are nothing but trouble."

"You're a real genius, aren't you? You asked your one question." She gestured with the pistol. "Now leave."

I checked out her machine. A glass dome covered a clockwork mechanism connected by copper tubes to the brass knobs. "I want to watch."

"I know you do. But this is different. This is a secret process."

"Like we don't know each other's secrets already." I motioned with my chin at Louisa. "What about her? She's not a telepath."

"She's my apprentice."

"I'm under the impression you need the 'touch' to be a telepath." I tapped my temple.

"You do, but you can learn some." Gladys traded glances with Louisa. "Learn enough."

"I'm not leaving until you show me."

"Why?"

"Just curious."

Gladys cocked an eyebrow and her temper cooled. "You've never been curious before. About this, I mean."

That was a sliver of information about the other Felix. "Humor me."

"The report needs to be transmitted," Louisa insisted. "You two can settle your differences later."

Gladys cut me with a resentful glare and hid the Cloverleaf under the table. She wound a key that stuck out one side of the dome and then adjusted a set of levers along the bottom. She gripped the brass knobs and closed her eyes. Her brow creased and her knuckles turned white. A crystal nested within the clockwork began to glow. The gears spun and clicked.

Sweat trickled from under her crown, and in the dusky light, I could see that the crown's sapphires were also faintly illuminated. Louisa stared at Gladys, fascinated, expectant.

Paper tape chattered out a slot in the dome and was taken up by a spool. Smoke swirled inside the dome from a stuttering key that burned symbols on the paper. With a burst of clicks and clacks, the clockwork fell silent and the crystal went dim.

Gladys released the knobs and shoulders sagging in relief, let out a sigh. She removed the crown. It left red imprints on her forehead.

I reached for the tape wound on the spool.

"Don't touch that," she said.

Louisa lifted the spool from its cradle and pulled at the tape. She studied the symbols and spoke in a hesitant voice like she wasn't sure what she was reading. "*La Poderosa* to Central Station. Time. Seventeen hundred forty-two." She recited today's date and our location in longitude and latitude. "Attacked by outlaw gang. Repulsed with minor damage. No casualties. Stop."

Gladys nodded. "Very good."

A length of tape dangled from Louisa's fingers. The symbols were clusters of tiny hash marks scorched into the paper.

"Those look like Sumerian cuneiform," I said.

Gladys's eyebrows arched. "Quite correct, my over-sexed *pistolero*. What's with this sudden outburst of knowledge? You sleeping with a schoolmarm or an archeologist?"

So I gathered the other Felix wasn't book smart.

Louisa continued reading. "Central Station to *La Poderosa*. Send more information about attack. Confirm suspects. Motive. Urgent. Stop."

Gladys steepled her fingers and her attention turned inward. She mumbled, "More information. Suspects. Motive." She lifted her eyes and clapped a hard gaze on me. "You're a detective. How about digging up some answers?"

CHAPTER NINETEEN

The steam engines quit pounding. *La Poderosa* abruptly slowed. Gladys, Louisa, and I traded concerned looks as the land yacht groaned to a halt.

"What's going on?" I asked.

"You tell me," Gladys answered.

I turned around, the grip of my Colt Navy scraping against the wall of the cramped compartment, until I faced the door. I pushed it open and leaned out. We were on a broad swath of flat desert with clear fields of fire for hundreds of yards in every direction. Below, Captain Labatut stood on the forward deck with a couple of his crew and Malachi, where they studied the landscape. The setting sun dragged long shadows across the terrain. Within a half hour, the shadows would fuse into twilight.

I shimmied down the ladders to drop alongside them. "Why did we stop?"

"Without scouts on the ground," Labatut replied, "it's too risky to proceed at night. We could topple into a ravine, mire ourselves in sand, or roll right into another ambush."

"If you need someone on the ground to lead the way," I said, "let me do it."

Labatut stuffed tobacco into his pipe. "I appreciate the offer, Mr. Gomez, but this night is not the ideal time for you to be wandering this desert."

For a human, not a vampire. But as I had to keep my identity a secret, I didn't press the matter.

He lit his pipe and flung the burning match overboard. Looking up, he noted Gladys and Louisa watching us from their roost. He yelled, "Steward!"

"Sir?" Gladys sounded strangely formal and obedient.

"What's your report?"

"Central Station is sending a fresh escort to accompany us to Guaymas."

"Very good. Amend your situation report and tell them we've halted for the night and will proceed at first light tomorrow."

"Aye aye, Captain."

Labatut next said, "Yeoman!"

Now it was Louisa's turn to reply. "Sir?"

"Assemble the passengers on the banquet deck." He yanked a gold watch from his breast pocket and read the dial. "In fifteen minutes."

Malachi and I started aft. Louisa climbed down and marched around the main deck, knocking on cabin doors to relay Labatut's instructions. As we waited for the passengers to congregate, Malachi and I leaned on a railing along the fantail and watched them emerge from their cabins and gather on the banquet deck. Hermosa mingled among them. Crewmembers remained in the gun tubs beside the cannon and Gatling guns.

Labatut and Gladys stepped onto a platform overlooking the banquet deck. The captain addressed the crowd. "Esteemed passengers, the exigencies of the recent assault against the yacht and our persons require that we take extraordinary measures to assure our common safety."

"What the hell does that mean?" a voice in the crowd retorted.

"It means that every able-bodied passenger must be armed

and ready to fight." Labatut cleared his throat. "You heroically braved injury and death earlier today, for you all rose like Spartans to the occasion. You have my sincerest admiration and I salute you." He waved his pipe and a murmur of approval coursed through the passengers.

Malachi whispered, "Our good captain knows how to shovel the horse manure."

"So let us," Labatut continued, "proceed with our Herculean endeavors and not allow our adversaries to engage us with an upper hand. To that end, everyone is to sleep in their clothes with their boots on. Keep your guns and ammunition handy."

"I didn't pay good money to risk my hide like this," a second voice protested.

"You've forgotten the fine print." Labatut pulled a folded handbill from his back pocket and snapped it open. "Your travel itinerary promised adventure and so consider this an opportunity to get your money's worth." He turned smartly and faced Gladys. "Steward, you may take charge." Labatut stepped off the platform in the direction of the wheelhouse, smoke trailing from his pipe.

Gladys waved a hand to clear the lingering tobacco fumes. "As of now, no more smoking while in the open. As it gets dark you don't want to draw the bead of a sharpshooter." She went on to announce that dinner would be served below instead of on the banquet deck. Passengers would be grouped into shifts and stand watch with the crew. She opened her ledger and called out names for guard duty. A tide of grumbling and excuses answered her.

"If I'm on watch, can I sit down? My feet hurt."

"I plan to get drunk. Hope that's okay."

I told Malachi and Hermosa to go below and eat without me. Besides, there wasn't anything on the menu that could satisfy my growing hunger. The crew set the heavy banquet tables on their side and arranged them in a circle for cover. At first everyone was vigilant, but as the hour dragged on, the passengers grew lax and spent more time gossiping and complaining than staying alert. Down below, a raucous card game in the galley provoked laughter and friendly insults.

Twilight eased into night and a vast canopy of stars shined above. I made my rounds along the deck, chatting up the gun crews and the passengers on watch to make sure everyone stayed awake. Shortly before midnight, the card game was disbanded and those off duty ambled back to their cabins.

Malachi joined me on the fantail. He chewed the nub of a cigar. We kept quiet, plumbing the dark silence around us. From deep in the bowels of the yacht, the burners rumbled as they kept the boilers hot. Sparks floated from the stack, carried by smoke that blended with the night and blurred the stars.

With vampiric night vision I noted the assorted critters crawling close or winging by. Then I caught the movement of larger animals approaching the stern. I studied their shapes and the surrounding emptiness in case they weren't alone. It was a pair of horses, plodding wearily toward us. My first thought was the return of the outlaws, but if it were them, they would've advanced stealthily. Slowly I made out the details of two horses, their halters and empty saddles. Both walked with their heads down, reins dragging in the dirt.

Malachi leaned against my shoulder and gazed down my line of sight. "What's got your attention?"

"A couple of horses," I whispered. "No riders, though."

"Maybe they dismounted."

I searched the surrounding ground. The only cover was grass, weeds, and scattered rocks. A lizard or a snake might have been able to sneak up on us but not a person, human or supernatural.

The horses halted about fifty feet behind the yacht, close enough for a human like Malachi to make out their shapes. They flicked their ears and shook their heads.

One of the crewmen—a teenager—was making his rounds and stopped to see what had our attention. He craned his neck to study the horses. He let the sling of his rifle slide off his shoulder and cradled the gun in his hands. "Where did they come from?"

"They just wandered in from the desert," I explained. "They must've been abandoned by the outlaws and followed us."

The crewman thumbed back the hammer of his rifle.

Malachi put his hand on the weapon. "Easy there," he admonished.

"There might be bushwhackers out there."

"We've been keeping an eye," I said. "So far, it's just these two hungry nags trying to find someone to take care of them. The first sign of trouble, we'll give a shout out."

The crewman relaxed the hammer and slung the rifle. "I should go tell the captain."

"We'll take care of it," Malachi said.

As the young man stepped away, he tossed a wary glance to the horses and the dark void beyond.

"Everybody else on guard should be as alert," Malachi said. "A herd of elephants could waltz right up on the rest of the lazy bastards." He resumed chewing the cigar. "So what's on your mind?"

"The captain warned that the night was too dangerous to go poking around."

"And you disagree?"

"Don't you?"

"Then what's your plan?"

"We take the horses and head straight to Guaymas. Along the way, we might pick up one or two clues about Ling Zhu Han."

"Beats cooling our heels on this barge." Malachi spit the soggy clump of tobacco over the side. "We best tell Hermosa."

The door into my cabin eased open. Hermosa shuffled in, a

cartridge belt cinched around her waist, the Merwin Hulbert holstered butt forward.

"What's this about you and Malachi riding off?" She nudged the door closed. A small candle lit the small enclosure with a flicking glow.

"It's a change in plans." I gathered my belongings into my war bag. Malachi had already packed and taken his. "You continue on the yacht to Guaymas. We'll meet there. Consider this a two-pronged approach into our investigation."

"You'll forfeit the passage fare."

"It's always about money with you, isn't it?"

"I've lived without money and I've lived with it. With money is preferable."

"And I know you like your creature comforts," I added. "Which you have on the yacht. Besides, there are only two horses."

Hermosa rested her hand on the grips of the revolver. She rocked back and forth in her boots. "What if the outlaws return?"

"With you standing guard? Then I pity the poor sons of bitches."

She smirked.

"Besides,"—I caught myself before I said Gladys—"the steward assured me that another escort would meet the yacht by noon tomorrow."

"When was this?"

"Right after the attack."

"You've been spending time with her?"

"Simply a professional visit," I protested.

"Any transaction involving money would make it professional."

"It's nothing like that," I countered.

"Go ahead then," Hermosa cracked the door open. "With you off this canoe, I'll have plenty of time to wheedle information from her."

"Have at it." Hermosa and Gladys in the same room would be like dropping a couple of cats into a sack. It wouldn't go well.

Hermosa slipped out.

I made sure Malachi and I hadn't left anything behind. I blew out the candle and hefted the war bag. Malachi and Hermosa waited at the fantail. The two horses stood at the edge of the gloom, more shadow than beast.

Malachi handed me the free end of a length of rope. "Tie this to the handles of your bag."

After doing so, he and I lowered our war bags to the ground.

"Ready?" he asked. He slipped keeper thongs over the hammers of his Schofields to prevent them from sliding out of their holsters. I secured my Colt Navy the same way.

Grasping the rope, I said, "I'll go first."

"The hell with that, *compadre*." Malachi yanked the rope from my hand and hooked one leg over the railing. Hermosa and I steadied him as he climbed over and looped the rope around his boots. "Time to shove off," he whispered.

Hermosa and I let go. Malachi dropped a few inches, then lowered himself nimbly and quietly to the ground. He let go of the rope, looked around, untied the bags, and waved the all clear.

I took slack out of the rope and wrapped it around my hands. Hermosa snatched a handful of my collar to give leverage before I swung my legs up and over the railing. She pressed against me and kissed my cheek. "Goodbye, just in case."

"In case of what?"

"In case I don't see you again."

"I'll see you in Guaymas," I replied, smiling. Once you got inside Hermosa's crusty shell, she had a very sweet filling.

"Guaymas," she whispered. "I intend to collect the rest of what Wu Fei owes us. So don't do anything stupid."

CHAPTER TWENTY

M alachi and I carried our war bags toward the two horses. They waited patiently, as do most put-upon beasts of burden. Malachi took the horse on the left. I stepped close to mine and since I had no clue about how to handle a horse, I watched Malachi to follow his example. He grasped the reins and stroked its head, uttered soothing words, then walked around patting its neck, shoulders, and hindquarters.

My horse tugged against its reins. Its large eyes glimmered in the starlight. I ran my hand across its smooth hide, feeling the heat and the suppleness of its muscles. Rather, her muscles. My horse was a mare, Malachi's, a gelding. As I examined the animal I kept a vigil on the fathomless murk around us. To our rear, *La Poderosa* loomed big as a mountain, and the soft rumble of its boilers pulsed like a heart.

My saddle was stained, hopefully with the blood of an enemy. The scabbard was empty, as were the large holsters draped over the pommel. Malachi's scabbard held a double-barrel shotgun. Neither horse carried saddlebags or appeared to be injured.

Malachi loosened the saddle's cinch strap, smoothed the

blanket underneath, and retightened it. He adjusted the bridle. I mimicked him and since the mare didn't protest, I surmised I was doing okay. We tied our war bags to the backs of the saddles. Malachi nudged my shoulder. "Here." He offered an apple.

"Where did this come from?" I whispered.

"Brought it from the chow hall."

"That's okay. I'm not hungry."

"It's not for you, dumb ass, it's for the horse."

Oh. Made sense. I took the apple and held it in my open palm. My horse drew back her lips and her big teeth snatched the apple. Mouthing it whole, she crunched, chewed, and swallowed. She nuzzled me in appreciation. I guessed we were now friends.

Malachi jammed his left boot into a stirrup and climbed onto his horse. I copied him, hoping I wouldn't mount the saddle backwards. Which I didn't, fortunately.

My horse shifted beneath me, and she perked up like she was expecting to go somewhere.

Malachi stood in his stirrups and craned his neck to ponder our surroundings. "Goddamn, it's dark out here." He snapped his reins and his horse started toward the west. "Let's avoid the yacht. Don't want some sleepyhead with an itchy trigger finger taking a shot at us. We'll stop at daybreak or when we find water, whichever occurs first."

Again, I followed his example and worried that if I did something wrong, my steed would buck me off. I swiveled in my saddle for a parting look at *La Poderosa* and to wave goodbye to Hermosa, who was lost in the yacht's shadows. I couldn't tell if she waved back.

With my vampire night vision I could've taken the lead and picked our way through the darkness. But while I knew our destination was Guaymas, I didn't know the way from here to there. So I pulled in behind Malachi and let him guide his horse over the uneven trail. Minute by minute the smothered groan from the *La Poderosa* faded until the only sound that accompanied us was the rasp of our hooves against sand and rocks.

We plodded in and out of one arroyo, then another. Night's shroud tightened around us. Faint sparkles provided relief around the brush crowding the trail. I thought the sparkles were reflections of starlight against shards of obsidian and quartz sprinkled in the sandy walls of the arroyo. Until I realized the sparkles were arranged in pairs. Like eyeballs. Set in faces.

My vampire senses pinged an alert, and reaching for my revolver, I noticed more faces to my left, and behind us.

"Malachi—" I began.

"Keep it quiet," he replied in an admonishing whisper. "You don't want to tip off anyone that we're passing through."

"A little late for that."

He stiffened in his saddle, looked to the left and right, then raised both hands.

About a dozen men materialized from the creosote and mesquite, advancing with rifles and carbines leveled at us. My kundalini noir sparked like a lit fuse, ready to explode. But even if I used vampire reflexes, at this close range and with so many guns trained on me, I'd probably gain my weight in lead before I managed to empty my revolver. And Malachi would be shredded to pulp before he even blinked. So I kept my hands up.

As the men crept into the weak ambient light, I could make out their plain, drab-colored uniforms. Some wore leggings and boots, others heavy sandals. Most had sombreros hanging by chinstraps behind their backs. Up close, their mustachioed faces were knots of hairy leather.

"*Sus armas,*" one of them growled.

They took our guns and reins and led us along the trail. Who were these men? Where were they taking us? They weren't bandits, since outlaws wouldn't have bothered with prisoners. Plus they moved in hushed discipline like trained soldiers. The one giving orders wore sergeant's chevrons on his sleeves.

Soldiers on horses emerged from the murk and formed a posse around us. On the sergeant's command, they started up a path that forked with our original trail. The column moved stealthily through the desert like a formation of ghosts, and Malachi's and my horse fell in stride. Our captors strung out ahead and behind us. Outliers silhouetted themselves against the stars.

On my own, I might've been able to escape. My boots still hid the dagger and hideaway revolver, plus I could unleash my talons and fangs. But I couldn't think of a scheme that didn't leave Malachi bleeding from a well-ventilated belly.

My thoughts of breaking away ended abruptly with a distant trumpeting. The eerie noise echoed from the hills to our right. Our horses shied and nickered in alarm. Soldiers around us shifted and readied their guns. They spurred their mounts to keep us on the move.

The trumpeting sounded bizarre and out of place, especially since I recognized the sound as coming from an elephant. What was an elephant doing in the Sonoran desert? And equally strange, our escorts didn't act astonished to have heard the trumpeting. They responded like they knew what made the sound and were taking precautions.

The trumpeting was answered by another, this one more distant. Its brassy echo faded but the mood remained brittle with dread.

We continued for another mile and entered a narrow gully. A trace of wood smoke tainted the air. Sentries watched from the high ground to our left and right. Upon rounding a corner, the trail opened onto a tidy camp encompassed by a rocky palisade. A small fire illuminated a pyramid army tent and flags stuck in the ground. More ragtag soldiers milled about, cradling rifles and carbines, some with machetes strapped to their backs, and greeted us with the circumspect stare of feral dogs. A couple of men tended to a large coffee pot hanging above the fire.

The sergeant and a couple from his posse dismounted. A squad clustered around Malachi and me. A man with corporal chevrons gestured that we climb to the ground. *"Bajense."*

Mounted soldiers took our reins and walked the horses around the camp toward a remuda on the far side.

The soldiers parted their ranks to let the sergeant escort Malachi and me toward the tent. Malachi whispered knowingly, "*Rurales.*" The rural militia.

I replied, "But is that good news or bad—"

Rifles prodded our backs, warning us to hold our tongues.

One of the soldiers wore a crown, and that made me give him ... rather her ... a second look. The crown resembled the one Gladys had worn during her duties as a telepath. A vestment stole embroidered with pictograms and symbols of the zodiac hung around her neck and was held in place by bandoliers crisscrossing her chest.

We proceeded to the tent and were halted midway between its door and the flags. I noticed something else propped along with the flags: three human heads impaled on spears. Their lifeless eyes gazed into the fire, its flickering light seeming to animate their dead expressions. Long braided plaits hung over their ears and past the checkered bandanas wrapped around their heads. Blue and white bandanas, the colors of our treacherous Apache escorts. Apparently the *rurales* had snagged this unlucky trio. Though I didn't see an extra spear for my skull, I was sure these roughnecks wouldn't have much trouble whittling a spare.

The sergeant rested a hand on the grip of his revolver. "*Manos arriba,*" he said. Malachi and I raised our hands. Four of his men flanked us.

The flap over the tent door was abruptly folded back. An older, wiry soldier stepped out, buttoning his tunic and adjusting a Sam Browne belt. The brass hardware on his belt and the insignia on his epaulets and collar reflected the campfire. His more formal attire and tall boots marked him as a senior officer. He raked a strand of thinning hair and smoothed the corners of his thick mustache as he watched Malachi and me.

The telepath stood beside the officer. She was a matronly

woman with a stout frame that reminded me of an ox. Her deeply hued mestiza features matched my own and those of most of the soldiers.

We stood still while our hats were whisked off, examined, and dropped upside down by our feet. We were patted down, hands emptying our breast pockets, then reaching inside our coats and tossing the contents into the crowns of our hats.

The soldier tugged at the chain looped across my belly and pulled my watch out of its pocket. But it wasn't the watch that caught his attention but the fob, specifically the medal.

He handed it to the officer, who palmed it, nodding as he showed it to the telepath. "You earned this commendation?" he asked me in Spanish.

"*Sí*," I replied, not knowing what kind of a response my answer would get.

"What unit were you with?"

"The First Battalion of the Thirty-first Infantry Regiment."

"Ah, the Chinese contingent. You were at the Meat Grinder?"

Immediately, Coyote's memories supplied the answer. The nickname given by survivors of the bloody amphibious assault on Shark Island.

Malachi answered, "*Ambos*."

The officer returned the watch and fob. He stepped toward one of the flags and unfurled its tattered cloth, revealing the emblem of the Thirty-first Regiment—an upright bear in a wreath of prickly pear, arrows and lightning bolts at its feet. "A souvenir from the war," he explained. "At the time I was a young lieutenant in the second battalion. It was your unit who rescued us from that disaster." He let go of the flag and extended a hand, grinning, teeth shining below his mustache. "Welcome comrades. *Hermanos*."

His sincerity calmed my fears and I relaxed. After shaking hands, Malachi and I introduced ourselves. Our host said, "*Coronel Cascabel*." Colonel Rattlesnake, of course, in keeping with our desert theme.

He asked us to collect our belongings, including our guns. We put our hats back on. An orderly brought a canvas safari chair from inside the tent and arranged it by the fire. Cascabel took the seat and pointed to the ground. "Sit, please." The telepath stood to his immediate left.

Malachi and I looked at the open dirt, then shrugged, and sat Indian-style. We were offered coffee.

"You wouldn't have whiskey?" Malachi asked. "Tequila? A little wine? After our trek through the wilderness I need a suitable libation to cut my thirst."

"Then you'll have to wait until we reach Guaymas," Cascabel replied. "We don't drink alcohol while on patrol."

Malachi reached into his coat pocket and retrieved a cigar pouch. "How about a smoke?"

"That is allowed." Cascabel lifted from his chair and reached toward Malachi to pluck a stogie from the pouch though I doubted my friend had intended to share.

"What the hell." Malachi dumped the rest of his cigars into his hand and tossed them to the soldiers. "Considering we might have easily been turned into sieves, I oughta show a little gratitude."

The telepath helped herself to the largest cigar. Another soldier lifted a burning stick from the fire and passed it around.

Cascabel puffed on his cigar and pointed the smoldering end of the stick at the severed heads. "You recognize my other guests?"

"Sadly for them," I answered, "I do."

"My apologies," the colonel added.

"What for?" Malachi chewed on his last cigar.

"We received the order from Central Station to assist you earlier this evening." He gestured to the telepath. "But too late to prevent the attack by the outlaws. Otherwise there would be more heads decorating my camp." The colonel handed the burning stick to an orderly.

"What happened to the rest?" Malachi asked.

"When we found their assembly point they scattered like mice. Those criminals and their back-stabbing Apache friends are only interested in easy pickings." The colonel tapped his thigh. "Or are they?" His eyes narrowed. "Why did you leave *La Poderosa?*"

"You were watching?" I asked.

"My scouts were."

Malachi examined the ember of his stogie. "If you're implying that the outlaws had staged the attack for our benefit, that is news I'm welcome to hear you elaborate."

"Again, why did you leave *La Poderosa?*"

"We have pressing business in Guaymas," I replied.

"So pressing that you left the safety of the land yacht? Educate me, please."

Malachi tilted his head in my direction and raised an eyebrow. *Should we tell?*

Why not? I asked myself. Maybe the colonel knew something. "We're looking for a Chinese girl, Ling Zhu Han."

If Cascabel recognized her name, he gave no sign of it. Neither did the telepath.

"She's the daughter of Wu Fei," Malachi allowed.

The colonel exhaled a jet of smoke. "The Dragon?"

"The one and the same," I acknowledged.

The telepath bent over to whisper in the colonel's ear. He weighed her comment and whispered back. She straightened and resumed smoking her cigar.

Cascabel said, "Wu Fei casts a long and deadly shadow, and I feel its chill even here. How"—his gaze darted left and right as he searched for words—"interesting that you're looking for her on his behalf."

"That is one angle to this mystery," Malachi replied.

"And her trail leads to Guaymas?" the colonel pressed.

"Actually, to *Isla Tiburón,*" I said.

He grimaced painfully, like an old bullet wound had suddenly torn open.

"You have something to share?" Malachi asked.

"Foremost, that you should consider not going."

"A bit late for that," I said.

"Other than the memories, what's so forbidding about the island?" Malachi asked.

"I can only relate rumors. The island is the enclave of the Dowager Engel, and she guards her secrets." Cascabel leaned forward and anchored his elbows on his knees. "Did you hear the trumpeting earlier?"

"Elephants?" I inquired.

The colonel shook his head. "If only. No, that sound came from other fantastic creatures. Rogue beasts that escaped her island and have wandered this far inland."

"And you've seen these beasts?" Malachi asked skeptically.

"I've seen their tracks, their victims," the telepath said, an Indian lilt in her Spanish. "Men ripped to pieces. War has turned this region into a vast cemetery, and now we have these monsters adding to the horror."

"Is *La Poderosa* in danger?"

"Probably not," Cascabel answered. "The weapons she carries should protect them."

"Why weren't we warned?" Malachi continued.

"The government in Guaymas suppresses all news about the Dowager."

"Why?"

"When you get to the city, you will see."

CHAPTER TWENTY-ONE

Cascabel dismissed us and returned to his tent. His orderly led Malachi and me to the palisade and showed us where to put our blankets. After retrieving our war bags, bedrolls, and saddles, we tossed our gear on the designated spot. Malachi kept his clothes on and lay on his blanket. Hat over his face, he rested his head against his saddle. I was spreading my blanket on the ground when the orderly returned.

"Señor Gomez," he said, "*Doña Luz* wants to see you."

Since the only woman I had seen at the camp was the telepath, I assumed "Doña Luz" was her. I rose to my feet, mindful that despite the colonel's show of hospitality, the *rurales* might be separating Malachi and me for a double cross. A glance at my friend confirmed that he was thinking the same thing as I caught him sliding an unholstered Schofield under his saddle.

Two soldiers tending the coffee pot watched me as I followed the orderly to the other side of the camp. The campfire had died down, and the glow from the coals in the pit dappled their faces with orange light. *Rurales* snored, burrito-wrapped in blankets along the periphery of the cul-de-sac, their naked feet pointed toward the campfire. Horses nickered softly in the remuda.

Above on the canyon walls, sentries stood silhouetted against the Milky Way.

The orderly halted at a semi-circle of small rocks arranged around a canvas lean-to pinned to the rock wall. The rocks must've marked a perimeter he wasn't allowed to cross. I smelled a faint trace of burning sage, tobacco, and hashish.

"*Siga*," the orderly whispered, pointing at the lean-to.

"What does *la doña* want?"

"She'll tell you." He turned back toward the campfire.

This late at night, I hoped the reason for my visit was a booty call. The telepath wasn't my type, but if getting between her big legs helped keep the peace between Malachi and me and the *rurales*, then I'd do my duty.

Just in case I tripped some kind of trap by crossing over the rocks, I primed my gun hand and my talons. Stepping to the nearest end of the lean-to, I crouched and whispered, "Doña Luz?"

"Oh Felix," she answered, "since when are you so formal? Get your ass in here."

Crap, yet someone else in this crazy place and time who's got me confused with the other Felix. Goddamn him, wherever he was.

I lifted the lean-to's flap and fragrant smoke rolled around me. Though plenty dark inside, I saw Doña Luz sitting cross-legged on a buffalo robe. Her telepath's crown glinted in the meager light. Her braids were undone and her hair fell loose over her shoulders. She had stripped out of her uniform and her large breasts sagged against the white tunic draping her torso. Gear and weapons lay piled around her. Scooting close I smelled fresh human blood. She clamped one hand over her other wrist, which was bound in a cloth bandage.

"I thought you might be hungry." A native accent added a musical cadence to her Spanish. She lifted a cup fashioned from a tin can.

My kundalini noir quivered in alarm. She knew I was a

vampire. Then I remembered that Gladys and her assistant Louisa knew I was a vampire. I suspected that O'Laughlin—Wu Fei's telepath—did as well. Maybe their access to the supernatural realm clued them about my true identity. But why keep the secret? Perhaps they shared a vow of silence about us vampires, a condition for their access to mystical knowledge.

"*Gracias*," I said, taking the cup. The metal was warm, the aroma appetizing.

Luz reached for a thumb-thick blunt smoldering in a small dish by her knee. She filled the enclosure with a blast of smoke.

The strangeness of the situation made my kundalini noir bristle. Sipping the blood, Coyote's implanted memories told me I tasted notes of dog meat and gopher, plus sage, wild onion, and dandelion. The blood flowed like nectar down my gullet. A comforting sensation ebbed out from my belly to my limbs.

Now for business. "Why did you ask me here?"

"To tell you about the Dowager Engel." The telepath stared, her eyes reflecting the red ember of her blunt. "She is dangerous, a devil, *vampiro mio*, a devil dressed in silk and satin."

"Can you be more specific? Most of the devils I know are fond of silk and satin. And lace."

Luz chuckled and pointed a finger. "Always with the jokes, Felix." She reached under her tunic and from beneath one of her heavy breasts, fished a scrap of paper. "You'll need this." She pressed the paper into my fingers.

I held the note to a crack of starlight and read *los zorros*.

"The foxes?" I asked.

"Actually, only one fox. Alicia Zorro. When you get to Guaymas she'll help you."

"Who is she?"

"The port harbormaster."

I hadn't expected assistance from such an official. "What does she have to do with the Dowager Engels and Ling Zhu Han?"

"It would be better that Zorro explain that to you." Luz

tapped her blunt into the dish. "However, I can tell you why Ling Zhu Han went to *Isla Tiburón*." She took another hit of tobacco and hashish. "The Papago who helped her flee from Tucson told her they had sisters on the island."

"Doing what?"

"Working for the Dowager Engels."

"What kind of work?"

"What uneducated young women end up doing. Sadly."

"Prostitution?"

"More like sex slaves. And worse. Ling Zhu Han said she'd help them escape."

The more I learned about Ling, the more her character began to take shape. Anyone except for her would've considered themselves lucky for escaping the robbery and kidnapping, and laid low for a while. But she didn't falter in her calling to help other women. And it was especially interesting that she was directed to *Isla Tiburón*.

I asked, "How do you know all this?"

"The Papago told me. What I can add is that you, *chupa sangre,* and your *güero* friend Malachi are on the right trail."

Her reply was mildly reassuring. Without thinking, I blurted, "You sound like Coyote."

"Coyote?" She sat up. "Where is he?"

"I don't think we're talking about the same Coyote."

"If he's a friend of yours, then it's the same scoundrel." Luz scrambled for a leather possibles bag and upended it over the buffalo robe. She sorted through the spilled contents and gathered small wooden chits. "IOU's from that son-of-a-bitch. He owes me." She tossed the chits and they clattered around my boots.

I picked at the chits, small flat pieces of wood, each scratched with a number. "What am I supposed to do with these?"

"Give them to Coyote the next time you see him."

"That might be a while."

"Not my problem. In the meantime, you owe me."

Damn. Even across the supernatural void, Coyote managed to drain my wallet. But more importantly, Coyote had been in this realm. "When did you last see him?"

Luz wrinkled her brow, causing her crown to slide down her forehead. "Months?"

In that case, he might be close.

"Years?" she amended and straightened her crown.

"What was he doing?"

"Don't change the subject. I want my money."

I considered the telepath. Evidentially she could pull strings to help or hinder me. "How much?"

"Quite a lot."

Even with my share of Wu Fei's reward, by the time I was done with this case, I'd be lucky to end up broke.

"Forty-six Sols," she said.

That's it? I didn't like it, but I could part with that sum. "I'll have to get the money from my saddlebags."

"How much do you have on you?"

"Eleven dollars," I lied.

"That will do. As long as it's gold or silver. Paper money isn't good enough to wipe your ass."

Grimacing as if each coin was ripped from my pockets, I collected a ten-dollar gold piece and two silver half-dollars. "Here you go. Are we square?"

Luz cupped her fingers, and I dropped the coins into her hand. She bit them each in turn and let them fall into her possibles bag. Leaning back, she stretched her legs and pushed the soles of her calloused feet against my knee. "Enough talking. Time for sleeping. *Mañana entonces.*"

I turned to leave when she said, "One more thing. When you see Coyote, tell him that I miss him."

Holding back a chuckle, I crawled out of the lean-to. For some reason, women had a soft spot for ugly dogs and Coyote.

When I reached my blanket I sat and hissed at Malachi to

get his attention. I wanted to share the note, but his snores told me to wait until tomorrow. So much for his vigilance.

Lying on my blanket, I watched the constellations tilt across the sky and tried to fathom the mysteries of this perplexing world and my place in it. Seemed in my quest for Ling Zhu Han, for every question answered, another two piled in its place.

When the sky was at its darkest, and the air chilled sharp as broken ice, the *rurales* sergeant made his rounds to roust his sleeping men. They crawled from under their blankets, grumbling and cursing, and shambled against the palisade to piss on its rock walls.

Malachi stirred and threw aside his blanket. He staggered away to take care of his morning business. Upon returning, he rummaged in his war bag for a can of tooth powder, which we shared. I used my toothbrush to give my fangs a good polishing. When done I shared with him what the telepath had told me.

He spit and wiped foam from his mustache. "The harbormaster is going to help us? That's welcome news." He rinsed his mouth with a pull from his canteen. "What exactly did *Doña Luz* say about the Dowager Engel?"

"That she was dangerous."

Malachi corked the canteen, stared at me, and smirked. "That's why I like hanging out with you. Between the two of us, I'm never mistaken for the dumb one."

I knelt to fold my blanket and ground tarp. "You should be as good with a pistol as you are with that smart mouth." As I explained why Ling Zhu Han had gone to *Isla Tiburón*, Malachi nodded and said things like, "That's good to know ... interesting detail ... a right peculiar wrinkle."

A detail of *rurales* dropped logs on the fire and when its flames licked high, they heated coffee pots, kettles filled with meat, and a *comal* to heat tortillas. The colonel's tent was struck. The spears with the Apache heads were yanked from the ground and taken away. The soldiers filed past the campfire for breakfast, and the orderly brought us hot stew slopped over tortillas. Still satiated with Doña Luz's blood, I gave my meal to Malachi.

By the time the dawn limned the top of the stony cul-de-sac, everyone had their bedrolls and saddles cinched on their mounts. The sergeant shouted a command, and the *rurales* climbed on their horses.

Colonel Cascabel guided his horse close to Malachi and me. His khaki uniform was brushed clean, his boots and brass polished. "My detachment will meet *La Poderosa*. Corporal Ruiz and his squad will escort you to Guaymas."

Corporal Ruiz watched from his roan, looking impatient. He resembled the stern-faced leathery sergeant and might have been a younger cousin.

Cascabel waved to the sergeant, who in turn shouted, "*En fila india. Adelante.*"

Two men of the vanguard rode for the narrow gap between the canyon walls. The colonel started after them. Without acknowledging me, the telepath trotted her horse behind his. The color guard followed, flags furled. The Apache heads dangled from saddle horns. The detachment emptied the remuda single file. The clomp of hooves, the creak and jangle of tack, the bouncing step of donkeys laden with baggage made the scene appropriate for a Hollywood western, minus the rousing *Beef-it's-what-for-dinner* soundtrack.

Malachi and I let the dust settle, then saddled up. Ruiz led our party from the canyon, out of the shadows, and into sunlight that was already punishingly bright. The *rurales'* umbrella-wide sombreros dropped big circular shadows over their torsos. We proceeded along a path weaving through a line of hills. To the east, a dusty haze marked the colonel's progress across the rolling desert.

One of the corporal's men rode ahead as point, and another lagged behind as the rear guard. We entered a trough between the rising scrabble. Mesquite and chaparral gave way to willows and cottonwoods. A damp smell lifted from the ground. Our horses' hooves began carving Us in moist sand. Water seeping from the earth grew into a trickle. Soon our horses splashed through a stream that grew wider and deeper, and we left the flowing water for a parallel trail. Frogs plopped into the cattails, and rabbits scurried into grass. We ambled through pockets of refreshing air beneath the canopies of leafy trees.

While the atmosphere seemed bucolic and peaceful, the *rurales* carried their Springfield rifles perched on their pommels. Malachi and I flipped our coats back over our revolvers. For mile after mile, we traveled in silence, stopping only to water our horses in the stream.

Malachi rode behind me, and I turned to watch him and consider why I was partnered to him. In the other world, since I'd been turned, I'd grown more calloused to humans. I'd come to regard them as feedbags at best, enemies at worst, and nuisances the rest of the time.

But Malachi—and Hermosa—were different. I depended on them, and they depended on me. Rather, on the other Felix. Then Coyote sent me here with some great task in mind, and as usual, his reason was garbled in transmission.

Malachi caught my gaze, and he spurred his horse into a canter until we rode side-by-side. "What's on your mind?" he asked in a low rasp.

"Nothing in particular. Simply wondering how you're doing."

"Lousy. And unless you've got a spot of tobacco to help ease this monotony, then don't bother asking."

"With an attitude like that, I might not be so forthcoming the next time you need help."

"Ha," he snorted. "I'm the one holding your hand." He dug into his vest pocket and flipped a gold coin that flashed in the sun before it landed back in his palm. "Seems that in our contest, I'm ahead. You want to keep financing my whiskey habit, let's make another wager."

"All right. I'll find Alicia Zorro before you do."

His mustache twitched. "Ten dollars this time." He tugged his reins. His horse slowed and fell in trail.

The silence returned and it seemed to swallow every sound we made. The quiet became an oppressive weight. Along the way I remembered my geography. No one to date had mentioned Hermosillo, the capital of Sonora, which straddled the north-south, east-west corridors through the region. The city should've been the next resting stop.

After another hour of our march, we reached a basin surrounded by dusty slopes, random conical hills, and distant rocky spines. We passed the eroded remains of one adobe cabin, then another, then a tumbled-down barricade, and more and more of the same, all pockmarked with bullet holes and starbursts of artillery shrapnel. Rusted cannon and wrecked caissons lay everywhere like a giant's broken toys.

The trail widened into an abandoned road. Blackened traces of wooden structures alternated with brick and adobe ruins, now arranged to form a city grid.

Hermosillo. What was left of it.

Wooden poles jutted in interrupted rows across block after block of bleak wasteland. The wizened bullet-riddled carcasses of men and horses—mummified by years of dry heat—littered the streets, their corpses more or less intact. Scavengers should've scattered the remains, but apparently the savagery of the battle lingered years after, spooking even the vultures, coyotes, and rats.

The stream meandered through the city, turning brackish and giving way to foul-smelling mud flats. At any moment I expected a flock of ravens or buzzards to rise from the ruins in a burst of flapping wings. Aside from us, nothing living stirred, not a mouse, nor a snake, a lizard, a grasshopper. A breeze kicked up dust and from deep within the desolated city, a hollow clacking —like a string of skulls—echoed up the streets. Each of us gripped our weapons, ready to start shooting and bolt away.

Our horses whinnied and tried to bunch up. Even I as a

vampire got the heebie-jeebies. One of the soldiers drew a
crucifix from inside his shirt and kissed it. Malachi slowed his
horse and leaned forward in his saddle to study the devastation.
He halted, then plucked a pad and a pencil from inside his coat
and scribbled.

I broke ranks and rode to him. "You putting this in your
memoirs?"

"Have to. My wife is from these parts."

My gaze ranged over the destruction. "Some legacy."

"Remember that battlefield we passed through while on *La
Poderosa*? That was mere practice for what was done here. The
only blessing is that we missed it."

The corporal and his men waited. He yelled to us. "*Apurense,
güeyes.*"

Malachi put his things away and we trotted to regain
our place.

I glanced back to what was left of Hermosillo. "Do you
believe in omens?"

Malachi kept his eyes on the trail ahead. "I believe in staying
ready."

CHAPTER TWENTY-TWO

The road out of Hermosillo narrowed to a trail we followed to another creek that wound into the hills. Gradually, life returned around us. First weeds, scrub grass, and small cacti, then brush and larger cacti, then stands of juniper and copses of leafy trees. Fish in the creek darted from our shadows. Bees and butterflies flitted about, and our horses tossed their heads, acting relieved to have left behind so much death and decay.

We rode hard through gaps in the rugged earth, winding between steep walls shaded by stands of pine trees and cedar. Malachi mentioned that we traveled on a shortcut through Devil's Canyon, scene of many an ambush and murder.

We continued south past sunset, and when the horses had trouble finding steady footing in the dark, the corporal gave the order to stop and make camp. We spent a cold night in a rocky draw, with no fire for warmth or to heat water. Despite the discomforts, I managed a nap.

The yapping of coyotes woke me. A silvery quarter moon floated above the horizon, and the coyotes' ragged chorus added to the lonely vista. Then the eerie trumpeting of the elephant

creatures reverberated through the darkness and immediately
the coyotes fell quiet. Around Malachi and me, the *rurales* slept
uneasily with their rifles clutched tight. I offered to stand watch
and climbed on a bluff that overlooked the draw. I was curious
about these mysterious beasts but couldn't pinpoint the source
of the echoes bouncing across the inky landscape. The next
morning Ruiz mentioned we were forty miles from Guaymas and
told us to prepare ourselves for a long day in the saddle.

Late in the afternoon, when horse lather soaked though our
saddle blankets, we plodded free of the tangled hills and onto an
open trail. The sight of a small boy herding goats put us at much
needed ease. Huts made of grass and wattle collected around the
road. Men tended to burros hitched to carts. Women stoked
outdoor stoves. Others labored under canopies of woven palm
fronds, grinding corn, making tortillas, or scrubbing clothes.
None seemed bothered by our passing, as if smelly and heavily
armed men routinely emerged from the wilderness.

The point and the rear guard closed ranks, and the six of us
rode two-by-two in tight formation, Malachi and I bookended
by the *rurales*, Ruiz at the lead.

The trail widened into a well-used dirt road. Crude shacks
cobbled from scrounged material accumulated into a vast shanty-
town. I couldn't believe this settlement of hovels was our prized
destination, Guaymas.

Apparently neither did Malachi, and he panned the squalor
with a puzzled look.

Where in this would we find Alicia Zorro, the harbormaster?

As we proceeded down the road on the other side of the hill,
brick buildings towered over the impoverished neighborhood.
Women swept the fronts of ramshackle cottages. Laundry hung
from lines stretched across alleys. People filled buckets with
water from public taps. Men and women crisscrossed the road in
a bustle of commerce. Those in stylish dress clutched portfolios,
while those in work clothes carried baskets or pushed wheelbar-
rows. Some led goats or swine, no doubt to a butcher's shop.

Horse-drawn wagons and ox-carts laden with goods crowded onto the road. Though the air smelled like a musty towel, the industry and life was a welcome contrast to the depressing desolation of the journey here.

Young women ceased their work and shaded their eyes to track us. The *rurales* rode a little taller and adjusted their sombreros though they feigned indifference to the attention.

We crested a second rise. Malachi and I halted, stunned by what opened before us. The slum town pressed against a lofty wooden fence. Behind the fence rose a colossal wall of gleaming white marble. From behind the wall jutted a confusion of spires, domed roofs, and belfries. Flags and banners fluttered from the wall and the buildings. And behind the walled citadel, a turquoise panorama—the Gulf of California—spread into a bright haze that smothered the horizon. Tiny ships in the distance cruised the open water. The entire scene came at us in one gigantic burst of texture and color.

"A might impressive," Malachi deadpanned.

The *rurales* following us barked orders to catch up with the corporal.

More and more wagons and carts queued onto the road, all headed to the city. As we rode, Malachi and I kept glancing to the right, northward, across a sweep of beach that curved toward a smudge in the haze. *Isla Tiburón.*

I felt as if I was falling into myself. Suddenly, I was back on that beach. The undulating motion of my horse gave way to the sensation of being carried flat on my back. Malachi trotted in front of me, head down, burdened with one end of my stretcher, where I lay with my belly ripped open. The air was a black curtain of smoke from the assault ships burning in the water, the surf red with blood. Flaming streaks arced between our ramparts and those on Shark Island.

Children called to me. I blinked, and the horrific spectacle vanished from my mind. Barefoot urchins in rags sprinted beside my horse, the expression on their dirty faces beseeching for handouts. I tossed a handful of small coins to the side, and the little beggars swarmed after them.

The road became a hard-packed avenue leading to an immense iron gate set in the wooden fence. On either side, an open-air market heaped with goods of every kind pulsed with hagglers and hawkers like a grand bazaar in a Moroccan casbah. Women in shawls held up loaves of bread and pans of steaming food. Men wearing gaudy straw hats passed out handbills that promised iced drinks, honest games of chance, and *chicas bien joven y apretadas* at the Integrity Gambling Hall and Hygienic Bordello.

Guards in blue uniforms and white pith helmets watched traffic queuing for the gate. A weather-beaten sign on the fence said in Spanish and English. *Transfer Zone. Have your documents ready for inspection.*

Corporal Ruiz threaded our party through the line. At the gate, he saluted a pair of guards who waved us along.

Inside the zone, the odor of horse manure and coal smoke clotted the air. Wagons clattered from the gate in random directions across a wide dirt track between the fence and the wall. Steam-powered trucks chugged along the track. The trucks and wagons stopped side-by-side in sheds marked with numbers. Laborers transferred cargo from the wagons to the trucks, and vice-versa as men and women in fancier clothes supervised. Loaded wagons headed toward a second gate marked Exit. I couldn't fathom a reason for the transfer zone as it only added a layer of complexity and middlemen to the market.

Ruiz pulled up to an arrow painted on the fence. It pointed to the right, and the caption below read: *Cuartel General. Fuerza Rural. Batallón Provincial.* He said, "I delivered you both to Guaymas alive. This concludes my services, *señores.*" He touched the brim of his sombrero. "*Adios.*" He and his party trotted to their headquarters.

I contrasted the difference between the city and encompassing slum, and thought aloud, "Even here, it's the first world and the third world."

Malachi cocked an eyebrow. "First world? Third world? The hell you talking about?"

"It's something complicated that I read in a book."

"Complicated?" He smiled. "Why don't you leave the heavy reading and big ideas to me?"

"Okay Mr. Big Ideas," I replied. "What's next?"

"If I stink as much as you, then a bath is a priority. Followed by a shave. Once we look decent, then we're due a meal, whiskey, and a cigar."

A bearded man in greasy overalls walked by hefting a toolbox.

I called to him in Spanish. "Where can a man get cleaned up?"

Without pausing, he pointed toward our left. "At the reception port for Central Station." Before I could thank him, he hustled away.

Malachi and I continued through the crowded zone, occasionally hurrying our mounts, or yanking back on the reins to avoid colliding with a wagon. Up ahead, the masts of land yachts came into view, but none of them was *La Poderosa* as it hadn't yet arrived. Passengers and crew meandered on the elevated docks. Boom cranes swung cargo nets. Steam trucks carried stacks of Wonder-fuel, which were loaded by conveyor belt into waiting yachts.

An inclined walkway connected the platform to a cluster of shops and salons. We left our horses, saddles, and bedrolls at a stable. War bags in hand, we headed toward the shops.

An hour later—bathed, shaved, fed, boots shined, and in fresh clothes—we strode through the transfer zone. Our next stop was the harbormaster's office and a chat with Alicia Zorro.

CHAPTER TWENTY-THREE

Now Malachi and I had to get into the city.

Horse-drawn carts and steam-powered wagons top-heavy with cargo lumbered around us. An elegant open carriage rumbled close. Half a dozen passengers sat inside the boat-shaped body painted emerald green and festooned with gleaming brass fittings. The driver sat over the rear-mounted engine compartment, and he steered the carriage toward a sally port in the city wall.

"Let's go," I said to Malachi.

War bags in hand, we ran after the carriage. When close, we tossed our bags into the carriage and leapt after them, bounding over the side and landing between the passengers. Malachi staggered into me until he found his balance. We stood between the two rows of passengers, in forward seats facing backwards and in rear seats facing forward. They gave us a collective glare, but no matter, my friend and I wedged our butts onto opposite-facing velvet seats and gathered our bags, which we set on our laps.

The driver yelled to us, "This is a private coach. You can't just hop on board."

"We just did," I replied.

Lips pruning, he gave his head a dismissive shake and dropped the matter.

Even in our neat and pressed coats, compared to everyone else, Malachi and I looked like shabby cowpokes. The other passengers wore sharp outfits of fine cotton and worsted wool. Silver, gold, and ivory fittings decorated their canes, handbags, and revolvers. The four men donned fresh-looking derbies or top hats. One of the women wore a silk bonnet to complement her billowing dress, the other a pith helmet to match her khaki safari clothes. Gauzy veils covered their eyes. The whole group looked bothered, like we had crashed their intimate party.

In a gesture of goodwill, Malachi reached into his coat pocket and offered cigars to the passengers at his left and right. The man on the left acted as stiff as his starched collar.

"I don't smoke," he sneered. "It's a filthy vice."

"Perhaps," Malachi answered. "But as our departed President Abraham Lincoln once said, 'A man with no vices has few virtues.'"

The woman on his right, the one in khaki, chuckled and accepted the proffered cigar. She spooled a gold chain to tug a cloisonné lighter from her coat pocket. After lifting the veil to reveal a pair of sparkling sapphire eyes, she lit her and Malachi's cigars.

I grinned, smug that Malachi and I would enter the city without a problem.

But I was wrong. Our carriage stopped in the sally port. The other passengers brandished small numbered cards for the customs guard. When he asked for our cards, Malachi and I could only shrug. He promptly ordered us off the carriage and pointed to a bench beside a door in the sally port wall. The door's window said *Jefe de Guardia Aduana*.

Mr. Starched Collar sneered as the carriage rolled away, leaving us frustrated in its swirling plume of smoke. The guard opened the door and reported to someone inside.

A wiry lieutenant bolted out, barking at Malachi and me like a terrier. "You can't get inside the city without a voucher."

I said to Malachi, "I'll handle this," and turned to the lieutenant. "Perhaps if I can explain."

"Explain what?"

I gestured that he lean close. When he did so I whispered into his ear, "We have business with Alicia Zorro."

He glowered, skeptical.

"Of the Harbormaster's office," I added.

"I know who she is." He straightened. "Why didn't she issue you passport vouchers?"

"I don't know. She only told us to see her as quickly as possible. Said it was an emergency."

The lieutenant regarded Malachi and me. He could tell we were rough men, and I guessed that someone from the city government didn't ask for a pair of guys like us unless the situation called for hush-hush dirty work. I could see the dilemma in the lieutenant's eyes. On the one hand, he had to keep the riffraff out of Guaymas. On the other, when a local big shot said jump, he had better jump.

"I'll need to verify that, *señor*."

I motioned to the door. "By all means."

Malachi waited outside while we entered his office. I closed the door behind us and on the sly, lowered the curtain over its window. Posters, announcements, and chalkboards covered with abbreviated messages hung from the walls. Arranged on his desk rested a blotter, a battery of stamps, a folder stuffed with forms, an ornately painted box, pens and an inkpot, and a small brass statue of a naked maiden.

I sat in the chair in front of the desk. He sat in the swivel chair on the other side. Reaching to the box, he depressed a lever, and a cigarette popped out. He lipped the cigarette and grasped the statue. Pinching her legs together caused twin flames to jet from her nipples. He lit his cigarette and puffed like he wasn't yet ready to get involved in what Malachi and I were up to.

I fingered the stamps and asked, "What do we need?"

Pulling the stamps out of my reach, he selected one and a couple of forms, and slapped them on the blotter. "These," he blurted, "but let's not get ahead of ourselves."

Outside, vehicles rumbled to a halt, then continued. Meanwhile, I played with the lever of the cigarette box and ejected cigarettes across the lieutenant's desk.

Fussing with the cigarettes, he admonished, "Keep your hands away from my things." He plucked a slip of paper from his desk drawer. "Now tell the guard to come in here. I need him to run a note to the Harbormaster's office. When he returns," the lieutenant's eyes bore into mine, "with confirmation about your business, then you and your friend will get your vouchers. I'm not sticking my neck out for anybody." He rested his cigarette on an ashtray and dipped a pen in ink.

I picked up the statue and clicked her shapely legs to admire the flames shooting from her boobs. I let the statue slip from my hand and clatter to the floor. "Oops."

The lieutenant jammed the pen into a holder. "*Cabrón*. I should throw your ass out and have *Señorita* Zorro take care of this herself." He sprang from his chair and stomped around the desk. When he crouched to retrieve the statue, I pounced on his back, fangs extended. I bit the side of his neck and pushed him to the ground. Warm blood filled my mouth. He struggled for brief heartbeats, then collapsed. I withdrew my fangs, pulled at his collar, and twisted his head to better expose his throat.

I'd only intended to knock him out but the rich taste of fresh human blood stoked my appetite. My last blood meal had been two days ago. I helped myself and in the meantime, pumped him full of amnesia enzymes. I hoisted him upright and left his ashen-faced body slumped in his chair.

Studying the forms, I figured how to forge the entries. With the quill I completed the necessary forms and gave them the official stamp of approval. I tore the vouchers from the bottom of the forms—one for me, one for Malachi—stuffed the forms into a file drawer, and straightened the lieutenant's desk. When he woke up, the last thing he'd remember was whatever he was doing before his assistant interrupted him. On the way out, I set the lock on the door so it bolted shut behind me. I told the customs guard, "The lieutenant is quite upset. He said not to bother him any time soon."

I showed the guard our vouchers, which he accepted with a cursory glance and shrug. I gave Malachi his voucher. We carried our war bags out of the sally port to where the entryway intersected a wide boulevard. We found ourselves in a canyon of polished marble walls, the gleaming white relieved by splashes of color from awnings, banners, and lush plants in window gardens. Traffic of all type—surreys pulled by magnificent trotting horses, shiny brass cars shooting sparks and smoke from chrome exhaust pipes, lumbering trucks laden with goods—passed by on the cobblestone roads, the stones polished flat and even. Malachi and I were the only pedestrians but even so, Guaymas, our forbidden destination, seemed as welcoming as a resort.

Malachi panned to the left and right. "Appears a touch different from what I remembered."

Certain the last time the other Felix had been here was during a war, Guaymas must've been a battered and miserable place. But unlike the desolate and abandoned Hermosillo, this city had rebounded and flourished.

Malachi patted his coat pockets. He found a cigar. "What the hell did you tell the lieutenant?"

"The usual. Showed him the advantage of helping us cut corners."

Malachi lit the stogie with a lucifer and tossed the smoldering match to the sidewalk. From behind us, like he'd been conjured out of thin air, a man in white overalls dashed forward, hissing like an angry cat. Wielding a broom, he whisked the match into a dustpan and scurried into a corner, where he blended into the white marble.

Malachi glared at him. "Well pardon me. You don't like people littering, then post a goddamn sign."

The man hissed again and jabbed his broom toward a shingle above our heads. It said in Spanish, English, French, German, and Chinese. *No Littering.*

"Okay, so I won't litter," Malachi grumbled. He looked at me. "Which way?"

Since we were looking for the Harbormaster, I'd bet it was next to the water. I looked about to get oriented and proceeded south.

We walked several blocks, coming across plazas teeming with people, some strolling, others resting under café umbrellas. Everyone appeared prosperous and content. However on closer inspection, some were wrapped head-to-toe in bandages beneath their clothing. Even so, they lounged about, casually like nothing was wrong.

"I was starting to admire this place," Malachi allowed, "until I saw those living mummies. What do you think?"

"I'm not sure." I figured Guaymas was a giant gated community, constructed to protect the pampered sensibilities of its wealthy citizens and visitors. But the bizarre sight of people wrapped in bandages told me the city had secrets yet to be revealed.

"Think this has anything to do with Ling Zhu Han?" he asked.

My kundalini noir tingled. "Until we learn otherwise, let's assume that it does."

At the next block a steam car honked its horn and cruised to a stop beside us. A plump-faced driver in the front of the cab opened a window. He grinned from behind goggles. "*Señores* Hunter and Gomez?"

How did this stranger know our names? My senses plucked an alarm.

"I'm here to take you to the Hotel Celestial," he explained.

"On whose orders?" I asked.

The driver lifted his goggles, and his brown eyes shined with humor. "Come now, *señor*. You're asking obvious questions."

"Alicia Zorro?"

"If you have another benefactor within these walls, it would be news to all of us."

I paused to let my kundalini noir braid around the moment. For all its beauty, Guaymas seemed as treacherous as a femme fatale. I appraised the driver and let my sixth sense range over the vehicle to probe for clues about a bomb or some other infernal device. Convinced we were safe, I opened the cab door, dropped my bag on the floor, and climbed aboard.

Malachi tossed his bag on top of mine and joined me on the rear seat. He drew his Schofield and set the big revolver on his lap.

I nudged him and whispered, "What gives?"

"Travelers insurance," he mumbled. "This place would creep out a tarantula."

The driver lowered his goggles into place. "Hang on, *señores*. I am the fastest chauffeur in town." He braced himself over the steering wheel, yanked on levers, and we zoomed forward. The steam engine behind us rattled and chugged. We careened around corners and raced past other vehicles, horns and curses echoing in our wake.

"Fastest chauffeur?" I asked as I jostled side-to-side. "I'd prefer the safest."

The car rocketed into a cul-de-sac and screeched to a halt in front of an imposing building with tall columns and rows of palm trees. A dark blue banner decorated with stars fluttered from a pole set into a wall and it said *Hotel Celestial*. From where the car idled, our view opened to a broad vista of the sea, the harbor, and the adjacent coastline. Malachi holstered his revolver.

I started to climb out when the driver reached and gripped my arm. "Not you, *Señor* Gomez."

"What gives?"

He nodded to Malachi. "*Señor* Hunter can take care of the arrangements. Our benefactor is on a tight schedule, and she requested you."

"Why can't we both go?"

"I suppose you can. But her instructions only mentioned you."

"Go on," Malachi said. He stepped forward and patted the driver's shoulder. "I never got your name, sir."

"Pasqual Diaz," the driver answered proudly.

"*Entonces, Señor* Diaz, *que guardas mi compañero. Para tu salud.*"

"*Lo entiendo.*" Pasqual gulped.

Malachi patted his shoulder again. "*Eres un hombre bien listo.*"

My friend collected both of our bags and jogged up the stairs to the hotel entrance. A bellhop held the door open.

Pasqual sighed. "Your companion is wound a bit tight, *Señor* Gomez."

"Let's get going," I ordered.

He put the car in gear, and we rolled out of the cul-de-sac and down the hill. As we continued down the slope and closer to the wharf, the buildings became more industrial and grimy, and the fancy passenger cars and coaches gave way to hulking cargo haulers. The odor of coal and wood smoke, oil, and fish added a greasy tang to the sea air.

"Draw the curtains," Pasqual said.

I pulled the curtains across the side and rear windows and kept myself hidden in the cab's shadows. I watched over Pasqual's shoulder to see where we were headed.

We approached a wire fence and slowed at a gate. A sign on the fence said in Spanish and English *Office of the Harbormaster. Access controlled. Trespassers will be shot on sight.*

CHAPTER TWENTY-FOUR

Pasqual Diaz halted the taxi at the gate. Through a gap in my window's curtains I saw a man in uniform walk out of a guard shack. The guard stepped close to Pasqual's side, stopped, and glanced in my direction. I pushed back into my seat to remain in shadow.

"*Buenas tardes*, Armando," Pasqual said.

So they knew each other.

"Another off-the-books guest?" Armando asked. "Who for, Pasqual? Some afternoon delight for the commodore?"

"I wouldn't know." Pasqual slid an envelope toward Armando, who cupped it against his waist. Armando straightened and waved to a comrade in the shack. A mechanism hissed and the barbed-wire gate retracted. The taxi grunted and lurched several feet before settling into a smooth roll. Pasqual cautioned me over his shoulder. "Stay hidden, *Señor* Gomez."

We drove into a lot where workers bustled in truck and equipment bays on the left. On the right stretched a long building with office fronts and a square-sided tower—it must've been six stories tall. Pelicans sat on fence posts. The lot sloped toward the wharf.

"*Señorita* Zorro ordered me to deliver you as soon as possible." Pasqual turned to the right past the tower and drove behind it where the lot appeared deserted. "Up ahead. There's a door. Go through it and make your way to the top floor of the tower. You'll find *la señorita* there."

He braked. "It's all clear. Go. Go."

I hustled out of the taxi, darted around scattered junk, and pressed myself against the door. The taxi rattled away in a cloud of steam and smoke. I opened the door and stepped into an empty stairway. To my right an elevator clattered behind the wall. The stairs led to the basement and up the tower, the long isolated flights a perfect place for an ambush. I wondered why I was so trusting of a person I didn't know, but I had to follow this lead.

My sixth sense on alert, I climbed to the sixth floor, fangs and trigger finger poised for action. I exited onto a small foyer and faced a wooden door with a frosted glass window decorated in gold-leaf lettering: *Alicia Zorro, Director del Puerto, Harbormaster.*

Approaching the door, I listened, heard nothing, and knocked. A delicate voice invited me in, and I tried to form a mental picture. *Señorita* implied an unmarried woman so I imagined a young Alicia.

I was wrong. Upon entering I saw that a petite, elderly woman occupied a big leather swivel chair behind a large desk, and she gave the impression of a queen cat guarding its domain. A bowl-cut hairdo streaked with gray cupped her diminutive face. Shiny dark eyes studied me from behind circular, wire-rimmed spectacles. Her complexion was a deeply hued brown, and a shawl woven in a Mexican-Indian design draped her thin shoulders. An assortment of knick-knacks cluttered her desk.

The office smelled like a smoker's lounge. Sunlight blazed through windows. Furnishings included leather chairs, bookcases, a globe on a pedestal, and a brass telescope aimed out one window.

Walking closer and treading over a sumptuous Persian carpet, I noticed she cradled a small gray fox in her lap.

"Felix Gomez, finally, we get to talk," she said. "I've been looking forward to meeting you face-to-face." Though her Spanish diction was precise, certainly better than mine, it still carried the melodious trace of a Tarahumara accent.

I touched the brim of my hat in salutation. "Same here, *Señorita* Zorro," I replied, certain that she and I—rather the other Felix—didn't have a history.

She leaned to one side and dropped the fox into a padded basket on the floor. "Did anyone see you enter the building?"

"I don't think so."

She nodded.

"Before we continue," I asked, "how is it that you know me?"

"That's not important," she replied crisply. "Let's get to the reason you're here. Ling Zhu Han."

I asked, "Would you know if she's alive?"

Before answering, Alicia plucked a small clay pipe from a stand on her desk. She opened a round tin, pinched tobacco, and stuffed the bowl of the pipe. She tipped the container toward me.

I shook my head.

Alicia lit a match and sucked on the stem of the pipe. "Is she alive? That I don't know, but there is someone who does."

"Let's make sure we're talking about the same Ling." I reached into my jacket for the tintype of Ling and dropped the picture on the desk.

Puffing smoke, Alicia nudged the picture back to me. "I never met her. I only know she was here."

I put the tintype back in my pocket. "Then how do you know it was her?"

"Young women pass through Guaymas like flocks of migrating birds, but only one was Wu Fei's daughter."

"Wu Fei," I replied sourly. "So you're aware of what's at stake for me?"

"Quite. In fact let me show you a picture of my own." She opened a desk drawer and handed me an envelope.

It contained a photo of two men's heads, severed and resting on platters. Should something go rotten in our search for Ling, those two heads could be Malachi's and mine. A third platter held a card hand-lettered with the name Flor Horgersen. "Who is Flor Horgersen?"

"My companion." Smoke clouded above Alicia's head.

"Was this a warning from Wu Fei?" I returned the envelope and photo.

"No. It's the calling card of the Dowager Engels and a reminder to not only think of myself but Flor as well. Those two unfortunates had been working for me and this is what befell them."

"I think what befell them was an ax to the neck. What were they doing?"

"Digging into the dowager's business." Alicia put the photo away. "What do you know of her?"

"Almost nothing. I didn't even know she existed until two nights ago. Thanks to Doña Luz."

Alicia nodded, evidently pleased that Doña Luz had passed along the mention. A breeze wafting through an open window rattled maps on the walls and cleared the smoke.

"Let's back up," I said. "How do you know me? How did you know I was on my way here?"

"I have spies, minus two thanks to the dowager. As the harbormaster it is my duty to watch who comes into this city whether they arrive by sea or by land."

"Spies watching me?"

"Indeed, from every direction." Alicia chuckled as she struck another match to relight her pipe.

"You summoned me and here I am," I said. "Now what?"

Alicia pushed up from her seat. "This way." As her pleated dress billowed around her short legs, she seemed to glide toward a window. The little gray fox tracked her from its basket.

I followed Alicia. The view overlooked the crowded wharf to the southwest.

She pointed with the stem of her pipe. "See that white steamer?" A large white ship was berthed alongside smaller passenger vessels. "That's the *Empress of St. Petersburg*. It arrived yesterday."

"And?"

"That ship arrived with passengers representing the richest houses of Europe. The Windsors, the Hapsburgs, the Romanovs, Krupp, Lichton, Borowski, Osorio."

"That's no surprise. Your city is a beautiful destination, but I still don't understand what this has to do with Ling Zhu Han or the Dowager Engels."

Alicia walked across the room toward the window with the telescope. "Take a look." When I stood behind the telescope and realized what it was aimed at, a chill torqued my bones. Shark Island.

Alicia began, "The Dowager Engels lives there, on *Isla Tibu*—."

"I know the place," I interrupted.

Alicia studied me as if waiting for another outburst.

Recovering my composure, I explained, "Bad memories. The war."

"Plenty of those to go around," she muttered. "Since then, the island has changed much. I've never visited but am told it makes Guaymas look like a slum by comparison."

"And that's where the rich go?"

"For more than the ambiance."

"Which is?"

Alicia approached a cabinet behind her desk. She opened the cabinet and removed a bottle of Kilbeggan Irish Whiskey.

"With hooch like that," I noted, "this conversation has taken a more serious turn."

She poured a half-inch of whiskey and a splash of water into each of a pair of short heavy glasses. We raised our drinks in a silent toast. I sipped and let the whiskey give a comforting burn. Malachi would've approved.

"While you were in the city," Alicia said, "did you notice people wrapped head-to-toe like mummies?"

The question stopped me mid-sip. "What's that about?"

"The reason so many wealthy people visit this part of Aztlan. The Dowager Engels offers them medical therapy that promises a true fountain of youth."

"Does it work?" I asked.

"I'm skeptical."

"People fall for all kinds of scams," I offered. "If she fleeces the pockets of the rich, then good for her."

"It may be a scam, or not," Alicia said. "Regardless, it's a secret the dowager protects with murder."

"Then why not use the judiciary to investigate?"

"Because that island of hers is guarded by something more formidable than schools of sharks, than her army of thugs, than walls of granite and steel."

"And that would be?"

"Piles of money. Who she decides not to murder, she corrupts with cash."

"What did she offer you?"

"A fair question," Alicia replied. "The answer is that I'm not for sale. My people will never get anywhere if we don't stand on principle."

"So the dowager resorted to threats against your companion."

"Flor is out of harm's way. For now."

"I don't doubt that the Dowager Engels is a dangerous woman," I said. "But what's the connection between her and Ling Zhu Han?"

"One of my spies"—Alicia glanced to the drawer where she had deposited the photo of the heads—"saw the girl on the island."

"What was she doing there?"

"She had arrived with a group of young women. Working girls lured by the promise of easy money."

"And then they're trapped as sex slaves. Doña Luz told me."

"Information I passed to her," Alicia replied, then held up a hand. "And before you ask me why I haven't interceded, remember, I am powerless to keep the Dowager from murder, much less save girls she's trapped into whoredom."

"Before Ling showed up here, she was last seen escaping from Tucson, Arizona," I said. "Supposedly she was murdered during a robbery but that's not what happened. She was traveling with the Continental Sisters of Benevolent Light. It's a philanthropic organization that helps women escape prostitution. Ling was kidnapped but allowed to escape."

"Allowed to escape?" Alicia puffed on the pipe.

"I'm convinced that Wu Fei set up the scheme. The robbery. Ling's supposed kidnapping. That put her on the path here, to look into the girls trapped as sex slaves and help them escape."

Alicia studied me skeptically. "Why put out the word that she was dead?"

"Maybe as cover to her. If people heard she was dead, they wouldn't be on the alert for her."

"Or," Alicia began with an ominous tone, "she may be already dead. Just not at the place you originally thought."

"We can speculate all night and still not get any closer to the truth. Perhaps if I can find one of the girls who met Ling. Someone in Guaymas."

"Not possible. Only the Dowager Engels, her entourage, and rich guests leave the island."

"How many other girls have become sex slaves?"

"At least three hundred and fifty-one. And many were murdered when the Dowager no longer needed them." Alicia opened a folder on her desk and showed it to me. The folder contained lists of women's names with a recent date beside each. "Families have made inquiries about them." She opened a large envelope and dumped pictures of young women's faces. Some were formal portraits, others cropped from larger photos, and others crude drawings. "Your mission, Felix, has taken on a larger dimension. You are more than a hired gun for the Dragon, you must be the agent of retribution for what happened to all these women."

"That's a tall order. I doubt the Dowager Engels will cooperate."

"Which is why this assignment calls for rough men like you and Malachi." Alicia reached down, unlocked a drawer, and heaved a leather bag on the desk. It landed *chunk*. "Six thousand dollars. Add this to whatever lucre Wu Fei offered you. Find what happened to those poor young women and bring those responsible to hard justice."

"If by 'hard justice' you mean put bullets in bodies, I can do that."

"There's something else," she said.

"I'm not surprised."

She walked to a bookcase, pressed a button under a shelf, and the bookcase slowly rotated. On the reverse side hung the skull of a huge creature. "Do you recognize that animal?"

"An elephant?"

"Mammoth to be precise."

The skull was not a fossil. "It looks fresh." My kundalini noir quivered an alarm.

"It is. That animal was killed a month ago."

"Where?"

"In Devil's Canyon."

I remembered the trumpeting of strange beasts in the wilderness on the way here. Those were mammoths? I was about to ask, How is that possible? when I paused to reflect on where I was. *Really Felix? You're a vampire. And in this world you've met telepaths and werewolves. Why wouldn't mammoths be possible?*

"They were extinct," Alicia said, "but not anymore. The Dowager Engels is conducting infernal business inside her island fortress. Young women disappearing by the dozens. Bizarre experiments on her rich patrons. Plus resurrecting prehistoric monsters such as this one."

"She made those animals on *Isla Tiburón?*"

"As far as I know, yes."

"How did they get off the island?"

"That is another mystery."

I gulped what remained of my whiskey. How much did Alicia know about me? "Any other fantastic creatures I should be aware of?"

Alicia puffed on her pipe until smoke fogged the air. "A few, but I have no proof they exist."

"Such as?"

"Such as saber-tooth tigers. You and Señor Hunter are going to earn your money."

CHAPTER TWENTY-FIVE

U pon reaching the hotel, I learned from a desk clerk that my room was on the third floor. There, I found Malachi sitting at a small table beside a window, a lit cigar in one hand. Hermosa Singer, still wearing safari clothes, was with him. A half-empty bottle of rum, a pitcher of iced lemonade, and glasses stood on the table, beside her gun belt and hat.

"Malachi was filling me in on your adventures since you left *La Poderosa*." Hermosa stood to greet me. "He told me you went to see Alicia Zorro, the harbormaster."

"She and I talked," I replied. "How was your trip?"

"Peaceful to the point of being dull," Hermosa answered, "thanks to our escort, Colonel Cascabel and his *rurales*. I met Doña Luz and she told me about the Dowager Engels. However, we did have one disaster."

"Which was?"

"Remember our battle with the outlaws? Their bullets tore through the land yacht's whiskey barrels and so the last day of our trip was miserably sober." She teetered in place. "A condition I've managed to rectify."

Malachi tapped cigar ash out the window. "What did the harbormaster have to say?"

"Plenty." A knock on the door stopped me from explaining. Malachi dropped a hand to his holstered Schofield.

From the hall, a man called out, "Luggage for *la señorita* Singer."

Hermosa answered the door and a bellhop wheeled in a steamer trunk on a dolly. "Right over there," she instructed. The bellhop wrestled the trunk to a spot by the dresser.

"Wait a minute," I protested. "Why isn't the trunk going in your room?"

"This is my room," Hermosa answered. "It's not up to my standards but will do."

The bellhop cleared his throat.

Hermosa said, "Felix, if you wouldn't mind. I don't have any change."

I turned to Malachi. "What about you?"

"You're closer to him," he replied.

I dug into a trouser pocket and handed the bellhop my smallest coin, a silver half-dollar, probably a day's pay for him. Smiling effusively, he dragged the dolly out the door.

I panned the two beds in our room before turning to Hermosa. "Where are you going to sleep?"

She plopped on the larger of the two. "This one looks more comfortable." She kept a straight face though her eyes brimmed with sarcasm. "There's plenty of room on the other bed for you and Malachi provided neither of you hogs the mattress. Or you can sleep on the floor. The rug looks reasonably clean. Your choice."

"The hotel clerk didn't object to you sharing a room with two men?"

"This is Guaymas. I'm surprised he didn't ask, 'only two men?'"

Malachi snorted in disgust, then said, "Let's get back to Alicia Zorro."

"She's certain that the Dowager Engels is responsible for Ling Zhu Han's disappearance." From my pocket I pulled out a photograph Alicia had given me and passed it to Malachi. "That's the Dowager Engels."

The picture was a hand-tinted image of a striking and elegant woman standing in front of a garden trellis and dressed in a waistcoat over layers of ruffles and a pleated skirt. A wide-brimmed hat sat cocked on her head of light-colored curls. Small eyes gazed from alongside an aquiline nose, and her square face tapered to a strong jaw. Gloved hands clutched a closed umbrella that she leaned on like a cane. She stared at the camera with a playful smile. "Don't be fooled," I said. "I doubt she had that expression when she ordered the decapitation of Alicia Zorro's spies."

Hermosa wandered from the bed to look at the photo. "At least she didn't get any blood on that outfit of hers."

Next I related what Alicia shared about the hordes of wealthy tourists eager to try the dowager's magical youth regime, her use of money and murder to coerce the local government, the disappearance of hundreds of young women, and her menagerie of formerly extinct prehistoric creatures.

"What else did you learn about her?" Malachi asked.

"She arrived in Guaymas five years ago and reclaimed the old fort on Shark Island."

"Just like that?"

I knew what Malachi was getting at. During the war our side had thrown wave after wave of landing parties in a futile attempt to neutralize the fort so we could capture the island. Then after the peace, the dowager had simply plunked down a pile of cash and taken over.

"Since then she's built up the amenities," I said, "to include secrets worth murder to protect."

Hermosa pinned me with a probing stare. "Secrets that cost Ling her life?"

"Possibly so." After days of travel and searching for clues, we were on the threshold of learning what those secrets were. But the immediate future loomed like a dark cave full of traps, and a voice in the back of my head whispered to tread forward very carefully.

"Now that we know what she looks like," Malachi fanned the photo, "do we still need this?"

"I don't," Hermosa replied.

I shook my head.

He touched a corner of the photograph against the end of his cigar. He sucked on the stogie until its ember burned an incandescent red and made the paper smolder. When the photo burst into flame he dropped it out the window. As we watched the burning paper flutter in the breeze, then disintegrate into smoke and ash, I knew we all hoped this was an omen for the dowager and not us.

One last item of business remained from my conversation with Alicia: the reward she had offered. "Alicia Zorro promised six thousand in gold if we find those responsible for the missing girls."

"What did she mean by find?" Malachi asked.

"She meant make dead."

"Six thousand. That's two for each of us." Hermosa looked me up and down. "Where is this money?"

"Locked in her office."

"Can you trust her?"

"For now, we have to."

"The trick will be getting on and off Shark Island unscathed," Malachi said.

"Seems only a select few are allowed that privilege."

Hermosa handed me her glass. "Felix, be a hero and refresh this for me. No ice. And don't be stingy with the rum." She hopped on top of her steamer trunk and sat, legs crossed. "This calls for a woman's cunning. Allow me to ponder our situation."

I poured equal measures of lemonade and rum into her glass and gave it to her. Malachi declined another drink and finished his cigar. As I emptied my glass I thought about my prospects of finding a nice tender neck to feed from.

Several minutes passed without Hermosa saying a thing. She remained on the steamer trunk, sipping from her glass, her expression set in deep concentration. She began rocking and murmuring.

"What's with you?" I asked.

"Shush," she snapped. "I'm channeling Melpomene."

"Who?"

"The Muse of Tragedy," Malachi replied. "And inspiration to the poet Horace, among others. If you read something besides a sportsman guide to whorehouses you might know that."

Hermosa reached to her right boot and brandished a dagger. "The Muse spoke. She said listen to Náttih Nayáwsa', the Great Woman Cantor of the Caddo people." She brought her legs up and stood on the steamer trunk. The top of her head brushed against the ceiling. Drink spilled from her glass. "I wield Melpomene's blade and bring doom. *What a storm of death for Troy race in movement thou dost set.*"

"You might want to go easy on the rum," I said.

She quaffed what was left and tossed the glass for me to catch. She hopped off the trunk, and her boots banged on the floor. "You asked about a plan. Náttih Nayáwsa' gave me a plan."

Muffled thumping rose from the floor, as well as a muted, "Keep it quiet up there, *cabrónes.*"

She plucked the hat off my head and masked her face with it. "The plan"—she peeked around its brim—"is to sneak onto *Isla Tiburón* in disguise."

CHAPTER TWENTY-SIX

I took my hat back from Hermosa and said, "Sounds simple enough, sneaking onto *Isla Tiburón* in disguise. Give us details."

"Such as," Malachi added, "disguised as whom? And once disguised how are we going to get onto the island?"

"You're both talking like we haven't done this before," Hermosa replied.

"That's because we haven't," I said.

"Then we'll improvise." Hermosa snapped open the latches of her steamer trunk. "I need to freshen up and change. Meet me in the hotel lobby."

Malachi and I headed downstairs. Considering Hermosa might be a while, we decided to wait in the hotel bar, a mezzanine above the lobby. French doors opened up to a balcony that overlooked a courtyard garden. Terraced balconies faced the courtyard. Orchids, ferns, and lush flowering plants gushed from dozens of planters. We sat at a café table along the balustrade and ordered two whiskey and sodas.

Malachi fired up a cigar. "Looks like the Hanging Gardens of Babylon."

As he traced a finger across a menu my stomach rumbled with the need for blood. Opposite from us, a maid emerged from one of the rooms and unfurled a tarp to screen the balcony. Many of the other balconies were similarly covered. Only a small wedge of sunlight reached the courtyard so the tarps weren't meant for shade.

The waiter brought our drinks.

"What's going on there?" I asked.

"I'm not supposed to say, sir."

I placed a two-bit coin on his tray.

He whispered. "That wing is for the special guests. They insist on privacy."

"Special in what way?" Malachi asked.

"They arrived today on the *Empress of St. Petersburg*. That should tell you." The waiter pocketed the coin.

He was about to leave when I grabbed his wrist. "Hold on."

Through gaps around a tarp at another balcony I discerned somebody moving and sitting on a chair. I could make out that this person was swaddled in bandages and most certainly one of those recovering from the mysterious Fountain-of-Youth therapy.

"How would I get on the *isla?*"

The waiter kept quiet and opened his hand, palm up. This time I gave him a dollar.

He answered using a low tone. "You must board a special ferry. With the arrival of the *Empress of St. Petersburg*, the next one is tomorrow."

"So we have a way on the island that doesn't involve swimming past the sharks."

The waiter cleared his throat, nervously cut his eyes to the left and right, and then looked at me. I readied another dollar, but he closed his hand as he left the table. "I must tend to my duties, *señores*."

Malachi watched him leave. "The next move is to figure out how to catch that ferry." He scrubbed the nubby beard on his face, "In the meantime I could use a shave," then flicked his spent cigar into a rose bush. "And a fresh smoke."

While Malachi headed to the hotel barbershop, I started for our room to see if Hermosa was there.

"*Señor* Gomez." Hermosa beckoned from a plush armchair in the lobby. She had changed into an expensive-looking dress with matching waistcoat. Stray strands curled from under the hat and veil pinned to her hair.

She kept company with a stern-looking matronly woman in a pale yellow dress and matching broad-brimmed hat. In the love seat to her left, a reedy younger man slouched cross-legged on the velvet cushions.

Hermosa snapped her fingers that I hurry over. "Felix," she said, "this is the Duchess Juvante of Monaco."

Powder and rouge caked Juvante's pulpy face. Gobs of heavy mascara made her wrinkled eyes resemble old prunes. A necklace of rubies and diamonds and a similar brooch rested on top of an exceptionally large pair of breasts that stretched the pleats in her blouse. Her fleshy hips filled the armchair like rising dough in a pan.

The man wore a tailored black suit complete with a white silk cravat and an emerald stickpin. A pencil mustache decorated his upper lip beneath a twitchy, possum-like nose. His blond hair was a glossy cap shellacked into place.

I extended my hand but the duchess didn't accept my offer. After waiting an awkward moment, I turned to her associate.

Not bothering to uncross his legs, he introduced himself in a dismissive French accent, "Monsieur Étalon." A wino's burst capillaries blotched his alabaster-hued cheeks.

"You her valet?" I asked.

Juvante cleared her throat, and it sounded like someone cleaning the spit valve on a tuba.

Hermosa explained, "The monsieur is the duchess's *galant*."

Ah, her gigolo. "Welcome to Guaymas."

He blinked like he wasn't used to being out in the light of day.

"The duchess has freshly disembarked from the *Empress of St. Petersburg*," Hermosa said. That's all she needed to relay that the duchess and her boy toy were on the way to *Isla Tiburón*.

My kundalini noir pinged in suspicion. Something about these two wasn't adding up. Étalon's cracked patent-leather shoes. His wilted boutonniere. Her frayed lace collar. I'd bet if I tested their gemstones they'd be nothing but paste.

I decided to bait them. "You have rooms?"

Juvante pointed a gloved finger to the ceiling. "We're on the top floor right above us."

"I thought passengers from the *Empress* were given accommodations in the other wing of the hotel."

"Why be extravagant?" she replied, laughing too forcefully. "We'd rather save our money for the important diversions of our journey. Not that we need to count our coins."

Étalon inspected his fingernails. One of his cufflinks was missing a stone.

An older woman of dubious wealth teamed with a lover on retainer, these two were definitely swindlers on the prowl. Juvante was as much a duchess of Monaco as Étalon was the King of France. I was familiar with the type. She wasn't here for the Fountain-of-Youth treatment but to scam the dowager's clientele.

"We have nothing on our schedule until tomorrow," Juvante offered.

Étalon gave a sly look. "We're looking for entertainment to help occupy our time. Something exotic. Provocative."

"How adventurous are you?" Hermosa asked.

"We'd like some local color," Juvante said. "Savages doing their dances. A bullfight."

"A donkey show," Étalon blurted, his French accent lapsing into native English.

"You're in luck," I noted. "All that is available. How about we begin with a tour through our Chinatown."

"Chinatown?" The duchess's smile flaked rouge from her cheeks. She leaned toward Hermosa and whispered, "Opium?"

Hermosa glanced at me, and that furtive look alerted me that our plans were in sync. She could easily fit into Juvante's voluminous clothes. Though I couldn't squeeze into Étalon's suit, I'm sure I could pass myself off as a stud for hire. I nodded.

"Absolutely," Hermosa said. "The finest."

I chimed in, "As soon as our escort arrives, we can go."

"Escort?" Juvante asked.

"In the interest of safety," I said, "we should employ the services of a Kansas Ranger."

Étalon pressed, "Isn't Kansas far away?"

"Indeed, sir," Hermosa replied. "However this one is here on special assignment to help clean up this city."

"He is a marksman and a lawman without peer," I said. "If there is one man who can assure that we negotiate the dens of iniquity unscathed, it is Malachi Hunter."

CHAPTER TWENTY-SEVEN

T he dockworker pushed his cart behind me as we strode across the wharf. I'd hired him to carry the "Duchess" Juvante and her paramour Étalon from Guaymas's Little Chinatown. The cart's wheels clattered over the uneven planks and the motion jostled Juvante and Étalon, who lay sprawled together in a tangle of arms and legs. They were barely conscious, and their glazed, dilated eyes resembled black marbles. They reeked of opium, a good thing since the cart stank of fish guts.

Malachi hailed me from the end of a pier. He'd left us to find a boat and was negotiating in Chinese with the skipper of a fishing junk. The old salt was surrounded by his barefoot crew. Looking up at us from the deck, he removed a faded and misshapen navy officer's cap to wipe his tanned, bald head. Malachi translated for my benefit. "He won't be party to a shanghai."

"We didn't kidnap these two," I said. "They obviously can't take care of themselves. Guaymas is not a place for anyone in their condition."

Malachi translated, and the skipper grunted in skepticism.

"Show him the money," I said.

Malachi bounced heavy coins in the palm of his hand. He switched to Spanish. "Take them across the gulf to Punta Chivato, or better yet, Imposible."

The barefoot crew whispered excitedly to their skipper. We were probably offering the same as the profit from a day's hard work. Two of them leapt onto the pier. They grabbed Juvante by her ankles and wrists. Scowling, the captain barked in Chinese. His men froze.

He stared at the coins and by the way the gold glittered in his eyes I knew he was taking the offer. But he crossed his arms and stared at Malachi. "What have they done?" he asked in Spanish.

Malachi answered, "If you really want to know, the answer will cost you." He plucked one coin and moved to drop it into a coat pocket.

The captain raised a hand. "Never mind. We'll do it."

His crew replied with hurrahs. The two holding Juvante lifted and swung her to the boat, where she plopped on a heap of fishing nets. Another two crewmen scrambled onto the pier and seconds later, Étalon tumbled on top of her. On the captain's orders, the crew stretched a canvas tarp over them. "So they won't get sunburn," he explained.

Malachi paid the captain, who shouted orders. Smoke and sparks coughed from the boat's funnel. The crewmen untied the hawsers and in short order the boat surged toward open water.

Returning to Little Chinatown, Malachi and I found Hermosa where we'd left her, in the parlor of an opium den. Sitting on a couch, she was picking through the contents of Juvante's purse, Étalon's wallet, and the belongings we'd taken from their persons: loose change, jewelry, miniature stilettos, a derringer, and papers scribbled with cryptic notes.

She jangled a hotel key attached to a brass fob. "Room 611. My new accommodations courtesy of the Duchess of Monaco."

She scooped the rest of the items into the purse, and we

proceeded to the hotel. Once in the room we ransacked the suit-cases and a large steamer trunk.

A half hour later Juvante and Étalon's wardrobes spilled across the room. Of special interest were wigs, corsets, and garter belts with sheaths and pockets, and women and men's hats with secret compartments.

Étalon's clothes were too small and foppish for me. In his shaving kit I discovered French love letters in cellophane pack-ets. Plus notes in women's handwriting. The missives to him were in a variety of languages, but from those penned in English and Spanish, I deduced that they all said the same thing. *My darling, I trust you.* Apparently Juvante didn't hesitate to pimp her companion as bait for their scams, and the condoms were used to seal the deals.

Hermosa had stripped to her chemise and long drawers to try on outfits. What clothes struck her fancy were piled on the bed.

As for money, we found a disappointing cache in French, Russian, and English currency: a few bullion coins and a stack of notes. Hermosa riffled through the paper money and selected one bill at random. She licked her thumb, rubbed it against the note, and held the money to the window light. "Bah." She flung the note. "Counterfeit."

I tore open the trunk's lining and discovered a trove of diplo-matic papers—*Writs of Passage* and *Letters of Transit*—which were probably as fake as the paper money.

Malachi placed a large envelope on the table. "This looks useful." We sorted through the envelope's contents of tickets and travel documents from the *Empress of St. Petersburg* and a smaller envelope addressed to Madame Juvante, Arrondissement du Panthéon, Paris. From inside this envelope I withdrew a brochure and an itinerary provided by the Temple of Enlighten-ment, Grace, and Futurism located in Guaymas.

"Look who heads the temple." I showed these papers to Malachi and Hermosa. The brochure offered a welcome message from the Dowager Engels, alongside a photo identical to the one Alicia Zorro had provided.

Malachi read aloud from the brochure. "Partake in scientific breakthroughs ... the wonders of tomorrow ... indulge in miracles made possible by the newest of inventions ... we've tamed the secrets of nature." He snorted in derision.

The itinerary listed tours, social hours, spa treatments, and several gala balls.

"Seems like *Isla Tiburón* is a nice vacation spot," Hermosa said, "if you overlook sex slavery, murder, and medical quackery."

"Any mention of her Fountain of Youth?" Malachi asked. "Prehistoric monsters?"

I perused the itinerary and brochure. "Nothing."

Hermosa sat on the bed. "When do we leave?"

"The ferry to the island boards tomorrow at Pier Seven, 11:00 AM," I said, "and departs at noon. Juvante paid for six days and five nights for herself and Étalon."

"Perfect. Felix and I will go as the duchess and her escort."

"Won't anyone recognize the difference?" Malachi asked.

"I'm guessing those two kept to themselves. Types like them don't like to be remembered." Hermosa tossed coins to Malachi and me. "Felix, go buy yourself nice clothes. After all, you are escorting a lady of fine breeding." She preened and batted her eyes. "Malachi, order dinner and have it brought up here. We need to mince through our plans in private."

When Hermosa is present, you don't argue over who's in charge. Malachi and I left the room, and he accompanied me to a tailor shop. While I was getting fitted, he continued on his own. When we met later, he brought a map of the Gulf of California.

"You barely picked at your meal," Hermosa said. We were arranged around the room's small table.

"I wasn't hungry." At the moment, only blood would satisfy my appetite.

Malachi opened a fresh bottle of wine and refilled our glasses. Three empty bottles stood among our plates.

The map was spread on the bed, and we used its rendering of *Isla Tiburón* to plan our operation. Once on the island, Hermosa and I would give ourselves two nights to search for Ling Zhu Han and the missing girls. Any longer than that and we risked blowing our cover. Malachi would stay on the mainland. His job was to provide a boat for our escape. During the first night, I would signal him using a lantern to indicate a pick up from the island's dock. If that wasn't possible, we'd head to the north end where he could stage a rescue from Arenas, a small fishing village on the mainland, opposite side of the channel from the island.

"Tomorrow night," Malachi asked. "What time will you signal?"

"I don't know," I replied. "You got something else going on?"

"It's all a bit loosey-goosey for my comfort."

"Since we'll have to improvise as we go along," Hermosa said, "there's no point in planning too many details."

Malachi read his pocket watch. "It's a quarter to midnight. I'm going to turn in. There anything else?"

Hermosa and I shook our heads.

He folded the map into a coat pocket and walked to the door. I got up to join him.

Hermosa said, "Felix, stay here. For appearance's sake. I doubt the duchess slept alone when Étalon was around."

Malachi smirked as he left. "I'll see you two canaries in the tomorrow."

Hermosa propped an elbow on the table and grinned. "You know I'm drunk?"

I didn't answer because I knew what was next.

"Wine sets loose the vixen in me," she purred. "With only one bed, there's no mystery where you're going to sleep."

"On the bed. What about you?"

She gave my thigh a playful swat. "After all we've been through? What's the harm of romance before the start of our adventure? For good luck."

She leaned forward and her breasts threatened to spill from the top of her chemise. My kundalini noir retreated. I am a vampire with all manner of powers, but Hermosa and her wiles had tripped me up too many times before.

"We're going to spend plenty of time together on the island," I said.

"Wouldn't hurt to practice."

"I'm sure the parts still fit."

When she tried to rise to her feet, she about toppled over. I helped her to the bed and she crashed onto the mattress.

"Felix ..." she drawled.

I locked the door's deadbolt. "What?" When I looked back at her, she was snoring.

I doused the lamps and kept watch. The view from the window overlooked the courtyard. From this high angle I couldn't see the garden below but did notice several of the mummy people backlit behind their privacy screens. Occasionally, footfalls traversed the hallway, some were quick and light—a woman's—and others, heavy and deliberate—a man's. Hand on my revolver, I listened to the steps, waiting to see if any stopped at our door, but none did.

I spent the time wondering what traps waited for us on Shark Island. We couldn't assume the dowager's spies hadn't alerted her about us. And considering all these people in bandages, perhaps her youth therapy, wasn't a trick. In my life—undead and previous—I've witnessed all kinds of supernatural monkey business.

At last the pink light of dawn seeped across the rooftops. Figuring that trouble would've arrived by now, but hadn't, I lay in bed next to Hermosa and scooted close to enjoy her warmth.

A metallic clicking awoke me. I opened my eyes, startled to see Hermosa in a blond wig, the same color as Juvante's hair.

STEAMPUNK BANDITOS   221

Hermosa was wearing her travel clothes, a jade-green skirt and waistcoat with a pale yellow blouse. She spun the cylinder of her Merwin Hulbert revolver to inspect its cartridges. A derringer and another small revolver rested on the vanity. I sat up and the bed covers rustled around me.

"Keep the noise down," she muttered. "I've got a headache that's making me regret that God ever made grapes."

The bellhop brought the frock coat and shirts I'd ordered. I changed into one of the new shirts and Hermosa tied a silk cravat around my neck. She fixed it in place with Étalon's emerald stickpin. I tried on the new coat, black worsted wool with a matching velvet lapel. I put my extra shirts in the trunk. The bellhop opened a small package that contained a fresh boutonniere, which Hermosa pinned on me.

"You look almost respectable." Then addressing the bellhop she said, "Take our luggage for transport to the ferry at Pier Seven."

The bellhop replied that he was going to get a dolly and dismissed himself. Hermosa pushed me out the door after him. "Get a shave. I'll see you downstairs."

Malachi was in the hotel barbershop, already groomed and helping himself to complementary coffee and a cigar. Vapor wisped from the towel steamer. Besides tobacco smoke, the shop was perfumed with the masculine scents of hair tonic and men's cologne.

I hung my coat on a hook, removed the cravat, and loosened my shirt. One of the barbers directed me to a chair, then draped a cloth over me, and tucked it into my collar. First leaning the chair back, he curled a steaming towel on my face, leaving a gap for my nose. As he gossiped with coworkers he worked up lather in a cup of shaving cream. After removing the towel, he brushed hot lather across my jaws, chin, and neck, but left my mustache alone. He stropped a straight razor and leaned close. With a thumb, he pressed upward against the bottom of my nose and brought the razor to my neck.

Hermosa announced, "Shave his mustache."

Shocked, I started to sit up but stopped when I felt the cold edge of the razor. The barber's thick eyebrows danced in bewilderment.

Hermosa ran gloved fingers across my mustache. "I want him looking like this. Sophisticated." Looking up out the corner of my eye, I saw that she pointed to a chart of facial-hair styles and selected a pencil-thin mustache exactly like the one Étalon had sported.

"No," I warned the barber.

Hermosa flashed a gold sovereign. "You want this, do as I tell you."

I gestured to my coat. "I'll match that and more."

"Don't believe him." She pressed a hand on my forehead to keep me still. "He's broke."

The barber brushed lather over my mustache. "My apologies *señor*, for this is a magnificent growth of manly hair. But I do have to make a living."

CHAPTER TWENTY-EIGHT

Hermosa, Malachi, and I walked through the hotel lobby. He strolled beside me, percolating with giggles. "That's very unmanly of you," I said.

He removed his derby and paused to give an exaggerated bow, his eyes fixed on what was left of my mustache. "Monsieur Étalon." He'd break into chuckles, walk ahead of me, and repeat the process, "Monsieur Étalon."

I hadn't been in this world two weeks, yet in that short time I'd grown fond of my bristled flavor savor. With it gone, my upper lip looked the size of a billboard. This puny Dirty Sanchez was a poor substitute.

Malachi rushed ahead to give another bow.

"This is getting old," I said.

"No it's not, Monsieur Étalon."

We stopped at the entrance to exchange goodbyes. He struck a lucifer to rekindle his cigar.

"You know those can kill you," I said.

"Perhaps. But when I meet the Almighty it'll be with the knowledge that I never had something like that skinny caterpillar desecrating my visage."

I glared at Hermosa. "This is your fault."

Her lips pursed as she tried to hold back a laugh. "Consider it a necessary sacrifice."

Malachi dropped the match into a cuspidor. "Fear not. Eventually your lip toupée will return to normal size." He slapped my shoulder. "Good luck to you both. I'll be waiting for your signal."

Hermosa and I nodded and continued out the door and through the portico. From there we spotted a gaudy steam-powered tram idling at the bottom of the steps. A crowd waited to board, dressed in their finest plumage, the women in fancy hats and dresses, the men in expensive suits, all eager to show off their elevated station in life.

I guessed that most of the travelers were Old World aristocrats. Who had been in Juvante and Étalon's social circle on the voyage here from Europe? Surely they had made a few acquaintances, for if nothing else but to con them later. And once on the island, what was their plan? Who did they want to steal from? And steal what?

We made our way to a booth, where the clerk accepted our stolen travel documents without suspicion and issued a pair of tickets. A bell on the tram rang, and a steward in uniform shouted, "Now boarding for Pier Seven."

Hermosa and I queued with the others and climbed into the tram's plush, leather seats. She dumped her attaché bag and parasol on my lap. Despite the tight quarters, the mood among the passengers was festive. When the tram lurched forward, a cheer rose from many of the women. *Let the party begin.* Obviously they expected a better stay on *Isla Tiburón* than what Hermosa and I had in mind.

During the ride to the pier, she began to fidget. "It's these damn pins in my dress," she complained. "They've gotten loose and are poking me every which way." She didn't have time to tailor Juvante's extra-sized dress and had to pin it into shape. Hermosa kept digging at her sides like she was suffering from an infestation of ants.

The sloping road toward the wharf allowed for a good view of the harbor. Cranes and an army of stevedores attended to large merchant ships along one pier. To my right, the Harbormaster's tower loomed above the buildings of the wharf district. I waved my hand just in case Alicia Zorro watched us through her telescope.

Arriving at Pier Seven we climbed off the tram. The long wooden pier led to the only ship tied up, the ferry to Shark Island. Passengers sauntered down the pier, porters carrying their bags. Horse-drawn wagons laden with steamer trunks, luggage, and crates clip-clopped past us. Several coaches paraded past and though the passengers were hidden behind drawn curtains, I managed to glimpse mummified people on their way to see the Dowager.

The closer we approached the ferry, the more I appreciated its immense size. *La Alma Roja* was written in gold paint on the red bow. The white superstructure and bridge towered four stories above us. Smoke wisped from the twin stacks. Enormous sponsons covered the paddlewheels jutting from each side of the hull.

Wagons laden with cargo proceeded up a ramp into the hull. We passengers were diverted up a boarding plank to the main deck where a ship's officer greeted us. He read our tickets and ushered Hermosa and me between ropes along the side of the ship to the rear deck. Those deemed the elite remained on the forward deck and were directed into a shaded area beneath an awning. Waiters circulated among them, serving chilled drinks from trays.

All of us unwashed ticket holders milled about on the rear deck. A blast from a steam whistle announced that we were about to set sail. Like most of the other men, I found myself checking my watch to see how punctual our noon departure was. A fat fellow groused that we were two minutes late, but my watch said we were on time.

The deck beneath our feet vibrated from the steam engines.

The side paddles began churning and propelled the ferry backwards from the pier. We cruised about a hundred yards then
drifted. The paddle wheels churned again. The ferry rotated to
the left and steamed from the pier. Once clear of the harbor, we
accelerated to a brisk clip over the calm waters. Specks of soot
swirled down from the funnels and we swatted cinders from our
coats and the backs of our necks. The first-class passengers on
the forward deck were undoubtedly spared this nuisance.

Hermosa dug into her attaché bag and gave me a pack of
cigarettes. "These were Étalon's." The lettering was in French
but I was able to read *Salome* and appreciate the comely young
woman on the label shedding her veils, diaphanous as smoke.
Hermosa reached back into the bag and produced a long
cigarette holder made of gold and jade. "This was his, too."

"How do you know it wasn't Juvante's?"

"He had smoker's breath. She didn't." She slapped the
cigarette holder into my hand. "Get busy and light up."

In the short time I've been in this world, I'd gathered that
true men smoked a pipe or a cigar, and cigarettes—especially
ones in a flamboyant holder—were for the effete dandy. "No
thanks."

Hermosa leaned menacingly close, glared, and whispered
through clenched teeth, "Get in character, Monsieur Étalon."

I waved the holder's nicotine-stained ivory mouthpiece. "You
expect me to put my lips on this?"

"You've put worse in your mouth."

Fair enough. I regarded the mouthpiece, speculated about the
gigolo's sexual fetishes, then lit up. Malachi's choice of tobacco
was at least aromatic. Étalon's reminded me of rotting hay and
horse manure.

Hermosa swatted my leg with the parasol. "Go make yourself
useful. Look around. Learn something."

I headed to the railing just aft of the starboard paddlewheel.
I remained there, enjoying the slow roll of the hull, the rhythmic
pounding of the paddles, and the mist thrown up from the froth.

Drawing the foul smoke through the holder, I surmised, what would Étalon do at this moment? Certainly he was always on the prowl, but he must've had times when he paused to enjoy the mood. I stood, hands in my trouser pockets, and rocked on my heels to contemplate the scene.

I took in the vista, the rugged coastline, gray and brown along the shore, shades of green in the hilly backdrop. Fishing skiffs bobbed in the water to our side. Seagulls glided on the ferry's slipstream, hovering close enough to touch.

With the impending return to *Isla Tiburón* I should be overcome with dread. Now that I was almost there, I surrendered to a serene calmness. Was this me, or the other Felix?

Day by day I felt myself growing into his skin, his flesh becoming mine, his habits melding into my own. What remained out of reach were his memories and as my recollections from the otherworld became less relevant, I began to feel like I was in a permanent state of amnesia.

I tried to imagine the other Felix immersing himself into my life. Had he taken my place with Carmen? Or Jolie? A pang of jealousy twisted my guts like indigestion.

But I thought about the people I'd met here, humans ironically, and how much I drew upon their comradeship. Getting stuck here might not be such a bad thing.

The mystery ahead of us called to me. To better see the island I climbed a ladder to an upper deck on the superstructure. The bridge blocked my view forward so I circled to the right along a narrow deck against the railing and directly over the sponson. From this vantage I could see over the bow. Below me, the paddles pounded the water into foam that dissolved into our wake.

I let the cigarette burn out. Grateful to be done with it, I unplugged the butt from the holder, flung it to the water, and sheathed the holder in my breast pocket.

Slowly, in the distance, our destination coalesced from a smudge into a definite hump of land. Sunlight glimmered from buildings appearing in the haze. The buildings were a collection of fantastic shapes, and I got the impression of jewelry materializing from a velvety fog. Growing ever more curious about what awaited us, I wished for the spyglass I had stashed in my luggage.

"Passengers are not allowed here," a crewman said, appearing behind me and practically shouting to be heard over the noise of the paddlewheel. He was an older man with the dark skin and features of a local native.

I gave him my cigarettes as a peace offering. "I only wanted a look see. I was last here during the war."

"The attack on Shark Island?"

"Sadly, yes."

He rolled a sleeve of his jumper to show me a scarred forearm. "I crewed *La Decisión*."

He said this like it was supposed to mean something. When I replied, "I was with the Thirty-first Regiment," he grunted in appreciation.

He extended a hand. "*Espina del Nopalito*." Thorn of the Prickly Pear, interesting name. "Friends call me Espina."

I hated to say my new name but I had to. "Étalon."

"A Frenchman with the 31st?"

His question made me realize that this disguise and stolen name were going to trip me up. Before I could answer he said, "*Dommage que vous n'êtes pas doué comme un étalon.*"

He stared, waiting for a reply. Since I had no idea what he had said, I gave a Gallic shrug and answered with the only French I knew. "*Oui.*"

Espina laughed and slapped my back like we were old friends sharing a joke. He lipped one of the cigarettes and tilted toward me as if expecting a light. The camaraderie warmed between us. What else did we have in common?

I sparked my lighter and as I lit the cigarette the fraternity between us emboldened me enough to ask, "Would you know a young woman named Ling Zhu Han?"

The question stunned him like the blow from a mallet. His

face paled several shades. Eyes widening, he lifted his gaze towards me.

"What is it?" I asked.

He staggered backwards and as his mouth gaped, the cigarette tumbled down the front of his jumper. "*Peligro!*" he yelled. "*Matón! Asesino!*"

My mind sputtered as it tried to make sense of what was going on. All I could figure was that the Dowager Engels must've known she was on a hit list and so warned the crew that anyone asking about Ling Zhu Han was a threat.

Espina bumped against the wall, hesitated, then drew a knife from under his jumper. He lunged at me.

My instinct was to rip him apart with my talons, but I didn't want to spill his blood and make a telltale mess. So I smacked the knife from his grip. With my other hand I clamped his neck and drove him to the deck. But at the same time he pushed against me and slammed us both against the railing. I was about to pitch over the side so I released him and clutched the railing to keep from toppling overboard. But Espina slid under the railing and off the deck. He screamed as he fell but the noise from the paddlewheel drowned his cries.

I watched him bounce off the sponson and splash just ahead of the paddlewheel. He disappeared in the froth and I imagined the paddles smashing him into pulp. The foam roiled pink and I waited for his body to bob to the surface.

A moment passed. Still no body. Not even his shredded jumper.

I swiveled my head across the ferry to see if anyone noticed. Nobody. I kicked his knife overboard.

A shark fin sliced through the wake. Then another. What was left of Espina was being chomped to bite-sized pieces.

This trip to *Isla Tiburón* had claimed its first victim.

CHAPTER TWENTY-NINE

Half a dozen sharks raced in circles through the ferry's wake. Below me, passengers clumped along the fantail railing and pointed, entertained by the arrival of the fearsome predators, yet having no clue about what brought them here.

Espina was dead, that was certain, and I felt no guilt over it. He was the one who had pulled the cork of his own demise when he lunged after me with a knife. I only parried him aside, and it was his stupid luck that carried him overboard.

I took the opportunity for another look at *Isla Tiburón*. The island loomed ahead, a jumble of huge rectangular shapes veiled in haze. The sharp edges of the buildings reminded me of giant, mechanical teeth.

Crewmen scurried along the decks. I didn't know if they were preparing the ship for docking or if a search had started for Espina. But if I stayed here, I'd draw attention I didn't need. I hurried to the nearest ladder and descended to the after deck.

I lost myself in the crowd and searched for Hermosa. I found her as she was ending a friendly exchange with an elderly couple.

I caught her eye and nodded toward a secluded corner along the back of the superstructure.

"Who were they?" I asked.

"The Delaneys from Wexford County, Ireland." She showed me a pamphlet that described a magic-lantern lecture featuring the wonders of modern science as presented by the Temple of Enlightenment. She turned the pamphlet over. "It doesn't say anything about the Fountain of Youth, but the Delaneys said it was mentioned during a traveling lecture. They're so convinced it's true that they mortgaged their farm for this trip."

When I explained my run-in with Espina, Hermosa's expression flamed with alarm.

"At the very least," I emphasized, "the dowager knows somebody is after her."

"We need to keep our tracks covered." Hermosa composed herself. "In any case, I'm ready." She flipped one of her lapels to show me a syringe pinned underneath, identical to the one she had used to kill the werewolf Cicatriz.

A ship's officer shouted through a megaphone, telling everyone to proceed to the forward deck.

She extended an elbow. "Now, Monsieur Étalon, let's join the other passengers."

I took her arm and followed the crowd. They mobbed together along the bow, gesturing toward the island.

Hermosa and I shoehorned our way to the railing. The breeze buffeted her hat and she cinched the knot of the scarf holding it in place. Passengers gestured excitedly and shared glimpses of the island through opera glasses. Their good humor proved infectious and for a moment I let myself imagine that the near future was not going to involve more dead bodies, especially mine.

Two small steam launches approached from our left and right. The boats were painted in the same crimson and gold color scheme as the ferry. They circled around and escorted us through a line of buoys.

The paddlewheels slowed their rhythm. As we closed the distance to the island, the clutter of buildings became a village organized around a wide boulevard that led straight from the pier to an impressive citadel on the hill beyond. The corners of its walls melded into turrets. From inside the citadel rose a keep, the tallest structure of the port.

Every building seemed made of square blocks arranged into sections that alternated between brilliant white marble and a silvery material, perhaps polished steel? Hundreds of pennants and flags in a rainbow of colors fluttered from posts and lanyards. The hues shimmered and sparkled across the angled facades so that the village looked like it been carved out of opal. The tidy and fantastic assembly reminded me of the alien world I had once visited.

I let slip, "It looks like Planet Pleasure."

Hermosa shot me a quizzical look. "Planet Pleasure? What do you know of other planets?"

"I'm just guessing," I replied. "It reminds me of a picture from a book."

"You and a book?" She palmed my forehead with a gloved hand. "Are you running a fever?"

I pushed her hand away. "I read books."

She laughed. "Then you're not the Felix Gomez I know."

I wasn't, that was for sure, and I needed to be more circumspect about hiding my identity. I had no idea how such a revelation would affect my situation here, but my circumstances were already complicated enough.

Some crewmen asked us to step aside so they could take positions along the railing. One of them muttered to his comrades, "Have you seen boatswains mate Espina?"

"Not since we left Guaymas. Why?"

"Nobody's seen him since after we shoved off."

"Did they check the rope lockers? The old sot might be sleeping off another drunk."

Actually he was sleeping with the fish, specifically sharks, parts of him anyway.

The ferry blew several whistle blasts. People flinched and plugged their ears. The paddlewheels churned backwards, then stopped, then churned again as the ferry made minute corrections to line up with the pier. In an expert display of seamanship, the pilot touched the pier with a soft thump. Passengers applauded. The ship was moored, and soon the gangplank was extended and we disembarked.

A small fleet of steam-powered coaches sporting multi-colored bunting shuttled passengers toward a tented square that straddled the boulevard. Hermosa and I queued with the others and sauntered down the gangplank. We had the option of taking the shuttle or walking, and like many others, we walked to appreciate the splendor of the place. Ushers didn't let us stray from the boulevard.

Despite the unreal beauty there was no doubt Hermosa and I were deep in the belly of the beast. I let my kundalini noir quiver like an antenna to detect any threats in our unusual surroundings.

When we arrived at the square, Hermosa announced us to a receptionist, who gave us a map, a schedule, and our room assignment in the Zenith Hotel. Young women dressed in gold-trimmed togas carried trays of hors d'oeuvres and wine in crystal goblets. A string quartet serenaded us. The mood was like being at a swanky cocktail party, but I knew we were being watched, studied.

I gestured to the server girls as I whispered to Hermosa, "Might they be here against their will?"

One of them responded to my attention with a sly smile.

"Hard to tell," Hermosa replied. She moved between the girl and me. "And don't get tempted to ask. Not until we figure out what's going on."

Hermosa and I headed to the Zenith Hotel. It was like everything else we'd seen so far on the island, impeccably furnished and decidedly futuristic. Copper and brushed steel accents zigzagged in Art Deco-like patterns. Gas lamps inside colored, rectangular glass hung from the ceiling.

Our luggage and steamer trunk were in our room. We were on the third story and luckily our one window faced the channel so we could signal Malachi.

Hermosa checked the trunk. "It's been opened."

"How do you know?"

"The wax seal I dripped around the latches has been broken."

We inspected our suitcases and the trunk. Everything was there, including our small lantern and the spyglass, but that didn't mean someone hadn't gone through the contents.

I said, "I don't know if this was a routine search, or if they're on to us."

"No matter, we still have to venture like we're innocent." Hermosa sat at the vanity and read the schedule. "Our first event is a formal reception in the Hall of Magnetism. Six o'clock." She referred to the map. "It's in the citadel."

I glanced at my watch. "That gives us two hours."

Hermosa checked the private bath. I heard her call out, "The tub's big enough for two."

"If you're going to bathe, go ahead without me." One of the strongest memories that carried over from the other Felix to me, was to avoid getting intimate with Hermosa. Even under the best of circumstances, it never ended well.

Hermosa gathered a fresh change of undergarments, tucked one of her revolvers inside a folded towel, and returned to the bath. I retrieved the spyglass to scan the channel and familiarize myself with its details. I kept back from the window to stay hidden as I looked for spots where we could rendezvous with Malachi.

A faint buzzing started and I looked about for its source. No matter which way I turned my head, the noise didn't change pitch.

Then I realized the buzzing was coming from inside my

brain. My kundalini noir locked tight in panic. I collapsed the telescope and let it drop to the carpet.

The buzzing grew louder, louder still, and it stoked my appetite for blood. My nerves were like brass cymbals crashing together. My kundalini noir trembled so hard it practically made my spine rattle. The undead bloodsucker inside me strained to escape. I pictured Hermosa sloshing in the tub and a minute later the suds and water turning crimson with her blood. I clenched my jaw and my fists to keep my fangs and talons from showing.

Hands clamped over my ears, I fell to my knees. I begged for the sensation to go away. *Not this. Not now.*

The other time I'd been overcome like this Gladys Vesna was behind the spell. Thankfully the last time I'd seen her was days ago on the land yacht.

A cloying meaty scent tugged at my nose and I was drawn to follow it like a famished dog, powerless to resist.

I rose to my feet and stumbled out the door. All the care we'd done to protect ourselves was forgotten. Someone could've been waiting in the hall to clobber me with a sledgehammer and it wouldn't have mattered. The sound and the aroma beckoned. I staggered down the hall like a junkie consumed with scoring his next fix.

I half-stumbled down the stairs. At the second floor I proceeded to a door midway down the hall. I twisted the doorknob and toppled over the threshold, overcome and mad with blood hunger.

"Monsieur Étalon," a woman's voice announced. "Or should I say, Felix Gomez."

CHAPTER THIRTY

I knew the voice. Gladys Vesna. Even as I lay in my delirium, I wanted to draw my revolver and shoot her. Lifting my head, I sniffed the perfumed tendrils of opium smoke circling the room and that fragrance tightened her spell on me.

A blur of brassy hair and lavender silk, Gladys studied me from where she slouched on a chaise lounge. Between us a man lay sprawled on his back, unconscious, his shirt unbuttoned to show off his naked torso. The spell made the walls press in on me, leaving no space for any thought except to satisfy my lust for blood. I stared at the bare-chested man like he was a steak.

"Go ahead," Gladys slurred. "I brought him for you."

As I crawled toward him, I heard the door close behind me. I sensed two other people in the room but at the moment I didn't care about them, only this meal in front of me. I slid against my victim. This close, he smelled like beef that had been left out too long. Nevertheless, my fangs sprouted to maximum length, my vampire self-peeled free of its human shell, and I curled over my victim like a monstrous spider embracing its prey.

Blood oozed warm and satisfying through my mouth and down my gullet. My mind sifted through the flavors, analyzing, cataloging, as if I had no other purpose but to enjoy this liquid sustenance. As the hunger ebbed, the spell lost its power and my rational mind regained command of my thoughts. When the feeding was done, I lapped healing enzymes over the puncture wounds to hide evidence of my fanging. His aroma became a stink of musky perspiration and hairy armpits, and I retreated from the odor. I had no idea who this poor bastard was or why he was out cold.

"I couldn't decide whether I should open his shirt or drop his pants," Gladys said, her voice now crystal clear. "I would've loved seeing you feed from his spigot."

The room opened up around me. Sitting back, I straightened my clothes, ashamed, humiliated at my loss of self-control. With her pipe and secret potions, Gladys—at her leisure—could make the undead bloodsucker within me dance like a trained monkey.

Her hooded eyes remained on me, glistening in amusement. Her blond tresses flowed into the Mandarin collar of her silk robe, decorated with golden stars.

Rising to my feet, I staggered in place, sluggish from the blood sloshing inside my belly. "Do that again," I growled, "and I'll kill you."

Gladys drew a small puff and let smoke seep through her smiling lips, unimpressed by my threat. She and the other Felix had an arrangement that I hadn't yet figured out, but I knew I needed her in my corner.

I looked behind me. Gladys's two cohorts, the young delinquent Louisa Davidson, and their lieutenant, Sun Zhipeng, watched. Both wore the dark blue uniforms of the island's hired help. Louisa smirked while Zhipeng's worried expression told me he hadn't forgotten the pistol whipping I'd given him the last time we crossed paths.

I turned to face Gladys. "I see the gang is all here, Gladys, or is it the name you used on the land yacht, Vanessa Glades?"

"My current employer knows me as Vanessa, so let's stick with that."

"And by current employer do you mean the Dowager Engels?"

"Who else would I work for on *Isla Tiburón*?"

"Doing what?"

Gladys ran her hands down the length of her gown. "Rather magnificent, no? It's my garb as a telepath. The Dowager has a sudden need to augment her staff."

"Is she expanding her operations?"

"I assume so, but that doesn't concern me."

I pointed to Louisa and Zhipeng. "And them?"

"What accomplished professional goes about without an apprentice and a valet?"

"What do you want?" I asked.

"We need to discuss our plans." She tapped the bowl of the pipe over a dish on a nightstand. "It's quite simple." She refreshed the pipe with a pinch of tobacco and lit up. "The Duchess Juvante, Monsieur Étalon, and I had plans."

Juvante and Étalon, of course. I was naive to assume that I'd rid myself of them so easily.

Gladys continued, "Last night they were supposed to contact me, and when they didn't, I feared that misfortune had interrupted their visit. Then when I checked the guest register here and saw that both of them had indeed arrived, I needed to see why we hadn't connected." Gladys jabbed the stem of her pipe at me. "Lo and behold, I discover that through a quirk of fate, the duchess and the monsieur have become Hermosa and you. Their plans are now your plans."

"And what are those plans?"

Louisa parted the window curtains. Gladys gestured with her pipe that I take a look. The view overlooked more buildings and that told me this room was on the opposite side of the hotel from mine. A procession of small steam tractors pulled carts laden with strongboxes up the boulevard toward the citadel.

"Cargo from the ferry," Gladys explained. "Treasure."

"What kind of treasure?" Interestingly, I didn't see any guards.

"The dowager's services don't come cheap," Gladys said. "She only takes hard currency or precious valuables."

I turned back around to face her. "*And* you and the duchess aimed to steal it all?"

"Not all. We're not greedy."

"You expect to get away with it?"

"If it were otherwise, I wouldn't be here."

I stepped from the window. "Sorry, I'll have to pass on your offer. I have another, more pressing task."

"What if I ask Hermosa?"

"I'm speaking for both of us."

Gladys choked on the pipe smoke. "I doubt that any man ever speaks for her."

True. "All right, you can ask her."

"No," Hermosa said. She glared at Gladys but glowered at me, furious when I told her the truth, minus the supernatural elements, about the telepath and myself. We were in my hotel room, Gladys in the velvet armchair, Louisa beside her, Hermosa on the chair from her vanity. Sun Zhipeng and I stood against one wall, two bumps on a log.

"It's a lucrative opportunity," Gladys argued.

"No amount of money is worth compromising our deal with Wu Fei," Hermosa replied, sounding surprisingly reasonable. "We are finally on this island. Once we find what we need to know about Ling Zhu Han, Felix and I are gone."

Louisa perched herself on the arm of Gladys's chair. "What if we help each other? If Gladys and I keep our ears open about the Chinese girl we're bound to hear something important that we'll pass onto you."

I started, "We'll appreciate any—"

Hermosa gave me both barrels of her scowl and that made me clam up. Minutes ago I was a bloodsucking monster unleashed. Now I feared walking on the thin ice between her and me. She said, "Yes, any insights would be appreciated. But we won't jeopardize what we've come here to do, and that includes leaving Shark Island alive and intact."

"Which fits perfectly with my plans." Gladys spoke as she stroked Louisa's long black hair. "If I know Felix, sometime during your escapade here, the caper will explode into chaos. That will give me the opportunity to look after my interests while you look after yours."

"What's to keep you from pulling a double cross and turning us over to the dowager?" I asked.

"What have I to gain from that?" Gladys asked. "It's not the dowager's gratitude that I want; it's her money."

"Which brings me to why Hermosa and I are here," I said. "What do you know about the working women on the island?" I asked.

Gladys raised an eyebrow. "In what regard?"

"Prostitution."

"Ah," she replied. "Considering the entitled desires of the masculine guests, female company is one of the amenities." She glanced at Louisa and back at me. "One of Louisa's duties is accommodating those said guests."

"Are you okay with that?" I asked Louisa.

She sneered and stared accusingly at me. "I've done worse for less."

Gladys jumped in. "It will give her the opportunity to get a better idea of the layout."

"What about the girls?" Hermosa asked.

"I fear theirs is a dismal lot. As far as I've learned, they're basically indentured servants kept for sexual pleasure."

"And that doesn't bother you?" Hermosa rejoined.

"Is alleviating their misfortune the reason you're here?"

"Part of it."

"There are many wrongs in this world," Gladys explained, "and the only ones I'm obligated to act upon are those that affect me directly." She paused a beat. "But if the opportunity arises to be of help, I'll do what I can."

"Much obliged," Hermosa replied, her tone showing she remained unconvinced of Gladys's sincerity.

"So it's a partnership?" Gladys offered.

I didn't answer, preferring to let Hermosa seal the contract.

"I guess we have no choice," she answered.

"Very good," Gladys said. "I take it that Malachi's absence means he's on the mainland arranging the logistics for your escape."

"You could infer that," Hermosa replied.

"I'm sending Sun Zhipeng back to Guaymas," Gladys offered. "His Chinese compatriots could prove of use to Malachi."

Hermosa grimaced in displeasure. "Whatever larceny you're planning, you only have two nights. Felix and I will be off the island the day after tomorrow at the latest."

"Given that it's taken you this long just to learn what little you know," Gladys asked, "are you giving yourself enough time?"

"We better be. The longer we remain here the greater the odds we'll be discovered."

At six in the evening, Hermosa and I joined the other hotel guests queuing in the lobby, everyone dressed in their best. Silk and satin shimmered. Jewels and medallions sparkled. Anticipation threaded the conversations, even ours.

The concierge announced that it was time to leave and we filed outside to board gleaming, steam-powered carriages. Hermosa and I shared a coach with three other couples, who continued to gush excitedly about this trip and the chance to meet the esteemed Dowager Engels. Among the passengers were the Delaneys, the elderly Irish couple we had met on the ferry. I could tell by their giddiness that they expected their dreams of a Fountain of Youth to come true.

The carriages huffed up the sloping boulevard, between the shiny buildings and toward the citadel. Flames danced atop its crenellated walls. It was like entering a Babylonian fortress. Inside we were treated to a lush garden and enormous bronze sculptures of flowers and insects, which added to the unworldly aspect of our surroundings.

The carriages circled through a porte cochère of a ziggurat-like structure, each halting briefly for the passengers to dismount. Attendants in blue uniforms shepherded us toward gigantic bronzed double-doors. Above them, inscribed in granite: *The Temple of Enlightenment, Grace, and Futurism.*

Inside, more attendants kept us moving through a gallery showcasing models of fantastic devices that resembled Da Vinci-like flying machines. Gas lamps hissed beneath the ceiling. People clustered around what appeared to be a magnifying glass the size of a wagon wheel. The Delaneys took turns behind the lens and their images appeared suddenly spry and youthful as a teaser of what to expect. Onlookers *oohed* and *ahhed*, and I had to admit whatever trickery the dowager used was amazingly convincing.

Gradually we made our way through another doorway and found ourselves in a cavernous banquet room. Ushers greeted us, checked our name off a list, and one led Hermosa and me to a table, where we took our seats with two other couples. A layer of cigar and pipe smoke shimmered across the room.

The tables fanned a stage. Conversations dropped to a hushed, reverential tone. Waitresses in local native costume— lots of feathers, geometric shapes painted on buckskin, garlands of seashells—brought bubbly fermented juice drinks and plates of oysters and crab. I studied these girls to see if any looked distressed as if kept against their will, but they all went about their duties with cordial attentiveness, the same as servers would anywhere.

When they stepped close, I noticed that each wore a pendant printed with a number. From a cup in the center of the table, you could draw a card and mark a girl's number for room service later.

Hermosa leaned toward me and whispered, "Might any of these girls know about Ling Zhu Han?"

"When we have the chance, let's ask."

The gas lamps dimmed, plunging us into a darkness relieved only by the red glow of tobacco embers.

Men and women in fantastic outfits that mimicked the wild colors of tropical frogs and birds appeared from the back of the room and wove between the tables. They assembled on stage, music started, and they began a choreographed dance, shaking the rattles on their wrists and ankles. Guests bobbed their heads to the catchy beat. Others, like myself, looked about for the source of the music. None of us saw an orchestra, and the more I thought about this, it sounded like recorded music piping through hidden speakers, technology that shouldn't yet be available.

Another detail bothered me. The song sounded out of place and I listened intently until I realized the tune reminded me of Django Reinhardt mixed with a strong percussive beat. In the timeline of my other world, music like this wouldn't be composed for another fifty years. Concern nicked at my kundalini noir and I wondered if the dowager might have a supernatural portal between our worlds.

The music grew louder and the dancers moved faster. They slapped hands and kicked the floor, shooting sparks that drew hoots of appreciation from the audience. The song ended abruptly and the dancers remained frozen in position.

Applause thundered through the banquet room. A man behind me shouted, "It's so tribal."

"Or so Las Vegas," I muttered.

"Ladies and gentlemen, honored royalty," a baritone voice announced from above as if from God. "Before you meet your gracious hostess, the Dowager Engels, let us show you the magic of electricity."

I heard a metallic thump, followed by a hum. An ozone smell pinched the air. Small globes in the center of the tables began a faint glow like vintage vacuum tubes. The hum grew louder, and the lights brightened to the intensity of candles.

From where had the dowager acquired all this technology? I suspected that the Fountain of Youth might not be just hokum.

Two spotlights burst on from a balcony behind us. The lights scissored dramatically before locking on the stage. The dancers were gone. Fog seeped from vents in the floor. A shape lifted from the stage, rising through the vapor. The shape glided forward, revealing it was a woman draped in a cape that dazzled like a shroud of sequins. More Vegas.

The fog dissipated and two attendants took her cape. In her wide, flowing skirt, she resembled an upside-down tulip. Her hair shimmered like spun platinum.

"Welcome honored guests," she said in English with a German accent. "I am humbled by your presence." She raised both gloved hands and diamonds sparkled from bracelets that covered her arms elbow to wrist. "Join me in our sojourn to the future. Follow me, the shaman enchantress who can make your dreams come true. I am the Dowager Engels."

CHAPTER THIRTY-ONE

The Dowager Engels extended her arms and tipped her head to acknowledge a thunderous ovation. But I remained stuck on what I'd seen so far. Jazz. Electric lights. It was as if the dowager had torn a slice from the future and brought it here. Maybe her Fountain of Youth involved technology that hadn't yet been invented where I was from.

A white curtain unfurled from the ceiling and it stretched behind the dowager like a sail ... or was it a movie screen? The lights dimmed. She stepped to one side and an out-of-focus red smudge glowed on the screen. The smudge sharpened into a line drawing of a white angel inside a crimson circle.

The audience quieted, fascinated. The angel flapped her wings and seemed to fly up and off the screen. People gasped in wonder. To me it looked like crude animation but to everyone else it must've appeared like the drawing had come to life.

The red circle faded, replaced by a black & white photograph of a young girl—six or seven years old—sitting on a stool. Adorned in a bonnet and an aproned skirt, she was smiling and holding a slate covered in geometry computations.

"Since my first days in the Kingdom of Württemberg," the

dowager explained, "I was fascinated with mathematics and science."

The picture disappeared, replaced by another of her—as a teenager—standing with a group of similar girls, surrounded by glass tubing, beakers, and bottles. She described her time at the University of Stuttgart and closed the anecdote by stating that as a woman she wasn't allowed to formally enroll, much less graduate.

"But that rejection only made me more determined to prevail, to show the world of academia that a woman, any woman, only needs the opportunity to prove herself the equal of any man. But I blazed no trail for I merely walked in the footsteps of the great female scholar Hypatia of Alexandria." A rendering of Hypatia's face illuminated the screen. "Imagine what new scientific harvests we'd be reaping if women were allowed to study mathematics, chemistry, astronomy, and engineering alongside their more privileged brethren?"

Slowly, a single pair of hands clapping broke through the hush, followed by another, yet another, until the banquet room was deluged by a second ovation, this one from the women. They bolted upright from their chairs and stamped their feet. Glasses on our table rattled and tipped over. Even Hermosa was swept up by the enthusiasm, and she stuck two fingers into the corners of her mouth to shriek an ear-piercing whistle.

The men around me slumped in their chairs and averted their eyes. I smirked. *Welcome to the future.*

The dowager let the cheers fade. A lively melody began, this one played by a violin, a cello, and a piano. She narrated slide after slide of her life, weaving an inspiring tale of her rise from ignored prodigy to scientist-millionaire businesswoman. If Bruce Wayne was auditioning for a sister, it would've been her.

For the final slides, she stood in front of the screen where the beam from the magic lantern hit her square and turned her into a dazzling, ethereal angel. My tablemates, even Hermosa, seemed enthralled in rapturous admiration.

The lantern dimmed and the room quieted. Eight tall boxes rose from the stage floor. They resembled coffins except for the tubes and valves attached to the sides. The dowager stood beside one of the middle boxes. Vapor feathering from the plumbing added dramatic tension.

"I present you, the Baroness Agafia of Bukovina," the dowager announced. A photo appeared on the screen, the image of a woman in her mid-fifties. A spotlight beamed on the box and its front popped open. *Ta-da!* Inside the box, a young woman stood, dressed in a simple white gown, and she winced into the glare. On the screen, a second photo appeared next to the other one, the before and after shots.

"Agafia," a woman shrieked in English from the audience, "can that be you?"

Tears glistening on her face, Agafia stepped out of the box. "Cousin Catherine, it is me. It's true. The Fountain of Youth exists."

Cries of astonishment echoed in the room. Excitement roiled from table to table, infecting everyone like the Holy Spirit in an evangelical tent revival.

The dowager revealed the next figure, Prince Ignacio of Catalan. On the screen, the before picture showed him resembling a withered pear. The after: a rakish man in his mid-thirties, clad in a shiny frock coat and matching trousers. And so the dowager continued with each box, showing off her creations.

I scrutinized each face as best I could considering the distance from my table to the stage. I wanted to roll with this magic show, but the skeptic within me kept pushing the brakes. With so much benefit to offer the world, why did the dowager resort to murder?

The screen retracted into the ceiling, and an attendant wheeled a waiters trolley to the dowager who said, "The wonder of turning back nature's clock continues. For the next to be blessed by science ..." She reached into a gleaming silver bowl on the trolley and plucked out a slip of paper, which she unfolded. "The Lady Amanda of Bedford."

Screams of delight burst through the room. A woman trotted from the tables and she lifted the hem of her skirt as she hustled toward the stage. An usher helped her climb its stairs. The dowager kept reading names, summoning more people. When she mentioned the Delaneys, the elderly Irish couple scurried toward her. People screamed. People cheered. The electric lights on the tables blinked. A symphony blared to pump up the carnival *Price Is Right* feel.

Ushers invited us to leave the table and crowd around the stage. Hermosa clasped my hand, only to lead me to the exit and back to the exhibition hall with its models of flying machines.

She whispered, "What a remarkable woman. It will be a shame if we have to kill her."

True.

Other couples milled about the displays. We weren't the only ones who chose not to mob the dowager.

"Something bothers me," I said. "Considering the expense of visiting this island, why wasn't everyone invited for the youth therapy?"

"I heard a couple at the next table explain," Hermosa answered. "The dowager can only treat a few people at a time."

"Let me guess," I replied. "Those with the biggest pile of cash get at the front of the line. So why come here at all?"

She waved her hand at our luxurious surroundings. "You get to see this. Even without the youth treatment, you're in an exclusive club." Her brow furrowed, and I could imagine deep thoughts cranking through her mind. "Knowing the dowager's story complicates matters for me. I hadn't thought much about her, and now that I know her struggles I'm inclined to be sympathetic."

"Inclined but not convinced?" I asked.

"There's the matter of Ling Zhu Han and the women who've disappeared. I'm sure the dowager has blood on her hands. All those bright lights and pretty music were great misdirection."

"You don't believe it was science?"

"Some of it. But it's too much razzle-dazzle to be legitimate. To see how this sleight-of-hand works," Hermosa said, "we need to see what's up her sleeve."

I noted ushers at every corner. "We can't do that here."

Hermosa agreed and together we stepped out of the ziggurat. The cliff-like walls kept us confined to the garden and we returned to the porte cochère. It was obvious that to learn more we'd have sneak into the forbidden areas of the citadel.

I told an attendant that we'd like a ride to the hotel. He led us to a waiting coach. "Which hotel?"

"The Zenith."

He grasped a knob on a device fastened to the side of the cab and twisted, dialing names that appeared inside a small illuminated window until he selected *Zenith*. We climbed into passenger compartment and when the attendant pulled a lever, the carriage proceeded on automatic control out of the porte cochère. We chugged out the citadel and down the boulevard. Looking out the windows, I saw that we were one of several carriages shuttling back-and-forth between the citadel and the port. The boulevard sloped down open ground before reaching the built-up area around the wharf.

On either side of the boulevard, a meadow stretched for hundreds of yards in each direction. A low moon washed the landscape in a silvery light and it would be impossible to cross all that open ground without being seen.

If we crossed on foot. A plan congealed in my head.

"Let's highjack this carriage. We might be able to drive about without looking suspicious."

Hermosa popped the door open. "Be my guest."

I swung out of the compartment and climbed into the driver's seat. A mechanism clicked inside a pumpkin-sized bronze dome in front of the seat. Rods protruded from the

dome and connected to a steering bar, and throttle and brake
levers. Hermosa clambered after me, her voluminous skirt
rustling like a banner in a gale.

As I tried to figure out how to disconnect the controls from
the dome she reached under her skirt to yank loose her petti-
coats and jam them under the seat. She fluffed her skirt to lay it
flat against her legs. "That's better. Now I can move without
sounding like a flock of geese taking off."

I sat up higher to see where we should go. Continuing
forward, we'd return to the hotel. But the citadel was where the
Dowager's darkest secrets were hidden. "We need to turn
around."

Hermosa glanced back up the hill. "Then let's do it."

"I will as soon as I can disconnect the controls."

She studied the rods shifting the controls. Grasping a
handrail and leaning back, she kicked one of the connecting
clamps and kicked again until it broke loose. The throttle swung
free and I grabbed it. She kicked the remaining clamps until all
the controls were free. No longer attached to anything, the rods
cycled crazily in-and-out of the dome.

I yanked the steering bar and heaved the carriage into a tight
U-turn. Our only lights were a dim white lantern at the front and
a smaller red lantern at the rear. We powered up the boulevard
and kept a good distance ahead of the closest carriage returning
to the citadel.

At the top of the incline, where the boulevard curved
toward the citadel, I kept on a narrow road that circled the
outside of the structure. Up ahead, a barbed-wire fence demar-
cated a wide perimeter behind the citadel. On the other side of
the fence, carriages similar to ours were parked in tight rows.
This must be a maintenance area. A guard tower overlooked an
open gate.

"Slow down just a bit," cautioned Hermosa. "And drive
straight inside."

At any moment I expected a searchlight from the tower to

blind us. But we passed through the gate without getting challenged.

Hermosa motioned to proceed beyond the other carriages. We continued past a wall at least a hundred yards long to where the back of the citadel blended into a jumble of square industrial-looking buildings. Light filtered through the occasional windows. Smoke from the many stacks obscured the starry sky.

I steered for a group of parked wagons and braked. Horses nickered from a nearby stable. From behind a bay door I heard muted clanking and the hiss of pressurized gas. Somebody was at work.

"Here we are. Up the dowager's sleeve."

Hermosa looked around and slipped off the car. "This way," she whispered.

We headed to a wall that jutted beneath an illuminated window above us. She put her hands against the stucco for me to boost her to the top. I scrambled after her. The wall was wide enough for both of us to crowd against the window and look down into a warehouse-like space. Laboratory equipment—glass beakers, tubing, and assorted bottles—were arranged on tables and shelves.

A worker in white overalls entered the room, pushing a low flat dolly. On the dolly stood a pair of tall boxes identical to the ones the dowager used on stage. He nudged the dolly into position against one wall and connected the boxes to a series of pipes. Tubes from the pipes ran into two sets of gallon-sized glass jars resting on shelves.

Another worker pushed in a wheelchair, occupied by someone in the mummy bandages, presumably one of the dowager's patients for the Fountain of Youth treatment. This second worker wore a white laboratory smock. He wheeled the patient in front of the dolly. The first worker pivoted the dolly so the front of the boxes faced us and opened the lid of one box.

A naked young woman—a teenager—was inside, enveloped in an apparatus made of rubber tubes with glass and metal fittings. Leather straps held her upright. She had Indian features and appeared unconscious though an expression of pain pinched her face.

The door to the second box was opened. It was empty, the apparatus inside hanging limp. The worker in the smock helped the patient in the wheelchair, who rose with slow and uncertain movements as if sedated. Using scissors to snip away the bandages, he revealed a nude older woman—I guessed around sixty—her hair gathered in a bandana, and some kind of strange goggles with microscope-like lenses covering her eyes. Metal sleeves had been clamped around her wrists and shins.

Carefully, the workers helped her into the empty box where she was turned to stand facing the lid. They connected the apparatus to the metal sleeves and cinched leather straps around her upper arms, waist, and both legs below the knees. After double-checking their work, the worker in the smock tripped a lever. Both boxes titled backwards to rest at an incline.

The workers fussed with valves on the pipes. Pressurized gas hissed. Needles on gauges swung. Fluid bubbled inside vials connected to the wall plumbing. The girl jolted but remained unconscious. Her apparatus throbbed, and a thick red liquid filled the glass fixtures, then coursed through the wall tubing and poured into the glass jars. The effect was like a mad scientist movie.

But this was no movie. That red liquid was the girl's blood.

With each passing moment, her complexion faded. When one row of the glass jars was full, she slumped against the apparatus.

The worker in the smock placed one hand on the throat of the older woman and peered into the lenses of her goggles. Though I couldn't hear what he said, I could tell he was relaying instructions to the other worker who busied himself working the various valves. Blood pumped through her apparatus to the second set of jars as blood in the first set was siphoned into her.

"No. No," Hermosa whispered. She brought her face so close

to the window she fogged the glass. Her eyes peeled in horror and disgust.

I pulled her from the window so she wouldn't be spotted.

She swatted my hands away as she said, "Now we know what's happened to the missing women. They're not just sex slaves but human sacrifices."

CHAPTER THIRTY-TWO

Hermosa turned as pale as the dead girl. In fact, Hermosa even looked a little green and nauseous. "We've got to stop the dowager." She slid from the retaining wall, and I dropped silently beside her.

Her expression roiled with anger and I cut her off before she lost control and gave us away. "Keep your wits." I advanced, ready to clamp my hand over her mouth if I had to.

She pushed me. "Can't you see what's going on? Can't you see she's using these girls for her experiments? Her Fountain of Youth is a death machine. The Dowager is nothing but a monster."

Grasping Hermosa's arms, I pressed her against the building. "I'm not arguing that." I kept my voice low. "The question is, what are we going to do now?"

"Get inside and rescue the girls. Those poor girls." Hermosa's voice cracked. "All my life I've seen Indian girls, half-breeds, women like me, get ravished. *Ravished?* What am I saying? *Violated! Raped!* Then cast aside like trash." Tears flooded her eyes. "And this is worse, if such a thing was possible."

I gave her a gentle shake. "I understand. Now settle down.

We've got to get back to the hotel to contact Malachi. Tell him what we know. Then we'll proceed."

She wiped her eyes. "And then what? What about the girls? Maybe there are more inside."

"We'll do what we can, *after* we make a plan with Malachi."

"*After?*" Hermosa smacked my chest. "*No. Now! Tonight!*" She seemed to swell like an angry puma, and her eyes burned with fury. "And destroy everything on this island starting with this building. Wreck it. Smash it. Torch it." She twisted her boot heel into the dirt. "Then grind the Dowager into the ash."

"What if the girls aren't here?"

"We won't know until we look."

"How?"

Drawing her Merwin Hulbert revolver, she thumbed the hammer. "We'll shoot our way inside."

That isn't a good idea, but I kept that to myself. Arguing with Hermosa was like tossing sparks onto gunpowder.

Looking up, the building rose three stories above us. I stretched my arms up high and hooked my fingertips into the wall. The bricks and the mortared gaps offered enough texture for my fingers and the toes of my boots to find purchase. I climbed up about two feet then dropped back down.

"You're going to climb to the top?" Hermosa asked.

"I'm considering it."

"What about me?"

"Let me get up there first and figure something out."

"You expect me to stand here and wait?" She turned for the corner of the building. "Fat chance, I'll see you inside."

Hermosa might have considered herself unstoppable but the guards would eventually overwhelm her. I resigned myself to the only practical solution. "Okay, both of us need to get on the roof."

Hermosa studied the wall and shook her head. "I'm no spider."

I faced the brickwork and stretched my arms up again. "Get on my back. I'll carry you."

"You're serious?"

"You have a better idea?"

She looked around, then decocked the revolver and thrust it back into her skirt pocket. "This is a night full of bad choices and I'll bet this won't be the worst before the sun rises."

I held fast to the wall. "Stop wasting time. Let's go."

"You fall and Sweet Jesus as my Savior," Hermosa said, "I will shoot you on the way down." She hopped onto my back, and my talons extended just enough for them to grip the wall.

I groaned. "You need to skip a few meals."

She looped both arms around my neck and clasped my hips with her legs. "Keep talking like that and I'll shoot you now."

I studied the edge of the roof above me. The climb was going to be tough but not impossible.

I reached with my right hand and anchored those fingers to the wall. Then raising my right leg, I groped for the gap between the bricks and set the toe of my boot into the wall. I repeated the process on the left, each iteration lifting us steadily up the wall.

Hermosa pressed her mouth to my ear. "*Shhh.* Guards."

Great. Pressing flat against the wall, I held still, certain that Hermosa and I were easy targets. Twenty feet below, a couple of guards chattered like irritated squirrels.

"*A dónde se fueron esos pinchi demonios?*"

The guards must've found the car we abandoned, and the demons they referred to were certainly Hermosa and me.

"*Pues dejaron el carro.*"

"*Si, me fije. No estoy ciego.*"

Hermosa clung tight and held her breath. What if they looked up? I'd have to let go and fall right on top of them. Of course, Hermosa might break a leg or worse.

"*Quizás se escaparon al bosque.*"

"*Vamonos. Las cosas que hacemos por nuestro jodido jefe.*"

I followed their footfalls as they tracked away from us.

About time. Resuming the climb, my hands and legs burned from the strain. With Hermosa on my back, my vampire strength began to ebb. As I stared at the roofline, I began to cycle every curse I could think of, in English, Spanish, Chinese, and even a few Indian dialects. I cursed the men who built this wall. I cursed the Dowager. I cursed Wu Fei. And most of all, I cursed myself for being the idiot climbing the wall.

At last, my fingers hooked onto the edge but if anything, the pain seizing my entire body had been turned up a notch, and it took the last reserves of my strength to hang on.

"We made it," Hermosa whispered and paused as if expecting me to finish the climb. When I didn't move, she scrambled off my back and over a short wall along the roof's edge. Even with her weight off, I remained too weak to move.

She turned around and looked past me to the ground. "Damn, Felix, that was impressive. You ought to be in a circus or something."

"A little help," I said, "please."

Grabbing my collar, she hauled me the rest of the way. Falling onto the roof, I retracted my talons before she noticed them.

Hermosa squinted into the darkness. "Let's look for a way in."

I flexed my limbs to get them working again. The quarter moon gave enough light for me to pick out a roof access hatch, a square iron plate attached to a metal frame. I slipped my fingers under the hatch and lifted, expecting it to hold against a lock. But it opened easily and I peeked underneath.

The chamber below was dark and appeared deserted. A metal ladder stood against one side of the access. Hermosa crouched and reached for it with her foot.

"Don't you think I should go first?" I whispered.

Without answering she climbed down and swung from the bottom rung until her boots thumped on the wooden floor. Once I joined her, we drew our guns and surveyed the room.

Meager light seeped around a closed door at one end and up a stairwell. I made out large spools of cable and bolts of cloth stacked in heaps.

"Which way?" she whispered.

I pointed to the stairwell.

We crept down the stairs, quiet as housecats. At any second I expected an alarm to sound, and my kundalini noir quivered with apprehension. Much could go wrong, and the further we descended, the more wrong it could get.

The stairs continued downward. Once on the landing of the ground floor, Hermosa stepped to the door. "The girls should be close. Let's get them."

I started to follow her when I heard a painful moan from below. The moan was deep and not human.

Hermosa caught my hesitation. "This way."

Something about that noise pulled at me, and I started for it.

Hermosa clapped my shoulder. "Where are you going?"

"Listen." I raised a finger.

Her forehead furrowed in concentration. "I hear it. But let's save the girls first."

Without explaining myself, I continued down the stairs. As Hermosa followed me, I could feel her resentful stare burning a hole in my back.

At the next flight, the moaning grew louder and the air thickened with a heavy moist odor like from a stable that needed mucking.

"It's coming from the bottom floor," I said, proceeding downward.

The last flight of stairs spilled into a wide hallway with a ceiling probably thirty feet high. *Why so tall?* Flickering electric lights illuminated the hall with an uncertain glow. The stable odor was strong enough to make my eyes smart. The moaning ceased. What made me continue was the row of barrel-sized glass jars along one wall.

Hermosa pressed against me. "What are these?"

I hunched my shoulders. Every jar was filled with a viscous greenish liquid and in each floated some type of creature in pale, fetal form, complete with a placenta. In various stages of development, they ranged in size from rat to a full-grown pig. But they were not rats or pigs. They had trunks and thick legs, not unlike ... elephants. Many were malformed with forked trunks, extra legs, or conjoined bodies.

Hermosa crowded behind me, and she waved her revolver like a talisman. "I don't ever think I've been spooked like this."

As a vampire, I was usually the chief source of the spookiness. Still, the bizarre and horrific spectacle unnerved me because I didn't want to end up pickled and preserved like these stillborn creatures.

The moaning started again, and its horrific tone was enough to rattle my kundalini noir. The sound definitely came from a large animal, and one that was suffering.

The clues suddenly fit together. During our journey here to *Isla Tiburón* I kept hearing the trumpeting of elephants. In Guaymas, the Harbormaster Alicia Zorro had warned me about the dangerous beasts on the island. Now we were deep in the Dowager's lair of mad science, replete with failed experiments at making elephants. But why go through all this trouble to make elephants when she could import them from Africa?

Hermosa pulled at my coat. "I don't like this frightful place."

I answered, "Neither do I but we have to see what is going on." And to spur Hermosa on, I added, "Maybe we'll find a clue about the girls."

We crept to an open door at the end of the hall, and with each step forward, the dreadful groan became louder, more horrific, more difficult to comprehend. When we reached the edge of the door, I heard men's voices—cursing and goading—but I couldn't tell what they were saying. Hermosa dropped to one knee so we could both look around the door at the same time.

The room before us was a cavernous laboratory. At the center of the floor, a gigantic elephant was bound to a large wooden palette. The creature—a female—strained against chains attached to a metal collar and matching leg cuffs. Its enormous trunk was secured by a pipe with spikes on the inside. Ropes bound its tusks to iron loops in the floor. Beside her, a man in a white lab coat stood on a stepladder to reach her torso. He adjusted rubber tubing attached to steel needles stuck into the animal's hide. The tubes were connected to a console festooned with gauges and pulsating electric lights. Another man, similarly dressed, manipulated buttons and small levers on the console.

The creature's muscles flexed against the restraints while her eyes shined in misery and desperation. But the more I looked at this animal—her pronounced domed head, the small rectangular ears, the long and wickedly curved tusks, and moreover, the creature's immense proportions—I realized what she really was.

"My God," I whispered.

Hermosa backed into me. "What?"

"That's a prehistoric mammoth."

"Mammoth? How do you know?"

"It's too big to be an elephant," I whispered, "plus the head is different and—"

"No, I mean, how do you know? Since when did you stop being an ignorant gunslinger?"

She was confusing me with the other Felix, again.

"I must've overheard something in a cathouse."

"If it's prehistoric," she asked, "why is it alive?"

"It's a her," I corrected. Looking past the mammoth and the two lab techs, I noticed skulls mounted on the walls. Most were the deformed skulls of mammoths, a catalog of experiments as the Dowager Engels perfected her technique in resurrecting these long extinct animals.

I found myself trying to swallow. My kundalini noir curled upon itself like an armadillo. The Dowager had turned science into a black art and this poor animal, as well as the Indian girls, were her doomed subjects.

The lab tech beside the mammoth said something that sounded Swedish? Norwegian? German?

The second man repositioned a lever. "*Ja*."

The mammoth groaned loud and stared in terror. Then she roared, a terrifying howl that made my bones tremble.

The sight of this tortured animal filled me with such outrage that my kundalini noir hammered like an exploding heart. My vision turned red, and I thirsted for blood. Jaw clenched to keep my fangs from showing, I pushed past Hermosa to charge into the lab. My vision focused on the tech by the cabinet and I raised my Colt Navy to align the revolver right on his face.

CHAPTER THIRTY-THREE

I had to give the lab tech credit for keeping cool. When he saw me enter the lab with my revolver pointed at his face, his eyebrows jumped a little before slanting into an annoyed *how-dare-you-interrupt-me* squint.

He was about to say something when I shot him. Flame and smoke burst from my revolver and as the air cleared he sank to his knees, hands clasped over his mouth, and collapsed against the console.

The second lab tech whirled from the mammoth, lost his balance, and tumbled off the stepladder. Hermosa pushed past me and tracked him with her pistol.

Bang! Bang! Bang!

He crumpled against the floor in a heap, blood staining his white lab coat.

The mammoth squirmed in panic, rattling her chains, as if certain that she was next on the list.

I patted her neck. "Easy girl." I yanked the nail-sized needles from her flank and tossed them on the floor. Hermosa busied herself doing the same on the other side. I loosened the snaps holding the spiked tube around the mammoth's trunk and let the infernal device clatter to the ground. Hermosa dropped to her knees and unfastened the iron cuffs around the mammoth's ankles. I untied the ropes holding her tusks and then climbed the stepladder to release the latch on her collar.

Now free of her restraints, the mammoth shrugged the collar from around her neck. I hopped off the ladder and joined Hermosa, not certain of what the mammoth might do.

She kicked loose her ankle cuffs and turned to face us, moving gingerly for such a gigantic creature. When she swiveled her head to regard Hermosa and me, then her surroundings, her immense tusks swept almost the entire width of the lab. Her big eyes expressed confusion as if she didn't understand why we had turned on our fellow humans.

Behind us, the first lab tech writhed on the floor, whimpering, blood oozing from between his fingers where his hands were clamped over his mouth. I felt no pity for the son of a bitch. He and his partner were part of the Dowager's evil crew.

The mammoth advanced toward him and slowly reached with her trunk. It forced past the man's arms, and coiled around his neck. The trunk tensed, there was a crack, and the lab tech slumped lifeless. She showed him more mercy than he had shown her.

"Now what?" Hermosa asked as she replaced the spent cartridges of her Merwin Hulbert.

The mammoth seemed to answer that question when she ambled to the enormous double doors at the back of the lab. They were barred with a pair of timbers the size of railroad ties, held in place by big steel pins. Hermosa and I pulled them out and when we struggled to slide the timbers through the brackets, the mammoth nudged us aside. She easily yanked the timbers loose, then bashed against the double doors and forced them open to reveal a ramp that rose toward a rectangle of night sky.

Far inside the complex, a bell rang. Then another. And another. From the hallway that we'd come through, echoed shouts and the tramp of boots scrambling in our direction.

Hermosa swatted the mammoth on the butt. "Get going."

The beast charged up the ramp. At the top of the ramp a guard sprang from behind a crate, revolver blazing. He shot the mammoth point blank. She in turn slammed him with a tusk, crushing him against the wall, and rushed outside.

Three, four guards clustered at the lab door and opened fire. Hermosa and I ducked for cover as I shot back, firing wildly.

I was certain I nailed one of them but in the chaotic crossfire, the air became thick with gun smoke, too opaque even for my supernatural vision. Flame from guns bloomed inside the smoky haze, but I was too busy dodging bullets to draw a good bead.

Slugs zinged past my ears and chewed into the wall behind me, biting loose chunks of concrete and shattering glass bottles on the shelves. Another volley tore at me from the left.

Hermosa bumped against me, her hands working feverishly to reload her revolver. "More guards are coming down the ramp," she shouted. "They have us cornered."

With guards covering both exits, I didn't see how we could shoot our way out. If we attacked one group, the second would drill us in the back.

I sniffed strong chemical odors. The smell came from liquid dripping from riddled cans and shattered bottles on the shelves around us. Under one bottom shelf, I spied a twenty-gallon drum labeled:

Peligro-Danger
Acetona-Acetone

We would burn our way out. With bullets whistling overhead and ricocheting off the walls, I crawled to the drum and tipped it over. I aimed it toward the door and shoved hard. "Get down," I yelled to Hermosa, "and cover your head." I threw myself over her and pressed us both as flat as possible.

When the guards saw the drum rolling at them through the

smoke, they shot it full of holes. Just as I planned, the drum exploded. Flames roared over us. The fireball rolled up the ramp while the rest was sucked up the ceiling vents.

At the lab door, men screamed and thrashed, their clothes and hair burning. I jumped to my feet and hauled Hermosa upright. Acrid, black smoke stung our eyes.

"I can't breathe," she gasped.

I didn't need to, but the smoke irritated my throat and I coughed to clear it. Flames crackled. The lab was in burning shambles. We had to get going before more guards arrived, or just as bad, we got trapped by the fire. I started up the ramp and pulled Hermosa along.

The opening at the far end of the ramp gaped with the promise of salvation. Cool air beckoned us forward. But when we reached the door at the top of the ramp, Hermosa wrenched free of my grip.

Two guards lay sprawled on the ramp, arms and legs akimbo in the dance of the dead. Another lay partway out the door. Smoke curled from his clothes and wide eyes blinked from a singed and blackened face. He waved his pistol in a pathetic gesture. Hermosa kicked it aside and stepped over him to go back inside.

"Where are you going?" I pointed outside. "We need to go that way."

"We're not leaving until we rescue the girls."

I stared out the door. At least the mammoth had escaped.

Hermosa and I hurried along the hall. We flung open doors as we passed them, hoping to discover the Indian women but finding only deserted labs, machine shops, and storerooms. Smoke and sparks spilled from vents. The drum of acetone must've started a fire that spread through the ventilation system to set the entire building ablaze. Wall sconces flickered, and the alarm bells sounded more urgent.

Through the din, I heard another set of voices. A chorus of women's voices crying for help.

I halted and raised my hand. "I hear them. The girls."

Hermosa spun in place. "Where? Where?"

I raked the air with my finger as if it was an antenna, then rushed toward a door up the hall. It was locked. I reared back to kick it open when Hermosa placed the muzzle of her revolver against the keyhole and fired. The report boxed my ears. The knob fell loose, and the door bounced open.

Shrieks from at least a dozen women greeted us, shouting in English, Spanish, and a smattering of native tongues. Hermosa launched herself over the threshold and I followed.

Women were bunched inside a long cage set along one wall of a laboratory. Their straight black hair and bronzed features confirmed they were some of the Indian females we sought, in ages from late teens to mid-twenties. One looked as young as twelve. All wore identical shifts of coarse cloth with numbers stenciled across the chests.

Hermosa ran to the cage and reached inside, reassuring the prisoners in a variety of languages. "We're here to get you out."

Several of the women pawed enthusiastically at Hermosa while others remained withdrawn. Their fearful expressions reminded me of a kennel full of abused dogs. Looking around the room, I saw what had traumatized them.

The corpses of naked women dangled inside glass cylinders filled with the same greenish liquid that we'd seen earlier. Some of the women were whole, others had tubes threaded through voids in their torsos or attached to the stumps of limbs or necks. The glass cylinders were suspended from hoists mounted in tracks in the ceiling. On work benches in the center of the room, severed heads, hands, and organs floated inside jars. Three of the coffin-like reanimation boxes stood empty, ready to accept their next victims. The boxes rested on dollies on an assembly line that ran to an exterior door.

I wasn't supposed to have a soul. But this sight filled me with such disgust and hatred that my undead lust for blood immediately heated to near boiling.

I counted thirteen women in the cage. Seven of them grabbed the door and pulled and pushed, shouting, "Get us out!" "*Sueltanos!*"

I tried the lock but it was too strong for my vampiric strength, or to shoot apart. Hermosa dashed through the lab, rifling desk drawers and boxes in search of keys.

The floor and walls shook from a distant explosion. The ceiling lights dimmed. More smoke belched through a ceiling vent. The women shrank from the commotion, then resumed trying to wrestle a way out the cage.

Hermosa thrust a metal bar into my hands. "Use this."

I fitted one end into a gap around the deadbolt and heaved. Neither the door nor the frame budged. I held onto the cage with one hand and pulled at the bar. I summoned my vampire strength until my kundalini noir burned in agony. Nothing. Hermosa tried to help, but after a minute of straining and groaning, we gave up.

She brushed a lock of sweaty hair from her face. "What if we tear at the floor and tunnel underneath?" She looked up. "Or where the cage attaches to the ceiling?"

I jabbed the bar against the floor and then the ceiling. Both were stout concrete. "If we had an hour, maybe." But the fire and smoke, or the guards, would finish us by then.

Scouting the lab, I searched for a way to spring open the cage. Maybe I'd find an explosive or an acid that would eat the lock work, but I was no chemist and the labels on the bottles were nothing but gibberish.

When I reached the exterior door, a solution hit me. "I'll be right back," I said to Hermosa over my shoulder.

"Where are you going?"

"To find a ride."

This door was locked from the inside, so getting out was no problem. I cracked it open and looked upon a broad courtyard in the center of the complex. Smoke and glowing embers haloed the citadel to my right. A large bell high in one wall clanged furiously.

Large steam-powered trucks rumbled through the courtyard, stopping to either disgorge a load of men or let another group clamber aboard.

One truck appeared through a sally port and headed toward me. I couldn't see past the dazzle of its headlamp to discern how many were onboard. To hide, I flattened myself into a shadow of the wall. When the truck passed, I saw that its only occupant was the driver. Perfect. I sprang onto the truck bed and fangs out, leapt for him.

A karate chop to the driver's neck stunned him enough for me to yank the brake. I clutched him by the shoulders and sank my fangs into his throat, giving him a quick dose of tranquilizing enzymes. When he went limp, I pushed him off the truck to take his place behind the steering wheel.

I fumbled with the controls, then backed up and aimed for a spot on the wall between the door and where the cage should be. Opening the throttle, I let the pressure build, then released the brake and braced for impact. The truck slammed hard into the wall, jarring my arms and shaking my eyeballs in their orbits. Concrete and plaster rained on me, followed by glass, greenish liquid, and cadaver parts that spattered everywhere. The truck plowed into the workbenches and got stuck. When I gunned the engine, the tires spun on the concrete, slick with liquid.

Hermosa ran to me, shouting, "Smash into the cage!"

The tires squealed in useless effort. "I'm not getting any traction."

Sensing that rescue was at hand, the Indian women howled in panic. One pointed and shouted to Hermosa, who nodded. Hermosa dug a heavy chain from the debris, looped one end around the cage door and the other over the truck's front bumper. She pumped a fist. "Go! Go!"

I wrenched the shift lever. The truck rolled backwards out the hole I'd created and continued until the chain jerked tight. I twisted the throttle full open. The steam engine grunted. The needle on the pressure gauge inched to the red.

Inches from me, a bullet punched through the side of the truck. We had run out of time.

CHAPTER THIRTY-FOUR

From three sides, guards approached in a U formation, firing their guns. A ragged volley of bullets zinged past my ear and I hugged the steering wheel.

Engine chugging like mad, the truck strained against the chain, keeping it as taut as my nerves.

I drew my Colt Navy and emptied the cylinder at the guards, keeping them back, buying myself precious seconds.

From inside the building I heard the groan of steel twisting and wrenching apart. Then the truck shot backwards. The chain and the cage door whipped right at me. Reacting at vampire speed, I spun the steering wheel. Momentum pulled the truck into a tight circle just as the cage door twirled past, inches from my face. The door shot to the length of the chain where it tumbled along the courtyard, sparking against the cobblestones.

I swerved in place, the chain lashing out, the cage door whirling through the air like a gigantic medieval flail. It cut a swathe through the guards, flattening some, dismembering others, before clanging to a stop.

I eased off the throttle. My kundalini noir trembling in

excitement, I took a moment to gather my wits and reload my revolver.

Smoke curled from the rooftops, and a blizzard of ash and embers swirled across the ground. Hermosa said we needed to torch this place, and without trying, it seemed we'd done it.

But the problem remained that Wu Fei had hired us to find Ling Zhu Han, and if there had been a chance to find her before, that chance was now lost in this chaos.

The Indian women emerged from the building and sprinted toward the truck to clamber aboard. Hermosa hurriedly stripped the fallen guards of bandoliers and guns. She tossed a shotgun and a Winchester and two of the older Indian women snatched them midair. Then she unhooked the chain, climbed on, and clutched a handrail.

I had four sally ports to choose from, all flooded with smoke. "Now where?"

The women huddled together in the cargo bed, pointing in all directions as they argued with Hermosa. She broke loose of the debate and shouted, "Head north."

Gunning the engine, I turned us around, and headed toward the north sally. We sped under the archway, knowing the burning building towering above could at any moment collapse on us.

Bullets pinged against the truck. One clipped my collar. Hermosa and the two-armed women returned fire and sent guards scrambling for cover. We raced clear of the complex and rumbled over a desolate field.

Driving into the night, I put more and more distance between us and the enemy. I didn't bother to see if the truck had headlamps. For one, I didn't need them, and more importantly, using them would give away our position.

We jostled over rough ground, and the open terrain turned into dense thicket. Our big iron wheels lurched and crunched over shrubs and cactus to flatten a trail even a blind man wouldn't have trouble following.

My thoughts careened in wild circles as I tried to figure out what to do next. I looked over my shoulder. Through the tangled branches of chaparral and desert willow, I saw flames lashing from the buildings and twisting into columns of smoke. A couple of hundred yards behind us, silhouetted against the flames, a squad of guards hustled after us.

Bullets slammed into our exhaust stack. I ducked as a second volley whistled overhead.

I pushed the throttle and we lurched deeper into the wilderness, barely lit by dim moonlight. We'd only rescued thirteen girls. How many did we leave behind? Dozens? A hundred? More? Of those, how many were trapped in the conflagration? I hoped—a false comforting hope for sure—that some of them would survive.

And what about us? Once we got to the north side of the island how would Malachi find us? Would we last that long? With every passing moment, the dowager's forces were regrouping, building strength, and using their knowledge of the island to trap us.

The truck lurched. Sparks belched from the stack. I glanced at the gauges. The pressure needle climbed into the red while the torque needle dipped toward zero.

The engine coughed and more sparks shot from the stack. Hermosa and the Indian women anxiously tracked the sparks, knowing they flagged our position. One of the women bent close to Hermosa. They chatted briefly and then Hermosa said to me, "Keep going this way." Another engine cough. More sparks. "We'll see how far we get before our ride gives up the ghost."

"And then?"

"The ground will get pretty rough and we'll have to proceed on foot anyway. The girl said there's a big motor balloon—"

"An airship?" Most certainly the one Alicia Zorro had mentioned.

"Yes, I suppose. She's hoping you can fly it."

"Of course," I replied dubiously. *Provided we get there.*

Nursing the throttle, I kept us crashing through the thicket.

A bullet ricocheted off the truck and whined into the night. The damned sparks above us had grown thicker and brighter.

Our wheels rumbled over stones, skidded into a rut, and climbed back out. The boiler's whistle shrieked as if in pain. I glanced at the pressure gauge, and its needle was pegged against the upper limit.

Hermosa banged the butt of her revolver against the boiler's whistle. "For God's sake, make it stop."

"Don't do that," I yelled. "Break the whistle and steam will scald your face." I wrestled with a valve knob beneath the gauge, hoping to release the pressure.

Steam filled the gauge, shattering the glass and sending the needle flying. The whistling became a demonic scream.

"Everybody off!" I shouted. "Run!"

We jumped and ran up a narrow trail. Behind us, the whistle increased in volume and pitch, and seemed to come at us from all directions. Then it stopped, and the silence became strangely tangible.

A thunderous explosion shook the ground and slammed the air, shaking branches and slapping our faces. Far down the trail, pieces of the truck spun upwards in a hurl of sparks. The blast echoed over the thicket, reverberating like a crashing cymbal.

I paused the group to let them catch their breath.

Hermosa counted noses. "Only thirteen. There are so many more."

"We'll come back and rescue them too," I said. "Some how. Soon. They won't be forgotten."

The two Indian women who had taken the rifle and shotgun stepped forward. Bandoliers, heavy with cartridges, hung loose on their slender frames. The shorter one said, "You must first escape. We will remain here and ambush the guards."

"You'll get killed," I replied.

"We must do our duty." She menaced with the Winchester. "Now go. Tell our people that we died without shame. Two sacrificed themselves so many can live." She and her companion touched foreheads and began chanting.

I fought with myself about remaining behind as well. My vampire powers would help even the odds, then again, Hermosa and the others needed me too. They could run into more guards up ahead. I couldn't be at two places at the same time. Reluctantly, I said, "Good luck. The rest of you, let's go."

The other women filed past their valiant sisters, kissing their cheeks, bidding them goodbye, and joined Hermosa and me on the winding trail.

A girl, the youngest of the group, led our way. She moved barefoot over the rough scrabble, hopping from rock to rock, dancing around cacti, nimble as a mountain goat. I told her to slow down or else we'd leave the rest behind.

Gunshots tore through the night and we walked a little more quietly. Some of the blasts were sharp—rifle fire. Others low baritone booms—shotguns. The gunfire intensified until it sounded like a string of firecrackers going off.

Then silence.

I was about to pray for the two Indian women when the gunfire started again. I imagined them shifting from cover to cover, confusing the guards, pinning them down.

"Keep going," I urged, knowing that staying put only wasted time.

The gunfire stopped. Then a pair of shots rang out, spaced apart like final heartbeats, and I knew the two Indian women had met their end. A dirge whispered through our ranks as we continued forward.

Desperation heightened my senses. Stars became needles of light. I tasted the burnt chemicals in the smoke lingering on my clothes. I smelled sage and mesquite, adrenaline and perspiration.

Resentment clawed through my anxiety. I am a vampire, the ultimate predator, but now I was hunted prey. I could leave Hermosa and the others, save my skin. But that's all I'd be saving because without honor and courage I'd be a barren husk. Tell me vampires have no conscience.

The trail inclined over terraced stone coarse as sandpaper. A fresh smell caught me. Blood. The girl on point was leaving bloody footprints. The meaty aroma tugged at my hunger, but I tamped it down.

"Let me carry you," I said.

When I tried to scoop her up, she struggled and gritted her teeth. "Put me down. I can do this."

"All right then." I set her back on the ground and let her soldier on.

The trail crested a low hill and continued through a craggy draw that kept getting deeper but not much wider. Hardly any of the meager moonlight filtered to us, and the women stumbled into one another. About a hundred yards into the draw, we ran into a tall barbed-wire fence erected between the rock walls. We bunched close but kept clear of the wire. The fence looked recently built and something about it made my kundalini noir tingle in suspicion.

"We can crawl through it," the girl said and dropped to her hands and knees.

"Hold on." I pulled her up and scrutinized the fence. A heavy wire ran from post to post and was looped tight around small glass bells—electrical insulators.

"Stay back," I ordered. "The fence is electrified."

I found a leafy branch on the ground and tossed it against the wire. Upon contact, the branch sparked. It bounced back at us, falling to the ground where it sputtered and smoked.

From behind us, a gruff voice carried through the thicket. Then another voice. The guards were closing in.

Hermosa groped one of the walls as if studying how to climb it. They were steep and barren and rose to at least fifty feet. I could easily get to the top, maybe the girl as well, but everyone else would be inching their way up when the guards caught them.

The voices grew louder.

From deep in the woods on the other side of the fence, a distant growl escalated into a roar, a ragged primordial howl that rattled my undead bones. A chorus of more roars added to the terror.

Several of the women hugged. Others picked up rocks. Hermosa pointed her revolver toward the noise as if her Merwin Hulbert could keep the beasts at bay. "Please tell me I'm hallucinating."

I answered, "I wish you were."

CHAPTER THIRTY-FIVE

At the entrance to the draw behind us, the Dowager's guards advanced cautiously through the thicket.

Another growl from the murk in front of us made my kundalini noir shiver, and the women gasped in terror. Even if we got through the electrified fence, our troubles wouldn't be over.

But we had no choice. If we stayed put the guards would kill Hermosa and most of the Indian women. The survivors would be taken prisoner and experimented on. Me? I wasn't looking forward to getting shot, maybe captured and vivisected. And I wasn't going to leave the others behind. Against the monsters—the prehistoric creatures Alicia Zorro warned about—we might have better odds.

I searched the ground for branches big enough to lever the wires apart but found nothing. My frustration rising, I thought about taking my coat off, wrapping it around my hands, and pulling a gap between the wires for everyone to pass through. It would be an act of desperation but we were desperate and time was running out.

"*Aquí estan las ratas. Fuego! Fuego!*" Rifles blasts echoed through

the draw. The Indian women dove to the ground. Some covered
their heads and screamed. The furious gunfire drummed like rain
spattering on a roof. What saved us from getting minced was the
angle of the draw that deflected most of the bullets.

Hermosa emptied her revolver at our attackers. "Goddammit
Felix, think of something!"

Any second now, the guards were going to crawl down the
trail while others advanced on the high ground on either side to
trap us inside the draw.

A few rounds pinged on the rocks above us and sprayed us
with fragments. One bullet ricocheted and struck the top of a
fence post. The glass insulator shattered and the wire looped
around it went slack.

An idea formed.

"Get back." I pushed Hermosa down. I unholstered my Colt
Navy and aimed at the glass insulator on top of the next fence
post. My shot hit square, smashing the insulator, and the wire
sagged into the barbed wire grid beneath it. Where they
touched, sparks and bolts of electricity lit the air. When the
barbed wire melted, its strands whipped free and flailed about. A
harsh tang of ozone and burnt metal stung my nose and eyes.
The loose barbed wire dangled onto the electric wire below and
shorted it out to begin another round of sparks and flashes of
electricity.

To speed the process I blasted the other glass insulators.
Within seconds the draw was lit by electric explosions. When
the bedlam died down, glowing wires drooped between the
wooden fence posts, themselves licked by flames. The commotion must've puzzled the guards because they held their fire.

Hermosa rose to her feet and waved a hand to clear the
smoke. She coughed. "Can we cross? Is it safe?"

"Safe enough." I holstered my empty revolver. "Everybody,
this way. One at a time." As each Indian women approached, I
grasped their hands, said, "Jump," and catapulted them one at a
time over the mass of twisted and smoking wires. When each

woman landed a few feet down the trail, Hermosa ordered her to keep running. On the other side of the fence, the draw opened into dense underbrush.

The guards wised up to what we were doing. Bullets cracked and whined high against the rock walls, and each fresh volley ratcheted lower.

Hermosa didn't wait for my help as she took a running leap to sail over the wires sagging across the ground. On the other side, she kept running and disappeared after the others.

As I readied to spring after her, I decided the guards were getting too close. I had to buy time.

I crouched low and reloaded my revolver. Above the wall at my right, a guard skylined himself and I shot him. With a grunt, he tumbled into the draw and hit the bottom, whimpering. That prompted another hail of bullets. I heard guards creeping toward me. I lunged forward, just enough to aim around the bend in the draw. Three men were hugging the walls and I hacked at them with blasts of fire, smoke, and lead. Shouting in panic, they retreated toward their comrades.

I backtracked to the fence, my kundalini noir coiling like a snake. My fangs and talons extended to combat length, and I was ready to go full vampire and take all the guards out.

A growl—sounding hungry, rapacious—rumbled up the trail. Hermosa and the women had fled one trap only to plunge into another. They would need my help.

I holstered my revolver and turned to run for them.

A bullet stabbed the back of my right leg, and the hot poker of pain jolted me off balance. I stumbled forward, tripped on wires, and fell across what was left of the fence. Sparks exploded around me. Demonic bolts of electric agony lanced through my body.

My mind detonated into a ball of light. My arms and legs flailed in spasms of agony. My kundalini noir twisted and untwisted like a giant wringing a dishrag.

Blam! An electric explosion sent me tumbling through brush to crash face down in the ground. I smelled meat burning and realized it was me.

The pain eased enough for me to hear women crying out in Spanish. "He's on fire!"

"Put him out! He's giving away our position."

Dirt pelted me. Someone grabbed my hands and I was dragged downhill through sticks, dust, and rocks, then let go.

"Felix," it was Hermosa, "get up. We can't stay here."

Nothing of mine wanted to move. I tried flexing my limbs, moving my head, even blinking to get my vision back. It was like everything inside had been disconnected. I could hear and feel but that was it.

She shook my collar. "Get up."

"He's been shot."

"Where?"

Everyone spoke in whispers.

"In the back of one leg."

Hermosa groaned for the both of us. "Oh Felix," I heard pity in her voice, "we have to keep moving."

"Pick him up," one of the women said. "We'll carry him."

Hands grasped my arms and legs. I was hoisted upwards and bodies shuffled under me. We advanced in a clumsy gait, my head lolling side to side as I floated in a black cloud of agony.

"Are the guards still after us?" someone asked.

"They stopped at the fence."

Nobody had to ask why. It was because of the monsters. The guards with their guns and superior numbers preferred to stay put. But moving forward, at least we were still alive.

"There's a cistern up ahead," the girl said. "We'll stop there."

We kept trekking and when we stopped, I was lowered to the ground like a bundle of broken sticks. The group rustled around me and dipped into the cistern.

Someone rolled me onto my back. A moist rag wiped dirt from my face. "Felix," Hermosa stroked my forehead, "we'll do what we can for you. Stay strong." She took my revolver and slipped cartridges from my belt.

"I need two of you to come with me," she said in a low voice. "I'm going to scout the trail ahead of us. The rest of you stay here and stay alert."

Hermosa and her party strode away.

I lay in the quiet, aware that someone else remained by my side. After many minutes passed, she bent close and whispered. "I am a sister-in-law to Doña Luz." Her breath puffed against my ear. "I know what you are, *vampiro.*"

Hearing that word, my instinct was to lash out, but I remained paralyzed.

Calloused hands cupped my jaw and forced my mouth open. Her wrist pushed between my lips and blood oozed down my tongue.

Each tasteless drop spread a cooling relief that spread from my mouth, down my throat, through my chest, and to my spine. The relief coursed to my brain, my guts, and down my legs. My fingers and toes tingled.

The beast inside me writhed as if fighting off chains. My fangs extended. Strength surged through my arms and I clutched her wrist.

She pressed herself against me, her voice breaking with pain. "*Fácil, vampiro.* Protect your secret."

I sank my fangs into her wrist, puncturing deep, and began sucking. Her blood flowed into me, like a flood drenching parched earth. My arms and legs flexed with renewed strength. I wanted to yank her neck back and greedily feed.

She hugged me tight. "Easy. Easy. Don't give yourself away."

The ache peeled away in layers. I sensed taste. Her salty blood.

Then odors, fragrances filled my nose. Her perspiration. The sage and mesquite around us. Fresh water from the cistern. Dirt. Charred clothing and flesh.

My sight remained blurry, and curious to see who had

doctored me back to health, I stared at the woman. She was a hazy outline, but I could tell she was stocky and the only one with wavy hair.

"What's your name?"

"Delfina."

I reached to stroke her hair, but she brushed my hand aside.

"What's the matter?"

"When the Dowager's men used me, the first thing they always did was touch my hair."

"I'm sorry."

"Don't be. It wasn't you."

"Thank you anyway, Delfina."

"Show your thanks by getting us off this island." She laid her wrist back across my mouth and I resumed drinking. With every gulp I gathered more awareness of my condition. I could feel my burned flesh healing but the wound at the back of my right thigh still hurt, well, like I'd been shot.

Realizing I had not given her any pleasure enzymes, I passed along a dose. Delfina quivered and rested against me. I quit feeding and she stirred. Her hand ran down my right thigh.

"Move your leg." Her fingers groped the back of my leg and found the hole in my trousers and the wound underneath. I recoiled in agony when her fingers dug into my raw flesh.

"Hold still." The bullet popped out of my leg with a gushy sound. She showed me the lead slug she had recovered. Then she brought her wrist back to my mouth. "Bite me again. Make me bleed."

My fangs reopened the punctures, and she pressed her bleeding wrist against my wound. The hot pain cooled and my flesh went numb.

Delfina withdrew her arm and sat up. My vision had sharpened enough that I could make out the features of her broad face. Behind her, the other women milled around a small stone cistern at the base of a stone outcropping. Interlocking tree branches formed an umbrella of cover.

The women turned as one to face the trail. Someone approached. When I tried to sit up Delfina pressed me back down.

Hermosa and her two companions hustled into our circle. She stood over me, her chest heaving from exertion.

"He's better," Delfina said. "The electric fence gave him a serious shocking but he's recovering."

"What about his gunshot?"

"It only nicked him."

I raised and bent my leg to show that it worked.

"That's good." Hermosa pointed down the trail. "We're close to the north side of the island."

"How near is the ocean?"

"I don't know. But we saw some buildings. It looks like a base."

"Did you see the airship?"

A new smell wafted through the darkness. Something feral.

A shape materialized in the shadows on the rocky ledge above the cistern. It slowly came into focus, a big striped feline. It's long fangs glistened like bayonets.

A saber-tooth tiger! Another tiger appeared beside it.

My kundalini noir shriveled as I grasped my empty holster.

Hermosa whipped around and froze. She swung my revolver from tiger to tiger, but as large as these creatures were, shooting them with bullets would be like hitting them with spitballs.

The tigers regarded us like prey, then locked their beastly stares on me. Their eyes caught the meager light and for an instant, they shined like green embers. The tigers sniffed.

One of them shrank back into the darkness, then the other, and just as mysteriously as they appeared, they vanished.

A muted thumping grew louder. A steam engine, and not one on the ground but in the air. The Indian women gazed upward in all directions, trying to see what approached.

"There. There," the girl exclaimed.

I pushed up to my feet and hobbled over to see.

Against the pale silvery clouds, a fish-like shape cruised toward us. A light beamed from the gondola underneath and raked the ground. Though the airship was still a distance away, we retreated under the trees.

I wanted to hope it was Malachi on the way to rescue us, but I didn't need supernatural powers to tell me I was wrong.

CHAPTER THIRTY-SIX

The airship floated closer, and the *chugga-chugga* from its steam engine pulsed against my kundalini noir. The gondola's search lamp stabbed the ground.

"Stay under the trees," I cautioned in a low voice even though the airship was hundreds of yards away. "If the beam hits you, freeze."

When the airship reached our position it hovered directly overheard. The growl of its propellers added to its menacing presence.

Why had it stopped?

A new worry amped my fear. Perhaps the crew had some kind of advanced sensors—advanced for this world anyway—that could see through trees. Thermal imaging. Microwave radar.

Two more search lamps snapped on, and the three columns of fiery light focused on the cistern. A bright glow reflected from the water. The crew knew we would've stopped here to rest and slake our thirst.

Like a gigantic shark trying to get a bearing on its prey, the airship pivoted above us. Its search lamps spattered through the layers of branches, painting us and the ground with shards of light, the pattern shifting and reshifting like the image inside a kaleidoscope.

The search lamps shut off as suddenly as they had flicked on. The steam engine accelerated and the growl from the propellers deepened. The airship lifted straight up, yawing as it climbed, and cruised to the south.

We remained still, each of us following the *chugga-chugga* as it faded to a whisper. Even then we didn't move, just in case a ground unit trailed behind the airship.

Hermosa was the first to step from under the trees. "Something is going on. The airship left like it was in a hurry."

"Let's take advantage of that," I replied. Delfina supported me as I limped toward Hermosa. With every step, my leg grew stronger and by the time I reached her, I pulled free of Delfina to stand on my own.

I asked for my pistol back. Hermosa armed herself with the Merwin Hulbert she pulled from a skirt pocket. Against the threats facing us, our revolvers would be as effective as rosary beads, but like rosary beads we held them anyway for reassurance.

The arrival of the airship had scared off the saber-tooth tigers, at least for the moment. We all gathered on the trail and the girl took her place at point. She told me her name was *Gah*, Apache for rabbit.

I massaged the back of my leg and put weight on it. "I'm ready. Let's go."

We hiked down the trail and for a good while the only sound that broke the silence was the scrape of branches across our clothing. Then a breeze stirred the trees, adding an ominous murmur that highlighted our anxiety. The wind brought the odor of smoke. Looking up, I saw smog dim the stars.

Hermosa hustled to me. "What's going on?"

I didn't slow down. "Something's burning."

She grasped my arm. "Could the fire have spread from the citadel?"

"Since the wind is coming from the south, I'm guessing yes."

"Maybe I can see." Gah started for the nearest tall tree and nimbly laddered upward branch by branch.

I holstered my revolver and followed her until the branches sagged under my weight. Gah was just above me. Flakes of ash fluttered around us. We were high enough to observe the ridge that we had cut through using the draw. Far beyond the ridge, flames licked into clouds of smoke.

I climbed down, carefully since I no longer had the powers of levitation to brake my fall. Gah dropped from a branch to land beside me.

I said, "It looks like the whole south side of the island is burning."

Hermosa smirked. "Good. The Dowager's bad luck works in our favor."

We kept hiking. The slope flattened and the trees and brush thinned out. Gah slowed and pointed toward lights in the distance. Haze clouded my vampire vision. The lights shined from a cluster of buildings in the center of a broad expanse of open, empty ground. Beyond that, starlight flickered across the gulf's water. We were looking northeast, toward the mainland.

Another set of lights, tiny because they were so far away, had to belong to the fishing village of Arenas, the place where Malachi was to stage our rescue. So we were right where we had to be. But the open ground teemed with a vibe that made my kundalini noir vibrate an uncertain but still sinister warning.

The eastern horizon faded from purple to blue. Daylight was about to break. I looked back at our party. Several of the women reclined on the ground, worn out by the night's ordeal. Others stood on tiptoes and craned their necks to scan what lay ahead. They were all tired, hungry, and thirsty. But with the gulf in sight, a feeling of hope buoyed us.

How to proceed? We couldn't cross the open ground without being spotted from the buildings.

"It will be a miracle if we can get off this island," I said.

"But a miracle got us this far," Hermosa replied.

"All right then, let's keep hoping for miracles. But once we get off this island, we still won't know what happened to Ling Zhu Han."

Gah spun abruptly toward Hermosa and me. "The Chinese woman?"

"You know her?" Hermosa asked.

"Yes, she was on this island." Gah pointed to the ground. "She was a missionary of some kind. She helped women escape prostitution and came here disguised as one of us to see what was happening. When she learned what the Dowager was doing, she escaped the island to get help."

"She escaped?" I asked.

"You saw her?" Hermosa pressed.

"Yes. I helped her sneak onto the ferry heading back to Guaymas."

"Why didn't you escape with her?"

"I ... I," Gah looked away and dragged one bare foot across the dirt. Her voice broke. "I made a bargain with the crew. Me in exchange for her freedom."

Hermosa reached for Gah.

"I don't need your pity." The girl bristled and stepped back. "It's over and done with, and there's nothing you can do about it."

I had more questions for Gah, but with those memories torturing her, I didn't ask. Each new revelation about Ling only led to another mystery. She had been here, she knew about the Dowager, and she had left the island, alive. And then? Maybe she wasn't dead after all. But if not, where was she? Hermosa queried the other women but we didn't learn anything more.

The gathering morning light sharpened the details around us. The buildings resembled those of the complex behind the citadel, and I wondered what gruesome experiments took place here. Perhaps this was where the monsters were created.

In a few minutes the sun would crest the horizon and though

in this world I had no reason to fear the dawn, a lingering dread still plucked my nerves.

So I closed my eyes and imagined that ball of fire cresting the horizon. Heat splashed across my skin. When I opened my eyes, I squinted and dipped my head to let my hat's brim shade my face.

Sunlight reflected off hundreds of polished white stones scattered around us. The rim at the far end of the open ground blocked our view of the beach, a quarter of a mile away.

The air rumbled. Vehicles were on the way. For a split second I wanted to believe that Malachi was swooping in to save us.

Then a trumpet echoed. It was the same sound I'd heard days ago in Devil's Canyon. Mammoths.

The noise of steam engines increased. To the right of the buildings, dust clouded the air. Slowly, shapes inched up from behind the rim.

Nervously, I thumbed the revolver's hammer, eased it forward, thumbed it back again. Hermosa's expression grew hard and troubled.

The trumpeting blared, and seconds later, large fearsome cats roared a reply. Big tawny shapes crept through the thicket in our direction. The saber-tooth cats were back.

The Indian women ran from the brush to the edge of the open ground. I raised my Colt Navy. The tigers growled and shrieked, announcing their presence, which caused us to keep our distance.

The tigers emerged from the brush and formed a semi-circle, the open end facing the force approaching from the beach. Then I noticed they weren't stalking us but herding us further into the open ground. They lingered in the low scrub, striped flanks blending with the dry grass and brush. Their bodies were packs of muscle, each torso as big around as a horse's. Immense furry heads sat on thick necks. Curved fangs as long as my forearm glistened in the morning light.

I turned toward the advancing force. The trap had closed and all I could do was wait for the Dowager's guards to arrive. Through the blur of dust and distance, I saw gigantic mammoths flank a column of trucks. Fighting against these overwhelming odds was pointless so I holstered my revolver. Minute by minute, they drew closer and I could make out the details of this strange procession.

Armed men rocked inside the howdahs strapped to the mammoths' backs. Their massive tusks swayed side-to-side in cadence to their majestic stride. Flags snapped from poles mounted on the howdahs and the trucks. Brass gleamed. Dust lifted from mammoth feet and truck wheels. Prehistoric mammals and steam cars—it was too surreal.

I noticed that the white rocks on the ground were actually bones, bleached by the sun. Hundreds of them. Human skulls. Ribs. Vertebrae. And animal bones. Mammoths. Saber-tooth tigers. Light reflected off the white dome of a mammoth's skull half-buried in the dirt. A round hole was centered between the eye sockets, like the hole had been made by a large, perfectly placed bullet.

I realized what my kundalini noir was trying to tell me. I was in the middle of a killing field, of humans and beasts methodically slaughtered.

The lead vehicle was an armored car covered in thick plates riveted together. A Gatling gun pointed at me from a squat cylindrical turret mounted on top of the cabin. Guards watched from inside open hatches. More guards waited in the trucks that followed.

Hermosa strode among the Indian women, yanking each one by the arm as she cursed in Spanish and their assorted languages. "Stand tall. Die like Indians. Proud. Defiant. Don't give these miscreants the satisfaction of thinking that we're scared of them."

"But we are," muttered Delfina.

The largest mammoth—a bull—led the formation. Smaller juvenile mammoths trailed the flankers, their mommas. Each bore a number tattooed on its forehead, numbers like the Ω 42 on the bull mammoth.

They slowed to form a wall of gray, wrinkled hide around the armored car. The air stank like a horse stall that needed mucking. Breath bellowed through their enormous trunks.

The airship's *chugga-chugga* returned. It floated low over the water and turned toward us. Out the corner of my eye I saw the tigers wince, then retreat and disappear into the thicket.

Steam wheezed from the armored car's grill. A side hatch opened and the Dowager Engels climbed out. She was dressed in white, and her tall brown boots matched her gun belt. Blond tresses spilled in sloppy, unkempt waves from under a khaki pith helmet, and her scarf twisted in the breeze.

She loosened her goggles and let them dangle around her neck. Dust circled her bloodshot eyes. She looked drained, pushed to the brink of exhaustion. Jaw clenched, she glowered at me for a long moment. "Monsieur Étalon, drop your gun belt."

Monsieur Étalon? Either the Dowager was playing me or she had no idea who I was. I released the buckle of my gun belt and let it fall to my boots.

She stared at Gah and Hermosa. "You girl, number 4317, join Étalon. Duchess Juvante, don't move. Monsieur Étalon, come forward."

I stepped from my belt and advanced a couple of paces. Gah stood beside me, on my right.

The Dowager nodded. A rifle shot boxed my ears. Hot blood spurted against my skin. Gah crumpled as blood gushed from her skull and streamed down her face. She toppled to the dirt.

The Gatling gun swung toward the women, warning that any brash moves would bring more deaths.

I raised my open hands, my kundalini noir burning with rage.

The Dowager raised a gloved hand. The two female mammoths on either side of me ambled forward and their trunks whipped around my neck and shoulders. I tried to fight them off but they coiled with an immense power I couldn't resist.

On her signal they lifted me. My body sagged and I clung to the trunks to keep from getting hanged. Even though us vampires didn't need to breathe, I felt myself gasping.

The Dowager set her hands on her gun belt and approached. "Monsieur Étalon, before my pets tear you to pieces, you're going to tell me everything I want to know."

CHAPTER THIRTY-SEVEN

The two female mammoths stood on either side of me, each as big as a house, Π 17 to my left, Σ 25 to my right. Their enormous trunks adjusted their grip on me, holding my head and torso firm so all I could do was swivel my eyes from side-to-side. I kept my talons retracted. Even if I could use them to tear free, I wouldn't get far before the bull mammoth finished me off. And I had to think about the Gatling gun trained on Hermosa and the Indian women. I was caught in a vortex of bad choices.

A breeze batted the Dowager's scarf and lifted tufts of dust from the ground. Guards shifted uneasily in the howdahs strapped to the mammoths' backs. The bull mammoth wrinkled his forehead, creasing the Ω 42 tattoo. The dirigible's steam engine groaned in the distance. But it seemed like time had stopped, like the clock was waiting for my death before continuing.

The Dowager Engels stepped away from the armored car, her boots crunching dirt and ossified bones. She brushed along one of Ω 42's forelegs and he shifted to let her pass. She appraised me with tired, bloodshot eyes. I thought she'd begin an interrogation, but she kept quiet, her thin lips cinched tight.

I struggled to get enough breath to start a conversation, get her talking, give me an opportunity to think of a way out of this. "Forgive me if I don't tip my hat."

The Dowager's face remained like stone. "Keep joking, Monsieur Étalon, that is until my pets rip your head and spine right out of your body. It's quite the sight." She raked one boot over the bones around her feet. "You won't die well. No one ever does."

I thought back to all the other times I'd found myself in similar straits, with the Grim Reaper's scythe tracing across my throat. "We can come to an arrangement. It so happens I feel like talking."

"I've changed my mind. I'm not going to waste time asking you questions. Once I make an example of you, I'm sure your companions will speak freely."

Death's scythe pressed a little deeper. My hands and feet tingled with dread. "Don't be hasty. I can be cooperative."

The Dowager's countenance brightened with perverse triumph. She waved her hand and Ω 42 ambled toward me. He could have easily gored me but his enormous scarred tusks passed alongside me until he pulled short about six feet from where I hanged between the other two mammoths.

The guards in his howdah watched uneasily. *Better you than me, stranger.*

My kundalini noir whipped inside of me, like a worm on a hook, stoking my panic as my mind lashed for ideas. Maybe Hermosa planned to do something but I couldn't turn my head to see what she was doing. I prayed that Malachi was on the way and he'd arrive like the cavalry, right in the nick of time.

The closer Ω 42 brought his trunk to my face, the more my panic morphed into terror. I felt myself shrinking from him, shrinking from the inevitable, imagining the agony when he yanked my skull and backbone out of my body.

I saw no point hiding my vampire nature if it meant getting decapitated. My talons strained inside my fingers, ready to snap out. When he reached for me, I would slash him and the other two mammoths. I had no chance of getting away but if I could create enough chaos, Hermosa might be able to lead the others to freedom. To die as a useful sacrifice seemed my only hope.

The end of Ω 42's trunk hovered inches from my face. Each oval-shaped nostril was as big as my fist and seemed ready to vacuum my eyes right out of my skull. The breath puffing against me stank of wet, spoiled hay. The tip caressed my nose and mouth; this colossus weighed probably ten tons and yet his touch felt delicate, bird-like. He withdrew his trunk to regard me with his large eyes, nestled inside wadded skin. His gigantic head tipped forward and his gaze broke focus to consider the bones scattered between us.

His trunk extended toward the mammoth skull half-sunk in the dirt to my left. The tip of the trunk formed a point that poked into the bullet hole in the skull's forehead, then traced inside the empty eye sockets. Did Ω 42 know this mammoth?

He swung his trunk to where Gah had fallen and held it over her corpse. He inhaled deeply as if studying her smell, then dragged the end of his trunk over her torso and through the blood congealing around her head. Flies buzzed away in random directions, then circled back.

Ω 42 brought the blooded tip of his trunk back to my face.

His eyes studied me for a long moment. Flies settled on his bristle-like eyelashes as his trunk swung side-to-side. His eyes revealed an intense curiosity but more than that, I got the sense he was trying to understand my part in this drama. Perhaps his as well.

The Dowager slapped his leg. "Get on with it, you stupid brute."

He chuffed and lifted his trunk, first to the left, then to the right. The female mammoths tipped their heads slightly, as if confused. He chuffed again. They uncoiled their trunks from around my body and I dropped to my feet, then toppled into the dirt. Ω 42 backed away until he was even with the rear of the armored car.

I sat up, astonished and confused, my kundalini noir still trembling, my neck aching, my body gathering strength.

The Dowager's face bloomed a bright red, and her face contorted in fury. She jabbed a gloved finger at me and shouted at the mammoths. "Kill him. I command you. Kill him!"

Ω 42 stood still. The two big females shuffled in place, their big feet raising dust.

"Very well, then" the Dowager said. "Use the electro-shocker."

One of the guards in the Ω 42's howdah crouched out of my view. Seconds later, the mammoth released a frightful bellow, an infernal sound that rattled me as if that pain was my own.

"Again," the Dowager shouted to be heard over Ω 42's cries, "until he learns to answer to his master."

Ω 42 trembled in place, his trunk jerking spastically, a spectacle of misery.

With everyone's attention on the poor, tortured beast, I scrambled back to my gun belt at vampire speed. In one quick motion, I lashed it around my waist and drew my Colt Navy. Thumbing the hammer, I trained the gun at the Dowager.

Hermosa screamed at me. "No! Take her alive. Take her alive."

The Dowager saw me and ducked toward the armored car. Its Gatling gun opened fire, barrels spinning as they pounded out clouds of fire and smoke. *Rat-a-tat-tat-tat.*

Hermosa and the others scattered, and the Gatling gun's bullets clawed empty dirt.

I shifted my aim to the guard in the howdah, the one manipulating the electric shocker. I held steady, and fired once, the cylinder and barrel of my revolver belching flame, the report clapping my ears. My bullet clipped the crown of his hat, and he slumped below the rim of the howdah.

Ω 42's pained cry deepened into a howl booming with fury. His trunk reached up and swept over the howdah. He snagged one of the guards and slammed him to ground. The other two guards levered the actions of their Winchesters and shouldered them to blast open the mammoth's skull. I shot at one guard, then the other, gun smoke swirling around me, pistol blasts ringing in my ears.

Time jumped into fast-forward and everything blurred together.

The two female mammoths began squirming to shake off their howdahs. The guards tumbled out to spill into the dirt. The juvenile mammoths crowded behind their mommas and trumpeted in confusion.

The Dowager beat her fist against the iron hull of the armored car. "They're going rogue! Wipe them out!"

The armored car swiveled its turret to the female mammoth, Π 17. The Gatling gun cycled through another volley, the air clouding with gun smoke.

Hermosa charged into the fray, pumping her revolver's trigger as she shot the panicked guards. The Indian women trailed after her, scooping rifles and pistols from the dead and wounded.

Slugs punched across the flank of Π 17. Her juvenile sprinted forward, shrieking what could only be *Momma! Momma!*

The Gatling gun strung a line of bullets across the young mammoth's head and rib cage. It stumbled onto its front knees, blood spurting from its mouth and trunk as it screamed in agony.

Ω 42 slammed against the armored car. He slid one of his tusks beneath the chassis and rocked it to one side. The car's turret rotated toward him.

I sprang onto the hood of the car and shoved the barrel of my pistol into a vision port of the turret. Firing blindly, I worked the trigger and hammer, the revolver filling the turret with smoke as I fired at the crew, the slugs ricocheting inside.

As Ω 42 kept rocking the car, its rear wheels spinning rooster tails of dirt, the car tipped over, rolling upside down. I jumped clear and reloaded my revolver. The car turtled onto its back. Steam whistled and jetted from the chassis, and the mammoth backed away. The car's boiler *Ka-Boomed!* and pieces of iron shot in all directions like shrapnel.

The Dowager picked herself off the ground and fired wildly as she screamed at her guards to rally and counterattack.

A shadow fell over us, and I looked up to see the dirigible lumbering in our direction. A Jacob's ladder scrolled from a hatch in the gondola's belly and scraped across the dirt toward the Dowager. Hermosa and the other women peppered the belly of the gondola with rifle fire.

Ω 42 lunged and swept his tusks over the ground, snagging the ladder as it dragged past him. He snaked his trunk between the rungs of the ladder and pulled out the slack.

The dirigible lurched to a halt, pitching forward. Ω 42 leaned backwards and began hauling it to the ground. When a guard appeared in a window to shoot at the mammoth, Hermosa and I picked him off.

Ω 42 shook his head and twisted the ladder. The dirigible dipped low, and the second female mammoth, Σ 25, rushed forward and stabbed the gondola with her tusks. She and Ω 42 wrestled with the dirigible, forcing it down, tearing the fabric, causing the contraption to wilt against the ground like a gigantic rotting melon.

Guards leapt from the gondola and sprinted toward the woods. Suddenly, they halted and turned back to what was left of the dirigible. Saber-tooth tigers pounced from the thicket, tackling the guards, pinning them to the dirt before fanging open their heads and chests in gouts of blood and gore.

Hermosa and I approached the Dowager. My kundalini noir relaxed like a spring losing tension, only to reset itself for more action.

Stumbling backwards, she threatened us with her empty

revolver. With trembling hands she fumbled cartridges from a pouch and spilled them on the ground.

Ω 42 turned towards her. Blood oozed from dozens of bullet wounds in his hide. More blood drooled from his mouth and he advanced in a pained wobble. After a few steps, he shambled to a halt. He stared at the Dowager. Blood frothed on his lips. Unable to proceed, he stretched his trunk toward her, grunting with effort but couldn't quite reach her. Wheezing, he tried one more time but failed. His trunk went limp and slapped the ground. He teetered off balance, his enormous legs stiff as Greek columns, and toppled onto his side. His body slammed heavily against the dirt. Breath gurgled and huffed out his trunk. It snaked toward me, the tip beckoning like a finger. His large eyes latched on me and slowly went dim.

Seeing him die overwhelmed me with admiration and guilt. I had at first called him a monster, yet he died saving us.

Rifle at the ready, Hermosa covered Delfina who stepped toward the Dowager and smacked the revolver from her hand.

"You're going to pay for what you've done to us," Delfina said.

The Dowager slit her eyes and smirked. Delfina slapped her. The women glowered at one another.

"Delfina," Hermosa barked as she poked the rifle into the Dowager's belly, "justice will get done."

"There's only one justice." Delfina stepped back as she traced a finger across her throat.

The groan of steam engines echoed from the direction of the beach.

"You won't get off this island." The Dowager stood tall and squared her shoulders. Slowly, she reached down and pushed Hermosa's rifle aside.

Hermosa's finger twitched on the Winchester's trigger but didn't squeeze.

The Dowager knotted the scarf around her neck and smoothed her hair. Dust, gunpowder soot, and flecks of blood soiled her white costume. This detachment of her guard force had been wiped out, her mammoths and tigers had turned against her, yet she remained defiant, even imperious as she looked down her long, regal nose at Hermosa.

"Those are my reinforcements." The Dowager smirked. "It seems we have a parlay. The only way you'll get off this island is if you set me free."

CHAPTER THIRTY-EIGHT

A steam whistle echoed from behind a line of sand dunes dead ahead. I held still and listened. The distant clatter of steam engines came from two directions on the other side of the dunes—the open water and from the beach to my right.

I knew the Dowager's men were advancing along the beach. That meant a boat was steaming close by the island.

Malachi. My kundalini noir spasmed in the hope that it was him. Otherwise Hermosa, the Indian women, and I were screwed.

But a profound sense of fatigue settled on Hermosa and the Indian women, as if after so much exertion and sacrifice they barely had the strength to continue.

The Dowager caught me staring into the distance, and she turned in the direction of the closest noise. Craning her neck, she stood on tiptoes, then relaxed to sneer at me. "Don't get your hopes up. The only way you and the rest of this dirty mob"—she panned Hermosa and the others—"will survive is if you give me up."

"The only way you'll live is if we get off the island." I grasped her wrist. "Let's go."

Hermosa and the Indian women judged me with expressions wrung dry from exhaustion. I began running and hauled the Dowager along. The others stumbled half-heartedly after me.

We crested a tall dune and the gulf's blue waters spread before us, stretching to the left and right against the hazy backdrop of the mainland. A stiff sea breeze carried the promise of escape. A paddle-boat plowing towards us through the rolling waters was still a good ways off. It wasn't large, maybe a thirty-foot launch. Smoke spooled from a stack midship. Even at this distance, I made out someone standing at the bow, but I didn't see weapons like Gatling guns or cannons.

The Dowager dragged her boots through the sandy slope, slowing me. Maybe two hundred yards separated us from the water's edge. She laughed. "Give it up."

Yanking her upright, I then studied the trucks racing toward us across the wide sand flats between the dunes and the surf. I counted six trucks, all packed with soldiers. After comparing the speed of the trucks and the boat, it felt like I was caught in a vice that was squeezing tighter. The Dowager's force would be upon us about the time Malachi landed.

Hermosa and the Indian women stumbled over the top of the dune, moving as fast as their weary bodies could take them. At the sight of the open water and the boat, some of them cried out in relief and the lot of them found the strength to sprint down the dune.

The women raced past me and reached the beach to sprint through the surf, diving into the water. Waves broke over them and tossed them back onto the beach, where they crawled coughing and gasping for breath. The others hauled them to their feet. They splashed along the surf, waving their arms, and hollering though the waves crashing around us swallowed their noise. The breeze lifted spray from the chop and misted us with seawater.

The trucks spread into a line that looped around us, each skidding into place about a hundred yards away, forming a horseshoe that trapped us against the water's edge.

My kundalini noir clenched into a tight ball of desperation. We were doomed rats caught in a barrel.

Hermosa aimed her Winchester at the trucks and fired, the report booming defiantly over the sound of the crashing waves. She levered another round and fired again. The Indian women with rifles joined Hermosa in shooting at the Dowager's men.

Gun smoke puffed from the trucks. Bullets whined overhead and tufts of sand kicked up around us. Delfina and another Indian woman grabbed the Dowager by her shoulders and held her to face the trucks. In her white outfit, there was no doubt who she was, and hopefully her men wouldn't shoot back at us in fear of hitting her. Sure enough, their firing stopped. I glanced to the boat and estimated how much time we had bought ourselves. Maybe a couple of minutes.

The Dowager jerked free but held her place. The sea breeze caught her scarf and twirled it over her pith helmet. She nabbed the scarf, pulling and cinching it beneath her chin. Smoothing her tunic and adjusting her belt, she snapped closed the flap of her empty holster. She lifted her chin and smirked, as if acknowledging there was only one way out of this dilemma. *Her way.* I hated her arrogance and fought the urge to kick her in the ass.

The *chugga-chugga* of the boat was now loud enough to serve as a backbeat to the rhythmic smashing of the waves. The boat was a hundred feet from the beach. Standing at the prow, Malachi clung to a short mast for balance, his wrinkled face hyphenated by his thick mustache that draped over a cigar. Behind him, smoke belched from the boiler. I wondered who he had convinced—or commandeered—to crew the boat. Expecting a clutch of roughnecks spoiling for combat, my kundalini noir sparked with surprise when I recognized Gladys Vesna tending the boiler. She wore a green silk robe, her uniform as one of the Dowager's psychic messengers. Beside her, a bare-chested Sun

Zhipeng shoveled coal into the firebox, his skin and dress trousers smudged with black dust. At the stern, Louisa Davidson handled the tiller, her loose hair spilling over the shoulders of her disheveled servants outfit. All three wore pained expressions like they'd rather be somewhere else, just like the rest of us.

Malachi's frock coat was folded over the ivory grips of his Schofield revolvers. His gaze lifted from me to the trucks then down to the water. He raised his hand and dropped it suddenly. Gladys yanked a lever and the paddle wheels quit spinning. The boat cleaved through the surf and lurched hard into the sand, halting thirty feet from the water's edge. In ones and twos, the Indian women splashed into the hip-deep water, fighting waves that drenched them. Close to the boat, they tossed their guns aboard and leapt for the gunnels. Malachi and crew grabbed outstretched hands and hauled wet bodies into the boat.

I pushed the Dowager toward Hermosa. "Let's trade." Hermosa handed me the Winchester. Shouldering the rifle as I backed into the water, I took well-aimed shots at the men advancing from the trucks.

Waves crashed over the tops of my boots, soaking my feet. I kept shooting and backing up. The cool water slapped the backs of my legs, rising higher until it curled around my waist. Glancing to the boat I saw Hermosa lifting the Dowager in a bear hug while Malachi and Gladys yanked her by the arms. Bullets cracked past my ears and forced my attention back to the Dowager's men.

Second by second, the situation was getting more desperate. My thoughts started to stutter, like my mind was getting unstuck. I lost my footing and stumbled into the surf. Using the rifle as a crutch I regained my balance and spat out briny water and blinked to clear my eyes.

Curtains of smoke clouded the sky. I blinked and the sky was blue again. Then another blink and the smoke was back, thick and so foul it stung my nose. I turned my head to figure out what was going on. Malachi's boat was gone, replaced by an armored landing barge. Bullets pinged off its iron plates. A Gatling gun in a small turret rattled smoky bursts toward the beach.

I was back at the ill-fated assault on the island.

My kundalini noir quivered in shock. I shrank in horror, the sensation was like buzz saws were whipping past me. Around my boots, the water churned red with blood.

Men—soldiers of my unit—hobbled past me, their screams of pain and defiance smothered by the thunder of artillery. Each scorching blast sucked the air out of my lungs. I grabbed men by their tattered uniforms and screamed at them, but my words were lost in the hornet-like whine of ricocheting bullets and the rumbling earthquake of exploding howitzer shells.

I was thrown against the front of the barge and it rose to smash me against the beach. I dug my boots into the sand and pushed against its iron hull. Waves doused me and I sputtered to catch my breath.

Then blue sky and clear water. I was pushing against the front of the launch. Malachi and the Indian women heaved against oars stabbed into the water. Delfina toppled as a bullet found its mark. The steam engine hammered at full speed, driving the side paddles that arced water from both sides of the boat. But we weren't going anywhere—the boat was firmly stuck in the sand.

Bullets nipped the wooden hull. The sand beneath my boots gave way and the boat lunged into me. I fell and jumped back up, water cascading over the soggy brim of my hat and down my face. When I blinked, I was in the battle. Back and forth I went between these two realities like the opposing universes had their hooks in me and were going to tear me in half.

More waves slapped into the boat and it pitched on top of me, forcing me underwater. The keel ground me into the sand, and I was trapped in a terrifying swirl of bubbles. Water flooded my lungs and had I been human I would've drowned. Flailing wildly, I wrestled free and struggled to my feet. I threw the rifle into the boat, hooked my hands over the gunnel, and hung on as

I vomited water. Bullets chopped at the hull, inches from my arms.

Another wave lifted the boat and flung us farther up the beach. Against the power of the surf I was nothing but a ragdoll. My legs dragged under the bow and I tapped my last reserves of vampire strength to keep from getting fed under the keel and crushed.

Every time doom was certain, the waves would relent, and I'd get another moment of respite, just enough to make me think I was going to survive. Then up we'd g, then down and I'd get dunked again, each cycle wearing me out as all I could do was clutch at the narrowing rim of hope.

My undead soul cried out for what God would never give me. "Mercy," I shouted. "Mercy."

CHAPTER THIRTY-NINE

My legs thrashed through the water as I held tight onto the boat. At any second I expected a hail of bullets to stitch me across the back. Then a strange noise cut through the din. A chorus of trumpeting.

I turned my head to see. Mammoths had charged over the dunes to rampage through the Dowager's force. The huge beasts slammed into their trucks, smashing and rolling them over. Men spilled to the ground and scattered in terror. But the mammoths didn't bother to chase the men. Instead the beasts trampled across the beach toward our boat, and my panic shot into the red zone.

Malachi seized my wrists and hauled me into the boat, where I plopped into the water sloshing across the bottom of our hull. The Indian women screamed in horror. I sat up and recognized the big female with the tattoo Σ 25 bearing down on our boat. Her two enormous tusks came spearing right for us as she stomped through the surf.

The boat lurched, and Malachi toppled over me. I expected the mammoth to overturn our boat and use her trunk to grab and smash us.

Instead Σ 25 pushed her forehead against the boat, keeping it level between her tusks as she bulldozed us off the beach.

Our paddle wheels bit the water and propelled us backwards, pulling the boat clear. Σ 25 continued to follow us, advancing into our wake. To our left and right, the rest of the herd—about thirty adults and young—also waded into the surf. Splashing into deeper waters, they submerged until only their eyes and tops of their heads remained above the surface. They swam with their trunks poking out of the water like snorkels.

"Swing around," Malachi shouted to Louisa. She levered the tiller, and the boat banked in a half-circle so tight that everyone clung to the gunnels to keep from getting pitched over. As the bow traversed from the island to the open waters and then straightened toward the smudge of buildings in the haze across the gulf, we all breathed in relief. I took a brief moment to acknowledge that I'd escaped death once again, and if all went well, that I was leaving the accursed *Isla Tiburón*. Hopefully forever.

But when Gladys glanced away from the steam engine's gauges, her glare was hotter than the boiler, as if blaming me for her troubles.

I studied her, Sun, and Louisa hard at work at getting us out of here. Knowing these three, they should've been sailing in the opposite direction of Shark Island and not bothered risking a hair to save anyone else.

For her part, the Dowager was looking back at the island, and from the firm set of her jaw I could tell she was already scheming to get back on her throne.

We were making slow but steady headway. The mammoths trailed in our wake, appearing like a group of stumps slopped over by waves. Occasionally, water spurted upward from their trunks. On the beach, the Dowager's men assembled around their wrecked trucks and lobbed bullets in our direction but we were out of accurate range. Smoke from the southern side of the island stained the sky.

I wanted to ask Malachi how he lucked into this boat and managed to lasso Gladys and her friends into helping him. But we weren't yet out of trouble.

Delfina lay on top of a canvas tarp draped over a platform in front of the boiler. Hermosa and the other women were crowded around her. I levered to my feet and splashed through the ankle deep water.

She rested like a corpse, legs straight, arms at her sides. Blood seeped through the pink stain of her water-soaked tunic. I waved a hand over her glassy eyes and noticed no reaction.

"She's gone," Hermosa said. "And we've still got troubles." She splashed her boot in the water. Seconds ago it had been ankle deep, now it was to her shin.

I saw the problem. The boat rode too low as it slogged through the chop. Every wave brought a fresh dousing of water. The sixteen of us seemed like the right cargo for the boat but for some reason we were overloaded.

Hermosa and two of the Indian women used buckets to bail the water. The others bailed with their cupped hands, the Dowager with her pith helmet. But minute by minute we were taking in more water than we were getting rid of.

"We got company," Louisa announced.

I straightened and panned the horizon, looking for boats.

"In the water," she shouted.

Large fins sliced through the water. The mammoths bellowed out their trunks. As big as they were, they were nothing but oversized lunch for the sharks. A hammerhead cruised beside our boat. When water sluiced over the gunnel, the shark seemed eager to slide into the boat and begin feasting. More and more fins sliced through the water around us.

Isla Tiburón wasn't done with us yet.

Hermosa and the Indian women argued about our situation. I didn't understand what they were saying, but when they pointed to their dead comrade, I understood their decision.

Hermosa grabbed Delfina's ankles. Someone else took her

arms and they heaved her over the side behind the starboard paddle wheel. Delfina floated just beneath the surface, her tattered and bloody tunic feathering around her. A small shark nipped her side then darted away. Another shark bit her, then another, each successive shark chomping harder, shaking her carcass like a dog until the water was clouded with blood.

We kept chugging away. Pink froth marked her position in the water, with fins and tails beating the surface as the sharks battled for their portion of human flesh.

I expected the Indian women to break out in a dirge but in typical native matter-of-factness, they returned to bailing out the boat. But it seemed futile. In a few moments, we would be swamped and in the water, tempting the sharks.

"We have to lighten the boat." My attention settled on the tarp stained with blood. "What's under this?"

Gladys hopped up from beside the boiler. "Leave that be."

I whisked the tarp aside. Beneath lay three iron strong boxes, each about two-foot square.

"Those belong to me," the Dowager exclaimed and tried to pull me aside.

The containers looked identical to the strong boxes I'd seen the first night Hermosa and I been on the island. Gladys and her gang must've stolen them during the confusion when the fire raged on the island.

I pointed to the boxes and asked Malachi, "You knew about these?"

"Wish I had. I would've left them behind." He lifted his boot out of the deepening water. "Seems we got no choice but to toss them overboard."

Gladys and the Dowager lunged for the boxes. "No!"

Malachi said. "Give me a hand." He grasped one handle on a box, and I grasped the opposite. We lifted. The heft strained my arm and I had to call upon vampire strength.

"Damn heavy," he huffed, face reddening.

The box must've held a king's ransom in gold. But no matter.

Malachi and I shuffled to one side of the boat while everyone else shifted to counterbalance the weight.

The strongbox was too heavy to swing and toss so we rested it on the gunnel behind the paddlewheel and slid it over the side. The box sank without a splash, simply disappearing into the foam and murk.

As the boat rocked steady, Malachi looked over the side. "That bought us some appreciable freeboard. The next two should fix us up."

After we had dumped the last box, I noticed that Sun and Louisa wiped away tears. A fortune that would've set them up for life was fathoms below us in the mud.

Gladys mouthed something, and I piqued my ears to sift her words from the background *chugga-chugga* of the steam engine. She said, "Each box held two hundred pounds. Thirty-two hundred ounces. Times three. Ninety-six hundred ounces of gold bullion."

The Dowager spun her head toward prominent landmarks, no doubt fixing landmarks and triangulating our location for a return to salvage her treasure.

With the boat riding safely over the waves, we could've pressed forward at speed but we hung back to remain with the mammoths. If the sharks returned, we'd do what we could to protect these proud beasts.

The mainland slowly materialized from the haze. First the green hills behind the beach, then the roofs of the settlement, and then sandy dunes flattening toward the water. The rumble of the surf grew louder. The fishing village of Arenas wasn't more than a collection of adobe huts and wooden shacks. People congregated on the beach.

Since we weren't sure about the intentions of our welcoming committee, we divvied up what ammo we had so that everyone with a gun could shoot if we had to.

Hermosa took the tiller from Louisa and guided our boat directly to the beach. A wave lifted and carried us forward. We smacked firmly on the beach and our paddlewheels chopped into the wet sand, making our boat stutter forward. When several of the paddles broke loose, Gladys cut the power. Malachi and I were the first to jump off, and the Indian women followed. We advanced from the boat, guns drawn.

CHAPTER FORTY

The villagers drew away from us, and I waved a hand to signal we meant no harm. Then I realized what frightened them.

From behind me, the mammoths emerged from the surf, water cascading off their immense bodies. Σ 25 walked a few paces from the shore and turned around, jabbing with her trunk as if counting. A smaller mammoth rubbed against her. The rest of the mammoths walked up the beach and stood still, their gigantic torsos bellowing deep breaths out their trunks. They all seemed as relieved to have survived the ordeal as did the rest of us.

Σ 25 and some of the larger mammoths wandered into the village. The people shied back, terrified at these monsters.

"What do we do?" A worried Malachi tensed his grip on his revolver.

"Let's see what they're up to," I replied.

Σ 25 poked her head under an awning made of woven palm fronds to explore the contents of several wooden barrels. When she used her trunk to siphon from the barrels I realized she'd found the village's cache of fresh water. The other mammoths joined her and in the process tore the awning apart and drank the barrels empty. They discovered a cart heaped with cantaloupes and gourds and wrecked it, scattering the fruit over the ground for the herd to enjoy.

All we could do was watch. When they seemed satisfied, Σ 25 trumpeted and started up a trail into the hills, the others filing behind her. Within a couple of minutes they vanished into the thicket, leaving behind great puddles of mammoth piss and enormous piles of poop.

"Smells like a circus," Malachi quipped.

The Indian women gathered driftwood and built a fire. They stripped out of their wet clothes and unabashedly naked, stood close to the flames to warm themselves as did Gladys, Louisa, and Sun. Hermosa only removed her coat, vest, socks and boots. She wrung her skirt and propped her boots and socks on sticks to dry them by the fire.

I regarded my soaked boots and decided that my feet would stay wet for now.

An older woman stepped close to us. Since she was the only one with a shawl draped over her shoulders I gathered she was the village elder. Though at first she acted scared of us, after the arrival of the mammoths, we seemed the lesser threat.

"We would like some drinking water," I said in Spanish. "If you have any left. And some food."

Malachi dug coins from his vest pocket, which he offered to the elder. "For your troubles." He winged a thumb at the boat. "Consider that yours."

The old woman took the coins and gave instructions to her companions. Soon, we were ladling drinks from clay water jugs, munching on tortillas, and roasting filleted fish. Hermosa bought some rags and borrowed a small can of oil so we could wipe our guns dry and lubricate them.

"I'm your prisoner," the Dowager asked, "now what?"

Hermosa answered, "You're going to tell me what happened to Ling Zhu Han."

Something about the Dowager seemed to shift. She was definitely still the same person, but there was something different about her, like she had instantly molted out of her skin. This new version of the Dowager appeared more vulnerable, more invested in her surroundings.

"Is your question concerning what that," she gestured to the distant smoke over *Isla Tiburón*, "was all about?"

Hermosa and I traded looks. I wanted to reply, *yes*, but knew that I was missing something.

"Tell me what you know," Hermosa said to the Dowager, "and then I'll answer your question."

"This is about Wu Fei, isn't it?" A tiny quiver floated through the Dowager's voice.

At the mention of the Dragon's name, my kundalini noir zinged with confusion and alarm. "What's he got to do with this?"

The Dowager gulped to regain her composure. Her fingers trembled and she stilled them by making fists.

"I asked you about Ling Zhu Han," Hermosa insisted.

The Dowager eased onto a log someone had dragged for the fire. She sat low, almost squatting, and with her rumpled and damp outfit draped around her weary frame, it was as if she was melting.

"My spies in Guaymas captured her," she said. "After she left my island but before she had a chance to share her story with the world. It was during my ... questioning that she revealed who she was—Wu Fei's daughter. I also learned it was Gah who had helped her escape, which is why when I captured you all, I had the Indian girl killed." The Dowager drew deep, troubled breaths. "Wu Fei had been keeping tabs on what I was doing and soon after I had Ling Zhu Han, my spies relayed a message from him that I was to take her to Los Piojos." The Dowager went quiet and stared past us with a blank expression.

Hermosa glanced at me. "Have you heard of Los Piojos?"

I shook my head.

"It's a tiny village," the Dowager gestured to the north, "that way a day's travels."

"And then?" Hermosa prompted.

"I took her there personally and handed her over to Wu Fei's henchmen. There were two of them. Then I returned to my island."

The Dowager's account tied my thoughts in knots. Wu Fei had hired me to find his daughter, but he'd mentioned nothing about this.

The Dowager asked, "Ling Zhu Han is why you came to *Isla Tiburón?*"

Hermosa, as dumbfounded as I was, could only nod.

"Then Wu Fei used you," the Dowager said, warming for a moment before growing cold again. "He and I were partners once. He financed my purchase of the island and the initial construction. But he insisted on running the show and I wasn't about to let go of the reins. I offered to buy him out but he refused. Those trunks of gold you threw into the water? I sent him two such boxes, full of gold. And still he refused, though he kept the money."

She stared at her fingers as she wrung her hands. "By then my dream was starting to flourish. I had power. When Wu Fei sent his emissaries demanding that I acquiesce, I returned them in pieces. I felt I was invincible." She relaxed her hands and lifted her eyes to Hermosa, then to Malachi, and fixed them on me. "Then you came, and it was my woe that I didn't recognize you for what you were."

The idea took a moment to sink in. "Are you saying that our search for Ling Zhu Han was simply a ruse for us to take you down?"

The Dowager shot upright. "That is it exactly, Monsieur Étalon or Felix Gomez or whatever your name is. You three are stooges of Wu Fei. You did his bidding. He promised revenge against me and you were it."

Malachi cleared his throat. "Well, considering we didn't know what we were doing, we did a rather decent job."

None of us said anything else, and I became aware of the surf, churning, churning, indifferent to our concerns. The Dowager sat back on the log. Hermosa remained standing, blinking.

Malachi and I left them to wander through the village and let our minds pick at this revelation. Wu Fei had orchestrated his revenge on the Dowager with artful finesse. He had manipulated Hermosa, Malachi, and myself like we were puppets. Every seemingly random development was just another step in Wu Fei's master plan.

What if Malachi hadn't arrived in time to rescue the others and me? "How did you get the boat? And get Gladys and her two thieves to crew it?"

He drew a leather cigar case from inside his coat and selected a stogie. He offered me one, and I shook my head.

"You have your key?" He reached into his shirt and showed me his FORTIS key.

I tapped my shirt to indicate I still had mine. "At least we have something to show for our efforts."

Malachi grunted in approval. As he lit the cigar and puffed at it, he said, "To answer your question as to how I met up with Gladys and her scalawags, last night, when the fire started on the island and I hadn't heard from you, then I knew tribulations had torn our original plans asunder. I sped to the pier looking for a boat and crew that I could convince," he slapped one of his holsters, "to aid in my endeavor to rescue you. Then, Providence smiled upon me when I ran into Sun as he was stealing a horse and wagon and heading to a spot on the beach by the pier. I watched him signal a boat and behold, Gladys showed up." Malachi's broad smiled appeared beneath his mustache.

"And the strongboxes?"

"Wish I would've known about them. That way some of

those gold coins would be in my pocket instead of at the bottom of the sea." He shrugged. "*Que sera, sera.*"

His words startled me. The past from my other life jolted through my mind, and I could hear Doris Day singing the lyrics. "You know the song?"

"What are you talking about?"

"Those words."

"Yeah? So? It's Mexican. Thought you would've heard them before."

"I have. It's that ..."

Malachi squinted, the cigar in his mouth pointing like a smoking gun. "I'm listening."

"Forget it."

He chewed on the stogie for a moment. "Then why are you talking like a mad fool?" He spit a bit of tobacco. "Honestly, ever since we left St. Charles, you've been acting like your brain's been twisted sideways. And let me tell you, our predicament is twisted enough as it is."

Seeing no point in arguing, I started up a tall sand dune. From the top, I spied a primitive road that ran south from the village parallel to the shoreline. In the distance rose a smudge of dust and smoke that told me to expect company. My kundalini noir twitched in the concern this might be yet another unfortunate twist in our adventure. "We got visitors," I shouted to Malachi.

He ran up the dune to join me. We squinted at the source of the dust and smoke until we recognized a steam car rumbling toward us.

"Any idea who?" Malachi asked.

I looked around to make sure the car was the only thing approaching. "It's coming from the direction of Guaymas. Who knows?"

We kept the car under surveillance until it was almost at the village. Sunlight glinted off the windshield as the *whompa-whompa* of the steam engine grew louder. The car was an open sedan, painted bright yellow. I doubted it was a taxi. Besides the driver, the car carried three passengers, but at this distance I couldn't tell much about them. "You go alert Hermosa and the others," I said. "I'll circle behind them."

Malachi hustled away and I stepped from the dune, moving to keep the car in sight as I skirted around the huts. The car veered across the flat sand to where everyone was gathered.

As the car slowed, the two passengers in the rear seat stood. The occupants—except for the front passenger—wore military-style hats and khaki uniforms crisscrossed with leather bandoliers. The front passenger was short, with a scarf cinching a hat. Large goggle-like sunglasses obscured her features, but I saw enough to recognize who it was. Alicia Zorro, the Guaymas Harbormaster.

When the car halted, the two in the back hopped out, rifles at the ready. Alicia Zorro opened her door and swung her legs out, the toes of her tiny boots reaching from under her pleated skirt. She slid to the ground and stood, all four-foot plus whatever inches. She peeled off her leather gloves, folded them into her waist belt, and loosened her scarf. Her driver climbed from the car and stood beside her. A large revolver filled his holster.

The Dowager remained steady. Hermosa stood beside her, holding the Winchester loosely in both hands. Malachi waited, watching and smoking his cigar. The Indian women didn't budge, only showing mild concern in this matter between Zorro and the Dowager.

Revolver in hand, I crept along the wall of a hut behind Alicia, keeping in the shadows until I could overhear their conversation.

"Engels is coming with me," she said in a voice remarkably hard and commanding.

"She and I still have business," Hermosa replied.

"You can petition the court for an audience with her."

Hermosa tipped her head toward the Dowager. "After I'm done with her, I'll personally deliver her to your doorstep."

"She's worth six thousand dollars."

"Like I said," Hermosa rejoined, "when I'm done with her, you can have her and keep the reward."

One of the Indian women murmured. Hermosa added, "Or give it to them."

"The Dowager is not up for negotiation. She must answer for her crimes." Alicia nodded to her guards. They clicked back their rifle hammers.

I stepped into the open, revolver up, my thumb poised over the hammer. Hermosa and the Dowager's eyes cut toward me. Alicia's guards caught the movement and when they started to turn around, I warned, "No sudden moves. These negotiations are over. We're keeping the Dowager."

Alicia slowly rotated to face me. Removing her sunglasses, she glared, saying, "Felix, after all that I did for you, I'm surprised by this show of ingratitude. Without my help, you and your friends would've been dead and buried days ago."

"My thank-you card is in the mail. For now, tell your guards to hand over their guns."

"Please reconsider what you're doing. If you don't cooperate with me, the law will come down hard on all of you."

Ignoring the threat, Malachi approached the guards and collected their guns and bandoliers. Hermosa extended her hand toward Alicia, who huffed indignantly before reaching into her cloak and withdrawing a derringer. Hermosa palmed the tiny pistol and shoved it into a vest pocket.

Hermosa examined the car, smiled appreciatively, and nudged the Dowager with the butt of the Winchester. "Get in."

"You'll regret this," Alicia said.

"Our regrets about this started a long time before we arrived in Guaymas"

Malachi piled the extra guns in the car and checked the coal box and boiler. "We got enough fuel and water." He slid into the driver's seat and adjusted the engine controls. Smoke puffing

from the stack belched and thickened. Hermosa prodded the
Dowager at gunpoint into the backseat.

"Gladys," Hermosa ordered, "come with us."

"Why?" I asked. Gladys appeared as surprised as I was by the
demand.

"We might need your services along the way," Hermosa
explained.

"But my companions," Gladys gestured to Sun and Louisa, "I
can't leave them."

"They can take care of themselves. If all goes well, you'll see
them again in Tucson."

"You won't get far," Alicia said.

"We'll get far enough." I climbed into the front passenger's
seat. "And when we're done with the Dowager, I'll make sure you
get her."

CHAPTER FORTY-ONE

Malachi drove up a wagon trail that led north from the village. We meandered through sandy patches and around rocky outcroppings topped with weeds and saguaro cacti. Rocks pinged against our undercarriage. While Malachi focused on keeping us on the trail and not dropping us into a pothole, I kept watch for anything suspicious.

Hands bound with rope, the Dowager sat between Hermosa and Gladys. For her part, the Dowager remained remarkably stoic. When we hit a smooth length of trail, she said, "What would it take for you to set me free?"

"Depends," Hermosa answered, "on what happened to Ling Zhu Han."

The Dowager's face creased with apprehension. "Like I told you before, when I found out she was Wu Fei's daughter, I personally took her to Los Piojos," The Dowager's voice cracked a bit. "She was alive when I left her."

"We'll see what we learn," Hermosa replied.

The trail wound up the hills, cresting over hills, dipping through sandy troughs beneath canopies of juniper, willow, and oak, skirting along rocky patches of cacti. Occasionally, we lumbered past the remains of abandoned wagons, leather harnesses, the scattered bones of horses and oxen, and crude crucifixes hammered into the dirt. We stopped twice to help ourselves to the water and rations in the provisions box at the rear of the car. As the sun eased below the hills, the shadows deepened and the air cooled. The trees gave way to clumps of shrub and the trail breached onto a plateau, its colors muted beneath a darkening sky. From this point, the trail traced straight across the flat high ground toward lights at the distant horizon. A rising crescent moon lit up the trail and extended the range of my vampire night vision.

A soft trumpeting rose about the rhythmic clatter of the steam engine, and the noise made my kundalini noir tremble.

"You hear that?" Malachi asked.

I was already looking for the mammoths. "I heard it but I'm not seeing any."

"Besides the mammoths and the saber-tooth tigers," Hermosa asked, "are there any other monsters you resurrected?"

The Dowager shrugged. "Does it matter? You destroyed my laboratories. All my research is gone."

Hermosa tapped her temple. "But what's up here hasn't been lost. Whatever you've done, you can do again."

"Assuming I live."

Another trumpeting echoed toward us but I couldn't tell if it was one mammoth or several. I wondered if it was Σ 25 and her herd or other mammoths that had previously escaped. I studied the brush and saguaro cacti spreading out across the flat expanse around us but saw nothing unusual. Still, I had to ponder what changes the Dowager had brought upon the world. With these prehistoric creatures it's as if she's folded time back upon itself, and that brought what unintended consequences?

Relentlessly we puttered toward Los Piojos. In the distance, a flickering light marked our destination. Rabbits and quail sprang from the weeds and darted in front of us. Sparks from our stack floated upward on our smoke and blended with the stars. About a mile from the village I spied that some of the saguaro appeared to move, and on second glance realized they weren't cacti but people watching us.

I tapped Malachi on the shoulder. "We're not alone."

He kept his eyes forward. "Keep me posted."

The closer we approached the village, the closer these sentinels stood to the road. Dogs ran out of the darkness to growl and bark at our car. A wall of cholla and tall misshapen prickly pear encircled the small collection of huts. A clutch of locals stood beside an open gate crudely fashioned from wooden boards. Behind them, a fire burned in the middle of the village, and the flames outlined their silhouettes. To our rear, more of the locals walked out of the wilderness and onto the road, their faces glowing orange from the fire. Other than primitive spears, none of them seemed to carry any other type of weapon. Because of the children among them I didn't get a sense of menace, instead I gathered that nothing much happens here so our arrival must've broken the monotony.

Malachi halted the car, and I hopped out. The locals wore mostly loose tunics over baggy trousers, gathered about the waist with sashes. Some wore straw hats or headbands, boots, others sandals, the children were barefoot.

An older, wizened man in a serape and tattered straw hat advanced from the group. I expected him to greet us, but he kept quiet.

In Spanish, I introduced myself and each of us in the car. When I mentioned the Dowager by her complete name, I expected the old man to acknowledge that he had heard of her, but he remained silent, his big rheumy eyes catching random slivers of light.

"Your name, sir?" I asked.

"Gonzales."

"You have a first name?"

"When you come to Los Piojos and ask for Gonzales, I'm the only one you'll find."

Fair enough.

"Which way are you going?" He stabbed a gnarled finger toward the north. "That way leads to Santa Ana and Nogales." He pointed to the east. "That way leads to Tepache and El Paso del Norte." He folded his arm back under his serape. An elderly woman beside him leaned close to his ear and whispered. He nodded but didn't share his thoughts.

"We're looking for a young woman." I reached into my coat, withdrew the small envelope, and handed him the tintype. "Her name is Ling Zhu Han."

From inside his serape he pulled out spectacles that he set on his big nose. He grasped the photo and lifted it so the firelight spilling over his shoulder illuminated the picture. Without comment, he passed it to the others who showed more interest than he did.

In English, Malachi said, "We need to get these proceedings moving. Tell him we'll pay for information."

Gonzales snapped his fingers to fetch the tintype and return it to me. "And how much will you pay to get these proceedings moving?" he asked in English.

I fished a silver half dollar from my vest pocket. "Have you seen Ling Zhu Han?"

He reached for the coin when I clenched it in my fist. "Tell us everything you know about her."

"Such information will cost you more than half a dollar."

"How much?"

"For five gold dollars I can show you where she's buried."

Buried? I traded shocked looks with Malachi and Hermosa. But after a moment, the realization that we had at last found her was tempered by the memory of all the wild goose chases we'd gone on since leaving St. Charles. If this was true, Ling Zhu Han certainly deserved a better end than being dropped into a hole in the middle of nowhere.

I kept tossing the details in my mind. I strung together the few facts with one conjecture after another. Ling had traveled to

Isla Tiburón to investigate the rumors of sexual slavery. Then she escaped the island, only to be captured by the Dowager and brought to this flea speck. And after all that, to be done in by Wu Fei's thugs.

Malachi flipped a large golden coin at Gonzales. "If it's not Ling, we want our money back."

The old woman beside Gonzales snatched it midair. She gave the coin a quick examination and then nudged Gonzales, who said, "She was killed."

"By whom?"

"Por dos chinos matónes."

"When?"

"The same night she arrived."

Hermosa poked the Dowager in the ribs with the rifle's muzzle. "You didn't tell us this."

The Dowager's knees weakened and she grabbed her side. "Ling Zhu Han was alive when I handed her to Wu Fei's men."

"And then?" Hermosa punctuated the question with another jab with the rifle.

The Dowager stumbled. "And I left that same night."

I turned to Gonzales. "Is this correct?"

"That is what happened. She gave the girl to the two Chinese men."

"How did you know they were Chinese?"

"By the same way I know that you and you," he gestured at Malachi and me, "are *Americanos* from north of the border. *Yanquis.*"

"Why was she killed?"

"That was none of my business."

"How was she killed?"

"She was shot."

"You saw it?"

Gonzales shook his head. "All of us kept away. But we heard it. *Un disparo.*"

"And then?"

"They told us to bury her."

"Where?"

Gonzales stepped toward my left. Hermosa pulled the Dowager by the arm and joined Malachi, Gladys, and me trailing behind him. Everyone else mobbed around us. The old woman shouted and several teenage boys ran off to return with burning torches. We followed a footpath between raised beds of maize and peppers.

We reached a shallow rise about fifty yards past the village, the high ground topped with small wooden grave markers. Gonzales barked some orders and the teenagers with the torches ran ahead to a grave, to illuminate its marker. Chinese characters had been painted on the wood. Though I couldn't read them, I knew they spelled out Ling Zhu Han.

Gonzales called out more instructions, and three of his men stepped forward with shovels and began digging at the grave.

Seems like Ling Zhu Han and we had gone on a wide circle. At the end of her journey she'd been handed over to her fellow countrymen, but instead of protecting her, they had murdered her. Why?

A shovel thumping on wood pierced my thoughts. One of the diggers said, "Here it is."

Gonzales, Malachi, and I inched close to the edge of the grave. The torchbearers leaned over the diggers to shine light into the hole.

The diggers scraped dirt off a long wooden box. When they exposed the sides, they heaved and lifted the crudely made casket. Malachi and I helped slide it onto the ground. The diggers climbed out of the hole and used their shovels to pry open the casket. The others hovered close, their expressions vacillating between curiosity and horror.

The groan of nails accompanied the casket lid pulling loose. The rancid odor of rotten meat puffed out. A shroud of rough cloth was tucked around the form of a woman around Ling's size. Worms dangled from holes in the tattered cloth. A black blotch

—from blood I was certain—marked the center of her chest where she'd been shot. The sides of the shroud were stained with grease from the body tissue dissolving.

"Who wrapped her?"

"The Chinese men did. And they brought the casket. But we buried her."

More details. More questions. And less that made sense.

I crouched beside the casket and tugged at the shroud but it seemed to have been sewn shut. Malachi used a pocketknife to slice open a seam.

I pulled the shroud apart. Light flicked over a face, turned black with putrefaction. Sagging flesh had pulled the skin tight around the nose, mouth, and cheekbones. But was this the body of Ling Zhu Han?

Ripping the seam even more, I exposed the top of a blouse and corset.

"Look for her ring," Hermosa said.

I felt along the shroud to find her right arm. Her hands rested together over the center of her belly. I lifted her right hand so that the silver and turquoise ring on her fourth finger caught the light. Finding the ring didn't confirm that this was Ling Zhu Han, but what fell from under her hand did.

A large coin plopped against her belly. However, it wasn't a coin but a medallion ... emblazoned with a Chinese dragon of green enamel inside a ring of fire. The symbol of Wu Fei. I am a vampire, yet the sheer depravity of what the coin meant sickened me.

"What is it?" Malachi asked.

I handed him the coin and wrestled against a storm of disgust and rage. My fangs started to extend and I clenched my jaw to keep them from showing as I struggled to keep from lashing out.

"Why kill her?" Malachi asked.

"So we'd look for her. Alive, she could unmask Wu Fei's scheme. Dead, she was a willing accomplice. He had his men leave that medallion to show us that everything about this monstrous caper was his idea."

We stood in silent contemplation for several long minutes, each of us grasping with this horrific insight into our employer, Wu Fei.

How could anyone be capable of such an infernal crime? As Wu Fei schemed to settle the score with the Dowager Engels, he shifted through every relationship and opportunity to use as a weapon. Nothing was off limits.

His one good deed in life was that he had fathered a decent girl, Ling Zhu Han, but he couldn't leave her alone. When he learned about her noble quest to save women from prostitution, he had her kidnapped—hiding his hand as he did so—and set her on a new course toward the Dowager Engels and the Indian girls kept prisoner. And to keep his secrets until he was ready to reveal them, Wu Fei had Ling murdered. All the while he left a trail for Malachi, Hermosa, and me to follow like hounds ... which we did.

At last Hermosa said, "Box her up. We're taking her with us."

"What?" I asked.

"Our deal with Wu Fei was to find his daughter and bring her to him. Nothing was mentioned about the state of her health or lack of it. Am I right?"

I couldn't argue.

"Now that we've at last unraveled the truth, there's one more thread that needs attending." Hermosa cranked the hammer of her Winchester and aimed it at the Dowager.

Hands raised and her voice breaking with disbelief, the Dowager retreated. "But I've come through. I brought you to her." She pointed to the corpse. "You realized that it wasn't me who killed her."

Hermosa kept her eyes fixed on the Dowager. "Don't forget the Indian women, the sex slaves, all those that you degraded and murdered. That was your doing, not Wu Fei's. I promised them that you'd pay."

She squeezed the trigger and a yellow blast tore through the night. That split second of light illuminated a wall of faces recoiling in shock. The sulfurous stench of burnt black powder stung our noses. The Dowager toppled backwards across Ling's now empty grave and fell to the bottom in a graceless tangle of arms and legs.

Hermosa kicked dirt over the corpse. "Dying among swine would've been more appropriate." She retrieved a small purse from her skirt pocket and tossed it to Gonzales. "There's three dollars and change. That plus what Felix and Malachi gave you should be enough to deliver the Dowager to the harbormaster in Guaymas. Might have to haggle for the reward considering the understanding was she had to stand trial. But I've seen corpses on the docket before so there's precedent."

"So we deliver Ling Zhu Han," I said. "Why would the Dragon honor his commitment to pay off the remainder of our bounty?"

"He'll pay, all right," Hermosa said. "Because we're going to deliver his precious daughter and a little something extra."

CHAPTER FORTY-TWO

Malachi backed a wagon against the door in Hop Alley off Larimer Street. With Hermosa at my side, I rapped my knuckles against the door and wasn't surprised when it opened right away. Wu Fei's spies knew we were coming.

Two of his burly, gigantic guards waited in the foyer. I pointed to the coffin in the wagon bed. In Tucson, we had transferred Ling Zhu Han's body into a newer coffin. Without saying a word, they stepped outside to retrieve the coffin. I proceeded to enter. Hermosa started to follow but one of the guards pushed her back.

"Malachi and I can manage," I assured her. Our plan to beat Wu Fei had been her idea, and now she might be the only survivor if things went south.

Malachi snuffed his cigar, climbed off the wagon, and joined me inside. Like my previous visit, the perfumed air couldn't completely mask the cadaver stink. Malachi gave the place a once over—the Oriental rugs, the delicate lacquered furniture inlaid with mother-of-pearl, the wall tapestries, the stairway balustrades carved to resemble carp, cranes, tigers, and dragons. Gas lamps hissed inside crystal sconces.

I contemplated the steps leading to the second floor and Wu Fei's office. My kundalini noir beat an alarm against my ears. The bodyguards shuffled into the foyer, the coffin carried between them.

Malachi cleared his throat, indicating that we better get a move on. We started up the stairs. The sensation was like we were headed to the gallows. On the landing I scoped out the familiar double doors and proceeded toward them. They opened abruptly. On the other side, his two nubile servant girls greeted us with polite bows. Not surprisingly, just as during my last visit they were barefoot and clad in abbreviated silk robes.

Wu Fei—that epic Mandarin reptile—watched from where he sat behind his immense desk. A brass plate covered the port in his desk, where I'd previously seen one of his victims stick his head through. Wu Fei's beady eyes were grotesquely distorted by his spectacles so I felt like a bug being scrutinized under a magnifying glass. Beside him sat Miss O'Laughlin in the azure tunic of a telepath. Her expression was brittle with dread. Living with Wu Fei must be like sleeping with a viper; it's in his nature to eventually kill you.

The bodyguards entered the office, their boots scuffing the carpet as they angled the coffin through the open doors. Malachi and I stepped out of the way to let them enter. The servant girls set up wooden stands close to the desk for the coffin. While they closed the doors, the bodyguards rested the coffin on the stands and backed away, each of them readjusting the large holsters resting on their hips.

Wu Fei stood and walked around the desk to approach the coffin at the side opposite me. A simple olive-green outfit clad his slender figure. Once at the coffin, his head swiveled back-and-forth to examine the polished lid before he asked in a high-pitched voice, "How do you know this is my daughter?"

I gave him her ring.

After a perfunctory glace, he placed it on the desk. "Show me Ling Zhu Han."

"First," I replied, "what you owe us. Ten thousand dollars in gold."

"No, you show me the girl."

Malachi took a place at the foot of the coffin, I at the head. Together we unfastened the latches, then lifted and removed the lid, which we propped against the stands. Ling Zhu Han's corpse was tucked inside a woolen blanket. A medicinal lavender fragrance masked her death smell. I could feel every gaze in the room reach toward her body.

I folded back the blanket where it covered Ling's head. Again, every eye focused on the face. If anything, she had decomposed even more since leaving Los Piojos. Out the corner of my eye, I noticed the bodyguards wince in disgust, while the servant girls tiptoed closer.

Wu Fei tilted his head and leaned over Ling's face like he was examining merchandise. Uncapping a fountain pen, he prodded her eyes and hairline with its golden nib. The spectacle lenses framed his pupils as they rolled up and down, left and right. He capped the pen and straightened. "This is Ling Zhu Han."

"About the money." I covered her and placed my left hand over the edge of the coffin to hook my finger into a wire loop tucked within the coffin's lining.

Wu Fei hadn't noticed what I'd done. Instead, a tiny smile creased his thin, bloodless lips, making him grimace as if this was an uncomfortable expression.

"We had a deal," I insisted. "One made in this very room. I find your daughter and bring her to you, in return for the remainder of the fifteen thousand dollars."

"She is dead. Why should I pay for a corpse?"

"You knew she was dead when you hired us because you killed her. All this," —Malachi waved his hands over the coffin— "was a display of wicked legerdemain to get Felix and me to exact your vengeance against the Dowager Engels."

"Your partner, Hermosa Singer," Wu Fei rejoined with an accusing tone. "Where is she?"

"Outside. Waiting for her share of the commission."

"She is waiting in vain." Wu Fei stared at me. "Why should I pay you? This deal is done. In fact, you and your friends know too much."

The bodyguards uncrossed their arms. Within the tight confines of this office, they could pounce on us before Malachi managed to draw his revolver. I had a fighting chance. The servant girls eased against a tapestry and slid their hands behind it. So it seemed that Wu Fei was about to add yet another double cross to his litany of treachery.

I lifted my left index finger to show the looped wire. "This is attached to a spring-loaded plunger poised above a cap of mercury fulminate. If I release the plunger it will detonate the cap and in turn ignite the thirty pounds of black powder that Ling Zhu Han is resting on. Plus we've laced the powder bags with arsenic."

Wu Fei squinted at the wire.

"This close to the explosion," I emphasized, "you won't survive."

His eyes lifted to mine. "And you, Mister Gomez? And your friend?"

Malachi rested his hand on my shoulder. "It's not us you should be worried about. Not that you were."

Wu Fei's smooth, hairless brow tightened. I could about hear the knives and razors in his mind clashing.

"You are bluffing."

Malachi slid his hand off my shoulder as he said, "Give us our due or get blown to bits."

Wu Fei's expression turned blank as stone. But the air in the room crackled with anxiety. O'Laughlin's eyes misted, and she pressed her fingers on the desk to keep them from trembling. The servant girls gazed at me as if I held their fates in my hand, which I did.

Then Wu Fei's thin lips curved upward. I expected a forked tongue to slither out. Then incredibly, he began to chuckle and it deepened into a laugh. His torso shook.

Still laughing, Wu Fei slid behind the desk and settled into his chair. Composing himself, he momentarily removed his glasses to wipe his eyes. "You have my praise, Mister Gomez. In the script I devised for this matter, I thought I had covered every possible contingency. But I failed to appreciate that men such as yourselves might prove even more devious than me. And here I am, threatened with annihilation," he pointed to the coffin, "by the instrument of my own making. Again, you have my praise."

He raised one arm, snapped his fingers, and gave an order in Chinese. The servant girls bowed and ducked behind the screen. A moment later, they emerged, shambling, and they hefted a strong box between them, which they rested with a heavy *thunk* on the desk.

I kept the wire taut. This could be yet another trick.

Wu Fei opened the strongbox and pulled out cloth sleeves that draped from his grip like thick sausages. He laid four of the sleeves on the desk and pushed them toward me. "The remainder of your commission, ten thousand dollars."

Malachi reached for a sleeve and loosened the knotted cord on one end. Out spilled several fifty-dollar gold coins that he collected in his hand.

"So we're square?" I asked, hopeful.

"Not quite," Wu Fei answered.

Malachi and I exchanged troubled looks. This bomb was all or nothing.

"Consider this a retainer," Wu Fei said, "for the next time, Mister Gomez."

CHAPTER FORTY-THREE

The flutter of window curtains awoke me. I was warm all over, inside and out. Just enough of last night's whiskey kept my thoughts loose. I kept my eyes closed to hold tight the traces of the fading euphoria.

After securing our reward, Malachi and I met up with Hermosa. We stashed the gold in our safety deposit box at the Confluence Territorial Bank and kept only enough money to pay for a good time. After making arrangements to meet at the Woodley Hotel for dinner, I searched for one of the painted ladies on Market Street to satisfy my undead appetite for blood.

After treating ourselves to a banquet, Malachi headed to his hotel room, with cigars, a bottle of ink, and a leather-bound journal on which to draft his memoirs. That left Hermosa and me alone. And despite remembering every bitter experience that Hermosa had caused me, and despite my promises that I wouldn't repeat them, Hermosa and I spent the night together.

This time it would be different. My loins stirred and I wanted a morning roll. Reaching for Hermosa's side of the bed, I felt nothing but the bed covers.

My kundalini noir flared with a damning realization, and I sat up, instantly awake, eyes wide open. Daylight filled the room.

Beyond the foot of the bed, my clothes and gun belt draped a valet stand. My hat hung from a peg by the door. But Hermosa's things were gone. Dress, cloak, hat, undergarments, boots ... all gone.

Not again, I cursed to myself, self-loathing keeping my mouth from forming coherent words. I slapped my chest and groaned as both the leather tie and the FORTIS safety deposit key were missing. I snatched my pocket watch off the night-stand. The time was 10:52.

Hurriedly I put my clothes on. After taking the key, Hermosa had but one destination.

Running outside, I headed along 20th Street directly to the bank. I darted between wagons jostling along. People criss-crossed the street or were strolling along the sidewalks. The placid morning routine mocked me, because it seemed like a hole had been cut into the surroundings and through it, Hermosa had vanished. Bursting through the bank's front door, I charged to the counter and pounded the bell.

A clerk jumped from beside the secretary desk. Pencil mustache twisted in annoyance, he sauntered behind the counter.

I blurted, "Was Hermosa Springer here?"

Another clerk rose from behind his desk. "Yes, she was here first thing in the morning. I allowed her into the vault."

"What did she take?" I yelled.

"Sir," the first clerk said, "please keep your voice down."

At the corner of the lobby, the guard thumbed the hammers of his shotgun as a warning.

I raised my hands to show they were empty. "My name is Felix Gomez. I'm a customer," I replied in a strained, controlled voice. "Just tell me what she took."

The two clerks looked at each other and shrugged. The

second one said, "That was none of my concern. However, I will say that she entered the vault with a large canvas tote."

Though I knew Hermosa was moves ahead of me I was still grasping with the implications of her betrayal. "Even if she had the key, she couldn't have access to the deposit box. To do so requires three signatures, hers, mine, and Malachi Hunter's."

"Oh no, sir," the clerk protested. "Only one signature was needed. Hers."

"Impossible. Show me see the signature form."

He pulled a folder from a file cabinet. Laying the folder on the counter, he opened it and with a triumphant flourish, pointed to the authorization signature on the form. It had only one name: Hermosa Singer.

But how could this be? When did this happen?

The form was dated three days ago. Where was Hermosa three days ago?

In Tucson, with me. We had just arrived from Los Piojos.

Hermosa couldn't have done this alone. I looked for the bank officer's name who completed the form.

Chester Dahlgreen, vice president. I visualized his over-fed, hamster face.

"Where is Dahlgreen?"

"Mr. Dahlgreen resigned the day before yesterday."

"Where did he go?"

"If he hasn't left town, he should be staying at ..." the clerk reached under the counter and thumbed through a box of file cards. "The Woodley Hotel. Room 112."

My kundalini noir slithered up my throat like it wanted to strangle me. Room 112 was the room Hermosa and I had shared.

The pieces to her treachery fell into place. After she learned about the commission Wu Fei offered, she had gone to the bank to cook up a scheme with Dahlgreen. He would forge a new authorization, which he would file upon her orders. When we arrived in Tucson, she had plenty of opportunity to either send a telegram ... or had used Gladys's services in exchange for a cut of our loot. That's why Hermosa insisted on Gladys accompanying us to Los Piojos.

Lusting for blood, my fangs wanted to snap out and taste fresh meat. I knew how to keep these looks under control, but my expression must have scared the clerk because he blanched like I was a wolf ready to bite him.

"P ... perhaps," he stammered, "you might be interested in this." He fumbled under the counter and placed an envelope labeled Malachi Hunter on the counter. "Miss Singer left this."

I snatched the envelope and ripped it open.

The clerk protested, "See here sir, that letter is not for you."

While he jabbered on I read a note in Hermosa's staccato writing:

Malachi,

I left your third of the bounty, minus our previous expenses, and upon your demand the bank will remit that sum in its entirety.

Simply,

Hermosa Singer

His third. How gracious of her. I knew she had absconded with my portion, but to make sure, I asked, "Did she leave anything else?"

"No sir."

I stumbled outside, the world around me a blur. When my head cleared up a bit, I was in the middle of street, being poked. An automatic steam buggy had stopped and its forward feelers prodded me, insistent like I was holding up progress. I stepped aside and let it pass. Soot spotted my coat like dandruff.

I returned to the hotel to freshen up and mull over what had happened. When I moved my toilet kit, I noticed a slip of paper tucked inside my shaving gear. It was a note from Hermosa and I opened it, wondering what other traps she laid before me.

Dearest Felix,

My regrets. I know it's my bad habit, but this time, this is the last time, I promise. It's that this money will give me the chance to set some other things right. Have you ever heard of Karma? It's an Oriental precept about how the universe will balance the bad and the good. In this case what I owe spiritually. So while I remain indebted to you, there is someone else who is in dire need of this money. So think of my taking of the gold as applying good Karma. From the both of us. Until next time.

Always,

Hermosa Singer

I folded the note and placed it on the dresser. *Until next time.* There won't be a next time. More than anything I wanted to go home. My home in whatever dimension I came from.

I set off for a market where I bought a bottle of rye and climbed the hill overlooking town. In the future—the future from my timeline anyways—where I stood would be called the Highlands, packed with medicinal shops, craft breweries, and hipsters. But at the present it was mostly weedy farm plots. I found a spot and took in the Platte River valley and Denver—rather St. Charles of the West Kansas Territories—spread out before me. I narrowed my eyes and could imagine high rises yet to be built.

"What's up, partner?" Malachi's voice interrupted my thoughts.

I turned to see him approaching from behind, a lit stogie under his mustache.

"How did you find me?" I asked.

"Because this is where you always wind up after Hermosa screws you over." He pointed to a discarded bottle of whiskey under a sticker bush.

I compared its label to the one in my hand. They were identical. My kundalini noir twitched in discomfort as I realized how much of this me wasn't me at all.

"That whiskey might be nice to look at," he said, "but it drinks even better."

I broke the seal and twisted the cork loose. I allowed him the first draw. I tried a sip, then recorked the bottle. The whiskey taste reminded me too much of last night. "I guess this is a time to get philosophical."

"Ease up on yourself, my friend. *What doth a man have to gain by taking heed of the world's inequities?*"

"Who wrote that?"

Malachi's eyebrows shifted. "Virgil, I think. And if he hadn't, he should've."

"So what now?"

Malachi puffed on his cigar. "Remember what the Good Book says. Job 5:7. *Man was born into trouble just as surely as sparks fly upward.*" He smiled and slapped one holster. "And those sparks are always coming our way."

ABOUT THE AUTHOR

Mario Acevedo is the author of the national bestselling Felix Gomez detective-vampire series and the YA humor thriller, *University of Doom*. His debut novel, *The Nymphos of Rocky Flats*, was chosen by Barnes & Noble as one of the best Paranormal Fantasy Novels of the Decade. He contributed short fiction to the anthologies *Nightmares Unhinged*, *CyberWorld*, and *Blood Business* from Hex Publishing, and *You Don't Have a Clue*, from Arte-Publico Press. His novel, *Good Money Gone*, co-authored with Richard Kilborn, won an International Latino Book Award. He edited the anthology *Found* for Rocky Mountain Fiction Writers, which won a Colorado Book Award.

Mario serves on the writing faculty of the Regis University Mile-High MFA program and Lighthouse Writers Workshops. He lives and writes in Denver, Colorado.

IF YOU LIKED ...

Sex Slaves of Shark Island, you might also enjoy:

Rescue from Planet Pleasure
by Mario Acevedo

Tastes Like Chicken
by Kevin J. Anderson

Monsterland
by Michael Okon

OTHER WORDFIRE PRESS TITLES BY MARIO ACEVEDO

Rescue from Planet Pleasure

Our list of other WordFire Press authors and titles is always growing. To find out more and to see our selection of titles, visit us at:

wordfirepress.com